Adam Roberts is a writer, critic, academic and Fellow of the Royal Society of Literature. He is the author of nineteen novels and many shorter works, including the prize-winning *Jack Glass* (2012). His most recent novel is *By the Pricking of Her Thumb* (2018). He is Professor of Nineteenth-century Literature at Royal Holloway, University of London, and has published critically on a wide range of topics, including nineteenth- and twentieth-century fiction and science fiction. He is based in the south-east of England.

Anthony Burgess – the pen name of John Anthony Burgess Wilson – was born in Manchester in 1917. He published his first novel, *Time for a Tiger*, in 1958. Diagnosed with an inoperable brain tumour and believing he had less than a year to live, he wrote six novels (*A Clockwork Orange* (1962) and *Inside Mr Enderby* (1963) among these) in short order, so as to provide financially for his wife after his death. Through the 1960s he published prolifically, establishing a reputation as one of the leading writers of his generation. Stanley Kubrick's film of *A Clockwork Orange* (1971) brought Burgess global fame, and the 1970s saw him produce some of his best work, including the historical novels *Napoleon Symphony: A Novel in Four Movements* (1974), *Abba Abba* (1977) and *Earthly Powers* (1980), considered by many his masterpiece. He continued writing, publishing and composing until his death in 1993.

THE
BLACK
PRINCE

A novel by ADAM ROBERTS

Adapted from an original script by

ANTHONY
BURGESS

unbound

First published in 2018

This paperback edition first published in 2019

Unbound

6th Floor Mutual House, 70 Conduit Street, London W1S 2GF

www.unbound.com

Text design by PDQ Digital Media Solutions, Bungay, UK
A CIP record for this book is available from the British Library

ISBN 978-1-78352-642-0 (trade pbk)
ISBN 978-1-78352-647-5 (trade hbk)
ISBN 978-1-78352-649-9 (ebook)
ISBN 978-1-78352-648-2 (limited edition)

Printed and bound in Great Britain by Clays Ltd, Elcograf S.p.A.

1 3 5 7 9 10 8 6 4 2

This book is dedicated to the memory of John Wilson.
Le maître.

CONTENTS

PRELUDE: PRANCE, NOAH!

There are many kinds of flood and not all are water. Here's France, green and grey beneath a sloping blue sky, and wholly submerged by war. The House Valois is a tall house, but only its rooftop tiles and the pennant flying from its flagpole remain visible, so high has the flood risen. Those who walk on the earth are drowned, the common folk, the men and women. Those who sail in ships float above the inundation. This castellated English ship, for instance, lively over the waves, and made of wood as a coffin is made of wood.

When he is on land this Black Prince rides a prancing horse; and when he is at sea this Black Prince rides a prancing ship. Clouds drag bridal trains of rain behind them as they sweep from sea to land. The Prince is on deck, unmindful of the drizzle on his face. He is looking forward. In between the folds of cloth-like rain he can glimpse fresh beaches, green fields.

The French coast.

The rainbow sign was a promise that there would be no more waterfloods, but this great wash is liker unto fire than water and there is no Noah (no, no) can save the French now.

King Edward, third of that name, rides a still grander boat, a wooden castle, a barracks, a stable, a storehouse. Below decks was coughing and demons, swearing and shitting and drinking, and tied-up horses skittering unhappily on the angling and tipping wooden floor. Hooves tattoo. Rat-tats that make the rats scatter. Too exhausted to whinny. Boys exhausted by trying to calm them. Wipe flanks with tattered cloths. The cabins at the rear of the boat are where the quality hunker, holding in the contents of their sloshy stomachs. Life on hard land has not prepared them for this. Now they are not on land, but over it: suspended many hundreds of feet over the mud and rocks of the channel bed, where strange sea life creeps and pulses, and immemorial weeds grow in sodden forests, and bodies lie thousands upon thousands, grasping at one another or at empty brine or phlebasing their way into oblivion as currents tug their bones apart and crustacea nibble at their flesh.

The king is helped through the slushy sand and foaming waves, up onto the beach. The drizzle is thinning and the sun is coming out. The horses are hauled, and pushed, and coaxed down planks to the dryness.

Mount! Mount!

Noah rides a high-stepping horse, draped and harnessed in finery. He is returning to the high ground where he first berthed his big boat. When I was last here, he says, and the wind sends his beard sideways, like a comet's tail, when I was last here this was the only land.

He has attendants, bannermen, servants, lords and high-born warriors, all clustering about him.

—Your Highness?

—Your Highness! Your Highness!

Under the sunlight, the view has the brightness and perfection of an illustrated manuscript: greens soaked in blue-light, silver shining armour, red and golden standards, all the colours new washed and gorgeous. The party rides, keeping the sea on their left hand. Light leaps, a gorgeous ribbon of prisming colour from cloud to horizon.

> *Think thou of all the bloating*
> *drowned Tangling below*
> *Who died before they ever saw*
> *This rainbow.*

It seems to me a cruelty of
That fierce judge who
Would take their all from them, and life,
And then this beauty too.

PART 1. CRESSY

Newsreel

A rooster, raucous in the rain. The symbol of France. But do not think this scrawny creature underdignified, for Saint Augustinus himself has declared that the cockerel stands symbolic of God's grace, and in no motion of these animals, unendowed with reason though they be, could there be anything ungraceful, for divine higher reason guides everything they do. Pope Gregory declared the rooster 'the most suitable emblem of Christianity', for a rooster is the badge of St Peter himself, his awakening conscience, the cry of God in the morning. The nation of France has taken the cockerel as its animal. And here it craws and crows and makes its tiny thunder in the dampness of this barn, like a door creaking open. Pokes its pathé head through the circle of this hole in this barn door.

WAR OF THE CENTURY!

Invasion of France ongoing

The banners of the English nobility, King Edward III, Edward Prince of Wales, the fighting Bishop of Durham, flutter against the clear summer sky. It is the very flower of English chivalry, the Earls of Warwick, Northampton, Huntingdon, Arundel, Pembroke, Suffolk, Oxford, each mounted on a horse and no horse here costs less than one hundred pounds.

> *And the Captain of this Company*
> *Was a-fighten in the lead*
> *Just like a trueborn soldier he*
> *Of them Frenchies took no heed.*

Sanitation neglected as the pressure of military necessity moves the force through hostile territory. EXPECT EVIL FROM STANDING

WATER. Dysentery: the word is the same in English and French, and derived from the Greek *dys*, bad, and *éntera*, bowels. Very bad the bowels of the English as they move through the summer. Very wretched their retching, or some of them. This farmyard is not so ruined, and serves as shelter. But the meat is maggotthreaded and the water is bad, and this poor man-at-arms, Geoffrey of Henley, is on his back and heelkicking the ground in his badbowel agonies.

The procession was magnificent in colour and splendour of cloth, armour silverbright and new scoured shining gembright. Lord Richard Talbot. Hugh le Despenser. John D'Arcy. Bartholomew Burghersh. Sir Robert Ferrers. Reginald de Cobham.

ENGLISH ARMY LAND AT SAINT-VAAST-LA-HOGUE

God on our side, claims Fighting Cleric

Landing on north French coast almost wholly unopposed. Five hundred Genoese crossbowmen desert King Philip of France for lack of pay.

PRINCE EDWARD AND CERTAIN OTHERS KNIGHTED IN NEARBY QUETTEHOU CHURCH

SUMMER SUN MAKES FRENCH COUNTRYSIDE AN EDEN.

Emerald green the fields, sapphire blue the sky. Let us never again be expelled from this paradise, for it is ours, and ours forever.

Hurrah! Hurrah! Hurrah!

Weather: intermittent rain, and sunny spells.

The procession continued with John de Sterling, Maurice de Berkeley, John de Montgomery, William Fitz Warren. And, braving controversy, John Maltravers, first Baron Maltravers, rode with the procession, under his device, a square rotated through forty-five degrees to stand on its corner, with two long bars crossways threaded through the diamond. Maltravers stood against Edward II, burned Bridgnorth, murdered the Earl of Kent and fled abroad. But he did the new king such service in Flanders that Edward III pardoned him. *Evil-traverse* men called him. Not to his face.

Inside the King's Tent, with our special correspondent. Cloth walls and a cloth roof, stretched and pegged and rich furnishings brought within, withal, that this mobile room is more sturdy and magnificent than most villeins' houses back in England. The map is drawn on a single sheet of parchment as big as a split cow can provide, and here it is, unrolled and re-readied. Fingers point, noblemen gesture with half chewed meatbones. This ring-encrusted hand clasping a bejewelled winecup is the king's own. Here is that place where they forded the Somme and so surprised the French, who thought their enemy trapped on the wrong side of the river. There Paris is, there Paree be, an inked and coloured citadel with little figures drawn poking their faces around the crenulations. Paris was used by Edward as a lure: he marched his army towards it and the French king panicked that his capital might capitulate and scurried, scurried. Then Edward swung his army about, the men grumbling and stamping, and swearing at the wasted journey, and running to the roadside with the shits, and losing their gear, and finding other men's gear and fighting over it, and archers accidentally snapping their bows and having to botch new ones from the local trees. Following the north bank of the river under cloudy skies. They arrived at Crécy a full day before the French, giving themselves time to rest and ready their formation.

Crécy town was on the map, but cartography did not record the surrounding terrain, and this was the landscape that truly mattered. A long hill filled the ground between the town to the south-west and the village of Wadicourt to the north-east. A shonky little windmill had been built upon this prominence, the better to catch prevailing breezes, although surely the miller swore often and loud in lusty French at having to drag grain and flour up and down! Who knows? He scarpered – as wouldn't you? – as twelve hundred men at arms, four thousand archers and four thousand Welshmen came marching up the valley and claimed the hill.

The king explains his desire as to the coming battle. His nobles all think variants of the same thought. They think *we have fewer than the ten thousand men we set off with; and they also think the French and their allies have ten times that number, and will crush us. We are far from home, and fighting for nobody is sure what, and they are in their own place and fighting for their own soil. The French king is a legend across the whole of Europe; the English king's only renown is hacking a number of barbarian Scotsmen in the barren northlands.* When a small and exhausted army meets a large, fresh and inspired army, and that latter army is defending its home ground, there is really only one way the battle can go.

Trumpets sound.

Camera Eye

the red dragon of Merlin waves in a strong wind   crumple and snap of bannercloth   the action of the air slackening and then tautening the cloth makes the wyrm's body undulate as if alive, and the camera pans down to show two mercenaries under it

What kind of armour is that, though?

Black to show off his white hair, wus

The sky is filled with greystone clouds filled and the full wind is the spirit of God moving through the falling waters   rain spits from the sky, and the drizzle fades, and then gains in intensity, and the Prince himself sits on his horse   where all can see him, gauntlets of copper gilt and lined with douce doeskin   the princely shield fashioned of poplar layered upon with canvas, gesso, parchment, and leather adorned with the sleek leopards predatory   black metal the chestplate and over it the red and blue velvet surcoat stuffed with wool and satin-lined   his esquire trots alongside to carry the helmet. He knows that every man-at-arms looks at him and sees: youth and nobility, bravery and God's Grace and beauty.

The camera's eye mounts up   droplets spot the lens, and shiver and dribble away with the motion   swoops and soars and we can barely hear the narrator's voice as he reads the list of French names   Antonio Doris and Charles Grimaldi leading the crossbows from Genoa   the Duc d'Alençon, son of the Count of Valois, in charge of the charging French cavalry   the Duke of Lorraine, Louis of Blois   his Majesty King Philip of France—   the royal commander rides a palfrey and is flanked by banners of the fleur-de-lys though the rain is drenching now and the banners hang poorly o que c'est beau schon prittie   his baggage train is behind him, much of it leagues away, struggling to catch up, and when he looks behind him he sees only giant black clouds reaching high over the horizon like winepurple mountains. Lightning itches at the belly of this cloud   and quick to follow the grumble of thunder that warns the king to rest his men   a flock of rainbirds tumbles out of the sky

There will be time for rest when the English have been smashed

smash agrees the thunder

crush agrees the thunder again

Lightning like stitchwork of bright gold thread in the black fabric, visible only an instant   a flock of ravens cawing furiously wheels over the French host. The king crosses himself

BLACK GEORGE

They had taken their positions and now they waited. One thing George learned as a young sprat on the Scottish campaign was: war is much more about waiting than it is fighting. Another thing he learned: men can stand the fighting much better than they can stand the waiting. The drizzle had thickened into pouring rain and in no way quenched the burning of anxiety in his gut. Like smouldering flax inside a sealed pot. How he hated all this.

—Sir Hugh de Cressi is *dis*pleased, said Ralf of Reading, to George's right. Declares it a poor omen that this place has his name.

—Why poor? He should be glad he's fighting for his name. What else do free men fight for?

Most of the group were not free men, and responded to this dangerous notion with grumbles. The rain shushed them.

—Is he from here, then, Cressy from Cressy? asked one of the Welsh, in Welsh, a little snatch of birdsong. *A yw ei deulu yn byw yma?* Nah, he's never dirtied his foot with France soil before in his life, has Sir Hugh. *Nid yw ffycin.* Very free with that *ffycin*, these Welshmen.

—He's a superstitious sod, said Black George. Superstitious sod howsoever rock built. The big ones are always so. And what does a battle ever do but wreck the place where it happens? Would you want that happening to your name?

Wet wet wet. Water running down George's back, under his clothes. Summer assuredly turning into autumn this late August day. Warmish rain, but an ache in the arse nonetheless. Stink of damp wool; hoods clutching their heads like giant tongues licking. Gleam of wet leather, like a tadpole's skin. Then the heavens opened again and the air went pewter and cool and everything was scratched and scrabbled with rainstreaks.

—I should speak confessio, look you all, announced one timorous Harlechian, in his church-voice. For I may die, this day. Not ffycin likely, yelled another. And why would death want hard Welsh bodies when there are so many ffycin soft Genoese to fill his gut?

Ralf of Reading, freeman, said: it makes a man contemplate his name. Still harping on Sir Hugh de Cressi was he? George's bowstring was wound around his cock, as the driest place he had about him. And also because the sensation was a pleasurable sensation. A sensual sensation. Sens sensualim. Threads of water dribbled from the rim of his hood. The cloth of heaven unravelling wetly. My name, Ralf said.

—You can read, said Sergeant Nim, as ever impressed at this fact. Or was he confusing Ralf's birthplace with his intellectual attainment? Nim's radish-coloured hair was absurdly thick and bushy, and disposed into three great clumps on his head like cockerel feathers.

—These Genoese, said Ralf. From Genoa. That a country?

—It's a town, said Black George. His attention was not wholly on what he said, because there was movement visible across the valley, through the mist of downroiling water. The French were readying an attack.

—Town?

—It's a town in Italy.

Oo, they said. Oooo. The Os stacked up. They had *heard* of Italy. The land of Pompey. And of Julius, the king aptly named Seizer for his skill at conquest.

—And Genoa the only town in Italy that breeds crossbowmen? Ralf asked.

—These fellows come from all over, all over Italy. Why we call them all Genoese is for, but George (standing now, and making bird movements with neck and head to try and descry the enemy's business) couldn't think what for. *What for* was on its way: 50,000 well-fed men, including 6,000 Genoese crossbowmen with the most up-to-date weaponry French gold could supply. Plus 10,000 French men-at-arms (O how the Os stacked, coins on a moneylenders' table) and 14,000 feudal militia from Luxemborg and Bohemia.

King Edward had marched his small force of 9,000 fellows on a sawtooth march down France up France down France up again, over the Somme where the mud stank of salty hell, through Cazentan where they'd burned houses and unshucked squealing brown-skinned nuns from their habits like conkers from their rinds. Now they were at Cressy, and everyone was tired. They'd rested a few hours, hardly enough. Fifty thousand men, eager to smash the English. And Edward with 9,000, if that. A thousand of them ffycin bastard Welshmen: brave, surely brave, and certainly violent, but not reliable, likely to rabbitbolt off if the fight went poorly, and the shout started up of *encil, Cymry! Encil encil!* Ffyc off, they would. Five and a half thousand longbowmen, that was something. Two thousand men-at-arms. But tired, and unhappy. Whereas for all

George knew the French had spent long days lolling in what had been, until few hours before, bright sunshine. Maybe they were eased and strong and would kill the army as swift as a pig is killed.

The smouldering flax inside George's pot-belly seared hotter. He felt, and suppressed, the urge to shit.

—Italy, I saw on the map. Ralf of Reading was being too matey, coming so close that George could smell his reek, even in the rain. George, wanting not to encourage his intimacy, pushed him an ell back with his elbow.

—Shaped like a leg, it is, Ralf said. With a foot and heel and toe at the end. Kicking in the sea, whatever they call the sea down there. South Sea, is it?

—Leg, Black George said.

—Genoa must be somewhere around the knee, I'm thinking? Is why it is so called, is it?

Rain, rain, rain.

—They come, somebody yelled. Everyone was peering down into the valley.

And the Genoese were indeed advancing, a shuffling carpet of men. George had once seen a great mass of spiders swarm from a woodpile as the fire was lit, and the advance of the Genoese looked like that. They came slow, mind, for it was look-you *difficult* passage over the muddy ground. But they came, and with one purpose only, to kill him. To kill *him*, and rob his family of a fine young fellow, brave and strong. The bastards!

There were shouts from behind. Orders. Trumpets sounded.

—They're coming, lads. Coming on, they are. Stand stand stand ready.

Horsethud on wet ground, near at hand. Muffled drumming. Never fear these Genoese, called out a bell-voiced rider whose accent provoked one bold Welshman to cry that he might *cusanu*, or kiss, his Cymraeg *anwsau*, or fundament, and thereupon impart a cleansing motion to that portion of his body with his fine English tongue (*lyfu gyda'ch tafod*). The young aristo, splendid in silver armour, the colours of his cloth bright enough to dazzle even through the rain, knew nothing of that language and remained beautifully innocent of the obscenity. He was riding a small white horse, one of the few not cached behind the hill with the wagons, and doing his piping and squeaking best to put fight into these men.

The English trumpets sounded again.

—Five hundred of the Genoese abandoned King Philip at Saint-Vaast-of-the-Hog, for that he has not paid them the silver he promised! They do not trust this French king, and will not press the fight for long!

—Since you're talking of honest soldiers being *paid*, O lordling . . . shouted one archer in English, and the others laughed. But the horseman was off, riding at a slow trot from the western group of archers, along behind the long ranks of men-at-arms, calling hootingly to them, heading for the eastern knot of archers.

The Genoese were visibly closer now. Black George could make out individuals amongst the mass of them, trying to hold capes over their heads, their crossbows draped about their necks like monstrously large crucifixes. Burdened by their crosses, symbols of redemption, or sin, or both, for how can you have the redemption without the sin along at the same time? Scowling and grinning and looking pensive, thousands of human faces worn in front of thousands of human souls. All coming to kill *him*. And what had he ever done to them, the bastards? Was it fair? It was not fair.

The rain grumbled at the ground, sodden hillside turf turning to mud beneath George's feet. Down in the valley it was very much worse, though: Black George could see the Genoese sliding and falling as they advanced through the valley. Under teeming rain. Some were trying to hide their crossbows under their cloaks, but that weapon is a big and a clumsy machine and it was not aided by *questa maladetta piogga – le corde sono inutile – inutile*. The shaft of a Balistai crossbow is as long as a grown man's spine and considerably more rigid. The string must be fitted and tautened in a frame, and set. It cannot be rigged on the hoof. Slushy rain, treacherous mud. Some of the Genoese carried additional quivers of darts; some had sacks of stone or metal bullets, but it would all go for nothing if the string be too – *sodden* – to—

Slithering in the mud while the rain pelted still. And waiting for them, Welshmen, bent against the downpour, grinning and chattering to one another, daggers ready. They do not look much like soldiers.

Heads of the French foot soldiers, soaked and disconsolate, were packed together like cobbles. The rain was easing. Sky lightening. The sheep look up. And an English voice sang out close by: string your bows, lads.

Soft ground made it more difficult than usual bending the shaft to snick the string on. Some found stones large enough to brace against, others used their feet as brace and pulled down their hand, some few tried to curve the bow with the ground itself as brace and only found it sinking into the mud. But at least the cords were dry.

A knight's sergeant came running along. Constable he calls himself, look-you, though his father was but a ffycin blacksmith – *and* bigamist they say, up Llandwrog way he was. Not a handsome fellow, mind. Boils bunched the skin at his Adam's apple like a chicken's wattle and one eye trying at all times to look at its corresponding ear, but he had a voice on him, bach, *a voice*. You wait 'til I give the word, he bellowed, this knight's sergeant, you bowmen. *Don't* you start shooting off like it's your first fuck and you can't hold it back. We all shoot together, see, and we'll stop those French bastards dead, see, and leave their corpses looking like hedgepigs, the way we did to those Scots bastards. See?

A number of the foot soldiers, being Scots, took vocal exception to this. The Welsh cheered, though; and the archers entered into the spirit. When *do* we get some fucking leave, Knight's Sergeant, how about our back pay, I've got this terrible pain in my *balls*, Knight's

Sergeant. At least the fellow was on foot, like an honest soldier of God, and not on a horse and gabbling half-French like those other fuckers. Aren't the Frenchies the ones we're here to kill?

Camera Eye

The French king is silent. His face huge   fills our vision.

The rain has eased off, and the clouds are moving away, giving the human actors below a little privacy. It is good that the rain has stopped.

Nearly sunset. The clouds are rolling away from a clear red sky. Bird flock, crying and sobbing overhead. For a moment Philip is bathed in brilliant light from the late sun   looks up the slope at the English, though the sunlight dazzles him   shades eyes with his metal hand   what's that?   blot against the light, a figure in black armour   servingmen on either side, one holding up the banner of Woodstock and the other the flag of Wales, that lean and violent dragon. The Prince's helmet still not on: it's a massy chunk of ironmongery and hurts the neck that bears it – and its bearer is only a child, Philip thinks, a boy, a youth, a page, un ganymède. He can't make out the face, but the long fair hair is lit gold by the light.

    a mouth is wide open, teeth bad (panning back) an English officer screaming an order (cut to) Philip can see the man, his mouth moving, but the words are muffled to grunts by the distance (cut to) Gloire! cry the French knights, Gloire!

English archers angle their bows up in unison. The blackarmoured figure raises his right arm— —drops his right arm: a cannon roars, all smoke and thunder and the noise rolling around the valley like a boulder in a cauldron. The French soldiery flinch and cannot help it

—Fire! cries the officer. Fire!

the air is full of snakes and hissing   Aaronic rods and hissing down

It is thousands of arrows all at once in a piercing shower. There is just enough of a pause before impact for the French and Genoese to look up into the sunset sky and see their deaths harrowing down upon them

arrows strike mud harmless as hailstones, arrows bounce from shields, or ram into shields and stick thrumming with their jags poking from the inner side, arrows strike horseflesh with the sound of a mallet hitting wood, or poke through armour as if it were parchment, or cut open the flesh of a mounted man and cleave a path to bone that is dry only for an instant before blood fills and overspills arrows jag into legs and stomachs a horseman is pierced in the eye   a crossbowman is struck twice, left shoulder right through right shoulder and the arrowhead sticks in the socket a rain of arrows flies heavenward and then, as one, the whole flock changes its collective mind and starts to come down

some of the horses are screaming now, thrashing and dancing in the mud, unseating their

unseating their

foot soldiers cower, but this doesn't stop arrows stabbing into and through them, shoulders, necks, bellies

the crossbowmen are getting the worst of it. (Cut to)

BLACK GEORGE

The rainclouds have all rolled away to the east. From his place halfway up the hill Black George has a spectator's view of the scene below him, weirdly lit by the strawberry sunset. The shadow from the hill draws a bow-shaped cape of darkness below him that encompasses most of the English force. Raindrops glitter yellow upon the bushes and grass, though the dip of the valley is black with mud. The screaming of the horses is very piercing and very loud, and horribly human-sounding, and it is very unpleasant to listen to.

—This is your chivalry, right here, he says. Down in that declivity, down.

Ssssssss, and another volley of arrows darkens the sky. It hangs, like a tent canopy, and then the canopy folds and falls. Though made-up of a thousand components, it comes all at once down like a giant executioner's blade, and the Genoese writhe and dance and flip with the multipoint impacts.

—I am by way of liking this slaughter, halloos one Welshman.

The Genoese advance has stalled, and barely within firing range, even had their strings not been rendered sodden and useless by the rain. God pours bloodcoloured light upon the crowd of them to mark their fate. Thwack and thwack and thwack, and they writhe and dance. Deathwrithe, deathdance. Though they duck down the arrows strike them, still them. Though they turn and lurch the arrows strike them, and cause them to lurch, and turn, and fall. They lying long do all die windily.

The forwardest are milling and backstepping. The ones at the rear are retreating back through the mud, making as slow a regress as they had made progress – slower, because now there are corpses and injured men laying in their way. The ones at the front are most exposed, and cannot get back because of the crush of bodies. A few of them scream at the English, yelling surrender rather than defiance. Several lift their crossbows with their left hand and with their right make display of a knife – cutting their own cords. Arrows find them despite their gesture.

Men are pierced through the bones of the face, in at the shallow V of the collar bone, through their quilted jackets and leather into the ribs. Men are pierced through the gut and howl in beastagony. Men are pierced at the wrist and ankle like Lord Jesu himself and fall to the mud.

—it is but Sunday practice, sang one of the archers.

The sun has gone and the sky is duskdark, but light enough to see the turmoil below.

Camera Eye

charge Philip knows that only a heavy charge will break these English – they are weak as willow branches, to be swept aside by great men armed on great horses

fury is proper to a king, thwarted, for it is not meet that the will of kings be thwarted arrows come from the hill and fill the sky with black constellations and tumble death down. The camera pans up with their ascent, and pans down with their descent.

the Genoese are cutting their own cords and throwing their crossbows away and holding them, broken, over their heads to show the English they are no threat, turning and running, trying to retreat   the press of foot soldiers and horsemen behind blocks their way

The Duc d'Alençon is in a rage and bellows and bellows *tuez-les! Ils empêchent que nous nous n'avancions!* It goes without saying that the Duc's order is the king's order.

The foot soldiers do as they are ordered, and thrust their weapons into the terrified faces of the Genoese

tuez-les!   the Genoese do nothing to divert the blows with swords and axes, and the spear stabs, and the half-dead bodies trampled into the mud

tuez-les!

as a wriggling duckboard for booted feet. Crossbowmen without their crossbows are but men, and their throats open bloody and they die quickly or a wound drops them and the mud goes down their throat and drowns them   as a beast of many limbs the army starts forward, and behind them, impatient, the cavalry

a rain of arrows pouring down

a rain of arrows pouring down

the way is made muddier by the churning of feet

and (a rain of arrows pouring down) hooves, and passage is hindered by the many corpses *avancez! allez! allez*. Horses go down and scream terribly, more terrible than men screaming for their lungs are much bigger, and hooves thrash and punch out on the horizontal and break unwary human legs. The army is one beast, and the panic that spread through the ranks is worse than fever in a body, the sound of squelching and the terror of the continual screaming and the snakes hissing thick *avancez! allez! allez* in the sky overhead

EDWARD, KING

From his vantage point, twelve feet up the windmill that tops the hill, Edward, King of England and France, terror of the Scots, observes the slaughter below. It is his land, he knows. It is all his.

To his right and left, halfway down the dark hill, are three-cornered formations of archers firing regular volleys into the dusk. Their targets are on the far side of the valley, advancing foot soldiers with mounted French knights proud amongst the mass. Nearer at hand, dead and dying Genoese, the yells and weeping of the latter distinctly audible. There is still light enough to see Welshmen breaking from the central formation of waiting soldiers to dart amongst the fallen, finishing off the injured with daggers, axes, short-swords, and taking from their bodies whatever is valuable.

Edward calls down to his knights, mounted below him. 'Those Welschmen,' he says, with a kick in his pronunciation upon the /ch/ sound. 'Call the scoundrels back. They'll break the formation, pardieu.'

The vanes of the mill, torn cloth full of holes tied over wooden frames, groan with sorrow at the deaths. I am the millstone, Edward thinks. Frenchmen the grain. By god they will be ground to the dust they are and to which they must return. By God they shall.

Sir John of Addersford shouts the order, and other officers, on foot no less, run down the hill to relay. *Stay within the ranks there!* But it does no good. One Welshman, grinning back at the knights, calls distinctly in English *I don't understand English, man*.

The French have cleared the obstruction caused by their own troops. They have done it by killing their own troops. So now they yell, and pick up pace. Edward looks behind, at the tenderly delicate lemon colour of the westron sky, and looks beyond the battle eastward where the sky is grape-black. The noise of the massed drumming of hooves is audible, just, over the screaming of the fallen mounts, and the serpent hiss of arrows sickening through the sky. Their pennants are drawn out behind the charging horsemen, comettails of cloth.

Edward see his son, looking up at him, waiting for his signal. So the King gives it, a nod, and for good measure lifts his right arm in salute.

The Welsh, hearing the coming French charge, or perhaps feeling the ground underneath them vibrate with it, are scrambling back from their pickings amongst the fallen. The Prince puts on his helm, and takes his lance from his esquire. The gilt leopard strains from the top of his body to move forward. The distance between father and son muffles the sound, but the King hears the call to advance, and sees the whole mass of foot soldiers shudder and launch forward. The Prince leads, his lance level now.

An arrow goes into the throat of a French horse, and it halloos a tremulous equine *non!* as it falls, resonant enough to rise above all the other noise. Its rider topples between its ears and the helmet striking the soggy ground is heavy enough to snapcrack the French spine of the Frenchman wearing it.

Welshmen surge forward.

The Black Prince's horse hurries, stops, hurries on, uneager to tread on the bodies of the dead and dying. The Prince pricks the beast's flanks in fury, and it starts up again.

The King can see his boy urging the mount. He has picked a target, a knight in the front rank of advancing Frenchmen. The blazon declares him to be Count Louis of Flanders – my land too, Edward thinks, angrily, since his treaty with Hainault. My Count, he should be. My liegeman. By God I'll grind him down. By God I'll grind all their bones into the mud of this field. The vanes of the windmill shudder in the coming night breeze, and with a devil's groan the whole mechanism turns through a yard, two yards.

Stops.

The light has taken on an eldritch quality. Two armies here have embraced. The French begin to draw back, as a wave runs back along the hissing shingle, repelled by the brute force of the English charge. Henry watches, and as he watches the French rally and push back. Now it is the English who yield, foot soldiers falling and surging back, the French knight swinging mace and sword left and right. The English push on again, and once again the French begin to crumple.

Edward peers into the melee, looking for his son's horse, his boy's splendid leopard helm. There! The lad is hardly yet a man, but he is fighting with such might as a sixteener can muster. He tries to strike the French knight, Louis, Louis, who hoicks up his shield. But young Edward's horse shies, and the princely sword stroke falls short. Louis has a moment to swing back, retaliates with a crunching blow. The King looks again, and his son is no longer in the saddle. Dead, then, he thinks.

Count Louis has wheeled his horse about amongst the scurry of foot soldiers all around him, and then he too disappears from the saddle – falling? No, dismounting, ungainly in armour. He seizes his enemy. Edward lets his gaze shift, across the whole of the battlefield, spears being heaved into flesh, swords clubbing down. He can discern no accompanying sounds to these individual warstrokes above the general clamour and the howling of the wounded horses. He can't make out what has happened to

—Sir!

his son, whether alive or

—Sir!

somebody is yelling, shouting at him from the ground. It is John of Norwich, running comically slowly and laboriously up the hill, his armour clinking and chiming like a blacksmith's forge.

—Sir! Sir! Grave danger to the Prince! Prince of Wales!

Already dead, Edward thinks. A death in the witchlight of dusk. He feels a tremor in his heart somewhere between sorrow and delight at the thought of his warrior son. Fallen in fair fight. God of Battles, God of Chivalry, receive him as my offering, as Abraham offered Isaac. Sir John has reached the foot of the windmill.

—The noble lord, the warlike Earl of Warwick has sent me to beg help.

The King looks to his attendants, shivering around him. He thinks: they will have to light torches soon.

It is a wrench, but he pulls out the words: is the Prince dead?

—No, sir.

—Is he wounded?

—No, sir, but it is a hard passage of arms.

—Tell him, says the King, something like rage swelling suddenly inside him. The King puts all his strength into his voice that it might carry far down the hill, if not to the melee itself at least to those troops yet to be deployed. Tell him that he must not ask for help. This day must be his day. Tell the Prince he is required to win his own spurs.

—Sir!

He looks again. The Prince is on his feet. His standard-bearer, and liegemen, have hurried to him, thrashing about them with their

26

swords and axes. The French advance has been checked. Their men are stepping back over corpses, and going back downhill into the sink of the muddier valley.

The archers have eased their volleys, some because they have exhausted their supply of arrows, some because the light is becoming treacherous and they do not wish to kill their own comrades. But some few are still picking out targets and loosing, loosing.

Edward sees Sir Hugh Cressi, that giant man, heaving his axe about him as he rides. He sees the French left flank collapse and scatter, in a single motion that is most beautiful to watch, like a wave at the seashore folding in on itself from left to right as it meets the slant shore. The English and Welsh push on – daggers slipped up in where the metal plates meet, clubs smashing home, swords going at flesh like raptors' beaks. Arrows fly. A foot soldier, wearing on his head a small metal helmet tight as the cap of an acorn fits its nut, pulls down the shield of a Frenchman (or Italian, or Bohemian) with his left hand and punches his knife forward with his right. The fellow vomits blood, though a second Frenchman has come behind and catches the English soldier with so hard a blow to the back of his head with a swung sword that the man's chin bangs sharp against his own breastbone and he falls. A horse, mad with pain, bites through the leg of a standing fellow, and the man's screams rise up, float, loud enough to be heard even from the windmill, over the battle like a kind of ghost. Ssssss, another volley. Men dance and crouch as arrows pierce them. One knight takes an arrow in his metal chest, and the bolt sinks two-thirds of its length into the plate. His horse, startled by the deathclench of the rider's legs, launches itself into a canter and collides with another horse.

Edward sees.

LITHES, AND I SALL TELL ZOW TYLL THE BATAILE OF CRESSY-HILL

Then Philip came, full hot for rout
With him many a comely knight,
And all upset the bare about
The bare made them in sunset light

He dealt them knockés to their meed;
He made them stumble on the soil,
But helpéd neither staff nor steed.
As Genoa did flee their coil.[1]

Beside Cressye upon the green;
Sir Philip wanted to be lord,
That well was on his semblance seen
With spear and shield and helm and sword,

With speech nor might he never spare
To speak of Inglissmen despite;
Now have him trim his bragging bare,
All the caitiff muzzled quite.

[1] Historians cannot agree on whether crossbowmen were known as 'Genoese' because so many of the serving mercenaries came from Genoa in Italy, or because so many of the bows themselves were made in Geneva in Switzerland. Historians can never agree. Professional historians are professionally disagreeable. The writing of history is a continual blind battle between opposing forces. Ignorant armies. Night. Right?

For arrows rose and arrows fell
And Franche-men piercéd died in dirt.[2]
And Welschmen hackéd pell and mell
Til Philip's arms were full sore hurt.

With eyes that durst nought sight abide
The King of Boeme was cant and keen,[3]
But there he left both play and pride.
And powered[4] his life upon the green.

Pride in press no praise I nought,
Amang their princes proud in pall;
Princes should be well bethought,
When kings should them to counsel call

If he be rightwise king, they shall
Maintain him both night and day,

[2] Arrows might kill immediately, but even trivial wounds would usually prove fatal in the medium term. Arrowheads were fastened to the shaft with animal sinew and glue, a copula which held well when dry; but often the bond made wet – for instance, by the blood inside a body – would dissolve. Pulling the arrow from the wound would remove only the shaft, leaving the arrowhead inside. With smooth round bullets or stones, such as were often fired from crossbows, this mattered less, since the body would sometimes be able to encyst the foreign body and restrict infection. But an arrowhead would result in too large a cyst, infection would spread through a wide area, and fever, gangrene and death almost inevitably followed. If you are shot with a medieval arrow, for God's sake do not try to yank it out. For God's sake, leave it alone, until you can cut the flesh with a knife and remove the whole lot. Are you listening to me, for God's sake? Are you even listening?

[3] The modern Czech Republic, ancient Bohemia, derived its name from the Gallic Iron Age tribe the Boii (singular: Boius), the *-hemia* suffix deriving from the same root as our word *home*. The Romans, who conquered the Boii in the 3rd century BC, believed these people to have emigrated from Boeotia in Greece. Most believe the name derives from the fact that they were a **bouios* or cattle-herding people. Other scholars have linked the word etymologically to the Indo-European **bhī-*, warrior. But, after all, the two words mean the same thing. What passing-bells for these who die as cattle? Cowhome. Warriorhome. Bohemia.

[4] 'Poured'?

Or else to let his friendship fall
On faire manner, and fare away.

Away is all you will, I wis,
Franche-man, with all the woe you fare:
Of mourning may you never miss,
That ye are cumbered all in care:

Ingliss-men shall set ye free
Knock thy pates or ere you pass,
And make you pollard like a tree;
And this is Ingland as it was.

JOHN THE BLIND

John of Bohemia's father was Henry VII – Holy Roman Emperor at a time when that title still meant something. And it was John's father who taught him that order was the logic of chivalry, and force its splendour, and as Emperor he tried, for nearly two decades he tried, to bring the poise of peace and the rigour of command to European turmoil. Henry intervened forcefully in an Italy racked by Guelf and Ghibelline civil war, and in doing so won the praise of Dante, no less. The Iron Crown of Lombardy was placed on his head one winter's morning in 1311, frost putting silver stars on the sunlit stonework. Henry pursued his right as King of Italy with a deadly suppression of opposing cities. Chivalry means: not flinching. Chivalry means: a strong ruler. John, fourteen years of age, watched closely.

Fourteen was the age when John was married to Elisabeth – tall, serious-eyed and nearly twenty, very old for such a bride. But daughter of Wenceslaus, King of Poland and Bohemia, and therefore descended from the fabled Good King W. of the Carol, no less! Though Elisabeth had endured trials in her youth sufficient to spoil the sweetest soul's wine to vinegar. Prague Castle burned to the ground in 1303, and she inside it and nearly killed. She carried a long patch of puckered skin on her left arm all her life. By thirteen Elisabeth was an orphan, and a counter in the dynastic marriage-games played by her ambitious siblings, Anna and Henry. Elisabeth, clever, tall and plain, grew increasingly to hate her brother and sister.

Brother Henry the Bohemian declared himself King of Bohemia, but was driven out by the larger army and superior strategic intelligence of Rudolf, Duke of Habsburg. Brother Henry and Sister Anna wanted Elisabeth to marry Otto of Löbdaburg, Lord of Bergova, but she refused – of course the match was proposed on purely political grounds, but it was on political grounds that the longer-sighted Elisabeth saw the foolishness of it.

Brother and sister had another go. They concocted Elisabeth's marriage to John, with the immediate aim of using the prestige of the son of the Holy Roman Emperor to help them regain Bohemia. It was a poor match, and Elisabeth found the boy stiff and unattractive. But it was better in so many ways than the proposed union with Otto, and she agreed. Soon after the September wedding John invaded Bohemia. Swift military action (John did as his father had taught him) and a sufficiency of eminent Bohemians welcoming his arrival made the country his in weeks.

The coronation of King John of Bohemia and Queen Elisabeth of Bohemia took place in February 1311 – only a few days, actually, after John's father was crowned King of Italy. Who could doubt that theirs was the coming family, the clan to back? Wife of such a man, Elisabeth was able to rid herself of her noisome siblings. Brother Henry and sister Anna fled to Carinthia, in the mountains of Austria, where Anna died soon after.

Military and political success barely compensated Elisabeth for the many bitternesses of her life. She was expected to produce a son and so ensure the Bohemian succession, but for six long years she bore only girls. Despite regular appointments in a shared bed, John and she spent much time apart. She and her young husband could not find even the courteous chill of common ground. He acted towards her with a pompous set of cod-chivalric mannerisms, unseemly in one yet a boy, infuriating and absurd in any husband. Elisabeth, having grown to adulthood without a mother to guide her, resented having to mother her new husband. He listened to her wisdom on politics and strategy, and then he ostentatiously disregarded it. She was driven to that most demeaning of female shifts, nagging.

John had been raised in Paris and taught by his father to take a pan-European rather than a narrowly national perspective. This did not endear himself to his new subjects. He spoke no Bohemian – Czech, we call that language now – and discoursed either in fluent French or stiffly correct, slowly-spoken Latin. He preferred the company of men to women, and attended his wife's bed only to pursue dynastic procreation.

And then John's father Henry died in Italy, of malaria. It was 1313. He was not yet forty years of age, and the work he had done to unify the peninsula under the iron sword of chivalry and realpolitik unravelled with a kind of slippery rapidity. John sent an embassy (four men and eight servants in a couple of carts, one with a dodgy axle that needed replacing three times as it crossed the Alps – the men, dressed in finery and carrying imperial parchments and seals, little suited to this carpentry) to claim the throne of Italy his father had occupied, but the men arrived to find Louis the Fourth of Wittelsbach had already been crowned Holy Roman Emperor. It had never been a title to pass automatically from father to son of course; but still John was filled with a tightly repressed rage. Had he not a better claim than fat Louis? Was he not a better king? It made no difference at all. It made no difference. Louis renamed himself Charles IV, and John had no choice but to swear binding oaths of loyalty to him personally and his position. It was that or open war, and such a war would not have been won.

Forced by events at home to concentrate on ruling, unsure of his own succession, John attempted to negotiate with his own bovine, martial barons. His Magna Carta, the Inaugural Diplomas, marked agreements with the Bohemian aristocracy to limit the power of the crown and guarantee the rights of lords to raise taxes and elect new monarchs. In return the aristocracy agreed to recognise the authority of John, and promised to supply him an army should the national need be there. John liked armies. One knew where one stood with an army. And he worked for a while to contain himself within the terms of the Diplomas. The barons, though, were delinquent. Diplomas signed or not, the aristocracy were loathe to subordinate themselves to this foreign king, with his French chatter and frequent absences from the land.

Matters improved, at least in a public sense, when the twenty-year-old King of Bohemia finally sired a son: Wenceslaus, a heavy, costive baby, red as the devil, named for his mother's own father. John had wanted to call him *Henry*, but had yielded to his wife's importunate insistence. She had, after all, finally given him the heir he had demanded. She had done so after much delay and wilfulness, but she had done so. Some of the chill came off his formal manner towards Elisabeth, and two more sons followed. He organised tourneys, and commissioned new armour, coats of arms, splendid helmets. Chivalry was spectacle, and overwhelming people with visible glory, and both politic and a pleasure in itself. The chill soon returned to the marriage of course, and that chill grew colder.

It took Elisabeth a while to realise that her relationship with her chivalric husband was defined not just by distance and indifference but by active hate. In the early years of the 1320s she – cautiously, tentatively, but decidedly – initiated a scheme to unseat John and put her infant Wenceslaus on the throne, his rule to be guided by the superior wisdom of herself as Queen Mother. A Bohemian king, with a good Bohemian name, to rally the national support, and John's pan-European dreams be damned.

When the plot was uncovered, as plots inevitably are, four-year-old Wenceslaus was taken away from Elisabeth and sent to be raised in France. She never saw him again. She wept a little at this, but then she contemplated her own fate and her tears dried up. She expected death, of course, a prospect dizzyingly exciting and terrifying in equal measure. But worse than execution was the relish with which John, his hair already starting to thin, his cheeks cratered with impetigo, adopted postures of perfect chivalric *politesse* towards her. He of course punished with death those aristocrats who had been party to the plot, but where Elisabeth was concerned he made a great and public show of mercy. Though he decreed the three eldest children (the two girls and Wenceslaus) should be removed from Elisabeth's custody, he made no other statements regarding her guilt.

Elisabeth lived under the thorny mercy of her husband's patronising pardon for months, but it was an intolerable situation. One day, pregnant with twins – her last children – and disguising herself as a common woman, she fled Prague in company of a small retinue of her most loyal followers and made her way to Bavaria. Royal letters followed her accusing her of desertion and treason, and requiring her to present herself to her husband for justice. She ignored them. But the birth, when it came, was a difficult one, and though the babies lived she herself suffered postpartum fever and infection. She improved a little, and then grew sharply worse. It became clear she was dying. Since John could do no more to her than she was already suffering, she agreed to return to Bohemia. A long, slow journey in a closed carriage, banging and rocking and swaying like a ship at sea, and every jolt causing her pain. When she finally arrived the king visited her and observed that she had become very thin.

John punished his wife's desertion by removing his favour and not allowing her any money, such that she was unable to maintain an entourage suitable to her prominence and nobility. It was a cruel manoeuvre. She lived in a mean house with low ceilings and no tapestries on the walls, and the common people passed to and fro outside her window laughing and chattering at all hours. Her hair came away from her head, and she felt the cold terribly. Her persistent cough began bringing up ruby-bright globs of blood, and the surgeon who attended her assured her that consumption would finish her in a short time and advised her furthermore to trust it as God's mercy. In the circumstances. In the circumstances.

A letter arrived from Paris. Elisabeth's steward read it, pausing and starting each sentence anew when his mistress's cough interrupted his words. It took a long time to get through the entire epistle. The letter was from Wenceslaus, her own, her darling boy. He informed her, in French, that having been raised with love and respect by his supremely admirable godfather Charles IV, Holy Roman Emperor, he had decided to alter his name to that of his patron. From this moment onward he would receive no message, and listen to no communication addressed to the name associated so regrettably with their backward principality, Wenceslaus; but kindly requested his mother write to him as *Charles* and think of him as a noble and European prince. Through the words Elisabeth felt the chilly formality of the boy's father. Outside her house the harvest was being gathered, hay sheaves stacked in regular order. Mice, breeding fast amongst the granaries, chewed the edges of her gowns in the wardrobe. The night air smelt of fruitfulness. The world was living and renewing itself which must mean that she was no longer part of the world. She coughed and coughed, and in the middle of the night dogs barked in joyous answer to her coughing. She slept only minutes at a time before coughing woke her again. She sucked small spoonfuls of air, and then thimblefuls of air and she never had enough air. All the fight drained from her soul, everything that had defined her as a human being during her forty

35

years of life. The sun set in red and lemon and grape-purple, and then the darkness came.

When her estranged husband was informed of Elisabeth's death, he announced to the court that he was distraught for the loss of his wife and manifested his feelings in mourning clothes. Courtiers were surprised. But then again, they had been married twenty long years. He remained completely himself apart from a brief time in Bohemia, and then he reconvened his court and never again discussed the matter.

Unloved in his own land, John was often abroad. He told himself that he was carrying with him his father's outward looking vision, bringing the whole of Europe together in a kingdom to mirror heavenly perfection. Certainly he was more gifted at foreign affairs than at domestic. He personally marched well-protected envoys into Silesia, Lithuania and over the Alps into northern Italy. The Silesian dukes swore allegiance to him, persuaded in part by his well-drilled military escort. Oh – brave? He was that. He made it a point of absolute honour to be brave. He took a force into Poland (a merely diplomatic mission, my friends; pay no attention to the gleam of my knights' armour, the lockstep of my foot soldiers) and the Poles begged him to receive a huge amount of money in place of his claim for the Polish throne. Money was always useful. Armies cost a great deal of money.

He was in his late thirties now, an old man by the standards of his time.

He led his army with unwavering courage, and his whole military strategy was: attack. Once, in Lombardy, when his advisers cautioned him against going into war, he dropped into Latin, for the greater dignity of the language. *Absit a Bohemis rex fugit pugna!* God forbid a Bohemian should ever flee from a fight.

And then, busy with battle and the travel that battle entails, his thirtieth birthday long behind him, in a blink it seemed he was on the very cusp of forty. Blink. An expedition to Lithuania saw him *blink* struck with a crust upon the *blink* eyeballs, and pus from the corner of the eye where he would not cease scratching and rubbing at it. How did it begin? Some said a mosquito bit the king close in at the bridge of the nose and that it was the fetid matter from this wound that spread to the eye. Some said he had received a wound in battle to the face. His surgeons begged him to have his hands bound to prevent him irritating the infection further by scratching. If he abstained from assuaging the ghastly itch during daylight, he could not stop his somnolent hands rubbing his face bloody when he slept. But – bind a king? Tie a king's hands, like a slave? Never!

Unable to ride home, but carried ignominiously across the bumpy tracks of north-eastern Europe in a carriage, John made his slow way to the warm south, and the Papal Court at Avignon. There he was attended by Guido de Cauliaco, the most famous surgeon in the whole of Europe, author, no less, of the *Chirurgia Magna*. Salves and bandages were applied. But when the scabs were washed away, the corneas of both eyes were so scarred and roughened that all vision was reduced to a pale white blur.

John the Blind he became, and as John the Blind he ruled for another long ten years. Fifty years old was dotage to most people, and blindness was common amongst the old. Besides what needed he eyes when he had ears, and trusted constables and assistants? His whole life has accustomed him to the assistance of servants. There was almost nothing he did by himself, in his private life, from reading his correspondence to dressing and wiping his Bohemian arse. Servants had done it all, and continued to do it all. Life did not change so very much. Mostly he regretted no longer being able to see the gorgeous colours of blazons and banners, men in gleaming armour, the bosses on their shields. But it was not so bad.

He began each day by listening to reports and epistles from around Europe (which is to say, from around the world). He would sit with his head angled back, warmth pressing on his face, staring straight at the sun with eyes open and suffering no further harm.

And though he was blind, he could still see feelingly – Europe, the whole body of the land, laid from the foamy breakers of Western France and Spain, where the Atlantic washed the head, to the heartlands of Bavaria and Bohemia. Here Italy puts out a leg; there Illyria the other leg caught up in the broad cloak of the Gothic lands to the East, and the whole standing on the broad plain of the Russians. It was a single land, the imperfect image on earth of the kingdom of God in the sky, whose head is the cool moon, whose heart the raging sun, and whose body is pinpointed by the clean stars. It is this that we serve, all of us.

The French King Charles died, and King Philip took the French throne.

Given the prominence of John's son in King Philip's court, and with his own upbringing and affiliation, quite apart from treaty considerations, inclining him to French culture and power, there was no question as to where his alliance would be when Edward of England, that wolf, crossed the French channel and landed in Normandy with a pillaging army. God forbid a Bohemian should ever flee from a fight. The English were an irrelevance to the splendour of Europe: a small, rainy and unfertile cluster of islands hidden in the fog, the very definition of marginal. Edward, a petty king, had absurd pretentions above his divinely appointed place. John would help Philip punish his banditry.

Philip, gracious in his gratitude, appointed John Royal Governor of Languedoc. English Edward wanted this land, wanted it greedily as a wolf wants prey, rich as it was with grapevines and olives. John took pleasure in denying it to him. John's chivalric motto was *Ich dien*, which meant I serve – not *I serve Philip of France*, for we are both kings together and brothers. But *I serve duty itself*. I serve chivalry and bravery and the right way of action. I serve my people, and am proud to be called King John the Blind of Bohemia. Is Justice herself not blind? Blindness would not stop him from service.

John marched with Philip, helped defend Paris, helped him chase the ragged English across northern France. By the time news came that the English had stopped on the hill outside a small northern village called Cressy, Crossi, something, John was in high spirits. He rode his horse, his firstborn Charles at his side, and their reins linked so that the son could lead the father through the hot autumn countryside.

Day passed to night, and the white fog in John's eyes became a black fog. Philip, King of France, came to see him. My brother, he said, and kissed John's old hands – more than fifty years of age, my friend, almost as antique as the patriarchs of the Bible! *You sir shall command my advance guard,* Philip promised. *To you shall be the immense honour of ordering the charge that shall crush the English and drive them from our land forever. Duke Charles of Alençon and Count Louis of Flanders are both leading large contingents, and these shall be yours to send forward to glory.*

Morning came, and the march resumed. The noise of the troop was all around him, as he trotted along, his son at his side: horses and men, and the rumblebang of carts, and the chatter of camp followers. Overhead birds unspooled silver threads of song. The fog in his eyes was gold-white. Then it cooled, and the fog went grey, and the rain began. No harm in a little warm rain.

They rested for a while, and fed the horses, and took sustenance themselves: some hard bread softened in wine. His blind fingers picked the crust from a cooked egg. The rain strengthened, and a servant painstakingly pinned a leather cape about the old man. Fifty years old, and his eyes white like two peeled hard boiled eggs, *œuf dur* they called it in France, odd really, for the texture of the egg, even long boiled, was actually as soft and pliable as flesh. Like an eyeball. Not hard like a stone. Hard like a stone. A stone. Patter of water onto the top of his hooded head. Hard could mean anything from folded, hammered steel to the pliability of a cooked and peeled egg.

'Father,' said Charles. 'The English have been spotted, camped on a hill north of Crécy. The King says we shall attack at once.'

'Good,' said Blind John. 'Strike at once is the start and end of military strategy. How many Englishmen?'

'A small force, a fifth the size of ours. Few horse to be seen, though they are presumably hid, beyond the hill.'

'Pennypinching English, they loathe to have the expense of horses mauled in a fight.'

'We shall trample them beneath our charge!' Charles sounded excited, younger than his years.

'What the time of day?' John asked, turning his face to where the foggy white was a little brighter.

'Some hours past noon. With God's help and our own courage we shall defeat the English before sunset!'

Spoken like his true son! *Absit a Bohemis rex fugit pugna.* 'We serve my boy,' he said. 'We serve a higher force. These English bandits cannot understand, God has banished their thin kingdom to the margins of the world. But God has arranged the world of Europe as it pleases him, and Bohemia is the heart of that, the warm and beating heart. Courage is a matter of the heart, not the head. We—'

'My lord,' said a different voice. 'Your son has departed, to take counsel of the King.'

'Good, good,' John said, too rapidly. 'That's good. Lead me to my horse.'

He is taken, and helped into the saddle, and the rhythm of riding settles him. He goes up a hill and down again, the rain in his face the whole time, and trickling unpleasantly underneath his cloak, down his torso. He feels the cold much worse than he used to. But he is a warrior, and growing old has not changed that about him. The quality of the fog in his eyes alters, thickening and taking on a pinkish tint. He is no longer moving. Somebody has stopped his horse, and is holding its bridle. 'Point me at the enemy,' he orders. 'Give me a sword.' But instead of this he is helped from his horse and brought out of the rain, into a tent. Humiliated he understands that he has been cached at the rear of the French lines, tucked away to keep him out of harm's way. Servants fuss about him, helping him from wet clothes, drying him, redressing him. There is no point in shouting at them; they can do nothing. It is his son who has ordered this, but the lad's solicitude only stings John's sense of duty. 'A king of Bohemia does not flee from the fight', he announces, from his chair, telling whoever it is who attends him, silent shadows feeding him broth. I am served, he thinks, and then he bursts into tears.

Then, because he is old and had ridden all day, he falls asleep, in his chair. When he wakes it is because somebody has placed a hand on his head and is muttering in Latin. It takes a moment for John to grasp the sense of the words. Prayer. A monk then.

'They were frightened at my weeping', John says, in the dog-growl voice of an old man woken from sleep. 'And sent for you.'

'My lord', says the monk, in accented French. Tuscan? Sicilian? 'I am to keep you company, and to pray with you.'

'And do my bidding. I am king, after all.' The monk coughs discreetly, and in that throatnoise John hears of *small Bohemia, though, not big France*, and his anger fires up again. God curse them all! He tries to get a sense of the man's face from his voice, but it's a fruitless business. 'How', he demands, 'is the battle going? Have I missed it, snoring here in the rear of the assault?'

'You are safer here, my lord', murmurs the priest.

'How', John snaps, feeling the power to command returning to him, that mystical ability possessed by the few, 'is the battle going?'

'It was a bad start, sir', says the monk. 'The Genoese advanced, with their crossbows, but they were driven back by English archers. The king, the French king', the emphasis on the nationality was an impertinence, surely, 'ordered the infantry to kill them.'

'Killing our friends', rages John, thinking not of mercenaries and strategic pressure, but of his times in Italy, his father's Iron Crown,

41

of service and chivalry. 'That is not war as we wage it in Bohemia. Where is my son?'

Eagerly now, to reassure the old man: 'he's in front, sir, in the thick of the fighting.'

'Old and blind as I am,' shouts John, getting to his feet, 'I will strike one blow against these murdering English.'

He strides about, runs his fingers over the cloth of his tent, turns and smacks the back of his hand against a metal chest plate, hung on a wooden stand. 'Dress me,' he commands. There is the sound of people all about him, but he repeats the order in his voice-of-command, and his serfs come to him and begin to strap him into his carapace.

A different voice at his ear, not the monk. Fluent French, and it takes John a moment to recognise it: Sir Guy, one of the knights assigned by Philip to attend him. 'But sir,' he says, 'but sir.' He does not dare lay hands on the old man, though. Does not touch the king.

'Quick! Quick!' The straps are tightened.

'But sir,' says the French knight. 'It is not seemly – you are the King of Bohemia, and as you say, you're—'

'Absit a Bohemis rex,' cries John, his blood pumping and the joy coming over him, the old joy. He commands those around him to lead him to a horse, and they do so; the air cooler outside the tent. 'Blind in my eyes, not in my heart. Old in years, not in courage. It is the duty of a king to serve, however old and blind he may be. Help me up – help me mount. Tie my bridle to yours and ride our horses to the fighting. Wait! My helmet – my standard.'

'The standard is here, my lord.' John knows its blazon without needing to see it: the three proud ostrich feathers, one for each of the holy bodies of God in the trinity; and the motto ICH DIEN. He feels the pressure upon and then around his head, and knows that his helmet has been fitted to his head. He knows the helm, too: iron, traced with silver and gold, and two metal vulture's wings on the top. A shame that his enemy would not see it in the darkness. But there was advantage, here, too. His enemy was as blind as he. 'On!' he commands, and the horse beneath him lurches into motion.

He rides along for a minute, and a second, and a third, and then feels the horse start to descend. A hill, they said; so this must be the valley. He draws his sword and shouts his war cry. Around him he can hear shouting, the screaming horses, the familiar sounds of men trying to kill one another. His heart is full to bursting with pride and delight, and then, suddenly, the tightness in his chest is a thorn of pain, a lion's tooth sheathed in his own flesh, so bright and sharp and ghastly a pain he is almost too surprised to cry out. His own heart flaps like a torn flag in his chest, and the pressure climaxes with a kind of inward ripping, or wrenching, the pain now everything that is and was and will be, his whole blind being.

THE BLACK PRINCE

The worst of it is his neck, sore from having supported his heavy helm all these hours. But the battle is over now, and he has handed the headgear to a page. He slumps in his saddle and lets his horse pick its way through the aftermath. Bodies of men and horses everywhere, some trodden into the mud and filthy, some so pristine it is surprising they are even dead. Two men walk alongside carrying torches. Behind him, the Earl of Warwick's horse coughs. It sounds like a branch breaking in the forest.

The torchlight slides egg-shaped patches of illumination over the chaos underfoot. Every now and again the light uncovers a Welshman finishing off a prone enemy. Sticking a sword or a dagger into a twitching body. The more experienced men use cudgels for this work; no point in getting blood all over yourself at this stage in the fighting. Picking booty from the dead. The Prince nods his fair head. Let them be clouded in the decent dark, with only the harvest moon for light. Some of the dying men sing their pain like swans, Edward notes. Some croak like toads.

A second patch of firelight is moving, floating over the cluttered ground. The King, also surveying the scene from horseback. Approaching slowly.

The Black Prince sees something, and dismounts. Not the usual trash of the battlefield. The Earl of Warwick, anxious that the lad not be surprised by some shamming Genoese or only-half-dead Frenchman – that he not get stabbed in the dark, after all they have been through that day – dismounts beside him and tests the corpses around with his metal foot. The boy is kneeling beside a fallen knight. More than a knight, Warwick sees: the banner half immerded in mud beside the body. The helm lying chipped to one side. The three feathers of an arrow-flight poke from the metal sheet of his breastplate.

The Prince has pulled the banner from the mud with his own hands.

—Who?

—A brave man, says Warwick. Old and blind, it is John, it was John, who was King of Bohemia.

The fact of this man's body being in this place, fully armoured, strikes him with deep feeling. A very brave man.

—Blind and old, but still keen for the fight.

—A death that does him honour. He has the best motto in Europe, or his house does.

Edward reads it aloud by the firelight. *Ich Dien*. Not French, he says.

—It means *I serve*.

The snort of a horse; the light has become redder, a little stronger. The Prince looks up to see his father.

Newsreel (2)

Come on and hear

Come on and hear

Come on and hear

PARIS SHOCKED AT LAST. Lamentation on the street of the French city as

> *In another place the earl of Alencon and the earl of Flanders fought valiantly, every lord under his own banner; but finally they could not resist against the puissance of the Englishmen, and so there they were also slain, and divers other knights and squires. Also the earl Louis of Blois, nephew to the French king, and the duke of Lorraine fought under their banners, but at last they were closed in among a company of Englishmen and Welshmen, and there were slain for all their prowess. Also there was slain the earl of Auxerre, the earl of Saint-Pol and many other. In the evening the French king, who had left about him no more than a three-score persons, one and other, whereof sir John of Hainault was one, who had remounted once the king, for his horse was slain with an arrow, then he said to the king: 'Sir, depart hence, for it is time; lose not yourself wilfully: if ye have loss at this time, ye shall recover it again another season.' And so he took the king's horse by the bridle and led him away in a manner perforce. Then the king rode till he came to the castle of Broye. The gate was closed, because it was by that time dark: then the king called the captain, who came to the walls and said: 'Who is that calleth there this time of night?'. Then the king said: 'Open your gate quickly, for this is the fortune of France.' The captain knew then it was the king, and opened the*

gate and let down the bridge. Then the king entered, and he had
with him but five barons, sir John of Hainault, sir Charles of
Montmorency, the lord of Beaujeu, the lord d'Aubigny and the
lord of Montsault.

PESTILENCE IN KENT AND ESSEX

Surgeons recommend prayer and abstinence.
Bury the bodies of loved ones, but burn their clothes,
no matter how expensive the cloth

words *bell* and *bellow* come from the same etymological Saxon root
term. Bells have a tongue, so that they might speak. Iron bells are
cheaper than brass, and can be more easily tuned. To hang a bell
from a wooden frame, in at the ceiling of your church, or in the
tower if your church has the wherewithal to erect a tower. Some
churches hang the bell and strike it with a hammer or rod from
without; but the sound is greater if a clapper or tongue is depended
within. The instruction that the bells be rung follows news of great
triumph in arms by our most glorious King Edward Third of that
name upon the green fields of France beneath the blue skies of God's
own glory. Hundreds of French Knights slain, the King of Bohemia
cut down, thousands of foot soldiers trodden underfoot

VICTORY AT CRÉCY

English troops keep discipline as the order was given
not to chase the routed enemy

King 'proud of his son'

Day After The Battle The Englishmen Discomfited Divers Frenchmen

We were slaughtering French
                on a moonlight night
You can hear the voices ringing
They seem to say
You have stabbed in my heart on the field of the field of the
    fight
Just as we sang
           love's

              old

                 sweet

                   songs

            On a moonlit night

Will the King first seize Paris? Or will he elect to secure the northern ports? DISCUSSION BY OUR EXPERT PANEL AT THE THIRD, SIXTH AND NINTH HOUR.

PART 2. AT BOWER

Newsreel (3)

WHITE FEATHERS FOR THE COWARDLY FRENCH

Three Plumes

Make a joyous sound unto the Lord. Such musical celebrations of the King's great victory as can be squeezed from bagpipes, citoles, clarions, cornets, crumhorns, drums, fiddles, flutes, gitterns, harps, horns, hurdy-gurdies, nakers, organs, pipes, psalteries, rebecs, recorders, sackbuts, shawms, tabors, tambourines, trumpets and whistles.

WAR, TRADE, SHIPS ON THE CHANNEL

The sea is a changeable medium and so is trade, the one fitted to the other, the mer in merchants tells us as much, and my fortune was made by the courage with which I embrace the sea, for I know men too timid ever to let the coastline out of their sight, and how can they ever build a great fortune that way? I was taught to use the astrolabe by a genuine Turk in Spitalfield, and it is a curious and miraculous device, and I know the moon and its triform and the tides that are the Great Ocean breathing, as a man breathes, or a woman. People say: did you see the monstrous sea pig of the Dutch Sea, big as a house, eyes all down its flanks and I say big as a palace, and tusks like spears I have seen it, but the truth is: I see the fog comes flanking down the grey sea, and I see the sand grey under the green water where the banks threaten my vessel, and I see the little waves like cobblestones, and I see the way salt rain falls sharp and slant out of the sky, and mostly I see the ports at Antwerp and Calais and Copenhagen and the end of my journey. English wool for European treasure, and I grow richer.

Put not your trust in princes, nor in the son of man, in whom there is no help. Psalm 146:3

What is the Trinity? Father son and holy ghost. *Are they then three things?* No, they are one. *Are they then one thing?* No, for they are no 'thing' at all, like a stool or a shrub or a steer. *Are they ranked, as father, head, son, body and ghost, breath?* By no means. *Are they all then three iterations of one another?* No, they are three. *Are they kindly disposed to man?* They abhor sin but do not abominate the sinner.

JURORS AT GATES OF BEEF BARONS

Hand by hand us shall we take,
And joy and bliss shall we make;
For the devil of hell is thrust in dark,
And Cressy field is made our mark.
A boy took arms amongest man,
In armour black as devil's dam
His hair as gold as ever was span
And in that child oure lif bigan.

A FEAST

Roast pork, cooked on a spit
Goose in a sauce of wine and pomegranate juice.
Roast smallfowl
Cony in a gravey of aylmond milk
A bake mete: pies of various meats
Bruce, a soup of tripe, chicken and wine
Elderflower fritters in honey
Salt cabbage
Pandemayne bread
Milk dough bread

Potage of Roysons: an apple-raisin pudding.
A Bake Mete: a pear and custard pie.
Gingerbread
Custarde
Goat Cheese Cake
Beer-frittered apples in crystallised honey
Bread
Wine
Ale, ale, ale, ale, ale, ale, ale, ale, ale, ale, ale, ale

The spitboy turns the handle. Cooking for such a large crowd is always a hurry. The chef cuts the innards roughly from the chickens and throws them in the humble pot for later, but he is rushed and some of the remnants miss and fall to the floor. Nowt so slippery as innards on stone flags, not helped by the dogs who have crept in to snaffle what food they can. The outer cabbage leaves, with the most holes and rotten patches, are used to wrap the roast smallfowl. To the king and his table it is plates – of metal, no less. A serving man carries one such, piled with brown, savoury smelling cooked birds, and nearly slips on a smear of rubyred viscera. Then, turning to the entrance to the main hall he fits the top of his shoe, snugly and entirely without intending to, into the elegant arch of a hound's underbelly that is nosing around there. It is a silver coloured hound, and it squeals at being kicked, and it writhes away, and the serving man totters and falls on his hip. The problem with metal plates is the noise they make when they strike the ground, like a gong. Hurryscurry to collect all the scattered roast smallfowl, the cook using spit and his uncleanly sleeve to wipe away the worst of the grit and dust that has adhered to their sticky little selves. Of all the folk in the kitchen only he has the authority to rebuke the serving man, so he half smacks, half punches the fellow, just above his ear, and the fool begins to snivel.

BRIAN OF BOWER

He had lived all his life at Bower. Of course he had. He farmed various things, as his father had done, but he had a special touch with chickens and so as much as he was anything he was a chicken farmer. Not his chickens, of course. His lord's. He owned nothing but his belly, as the phrase went. Still, his lord was a good lord, or at least better than some. Brian worked the manorial lands, and handed over his heriot when the law demanded it, and otherwise got on with life. He hadn't wanted to marry, and found women unappealing, physically, but his lord was entitled to more villeins to work his land and a court bailiff had come to Brian's cottage, unhappy that his fine leggings thereby became muddied, and informed him that the law required him to choose a wife, and that if he did not the court would choose for him. 'What if the wife I choose does not want me?' he asked. 'Then she will be fined,' said the bailiff, severely, 'and you too, and if you both continue to withhold consent you will be imprisoned.' This was a worrying thing, and would be a great shame, so Brian spoke to a neighbour after church on Sunday, and made a deal for the fellow's daughter: good white skin, though many big freckles like penny coins all over her body and hair almost as red as a rooster's wattle. She was thin, for which her father apologised, but though he did not say so Brian preferred it. He could imagine her a boy, and so husband her. She became quick with a child, and Brian got used to having a woman in the house with him. The child was born, and died within two days, but soon enough, she was filled up again with a child, and birthed it, and that one lived.

When he was thirteen he had broken his leg – a bad break, above the knee, and they had thought he would die. But he had not died. His leg was not crooked, afterwards, although it was two fingers'-width longer on the right, which he could never understand. A priest once explained to him that all bodily pain comes from the

Devil, who is the Father of Pain; that in the Garden when God made Adam and Eve there was no pain except one unique kind, which we all know, the pleasurable agony of anticipating delight. But when Adam sinned pain in its fullness came, and the Devils that are allowed by God a lease of time out of Hell, and will continue to roam the world until the Last Judgment, that is what they are. 'What they are?' Brian had wanted to know. This matter interested him very much. 'They are the pain we feel, the toothache and gout and megrim.' Brian hadn't known what this latter was, but from the way the priest talked it must have been a fancy French or Latin term for headache. 'When you broke your leg, that hurt, I think?' Brian nodded hard. How terrible the pain had been! They said you forgot pain, but he had never forgotten the fortnight he had lain up with that leg, nor the weeks after when his mother and father had bullied him out the house to help with the farm again, and the motion and action had caused his leg to scream silently up and down the long bone, and make him sweat with the horror of it, and the bruise the colour of a thundercloud that had swallowed all of the skin such that his parents had grown afraid that the leg would go rotten, and even permitted him back to the cottage to lie in the shadows. 'That pain,' the priest said, 'was a devil – an actual devil. Inside your leg. It was your sinfulness that let him in.' 'It was my bone breaking,' Brian objected. But the priest would not be diverted. 'It does not hurt now,' Brian told him, 'save when the weather is sharp frost or snow. So perhaps my sinfulness is less than it was?' 'Let me see,' the priest asked, so Brian unwound the cloth from his leg, and lifted his tunic, and the priest leant in, examining the wound. There was nothing much to see, but the priest stayed there a long time. Then, tentatively, he examined Brian's manhood, which responded in lively fashion. Then the priest kissed the end of the rod, and held it in his hand, and soon enough they were grappling together on the grass bank, and soon enough after this both were spent. It was not the first time it had happened with a man for Brian, but his previous partners had been sulky afterwards and liable to slink away, for it could be death if the law found you. But this priest sang and was jolly. 'It is only sodomy that is sinful,' he insisted. 'As you can tell, for that unnatural act is painful, as the devil of sin enters in through the fundament and takes up residence within. But what we have done with hands and mouths is natural, as King David found solace with Jonathan. There's no pain in it, only pleasure.' Brian had no opinion on this, one way or another. The sky was blue. The song of the linnet was sweet as wild honey. *E-leh leh lucklucklucklucluck*, the bird sang; *lightandlifeandlove*. The priest was a mendicant, but he was not displeased that Brian had no money to give him. 'You have given me enough, young man,' he told him, and soon enough he travelled away and Brian never saw him again.

Brian's mother had grown sick on account of a foulness that grew in her mouth. Her gums became very swollen on the left side, and then her whole face distorted gargoylish and horrid, and Brian could not stand to look at her. She died in the night, and Brian helped his father dig her grave, on the very limit of the churchyard. Brian had never seen his father show any affection for his wife, yet the old boy was cast into a great sorrow by her death, and sat for days inside without saying anything. Then he upped and left, told the boy that there was a call for serving men at Havering Palace, half a morning's walk away. Brian was puzzled, but kept his peace. It was the King's Palace, though the King was rarely there, for he favoured Windsor, wherever Windsor was. *That* was a name Brian had first heard as a young boy, on a cold December morning, when the wind had slapped his face red and made his cheeks and lips sore indeed, and ever since then the name had seemed like a bad joke. But now, word was, the King was favouring Havering-at-Bower, and might even be coming to stay in a week or so. Brian assumed the Lord of the Manor had given permission for his father to go seek service at the king's house, but then two ruffians brought his father back bleeding and with his left eye sealed shut, so it was clear that he hadn't had permission from their lord after all. He took to his bed, and Brian came and squatted on the floor beside him. This was before Brian had married, so it was just the two men in the small room. 'You were running off,' he said. His father said nothing. 'You weren't truly seeking service at the king's house.' Nothing. 'If you had got away,' he said, 'they would have fined me.' His father had said nothing for a long time, and then said: 'if God had blessed us we would have had a dozen daughters and a dozen sons.' He meant: but we only had you. Then he turned his face to the wall.

Brian worked half the day for his lord, and the rest of the time tended their own small farm, and looked after the chickens. Once he hit a fox with a hoe and killed it. That fox had a chicken in its jaw, and Brian considered offering it as heriot, in good conscience, but thought better. So he plucked it and gutted it and cooked it in the cottage pot. He offered the broth, and the choicest meat, to his father, but the old man professed perfect indifference to food. So Brian ate the whole pot himself – the entire pot, over three days.

Then his father had grown feverish, and his legs had swollen fat as hogbodies, and his fingernails had blackened and fallen away. He stank very bad, and Brian took to sleeping outside – it was a warm summer, and the nightsky was a canopy more magnificent than straw, and though he was stiffer in the morning than he was when sleeping indoors a little motion and kicking and leaping banished that from his arms and legs. His father worsened. Many people visited, though few stayed for very long: the stench was so bad now you could smell it from outside. Black spots had come all over his face, and blobs the size of goose eggs clustered under the skin of his neck. Magret, who was supposed to know about such things, declared these *gavocciolos*, and warned him to have a priest shrive the old man sooner than later. But such things cost money, and Brian was reluctant to part with the chickens necessary to raise the twopence to pay for it. He had more or less decided to do so anyway, as an act of filial piety, when the old feller died and it was too late to worry about such things. Brian wrapped the corpse in hessian and borrowed a wooden spade and dug a hole next to his mother and buried him. Stephen from the top of the hill, who had ten acres to Brian's two, had been ordered to kill one of his two pigs for one of the lord's infrequent feasts, so Brian was able to buy a scrape of hogfat for an obol, and this he mixed into a soap to wash the inside of the cottage. He spent a whole day doing this, but it still stank, so he continued sleeping outside the now empty house for a week or so more, until the weather started to chill.

He met with the lord, and explained the situation to him, and the old man expressed sympathy, but told him to marry nevertheless. Brian ignored this until the bailiff came, and then he married Alison, and life carried on.

The lord praised Brian's way with the chickens. 'Yours are the best fowl in the shire,' he said, 'and you can be proud of your way with them. Marry and have children, and you can raise many more chickens.'

'Yes, my lord.'

The old man pulled his long beard into two separate forks, and grew animated. 'At the moment, you put the chicken merde on your own garden, I suppose. My steward speaks well of you, you don't stint us your produce. But, my lad, with more chickens you'll have more merde than you can use, and this can be sold to others. Money, money, money.'

'Sell to who?' Brian asked.

'Always a good question,' cackled the lord. 'Really, it's the only question. Sell to whom, yes.' They were in the hallway of the manor, and the lord was on his way out to his horses, going hunting he was, so Brian was conscious of the danger of trespassing on his time. But he seemed happy to chatter on. 'To whom. I tell you what, you know, the King himself will be spending more time at Havering Palace. The royal kitchens will always need produce.'

'Yes, my lord,' said Brian.

'And that's another thing – what's your rate? Three a penny? I'm come from London, just this last week, and there chickens are two a penny. Two a penny! That's what you should charge the royal kitchens.'

It had simply never occurred to Brian that he might alter the price at which he sold. Prices were, he had assumed, simply features of the human world, like the eminence of the noble born and the lowness of the villeins. He was so shocked, indeed, to discover otherwise that he couldn't think of anything to say in reply, and so only bowed his head.

After he married, he and Alison alternated happy pregnancies with mortal ones, and soon they had three children wailing and eating and pissing on the bed, and soon enough the first-born was old enough to be given charge of extra chickens, and so Brian's stock grew. The King did not, in the end, favour Havering-at-Bower, and Brian did not have the face to insist upon two for a penny from his fellow villeins, so nothing changed for several years. Then the King was away, they said, in France, which was further off even than Windsor, and was a place full of the king's enemies.

A wolf harried the sheep, and the lord ordered a posse assembled to hunt it. Brian was given an old spear with a rotten wooden handle and a rusty head, but he repaired the wood with boiled sinews as glue and a wound cord around the whole length of it, and he scraped the blade clean with stones. He joined the posse like a Great Knight from the old stories. The wolf was finally caught in its lair, suckling its cubs, and they killed it and the lord had it skinned and the pelt cured and hung in his manor. After it, nobody mentioned the old spear, and so Brian wrapped it in cloth and kept it at home. Little Alison, their oldest, grew sick, and developed a cough that shook straw from the roof, and then she died, and her mother wept and grew thinner still. But then she grew fat once more, big with another child, and a son was born, and they called him Oswald.

E-leh leh luckluckluckluck
E-leh leh luckluckluckluck

Then, without warning, the King did favour Havering-at-Bower, and the Prince his son too, and they were often resident there. There were some great feasts. Several villeins asked permission to carry wares to the great house and sell them, and the Lord agreed, for a half of their money. The goods were all his, by law, so he could have asked for all the money; but of course then nobody would have wasted the best part of a day walking to the manor and back to sell the goods. Compromise is always the mark of a good lord. At any rate, Brian hooded two dozen chickens to keep them calm and tied their feet and slung them over a pole and walked all the way to Havering. He kept the birds alive so that they were as fresh as possible to sell. Alive so that the buyers could see how fresh they were. He had never visited the place before, and was amazed when he passed between the two big oaks that flanked the approach and saw it for the first time – it was four great manor houses crashed together into one enormous structure, surely bigger than any cathedral or palace, big as the whole city of London together, or so Brian imagined. He loitered for an hour or more because he was unsure how to approach such magnificence, or where to go, and fearful that he would be beaten for presumption if he came close. But then a man he knew, called Edgar the Nine-fingered, came by, herding two big geese with a stick. Edgar showed Brian which flank of the huge brick-built edifice to approach, and which door to wait at. 'Some say, knock,' Edgar noted, 'but I tried that in Trumpington, and a man came out and beat me with a cane. So I just wait.' They waited for an hour, until a maid emerged with a slop bucket, and she called the cook out, and he agreed to buy the geese and the chickens, the former live, the latter dead. 'I've kept them hooded and living,' Brian explained, 'to keep them fresh.' 'And I've kept my wits hooded and living,' the cook returned, holding his fist close to Brian's face, 'so as to not need the fucking obvious explained to me.

Wring their necks and I'll buy them at three a penny.' Brian might have gone along with that, if not for the fist. He kept his calm face on, but part of him wanted to smite the cook with the pole he was carrying, squawking birds and all. 'Two a penny,' he said. 'A shilling the lot.' The cook scoffed and rolled his eyes and turned his attention to Edgar and his two geese. Nine-fingered Edgar said: 'I can get sixpence a head for these in London.' 'You've never been to London, shit-tongue,' retorted the cook. 'You're a nobody. Me, I have seen the King himself as close to me as you are now. Threepence each.' For a while the two haggled back and forth. 'I might give you fourpence for that one,' said the cook, eyeing the larger of the geese. 'But then I'd only give you tuppence for that other, on account of it being so fucking scrawny.' 'Sixpence a head in London.' They settled on ninepence the pair, and the cook went inside and came out again in person with nine brown pennies. A maidservant shooed the geese round the side of the building, the birds hissing like rainfall as they went. Edgar slipped quickly away with his money. The cook saw Brian, still standing there with the pole over his shoulder and said: 'You still here? Go, go, fuck off, before I wake up the house mastiff and he comes out and bites both your balls off.' The cook went back in the house.

Brian sat down on the grass bank outside the door, and rested one end of the pole on the floor. The chickens were not happy. They kept opening their wings and clucking and shuffling. Brian did not move. It was some time after noon, and big clouds the colour of whitepink blossom were barging into one another overhead. The sunlight came round the edges of the clouds in long, straight lines, spears of brilliance reaching down from God to his green world. Away to the west some of the clouds had darker bellies, but they showed no sign of coming in this direction. Larks tumbled over one another in the afternoon sky, spilling their long and complicated songs. The wind was rising a little, and the trees all around shushed the birds. For a while Brian only sat. The clouds parted, and bright sunlight pressed a great flat-edged shadow onto the grass beside the palace.

A serving boy, who could surely be no older than six or seven, put his head round the door, saw Brian, and shrank back inside. The clouds came together again and the air grew chillier. Brian sat. The stonework of the wall facing him was a marvel of intricate placing. The builders had not only arranged the flints with an almost supernatural neatness, they had somehow embedded different coloured stones in the matrix to create diagonals, fine shapes, true beauty. For a while Brian tried to imagine the process involved, but the mere thought of it puzzled his brain. So he stared at the roof for a while, and pondered how he might arrange such solidity for his own cottage roof. It was clearly beyond him.

A maid, kitchen maid by the look of her, came out of the door. 'He says, take tenpence, do?'

'Shilling,' says Brian.

The maid slipped back inside.

A little while she re-emerged. 'He says, wouldn't pay a shilling even for a whole hog, nohow.'

Brian thought to himself that a pig could cost twice or three times as much, depending on the size of the animal, so clearly the cook was not telling the truth here. Tall Stephen, who had twelve acres to himself and gave himself airs (though it was all the lord's land, really, and no more Stephen's than Brian's two acres were *his*), had once boasted as much, or complained, when the lord had taken his best hog. A strange mixture of boasting and mourning. Brian did not reply to the kitchen maid, and she retreated back inside.

He waited a long time, and the sun started to go down. He would be making the last part of his walk home in dark at this rate. The wind got up, and some rain drops flew about, in an exploratory way; but no proper shower came. Finally the kitchen maid came out for a third and last time. She approached Brian in a rather timid fashion, and then held out her hand. A silver coin. Brian took it and looked at it. One side was marked with the cross, and dotted around the rim. In the centre of the other was the king, sharp-bearded and crowned with a huge crown, looking straight out.

'It's a shilling,' the girl said.

'I know what it is,' Brian said, although he had never before held such a thing in his hand. 'Here,' he added. 'You want me to bring these inside?'

'Says if you set foot over the threshold he'll kick your can't say where he'll kick you, maiden as I am.' She blushed, but smilingly. He smiled at her, too. Her eyes did not look in the same place at the same time, but otherwise she had a pleasant face. '*I'll* take them in,' she said.

'Shall I wring them necks?'

She nodded, and he quickly killed each of the birds in turn. Then she heaved at the pole, smiled at him, and dragged it inside.

He waited, and several servants put their heads out to look at him, and drew them in again, tortoise style. It did occur to him just to go, but he wanted his pole. Eventually the young boy from before brought him his pole back. He thanked the lad, and set straight off. The sun was setting now, and the quality of the light had grown denser. Older. He used the pole as a walking stick, and held the shilling tight in his left hand. To exchange a great weight for a lesser one, he thought. He felt a tremendous lightness in his chest.

He made quick progress, and the closer he got to home, the more confident of his way, the quicker he was. He arrived at his dark cottage and woke his wife. There was not enough light to show her the coin, so he made her feel it with her fingers, and that led to other kinds of feeling, and soon they were coupling, grunting, and the oldest girl was awake and wailing at the noise they were making.

The next day he hid the coin, and went up to work the lord's lands. He did the same the next day and the day after. Word got round of a great feast at the house, and he thought to himself: maybe the King himself ate one of my chickens.

The steward came down to claim the sixpence, and scowled when he saw the coin. 'You'll be wanting change of that,' he said. 'It's very far from convenient to give you change, you know. Couldn't you take your money in pennies?' But there was no helping it. He took the coin away and for a fortnight Brian waited for his change. He knew that if he reminded the man, he would be rebuked, reminded that everything of him and his belonged outright to the lord, and that included the whole of the shilling. But by not raising the matter he gave the steward no pretext to say any such thing, and finally the man came down to his cottage on the day after the Sabbath and counted out six ill-shapen brown penny coins.

These Brian cached in a safe place.

Within three months, though, the old lord was dead; and the young, new lord came riding down from Cambridge on a splendid horse that cost (so the rumour went) thirty full pounds, and as the boy – how young! – rode through he met nobody's eye. They were villeins and he was noble, they all understood that. But the old lord had treated them as people, not as chattel, and Brian felt the twist in his chest at the thought that those days were over now, and that the future was uncertain. Everybody went about their usual business. They worked the lord's land, and worked their own in their spare time. The young lord vanished – to London, some said, to Jerusalem said others, it was all one.

Then the young lord came back and the steward announced that everybody must give over half their produce for a great feast. Nobody was happy about this: half was more than the usual heriot, and nobody would be paid for any of the produce. There was grumbling, and villeins would gather in little groups and mutter to one another. Brian lost more than most, because his children were now old enough to tend the hens, and his success at selling them to the King's house had given him ideas, so he had hatched out four dozen of the silly birds. He wondered about dissembling this, but the steward was often down in his acres, and he did not think he would get away with it. It was a grim day when he killed twenty-four good chickens and hauled the carcasses up to the Manor. Alison was at the house helping the other women repairing the big tapestry, the one with parrots on it, that had gotten torn. When Brian got back to his own cottage, the children avoided him, on account of the anger in his face. He went inside and unwrapped his spear, and then he sat on the ground and laid it across his lap. His mother had told him stories of knights-at-arms, and quests, and fighting griffins, which he'd always pictured as chickens the size of a house, with claws and fangs and a poisoned beak. The blade was rusting over again, and he spent a long time scraping it clean. Then he wrapped the spear up again and hid it in the rafters, and went on with his duties.

The next day it rained hard.

Newsreel (4)

Joan: Belle, Full Pleasant and Sage

The Chronicle of the Four Leading Valois calls her *a lady as wise as she is beautiful*. In Kent, her own county, she is a byword for courtesy and modesty. Yet who is she really? Is she more than 'just a pretty face'? For the first time, our people have been granted unprecedented access, behind the public façade, and

SHIP SINKS OFF DOVER

those on land watched as white sail slipped from sight beneath turbulent waters as black as mud though all but one crewman clung to the wool bales from the cargo and were able to swim to

BUBOES!
BUBOES!
BUBOES!

ale to be sold freely to all that dwell in the borough on pain of a fine levied at 6s. 8d., and thereafter imprisonment, nor shall any citizen be denied good ale at any price beyond three gallons of small beer the penny, four gallons of strong beer for 2d. Two ale tasters are by law to be appointed to see that the ale sold be good and set, such persons being required to be sad and discreet individuals. So ordered

PART 3. AT SIEGE

Newsreel (5)

TAILLEBOURG TAKEN!

Bells sounded in London Rejoyce, declares Archbishop

Fall of Taillebourg

'They turned *taill*,' said the Earl of Derby, 'and *bourggered off*.' There was much laughter at the noble lord's witty words. The town resisted occupation, and one noble knight, Sir Edmund of Wokinghame, was slain by stones thrown upon him from the rooftops by villainous commoners. In response to this act of treasonous aggression, the Earl of Derby ordered all inhabitants of Taillebourg town executed, men, women, children, and all property seized to the crown, with the exception of seven nuns who kept a garden in the town and who were permitted to depart provided they swore upon the holy rood never to return. 'Taillebourg is clean now,' the Earl declared. 'We can *tally* one more *burgh* for the king.' There was much laughter at the noble lord's witty words.

STEP BY STEP THROUGH THE PAS-DE-CALAIS
diverse boats removed across the channel

that sulphur and saltpetre be mixed with pitch inside twopenny earthenware pots be used to fracture on impact once lit and hurled to spread Greek Fire upon

THOMAS OF ROLLESTON TO JOIN SIEGE
At his majesty's gracious command Thomas of Rolleston royal clerk is to bring twelve artillers and gunners to man novel weaponry at the ongoing siege of Calais which has wasted near eleven months of royal time these weapons together weigh near one thousand pounds

of iron and hollow like birds bones with an outlet at one end to spit fire and hells brimstone and propel boulders of stone or iron asked about his phallic weaponry Thomas Rolleston declare the penis is bad the gun is good frenchmen come from the penis royal victory comes from the gun

EXCESSIVE SNEEZING IDENTIFIED AS SYMPTOM OF NEW SICKNESS

land is hollowed out by war. We march through empty villages, cottages with the doors removed so be piled with goods and dragged behind. Every sisterfucking peasant has squeezed themselves in behind a city wall. The very wind pushing at the shaggy heads of the trees mocks us with its hissing and

CALL ALAS FOR CALAIS

catgut or foxgut for to restring mine lute

> *At Nightingales' song*
> *When woods grow green*
> *And leaf and grass throng*
> *It is the most beautiful*
> *Beautiful . . .*
>
> *. . . . . .*
>
> *. . . Beautiful thing I ever have seen*

BLACK GEORGE

The irony was: the part of war George hated the most was the waiting around. And now, somehow, he had acquired the reputation of an expert in prosecuting siege warfare, of all things, which was all waiting, all around. The campaign in Poitou had been going smooth enough, and that was when Old Orford, whom some said was called Oliver, though George suspected him of humbler origins than such a name implied, had taken a fancy to him. He'd been smacking some soldiers into order, as they gambolled about like lambs in the spring sunshine, bellies full, on the march up to Saint-John-of-Angels, but then he had given up, Orford the old, Orford the tired and complainy. It had provoked George to see those youngsters with no discipline, and he'd taken on himself the shouting and the smiting them with the flat of his sword to get them to line up right. Afterwards Old Orford had come over to him, complimented him. He had a face like a stone gargoyle that the rain had washed for a hundred years: round and white and ancient, with two great gullies creasing the skin down left and right cheek – they could almost have been honourable scars won in battle, so deep the wrinkles ran. He was bald like a baby, and there was a misty whiteness about his eyes that made George suspect his eyesight was going. Not that he'd admit as much, or he'd lose his place. But this might have been why he was so hospitable to George. 'Stick by me,' he told him, 'at the next town. See how a siege is handled.'

But in the event the burghers of Saint-John-of-Angels, watching the English army approach in good order and large numbers – twelve hundred men-at-arms and two thousand archers was the official count, so the actual army was probably the still-impressive strength of 800 and 1500 respectively – grew so terrified they capitulated without a fight. The Earl of Derby received six of the leading citizens in front of the whole army, and the Frenchmen wept real tears, and knelt on their knees like villeins, and begged for their lives and the lives of their townsmen. One of the Frenchmen kissed and licked the Earl's hand as a dog might, and the soldiers laughed heartily at that. And Derby, the old bastard, looked splendid in the special Roman-style chair, cleverly made to fold about its middle axis so as to make it more portable. He took that chair everywhere with him. Seated like an emperor of old, his moustache like two daggers, his long beard like a broad sword, God's wrath and justice mingled in his eye, the whole effect was only partly spoiled by the fact that he had a boil the size of a knuckle, red like a ruby and crusting black, on his cheek underneath his eye. Also he had drunk too much wine two nights before and been sick on his short-fitting armouring jacket and his servants had been unable entirely to wash the brownyellow stain from the red and white and blue embroidery. But the French were certainly tremblearsed with fear, and they swore to be good Englishmen from that day forward, as long as the English King, or anyone representing him, could keep them at peace with the French.

Then they marched on to a tight little fortified town called Neort or Nort or Nayert, and things did not go so well. The inhabitants refused to surrender, and Derby ordered an assault. It took two days to reassemble the trebuchet, fat lot of good that old sling ever did, and the carpenters worked too hurriedly to build a siege tower. When they tried to roll this forward two of its wheels sheared right through and the whole structure got stuck in the soil, and that assault was called off. The Earl was furious. Twice more they tried, and on the third assault Old Orford somehow stumbled onto the ground in front of the English archers, and got himself shot in the neck by his own side.

George took what valuables the old boy had about him (into safekeeping, he told anyone who asked) and then borrowed a broadhoe from the sappers to dig the old man a grave. When he returned from the woods, having performed this duty, the Earl's men grabbed him, and he found himself in a private audience with the lord himself. There was no opportunity to explain the state of affairs, and he listened in a flat panic as Derby told him they were abandoning the siege of pissing little Neort or Nort or whatever the fucking excrescence was called and moving on to Mont-Rail-Bonny, not a fucking mountain mind you, the Most Noble Peer assured him, despite the fucking silly name, but a town with low walls, should be a piece of fruit to be picked easy from the fucking branch.

That evening George went among the carpenters and sappers and tried to act like he had been expecting this preferment. Nobody seemed to resent him anything; indeed, over the following days, he began to understand that they were happy somebody else was in the line of the commander's fury. Orchestrating siegecraft was both dishonourable and dangerous work – not that George cared about the dishonour, particularly, but he was less than keen on the danger, which resulted less from enemy fire and more from the displeasure of impatient noblemen who wanted to knock towns down in short order like push-pin quoits. A nobleman's temper was a perilous thing.

So they came to Mont-Rail-Bonny, and there George's career in siege warfare could have ended, had his natural ignorance and incompetence become obvious to the nobles above him. Yet fortune rolled his wheel a quarter turn and lifted him up. The town contained a mint, and two hundred members of the guild of French coiners whose job it was to manufacture the French King's money. They sang and spat defiance from their town walls, and promised to defend their royal charge to the last man – and indeed it was clear that making money had made the town rich. Yet the walls were low, as the Earl had said, and there were many gates, including a river gate where ore and metal and seacoal was brought in by barge, and Derby was optimistic. Fiercely so. He ordered the carpenters to begin assembling the siege engines, in full view of the defenders, so that they might think the assault not yet ready to begin. And crafty Derby formed up his archers in the brakes and other coverts, so that when many of the Mont-Railers came up onto their battlements to fire arrows and bolts down amongst the carpenters, Derby ordered an immediate assault. The men were perhaps inspired by the thought of huge heaps of coins waiting just on the far side of the walls – houses made with roofbeams of silver, gold nuggets lying like pebbles in the street. At any rate they were fierce. The archers shot many men on the battlements and scared the rest away, and the walls were irregularly-made and with enough slope to enable soldiers to set ladders and to clamber up the rest of the way where the ladders didn't reach. George, meanwhile, took a team of sappers round to the river gate, under a canopy of shields, and bust the hinges. But by then the town had surrendered. Nonetheless, despite it really having nothing to do with him, the Earl was delighted with his work, and praised him verbally in front of a dozen knights, and gave him a silver shilling.

The town inside was well-appointed, handsome houses overhanging streets as often paved as not, and a fine spacious church. There were, of course, no great heaps of coins simply lying around, and this fact by no means sweetened the mood of the English. And whilst the Earl hurried with his best knights to take control of the mint he left the rest of the force to vent their frustrations on the town that had defied them. Men who tried to surrender were cut down with swords and then, later, as the swords became too blunt to cut, were clubbed to death. Women hid themselves in upper rooms, but gave their hiding places away by shrieking in terror at what they could hear going on outside. A soldier called Piers de Brunofeld occupied himself by throwing children in the river and stamping on any that made it back to the banks, and soldiers brought him children to dispose of in this fashion, held upside-down by their ankles like market fowl. Archers practised their aim. The best targets in terms of honing one's skill were those timid Frenchmen who peered round corners to see what was going on. Two brothers stood with axes by the open main gate and cut down any citizens who tried to run out: it was a game to them, to see who could tally the highest count. Since the town had been anticipating a long siege, there were good supplies of food and wine, and men become cruel when well-fed and drunk and bored. Cornish Peter, who had burnt his face quite badly at Saint Josse and now looked like a pig, went about telling anyone who would listen that the best strategy with the townswomen was to break their fingers first. Hold the hands down and then crush them with a sword handle or hammer or anything heavy. Otherwise they would scratch you with their sharp little *ongles* when you stuck it up them, and they might get your eyes or tender parts. But break their pretty white *mains* and all the fight went out of them, and you could do what you liked. Nob thought that a lot of faffing about: just grab her, do her, snap her neck. A Welshman chopped a merchant's arm off and fed it to the fellow's own dog, before his eyes. But the disobliging Frenchman died too quickly to see the hound feast, with the blood splashing out of him like a full bucket kicked over.

By the time my lord of Derby had finished counting the money in the mint, and securing the building, and came back out onto the street most of the townspeople were dead. He had not specifically ordered this massacre, but neither was he displeased it had happened. Then, the next morning, in one of those odd little ironies of war, the whole force witnessed the hanging of Piers de Brunofeld, who had done such sterling work the day before. In the night, though, he had discovered a young girl who had hidden herself, you have to admire her ingenuity really, *inside* a mattress. But Piers had found her, and pulled her out through the slit she had made, naked and covered in feathers. Which was a clever find. But then, somehow, during the course of that night, a madness had taken hold of him. He had dressed her and started calling her his lady and his belle and so on. A knight of the King's Guard, Sir Nevill de Brandin, told the fellow to cut her throat and bung her in the big pit the sappers had now dug, and he refused. When Sir Nevill repeated his command, the foolish fellow had struck him, actually boxed him on the side of his head, and tried to run from the town, with the girl and a stolen horse. He was caught, of course, and hanged in front of the whole army, and there was some grumbling at this because he had been a popular soldier, but then again, he'd obviously lost his mind, so there was that.

Next was Poitiers, a much bigger city, with sprawling walls and many gates. The citizens there were not numerous enough to man all points on the wall at once, and it was a simple matter to stagger assaults to cause them to run frantically from one side of their wide town to another. This soon panicked them, and when sappers (George watched in admiration) set a fire under the weakest gate with tar and saltpetre and sulphur, the masonry tumbled and soldiers broke in. The whole population abandoned their town with yells of terror and great bird-like shrieks. Some of the Poitiers men and women opened all the western gates and fled away. But there were too many of them to all get out before the English seized the town, and six hundred or so, mostly oldsters and the less fit, were put to the sword. It's a predictable feeder, the sword, and not in the least fussy. Whatever is put to it, the sword takes. It prefers to put its point in at the collar bone and go straight down, for that is quickest and makes least mess. But it is happy to crack down and into heads, or to chop at exposed throats – these might be sliced, or crushed, and either would cause a choking death. Forty citizens were kept alive so as to dig a pit for these bodies, to spare the sappers that labour (they had done such good work breaching the wall), and also to scrub the walls clean of blood with straw, and afterwards they were hanged, outside the city walls, and their bodies left as warnings. But the Earl was very pleased with Poitiers, which was rich and full of plunder, and for a week or more he picked amongst the spoils and sent some of the best stuff down river to the sea on small boats with orders to take it back to his estates in England. The town was picked so clean there was nothing left in it worth staying for; and it was too far inland, and the journey too far by sea, to persuade English settlers to come out and occupy it. So they left the town desolate and marched back to Saint-John-of-Angels, and there was prize money for everybody.

But it was no good pissing around in fucking middle-France like this, Derby said, when Calais is what the King really wants. A cannon pointed at the heart of France, the King calls it, and it's held out a fucking year or more, and think how pleased with me his Gracious Majesty Roy de Angleterre and Franceterre will be, said the Earl, waving a silver cup to emphasise his words and spilling spots of blood-red wine as he did so, when I deliver him Calais. Haven't we proved we can break any French siege? And yes my lord was heard and excellent my lord was heard and nobody said anything about Neort or Nort or Nayert, or about the fact that they had burned the town of Lusignan but not been able to touch the castle, or any of the half dozen counter-examples.

To Calais they went. Up the coast to Normandy, and then across to Calais. Normandy was all fucking forests and wild-eyed peasants more beast than men. Weeks, they marched. Weeks! But eventually they reached their destination. And now, Black George thought to himself, here I am: colder and more miserable and no longer in the Earl's good graces, for Calais was resolutely refusing to yield to the English siege, and nothing the English tried seemed to have any effect. And then the news was that the King of the Scots had been captured and the Scottish wars all but done, which meant that Edward himself was coming to Calais, and that only added to the general pressure and unhappiness.

And then the King arrived, and do you know what? He only brought the fucking Queen herself, may Christ and all his saints bugger me if he didn't, and her Majesty so heavy with child it looked like she had a cannonball stuffed under her kirtle. Black George didn't get close to the King, of course; nor to any of his retinue. But like the other freemen, he spied out what he could from a distance. The bright colours of the royal clothing, flapping and snapping like velvet jaws in the strong wind off the channel. It rained for three full days, and then there was a day of bright sunshine and the King inspected his six new cannon, specially brought over, and each

77

was fired – although only four of the six actually launched any cannonballs, the other two squibbed and failed. But the ones that did fire made a *fucking loud noise*, as Pauley No-thumbs eloquently expressed himself to George. A *fucking* loud noise. Then the royal figures, made miniature by the distance, rode back to the main camp, and George saw that the Black Prince was with them. And at sunset as Black George ate porridge in his tent with Parley and Nob and John-of-Scowl, he said to them, 'if I bump into his princely Majesty around the camp at all, as could happen—' could happen, agreed the others, faces over their bowls '—with his gold hair and black armour, well if I do meet him I can say to him, begging your Royal Highness' Pardon, but we fought together you know, at Cressy it was.'

'You never mentioned this before.'

'Most surely,' said Black George, ignoring their sarcasm, and gave them yet again the benefit of his choice memories of that day.

The siege was a bugger, though. The Calais walls were thick and high, and the population of the town large enough to keep all points guarded. The summer was warm, but not so hot as to mean foul parcels – rotting bodies, diseased animals – could be flung into the city to spread disease. Not that they didn't try that. They tried *everything*. The cannons, though the King loved them, were worse than useless: a mighty noise like the devil farting, and a huge rumpled white sail of smoke billowing out from the cannon mouth, which made anyone who breathed nearby cough and spit and swear, but no actual useful destruction when the ball hit the wall. The sappers, whose opinion George trusted, insisted that a cannon threw a ball with less force than a good trebuchet, and none of the many explosions and nonsense so much as knocked a single crenulation from the walltops of Calais. They tried tunnelling, but they were too close to the sea, go down only a little way and the ground was too sandy and wet to permit tunnels. They built three big towers and rolled them towards the walls: one broke and stuck in the ground a hundred yards from the hall, another the Calaismen managed to set on fire and the third started to come to pieces when shaken too hard by the fighting of English attackers and French defenders at the top. There were more senior people than George in charge of the siege of course, which meant that the displeasure of the higher-ups fell on their shoulders rather than his. He just tried to make himself useful, and keep out of the way. But he was as frustrated as any of them.

Then Sir Thomas Holland, who was one of the fucking heroes of fucking Cressy, they said – I was at Cressy, said Black George, and they don't call *me* one of the fucking heroes of fucking Cressy – took charge of the siege. It was a long game, see. Long game.

The worst thing was that supplies kept finding their way inside. The port was so easily suppliable by water, and two sailors in particular managed to sneak cargoes past the English. One was called Marant, who people called Marant the Mariner, and then there was his companion, called Menesterelle d'Abbeville. Who knows what riches in gold the Calaismen rewarded these two with, for they took insane risks. They were both nearly captured several times off the coast between Boulogne and Calais, but always escaped and slew many Englishmen. Eventually Monsieur Menesterelle's boat was sank, and he drowned; and by means of a fisherman intermediary Marant was bribed to sell his supplies to the English forces – at, George heard one rumour, the incredible sum of fifty pounds a cargo – and so the siege resolved itself into the oldest strategy of all, which was: starve them out.

Camera Eye

the camera sees only red, closer, and the red resolves into a matrix, grid, the ropes that interlock. But

stand further off, sirrah, step away, back off or my sword shall force you away as I am a as je suis un gentilhomme:
red cloth.

the sunlight still sifts down from the west as the sun sets, and the streets washed clean in the bloody light   Monsieur de Bainville, his new red cotehardie and hood, scarlet with fine dyes, and bought for twelve full *écus d'or* exactly one day before the English sailed into Calais Sound and shut the city up like an oyster

oyster the word, say it aloud and his mouth starts to moisten, oysters and black bread and a pat of new churned butter the size of his nose, and a glass of vin blanc and   but there   but there is no use in dwelling on

He wore his cotehardie with hood up through the winter, when there was still food in the city. Then he took it off when the summer grew hot. Oysters, wailed the young women, several of whom he had known before the catastrophe to be daughters of good family. Bread, wailed the young women.

wine, wailed the young women. Monsieur, you are a wealthy merchant, a fine gentilhomme, you can help us monsieur, to food, to food. One leapt on him, like a tiger, when he came out of his house, walking slowly because he was starving and his muscles were tired, and because he had no meat left on his feet so his footbones clanged comfortably on the cobblestones, and he had boiled his leather boots in a copper pot of water to try

for potage a fortnight earlier and she jumped his back
and near knocked him over   *msieur   msieur
msieur msieur msieur msieur msieur*   begging him
for scraps of food you are wealthy msieur you have
secret larder msieur I will pleasure you any way you like
msieur Christ will avert his eyes and the Devil himself
forgive us but we must eat

it was a bad dream he had once had, a mere child,
seeing the scarecrows on the Flanders road and then
seeing a frame with a murderer's withered corpse still
pinned to it, and the two getting muddled up in his young
head, and crying in the night and flooding his breeches
with piss at the slightest moment and his father beating
him and here it was, this scarecrow woman, her ribs all
palpable underneath her wool chemise, stretched and
loose as a nightgown   she rubbed her hips against him,
but without force or enthusiasm, and the shape of the
underlying bone was horribly evident, like a crab's shell,
and then the thought of crab made him start to salivate
again, and think of a seafood broth, and he could barely
push the woman away as he began to cry and stagger off

she had ripped his

he didn't care

The rats had grown wary, but his son Jean somehow
caught one, clever Jean, and brought it to his father, in
piety, a good lad, he regretted having beaten him so often,
but how else did one raise sons? So together they skinned
the filthy black pelt off the creature, and nicked its guts

out with a fruit knife, and it took some sawing to remove the head and the tail, and then in a pot with rainwater, for the river was full of corpses, and cooking it over a fire and the smell of it dear Mother of Christ in a Kirtle of Heavenly Blue how it smelled, and he drooled so much he made his beard wet, like a senile old fool. Gaston was dead and Marie was dead and Sophie was dead and his wife was long dead but Jean was alive and a canny and a good lad, a good lad.

It tasted bitter, and the morsels of meat were small as mousedroppings and there were hairs floating in the juice, for they had been over-eager and clumsy in flaying the beast but it was food, and they sucked at the bones and then both slept.

When he awoke he was hungry again, and it was dark.

He lay, sleeping, waking, fitful, unhappy, through the night   then, without any apparent interlude of time, the summer sun was shining bright, and there was singing in the streets and the bells were sounding. King Philip had come, people called, with a great army to raise the siege, and they were all saved, and he wept with gratitude to God   and went to his garderobe and took out his finest dress, his scarlet cotehardie and put it on. It hung off his frame now, and he must roll the sleeves and pinch it in at the nape of his neck with a pin, but he felt proud again.

Citizens crowded the battlements and looked across the sound at the flat lands of the northern spit, and there – there – were French banners shimmering with the breeze on the mount of Sangatte, between Calais and Wissant, and scores of men in bright armour on tall horses, and he couldn't help himself he looked at the horses and his mouth started to drip spit and he imagined cutting a large steak from the flank of one beast and cooking it on live coals and eating it then and there and thousands of men-at-arms behind them and the afternoon sun behind all adding splendour to their glory,

his belly twisted inside, loosened, he had to run for the jakes, but too late, and *le diarrhée noire* spatters and stains the hem of his red cotehardie. He limped home, his bowels clenching, and called for his manservant to ready a wash-bowl, for he had immerded his legs and wanted to wash, and then remembered that his manservant was dead and his other servants all fled away or dead or who knows what. He called for Jean, but he was not there. So, awkwardly, he fetched a washing bowl, but there was no more rainwater in the tub, since they used it all for the meal, so he had to go out and bring in water himself – like a child or a woman – from the river. He lifted his bright red clothing above his waist and scrubbed his legs with wet straw. Then he dipped the shitten hem of the cotehardie in the water and tried to get most of the foul stuff out. Then the *diarrhée* came on him again, and he got to his jakes just in time and squirted a thin stream down onto the street.

He was exhausted. He slept. He slept and woke more thirsty than he had ever been before, and he had no energy to go to the river, what did it matter anyway, so he drank from the muddy water in his pot, and fell asleep again.

where was Jean?

pains in his bowels woke him, and it was dark. There was a nasty squelchy coating on his thighs where he had disgraced himself. He tried to stand, but instead collapsed on the wooden boards. So thirsty he thought he would die of thirst, and reaching for the copper bowl his hand flapped and he spilled half of it, but managed to get more inside him. Then he crept like a worm over the floor board, and when a large splinter went into the skin just above his naked knee he barely felt it, the whole of his inner belly was on fire so badly, and then the loosening of his bowels and a stink so foul it made him weep with shame and disgust.   He woke again, and his whole body was in a paroxysm of thirst   the inside of his mouth and throat felt scarred over and dry as the sands of summer and his head hurt, and his bowels opened again and a liquid fire fell from them and there was a body in the room with him which was his body or another body he was too confused to know the difference but thin as a skeleton thin as a scarecrow and it rasped like a crow with a woman's voice *msieur msieur msieur msieur msieur msieur msieur* and he tried to lift himself, but the fluid part of his soul had all crusted and scabbed over, and all moisture had fallen through his torso and out his arse and there was a savage thousand-pin-prick glimmer in his chest that spread down his arm and then and the thirst was and the skeleton woman was wrapped in a kirtle of nightskyblack and came to lay on his spine every single knobble and contour of the vertebrae visible through his drumskin skin and *msieur msieur msieur msieur msieur msieur msieur* reached round on its neck long as a cockerel's and its mouth closed over his mouth

Newsreel (6)

PHILIP: FRENCH ARMY 200,000 STRONG
Relief of Calais: Latest Reports

the king of France has made the decision to go with his entire host to Calais, to raise the siege, sensing that his people inside were dreadfully constrained, and he had heard how access from the sea had been cut off from them, which meant that the town was in danger of being lost. And with him were the duke of Normandy his eldest son, the duke of Burgundy, the duke of Bourbon, the count of Foix, my lord Louis of Savoy, Sir Jean de Hainault, the count of Armagnac, the count of Forez, the count of Valentinois, and so many counts and barons that it would be a marvel to recount

Il sont sourds.
Je vous embrasse.
Le Coeur de Coeur est à vous.

TIMING, TIMING
Ripeness Is All, say Experts

Timing of the harvest is important. Harvesting should not be too late because of the risk of grain shedding and not too early, because the unripe grains may be crushed during threshing. Grain shattering is a genuine problem. Cut only the heads with a sawtoothed sickle sackle suckle seckle section sexton sacking sick sick sick

RIPE IS AS RIPE DOES
Soon enough the ripe fruit drops into the hands of the patient

ISTE EDWARDUS superius nominatus, qui post conquæstum tertius, Post deceslum vero EDWARDI Regis Anglia Francia, Hoc quoque anno Angli obsiderunt villam de Calais. vero illustris Rex

cut off their access by sea, he had a great castle constructed from long timbers, and had it made so sturdy that it could not be damaged. He had it positioned on the seashore and equipped with espringals, bombards, crossbows and other instruments, and garrisoned within it sixty men-at-arms and two hundred archers to guard the harbour and port of

PHILIP RETREATS

The king of England considered that the French could not reach him or the town of Calais except through the dunes on the coast, or from higher up, where there were a great many ditches, bogs and marshes and places of soft ground and dirt and treacherous pathways and only one bridge over which one might pass, called the bridge of Nieuley. So the king drew all of his ships close to the dunes and furnished them with bombards, crossbowmen, archers and espringals such that the French army might not pass. And he had the earl of Derby establish a camp on the bridge of Nieuley . with a great number of men-at-arms and archers, to prevent the French from getting through, unless they took the route through the marshes, which are impassable between the mount of Sangatte and the sea. On the other side of Calais there was a high tower from which twenty-two English archers defended the way through the dunes from the French, and they had fortified it very well, as they saw it, with double ditches. When the French were lodged on the mount of Sangatte, the commons noticed a tower there. The people of Tournai, numbering perhaps fifteen hundred men, advanced towards it eagerly. When those within saw them approaching, they fired at them, wounding some. Seeing this, the companions of Tournai were enraged and set to attacking this tower with gusto. But they were driven back, and many men were killed, and no matter how he might renew the assault there was no way through and so he withdrew. After the departure of the king of France, with his army, from the hill of Sangatte, the Calesians saw clearly that all hopes of succour were at an end; which occasioned them so much sorrow and distress, that the hardiest could scarcely support it. They entreated, therefore, most earnestly, the Lord John de Vienne, their governor, to mount upon the battlements, and make a sign that he wished to hold a parley.

PART 4. POITIERS

Newsreel (7)

NEW POET LAUREATE CROWNED IN ROME
Petrarchus declares himself 'pleased as punchinella'
De Vita Solitaria available from both good bookstores now

THE HORSE NO FLATTERER. They say and truly it is said that noblemen learn but one skill truly, and that is riding their horse, for in all else that they do, book-learning or languages, politesse or playing at games, they are surrounded by sycophants who will praise them whether they do well or ill, but when they mount a horse they meet a creature that does not know how to flatter them, and will throw them off if they ride badly. And so it is they learn to ride well. There is a powerful moral to be taken from this truth, sir, madam.

Intentio vero nostra est manifestare in hoc libro de venatione solum ea, que sunt, sicut sunt, et ad artis certitudinem redigere, quorum nullus scientiam habuit hactenus neque artem.

HAWKING FOR PLEASURE AND PROFIT.
Falconry in six easy lessons.

Glorios Dieus, don totz bens ha creysensa; Meravilhar nos devo pas las gens.

Barmy army
Barmy army
Barmy army
We are Edward's
            barmy army

JOAN OF KENT

They said of her, from a young age, that there was a strange grace in her eyes, and they did not mean it entirely as a compliment. Even as a young girl, she understood that flattery might express kindness or else envy, hostility and even fear. Even when she was a child she understood that. She watched and they did not like the way she watched. You are beautiful, they said, and it did not move her. She had the camera's eye, is the truth of it, and her gaze went where a modest girl, or a well-bred woman, ought not. It was a camera eye because it went into every chamber: inside huts and castles. Inside armours. Inside bodies and minds. As for actual *camerae*, for her own *camera camerarum*, at her father's house she had a room of her own, and her own maidservant in a small room adjacent. She knew without having to be told that most people did not live this way.

In spring and summer she spent as much time as she could in the gardens. The empty skullcaps of the bluebells. The cabbage-folds and inward reds of roses. The dropsical purity of lilies or the long green tubing through which bindweed blows its effortless white trumpet. 'A fair flower among the fair flowers,' said her mother. She never saw her father. A party of girls visited for her eighth birthday, amongst them Eleanor and Anne and they both talked endlessly about how important their fathers were. Mother didn't talk of what happened to her father, but she knew. The camera's eye (she didn't call it that back then, of course) gave her a series of vivid images, a man she did not recognise, in a loose chemise, with his beard tied up to leave his neck bare, and then a sword swinging through the yielding air. The sword changed colour, and it took her a long time to understand why the sword changed colour. It happened like this: the sword was a polished silver that shone for a moment so bright that Joan thought it might be a splinter of the same stuff out of which the sun was made. But then it passed through and came out blue-black and shedding little petals of purple-black, and there were many of these petals, so she then thought it was a limb or branch of some heavenly tree.

The severe-faced woman who called at their house, from time to time, was the Queen of England. She must curtsey when this lady came in the room. But she did not want to curtsey to the long face and its bad teeth, so she curtsied to the woman's rich dress, laced in and out with thread-of-gold.

On her eighth birthday Joan got a new dress, in blue with silver carbuncles, and then another new dress when she was nine, in green with a pattern of white embroidered feathers. The King came to visit after that, with, it seemed to Joan, a thousand people in his retinue. He had a long beard that smelled bad, old food going rotten, something decaying. She could not avoid the stench when he embraced her. 'How old my child?' Near ten years, Majesty, she told him, and looked at him. It seemed normal to her to look at people this way, although it usually upset them. She didn't know why. The King stared back, and then looked away. He turned to his queen. The camera's eye gave her a glimpse of the King as a baby, a grotesque old bearded baby, suckling at the breasts of a woman, not the queen. Both the King and the woman were naked. Sometimes the camera's eye showed her things she only partly understood. But this was rancid, she thought, though the camera's eye gave her no smell or other ways of feeling the occasion. She didn't like the image.

'I want you to think of me,' the King told her, without meeting her ten-year-old gaze, 'as a father. As indeed I am, father to the whole nation.'

'Your Majesty,' she piped, and bobbed down and stood up. Everybody applauded. Later there was a big feast, and lots of dancing, and musicians traipsing through the kitchens and stealing food, and dogs yapping, and a great deal of jubilation. The torches smelled of old straw and bad things as they burnt, and the King kept stealing suspicious looks at her. She couldn't help that, she thought to herself with a nine-year-old's haughtiness. It was their problem, not hers.

Sometimes Ned visited, usually with his mother, twice, when he was a little older, on his own, with his own retinue. She got on well with him, because he was not thrown by her beauty, or her way of looking, or her pristine detachment. He was one of the few she met who, patently, liked that about her. Liked her. Of course he was good looking, but that was true of everyone she knew. Except for the ugly people, and there weren't many of them. And the commoners, but they were neither beautiful nor ugly, since they were not really people. Sometimes her camera eye took her into a villein's hut or the field or a man selling fish on the street or something, but she was rarely interested in any of that stuff, and without the focus of her attention the camera tended to drift away.

Once the King visited with two of his yeomen, Nicholas Langford and John Payn, which made Mother angry, though she hid it (but Joan could still tell). She didn't know why it made her mother angry. Once she tried to tell her nurse about her camera eye. It wasn't easy, since she lacked a name for the experience, and it translated poorly into words. The nurse said something about the perils of bewitchment, and then put her fist in her mouth and went red, and then took her fist out and said that begging her pardon witchery could never touch one so high born it must be a sign of divine grace, and then ran out of the room, leaving her embroidery on the floor. Joan told her younger brother, once, and he only laughed. She found herself wondering why she felt the need to tell anybody, and, after thought, decided she wouldn't, actually.

There was never a thought of marrying Ned, of course: he was Prince of Wales and heir to the throne, and would marry a foreign princess, on account of diplomacy and war and so on. Not that she was unworthy of him, granddaughter of Edward I as she was. Mind you, it was daft to think of marrying Tom too. He was old: five and twenty, and she but twelve. Most of all he was below her. Simple as that. True, her father had lost everything when whatever happened to him, with the sword that went from silver to its shedding the black-red petals, had happened. And although Edward III had restored their family status and honour there was still a stigma, nebulous and noxious, attached to their reputation.

Sir Thomas Kent, a mere knight, was simply her inferior, socially. But he was a mighty warrior, they said, and Ned always spoke of him as a noble fellow and a fine fighter. He had gone to war once, in Flanders, and was going to go again, in France, to fight alongside the Prince of Wales. He told these things to her, as his serving man stood haughtily behind him. As for Joan, *well* – Lady Saint-Omer and her serving maid Betty sat beside her, in an upstairs room at the house in Mons.

Well?

Well, they said.

She had come to Flanders two years before, on a fine ship with bright-coloured pennants and a sail white as a summer cloud against blue sky. She was one of the Queen's party, along with the two young princesses. Joan stood on the deck and looked calmly over the scintillant grey between her and the diminishing land. Lady Saint-Omer was with her, and she gave vent to her own anxiety with repeated, slightly manic reassurances to her young charge. 'Do not worry, my lady. It is but a short crossing. The captain assures me the conditions are perfect. Do not worry.' Joan wasn't the one who was worried. Her camera's eye gave her swooping, bluemurky views of mudbanks under the crush of the water, brown and grey, bunched up against flat hillocks of stone shaggy with seaweed, and here and there the smoothed outline of a shipwreck, primped and adorned with spotty polyps and flatfish and weeds like a hundred great green tongues lolling in the half-light. But these sights did not disturb her. There was something delicious about it, really. A calmness. Noah steering his ark over bright flat waters, and all the animals within filled with joy. On this voyage, though, not all were joyous. William and Catherine Montague were belowdecks, moaning and puking, though the sea was flat as a table of green fields and the boat hardly rolled at all. It sailed briskly into a Flemish harbour before sundown. From there it was a coach trundling slowly inland until they came to Mons, or Monts, or Mounts, ironically titled whatever it was for the whole of Hainault was flat as Kent, and the mountain a mere hillock. They stayed in a nice house with three storeys, and Joan played with the children of the servants at running up and down until Lady Catherine stopped her. Everybody spoke French, almost – *almost* – like that spoken at home, except for the commoners, who spoke something else entirely which sounded in Joan's ears like *ach-ach* and *bar-bar* and gibberish noises of that variety. She saw little of the Queen, who was often away; and although she played with her cousins sometimes the girls struck her as flighty and shallow.

Lady Saint-Omer asked her whether her menses were in flower yet, and she had to have the whole messy business explained to her. Then there was Lord Bernard of Albrecht, comically fat of body and with enormous whiskers that contained hairs of four distinct colours. It seemed Joan was to marry his son, and thereby cement a vital cornerstone in Uncle Edward's plans to take his lawful possession of France, even though they weren't in France at all. The adults talked about this and broke off when they thought she was listening; but it all made perfect sense to her. Sometimes her camera eye showed her the whole of Europe as if from a great height, a sprawl of rubbles and soil, fields nibbling at the flanks of the hairy forests, and a lace frill white all round the coastline like a dress hem. One day she was sitting in the garden at the back of the house, and the cook's son came to chatter. Her stillness encouraged him, or to be more precise didn't *dis*courage his extraordinary boldness, and he chattered and chattered – it was probably, she thought to herself, because she was foreign to him. The English king had no chance in France, where he was looked upon as a petty duke from a cold and marginal land, the boy said. He had lost a hundred battles, and nobody wanted him as their lord, and he would soon be gone. Joan didn't say anything; she only looked at him. He became panicky, gabbled that everybody hated the English, even in Hainault, they only did trade because they needed English wool for their weaving and clothmaking, and trade was ignoble and base. She inclined her head, and said nothing, so *he* said, oh yes he knew she thought *him* ignoble because he wasn't a lord, but his father was a great chef and cook, renowned across northern Europe and anyway he was going to join the army and do great deeds, which was a greater honour than trade, and then he'd be a knight. Then, with a kind of desperation, he kissed her and put his hand up inside her skirt. Had she struggled, or resisted, or called out he would doubtless have pressed on; but she did nothing, and her impassivity spooked him and he ran off. When she saw him next he had been whipped, and the left side of his face was all swollen, and he skulked along the walls.

She was introduced to many noblemen, some older than her by a decade or more, some nearer her own age. She was formally introduced to Armand d'Albret, Bernard's eldest son, bosseyed, blotchy-complexioned and with a wispy moustache of hair so fine it could have been made of individual threads of silk. Her calm gaze made him uneasy, and he fidgeted, but it seemed that they must soon be husband and wife.

But then, she thought, she would have to stay overseas, and would not see her own mother again. And since everybody complimented her on her preternatural beauty, she wondered if it were vanity to want a better-looking husband. Tom was good looking: gentil and parfait and strong and, what was best of all, completely at ease around her. He was part of the King's household and so, notionally, under the charge of the Queen, but in fact he was here because he was preparing himself to go to war. It was his second campaign in northern Europe. He came to see Joan whenever he was in Mons, and she enjoyed his visits.

One day, as they walked the garden together, and their respective attendants stayed in the cool of the house, he said: 'you sit so still. Twelve years of age – never, never seen composure like it. Your serving maid fidgets like there are caterpillars in her clothes. Lady Saint-Omer performs as if she were a character in a morality play called Bored. But you just . . . sit.'

'It unsettles some of those who meet me,' she said.

'I can believe it. And your gaze! Your eyes are like nobody's eyes. I'm sure everybody compliments your beauty, but most of that is of the ordinary sort shared by many beautiful people. Your eyes are . . . otherwise.' Those were words that sank into her mind, and no mistake.

> Her eyes
> Otherwise
> Otherwise
> Her eyes

Then, later, he said: 'I will do great acts of chivalry and prowess on the battlefield, you know. I don't say so to boast. I am telling you.'

'I understand.'

'Will you, then, marry me? Of your own will, I mean? I am not a prince or a lord, but I love you more than any such could.'

She thought about this. Her camera eye gave her no insight or vision where Tom was concerned. All that she knew about him was what she had been told. That she could see no further into his life intrigued her. 'My mother would not agree. The Queen will not agree.'

'No,' he said.

She tried to imagine what people would say. But no image came. 'Very well. Marriage.'

He knelt before her then, he a grown man and she a twelve-year-old girl, and kissed her hands. Then he was away for a week, and he came on a Saturday and persuaded her to come on a tour of the city. She didn't tell Lady Saint-Omer. He and his man – also called Thomas, though not a knight – walked her and Betty, both veiled, through the streets of the town. They came to the box-shaped church, dedicated to a saint of whom she had not previously heard called Waudru, and Thomas proudly showed her the bans, posted beside the door, weather-stained. Their bans. She stood on his left side, facing the church door, and a priest married them there and then, outside, and then asked if she could write her own name in the big book, and she told him: yes. Then they went in and joined a general mass. Afterwards they went back to the house at which Tom was lodging, and went upstairs together. He undressed her, and then undressed himself, and they lay on the bed. 'Your blood hasn't come yet,' he said, and she didn't contradict him. He kissed her, and stroked her, but when he tried to put himself inside her he was as nervous as she, and in the end only rubbed on her belly until his seed came out – much more snot-like than she had been expecting. She had wondered if it must not be something dry, like the pollen of plants. But it was sticky as glue. Afterwards they dressed and he said: 'we must tell the world we consummated the marriage.' 'We must lie,' she agreed, but he thought she was rebuking him and became mournful, so she kissed his face.

Then she went back to the big house, her eyes gleaming, and marvelled that nobody could escry the great difference in her. The fortnight that followed was a period of luminous grace, for she held within her a secret that gave her the power, passively but with the strength of a great rock or oak tree, to resist attempts to impose a man or a life upon her. Thomas went away to war. When Lady Catherine told her that the Queen favoured the suit of Armand d'Albret, she mentioned, as casually as she could, that she had married Sir Thomas Holland, and sat, motionless and placid, in the midst of the great fuss she caused. People went to the church and spoke to the priest, and saw the charter of marriage, and quizzed her as to whether it had been consummated, and she said:

'Yes.'

So she was sailed back to England. Her mother was angry, with the sort of fury that simmers for months without either flaring up or dying down. Tom wrote to her saying he would petition the King in person to have the marriage recognised and legitimated, but the Flanders campaign went badly, and politics interfered, and in the event he went off on crusade instead. Since her menses had not commenced nobody expected a pregnancy; and then her blood did begin to flow, and her family decided that the whole misadventure with Sir Thomas of Holland from the north country was a kind of playacting, or little-girl naughtiness. The flow of blood wiped the record clean, as Christ's blood cleaned. Sir Thomas was away in the Holy Land, and few returned from such expeditions. Now that Joan was a woman, her future must be secured. Her camera eye gave her glimpses of the desperation-tinged negotiations with several noble houses. Naturally many people were tempted by the advantage of marriage to the king's niece, to say nothing of the dowry. Bigamy, however, was something else again. Finally, and with a well-placed gift to the cathedral, the Archbishop of Canterbury wrote that Joan's first marriage was null, and she herself virgo intacta. On this latter, he made no physical examination, but relied upon Joan's mother's oath. Her mother made no examination. Joan herself neither confirmed nor denied that her maidenhead had been breached.

Then, rapidly, she was married again: to tall William de Montacute, the son of the Earl of Salisbury. William was unfazed by her gaze – not, like Thomas, because he saw past it, but rather because he was perfectly oblivious to her. He was oblivious to most things, except the proper forms for behaviour, good manners and respect for his status. He took Joan's calmness to be a type of modesty, of which he approved in woman; and since she never contradicted, nagged or bested him he had every reason to be pleased with his wife. He was often away, as the wars were renewed in France, but she did not miss him. At the beginning the servants in her new house were awkward and surly with her, but such ill-temper is hard to maintain in the long run. She settled into a new rhythm of life, running a large manor house when her husband was away, and sitting quietly on his left hand when he was home. He consummated the marriage unambiguously enough, and the experience was physically painful and emotionally discomforting, for she felt it to be a betrayal of her true husband. But there was little she could do, as a woman. The second time was better, and by the third she was finding ways to enjoy the experience.

A child grew inside her, and then her husband rode off again to fight in France, and one night she had cramps and a wet gush of blood and the infant miscarried. 'You're too young, my hen,' the midwife said. 'I'd say wait a year, but I know how husbands are. Perhaps Sir William will stay away in France a year and give your body time to develop?' 'Or perhaps,' Joan agreed, smiling beatifically, 'he will die honourably in battle and never come home.' The midwife shrieked a little shriek at so shocking a statement; and then she laughed and said, 'I promise to keep my lady's secret!' Joan thanked her in a calm voice, and her camera eye showed the old woman breaking her ankle in a fall down a stairway – hurrying to attend a birth in the winter, and wetness on the stairs that had slopped down from a spilled bowl freezing slippy. And the old woman's ankle swelling black, big as a pudding, and then her leg going black, and herself sweating and feverish, and then her dead. She said nothing, of course; kissed the old woman and thanked her, and took a glass of wine, and slept for a day and a night.

The winter snow at dusk, when the moonlight teased a glimmer from the shadowed spread of white. Ducks on the manor pond, surprised at their own legs. She sang the old song

I am winter, that doth keep
Longing safe amidst of sleep.

She sang quietly, to herself, as she worked her needle in front of the fire.

The following summer it was so hot she took to bathing in the pond to cool herself. Her mother, who was visiting, told her: you are not like yourself today.

A puzzling thing to say, really. Who is ever like themselves? People are either themselves, or, as with William, not and therefore not anybody really. But likeness, similitude, approximation, these do not belong with the language of the self.

With the autumn came news of a great victory against the French at Cressy, which was, they said, actually not very far from Hainault. William wrote to say that he regretted not having been at the battle, but that duty had detained him in another place. But Joan's camera eye told her something that was later confirmed by gossip: that Sir Thomas Holland of Upholland *had* been there. Then news reached her that he had achieved gloriously on that battlefield; that he had personally led the Prince of Wales' vanguard – hard to think of sweet Ned as a fierce warrior, but so he was – and that he was now leading the siege of the city of Calais. His war was full of greatness and nobility.

And then further news reached her, by means of a letter secretly delivered to the manor by a friend of a friend of her true husband. Tom had visited the Pope himself, in Avignon, and petitioned him to have his prior marriage to Joan recognised. The Pope was considering it. Joan's mother came to stay, and so did William's father. 'It is not meet that you are so long alone, daughter,' the old man said, smiling mirthlessly at her. 'You shall come along with me, to my castle, and there I shall keep you safe.' It was imprisonment, and there was nothing to be done. She hid Tom's letter, with its formal French, and its seal, and along the margin a scribbled afterthought, *je t'aimeray toujoures; Je ne t'abandonneray jamaise.*

Another winter passed; another spring turned to summer. Her camera eye went not where she commanded it, but instead roamed promiscuously, often tediously, and for long weeks she saw nothing. William returned, and serviced her ponderously in their bed, but no child quickened inside her. Perhaps childbearing had been scratched out of her with the miscarriage. She was moved neither to sorrow nor happiness by this thought. The servants were careful not to relay any gossip to her. Or at least, the only gossip that penetrated Old Salisbury's keep had to do with the plague, and its horrors.

Then, one summer's day, it was over.

She was sitting, with Betty, in the sunlight, amongst the nodding flowers, the green bushes that gleamed as with a varnishing, under a great tree that swayed as if bowing with immense slowness. Courtiers came from the King himself to tell her that the Pope had declared her marriage to William null, and that she was once again a maid, and a carriage came and took her down to Kent.

Once again, polite society was compelled to welcome her, though it did so testily. At a royal dance, when her stocking slipped from her leg, she thought she could see lasciviousness in the eyes of the knights and nobles present – so-called Fair Maid of Kent, twice-married, who knew how often debauched? But the King took her side, though, which proved something, or meant something politically, or who knew what. That was when the Order of the Garter was announced, although it was a little while before the Order could be officially constituted, the arms and blazons designed, the first knights inaugurated and all that sort of business. Sweet Ned selected the designs himself, and one of the first knights to be honoured with the Order was Joan's former husband, tall William. But another, she heard, was Sir Thomas; so both her husbands were now brothers-in-chivalry. Back in her mother's house, she finally received a letter from Tom. He dared not come to England, for fear of the legal displeasure at having undertaken to marry her. But he promised he still loved her, and would not abandon her.

One day Ned came riding, unexpectedly – or, rather, came walking along the path leading a half-shod horse behind him – and gave her a silver cup. Her mother entertained Ned and his men, and a small feast was arranged, using whatever was in the larder. Her brother acted as head of the house, under her mother's benign eye, and welcomed the Prince of Wales and his friend the young Earl of Warwick and the others.

'I was worried, I do confess it,' Ned said, as they went into the hall to be seated. 'I am glad that the plague has not reached you, in here.'

'We are all healthy, your Highness.'

'High me no nesse,' said Ned, grinning at her. 'Were we not friends in childhood? I have known you longer than anyone, Joan. You were a pretty girl, but now you are the most beautiful woman in England, France, Holland – in the world.'

Another girl would have blushed. Joan did not, though she did lower her eyes. As they sat, Edward brought out the large silver cup that was his gift to her. It had fine tracery round its rim and jewels in its base. This he gave to Joan, in front of everybody, with a slight smirk at the foolish ostentation of the gesture. 'I brought it here myself,' he said. Then he laughed. 'What a fatuous thing to say! But – only, do you like it?'

'It is very beautiful,' she told him.

They ate, and afterwards a minstrel sang an old lay to them, accompanied by a recorder player and a tabor fellow. Then, and although the moment did not feel right (although it felt, perhaps, less completely inappropriate than any other moment), Joan said: 'Ned, you know of course that the Holy Father in Avignon has written that I must return to Thomas Holland, and live with him, he as my husband.'

She looked at him, with eyes capable of penetration. And she saw that though the prospect of physical hurt and even of death could never coax fear out of him, this licit affront to his own half-formed hopes did so. And how could they be anything except half-formed? The King would not give permission for him to marry a lass of Kent, when there are treaties to be formed and foreign princesses to be purchased. And yet, she saw, the shiver of despair in him, mixed with something else, which might even have been relief.

'Of course,' he said. 'Yes yes yes.' And then, nonsequitur: 'I thank you.' Feeling the oddness of saying those words to her, he turned instead to her mother, and said them again, in a clearer tone, 'I thank you, madam. Let me pledge you.' And he raised his goblet, and they raised theirs, and everybody cheered, and everybody drank.

Camera Eye

closes in   the veins of a human body, snaking tunnels, flooded with pisscoloured fluid and bumbling softbodied toruses of purple or red, always in motion, hurtling on and slowing and then pushing on faster, in the faster-slower rhythm determined by the everspasming heart itself.

You missed it. It zipped past too quickly to

Follow, follow. The camera catches up with the object. It is a curl of thread, pill-shaped beads strung together in a line and then bent sharp about, like a bishop's crozier. It twists like a worm, and   there's another.

Atra mors, in its unmediated form. The camera sweeps, turns, coasts its rolls up and round to the lymph gland. And here, a huge congregation of the segmented croziers, swarming now with complicated monsters head and tail, scorpion and asp and dire amphisbæna. The body sends in fat shaggy phagocytes to consume the intruders, hug them and absorb them and digest them, but the Y. pestis, once grasped, injects a protein into the phagocytes that messes up their function. Muddles and breaks them. Pores open in the pelt of the immune system cells, they cannot multiply, they flake away. And the Y. pestis keep on swarming and multiplying, and flooding the lymph with chemicals that inhibit the immune system signalling, and growing more. Soon there are so many that they begin physically to block the passages. From the nodes everywhere is open to them

The body responds with its repertoire of resistance. It heats everything up, to try and cook the invaders, but Y. pestis is not bothered. Tissue, great rippling sheets of cells locked together, swell and inflame. The lymph nodes in the neck and armpit and groin swell, infected, battlefield sites. Blisters push up the outer skin, and swell to the size of a duck's egg.

The camera soars into clean air. Here is a vast hollow cylinder, ten miles long and built of some clear, smooth plastic, or a similar substance. Fly along its shaft, and see a regular fanning pattern of subsidiary shafts, each proliferating into myriad interlocking meshes.

The camera is too close. It pulls away – a feather. A hen's feather, against a background landscape of particoloured flesh. The hand that guides it has not been washed. The sharp point, pressed into the outside of the bubo, breaks the skin, and hot lymph flushes out, a soup of millions of Y. pestis and stuttering white blood cells and bits and shard and fragments of the human body's inner congregation of cellular components. Hot fluid washes over the thigh and down. Breaking the bubo does the patient no good, whatever the doctor thinks. It does the patient no particular harm, either, except to open the chance of infection and inflammation to add to the already overwhelming crush of symptoms. The real effect of bursting the bubo is to put those around the patient at risk of infection. But the doctor does not know this.

Acral gangrene. Blood from the mouth. Black spots on the arm

no, these are not spots, they are flecks of dirt. And now clods of dirt, black in the dusk, and soon the whole body is under the ground and buried, clutching coldly at the other bodies in its pit.

JOHN WYCLIFF

Vanity, said the preacher. A crowd of perhaps twenty listened to him.

—Heaven, he said, is castigating man for his sins. Have we not been warned of the coming of this scourge – we and all Europe? The unseasonable rains, the pillar of fire that shone about the Pope's palace at Avignon, the noonday star in Paris, the showers of blood in Germany, fiery vapours spouting from the earth in Cathay and India – these were portents. Why here in England, at Chipping Norton, a doubleheaded serpent appeared with faces like those of a woman, and great wings like a bat. There have been innumerable miscarriages and monstrous births. God has warned us, and his warnings were not heeded. Now he strikes – strikes with deadly boils in men's groins and armpits, the spitting of blood, fluxes of blood from the bowels, unspeakable thirst, the black tongue, the putrid inflammation of the lungs, the pestiferous stench which infects the very air.

Wycliff was not the one preaching, but he was the one listening most attentively. The speaker was the great Thomas Bradwardine, newly returned from Rome and with the Pope's own chrism upon him. A great and holy man. Young Wycliff felt the tingle of awe when he watched his master address the people of Rochester.

The people of Rochester, though, seemed unenthused. The crowd was not large, and some of them drifted away in the middle of the sermon. The King had snubbed good Thomas – Doctor Profundus they called him – denied him the Archbishopric he so clearly deserved. The canons at Canterbury had chosen him, had they not? This, the man who heard the King's own confession before the great battle of Crécy! But now John of Ufford, that placeman, that reptile, was Archbishop of Canterbury, and Bradwardine was preaching the gospel of God's Wrath from a wooden stage in Rochester High Street like a wandering priest. Some of the worthies of the town listened attentively, and some of the commoners too, but the crowd was thin.

The crowd was thin because the population of the town was denuded. Later, in the inn-lodgings the Doctor Profundus had taken overlooking the water, Wycliff sat in a chair against the wall with three other clerics, and listened to Bradwardine talk happily of his time at Avignon. Oranges growing on the trees, swollen with sweetness and sunshine. The warm breeze. The Papal Palace as large as a mountain, and filled with earthly reflections of the splendour of God! Blessed by the holy father himself. And Wycliff felt the holy spirit inside him, that warmth curling in his breast, that told him a great ministry was about to begin. England had fallen from the truth path of God, but now this great and holy man was come from the Pope himself to bring the Father's cleansing blessing to every town and village, to every churchyard and country field, and to chase away the devil's contagion!

Wycliff bid his mentor a good night, and walked to his own (cheaper) lodgings on the far side of the town. It was a mild enough August evening. The star Venus looked down from her high and lonely place, and rabbits scuffled in the hedgerow. The German sea, flat and dark, washed at the coast. Hope, Wycliff told himself, was the greatest facet of love.

In the morning, after praying for a long time, John came back to see the Doctor Profundis. He was almost not allowed in at the front door. Bradwardine's attendants looked grave. He had passed a bad night.

Disbelieving these reports, he went up the creaking stairs and put his head through into the low bedroom. The Good Doctor was sitting up in his bed, his neck a ruff of grotesque bulges, his gaze sickly. He opened his mouth to greet his student and black bile and red blood dribbled out.

That night he was worse, the fever very great and the gavocciolos grew larger still. A doctor was called, but he had to come up from Gravesend, for all seven of the doctors native to Rochester had died. This fellow smelt of old wine, and his hand was not steady. He broke the buboes about Bradwardine's neck, and recommended a herbal posset and for the patient to drink clean red wine.

By midnight Bradwardine was dead.

They buried him, and prayed for his soul, and lit candles for him in Rochester's echoey cathedral, and went their ways. Wycliff prayed to reconcile himself to the will of God, expecting to experience the symptoms of the plague himself, and thinking on his many sins. But the plague did not seize him. His mind, not his body, became possessed, and that by a thought that would not leave him, day or night. The thought was this: how had the devil been able to corrupt the body and take the life of so holy a man? When he had the Pope's own chrism still upon him? Either the devil was stronger (as God permitted him) than the Pope, or the Pope was in some way weaker, or more corrupt, or more diabolical, than he pretended?

Wycliff rode to London on a small brown palfrey with a bad cough, all his worldly belongings in one saddlebag. He slept where he could, wrapped in his one blanket at the roadside, underneath an early September haystack by Catford, and finally, when he came into the city, at an inn. Prices were low, for there were so few travellers these days. As he prayed on his knees in his room at sunset a thought occurred to him: a body divided between two passions would wear itself to pieces. God's will manifested in the world through His proper authority, and men and women submitted their selfish desires to the law of God. Perhaps England suffered because it was divided, and so the grace of God was dissipated? There cannot be two temporal sovereigns in one country; either Edward is king or Clement is king. We make our choice. We accept Edward of England and refute Clement of Rome.

This was a very terrible thought, and it caused Wycliff to tremble with fear. He prayed and prayed, and eventually he slept.

Soon enough he rode north from London, heading for his home county of Yorkshire. To begin with he kept to the high road and away from villages. Then it occurred to him that this was a pusillanimity unworthy of a man of God, for the villages were where the plague was most severe. If he was to die of the plague, then that was God's will; and as a priest he had a duty to the people. He stayed his terror at the thought of blood spewing from his own mouth and staining his beard; or those hideous pebble-hard swellings in neck and armpit, and guided his slow horse into the next village.

A sluggish breeze, and late summer insects floating in circles through the warm air. Nobody about.

A wagon was parked underneath a large oak on the village green, and somebody was lying underneath it. The legs of this person were perfectly motionless, and remained so for as long as Wycliff watched. He conquered his inner fear, and walked his horse slowly down the main street towards this cart.

He saw: a dog drinking at the pond with a clip-clopping noise.

He saw: the cart, and as he walked past he could see the whole figure beneath it. Something had worked sharp teeth at the corpse's face.

Ravens bobbed and hopped on the compacted dirt in front of a small house, going in and coming out of the open front door as bold as if it were *their* house. The ones coming out had little shreds of dull red cloth in their beaks. It was not cloth that their beaks held.

Wycliff tied his horse outside the village church, and took off his hat and went inside. It was dark inside, and there was a bad smell. Something glooped stickily at his boots, and he saw he had trodden in a mess of blood. Not so old as to have dried completely, not so new as to be still flowing. The blood was shaped into a shield-shaped wedge on the floor, a black and shiny blazon that could only belong to the noble house of Death, and at the apex of this flat shape was the face-down head of a man dressed in an expensive green coat.

Wycliff washed his boots in the pond as best he could. The dog plodded off without giving him a second look, his tongue out like a strap of unbuckled belt.

On his way out of the village Wycliff found a pit, excavated, loaded with bodies, and then half filled-in. But the diggers had been interrupted in their filling-in, and corpses, some wound in sheets, some thrown in fully dressed to leer at the sky, tangled together in hideous intimacy.

He rode on, back into the innocent countryside, away from the dwellings of men.

A bullock eyed him from over a thorn hedge. The beast was still in harness, which meant that somebody had not gotten around to unharnessing him. The field he was in was unplowed. Maybe he had wandered over from another field.

At least there were no bandits or sturdy beggars to harass a humble traveller. Of course, Wycliff's greatest protection against assault was his poverty. But that was not a sure remedy against the more violent sort of ruffian.

He was going to stop and water his horse at a rivulet that ran beside the road, when he noticed several corpses upstream. Heads in the water, either to drown themselves in misery, or in the attempt to quench their thirst as they died. Wycliff rode up to them and prayed, trying to escry God's will – should he bury these poor folk? But he had neither shovel nor hoe. Or leave them to the dogs and the crows? But that seemed hideous. Then again, he thought, as he sat on the ground and ate the last of his bread, he could hardly bury *every* uninterred body between here and Hipswell North Riding. Who knew how many corpses this little river contained, upstream?

He regretted eating the bread as soon as he had finished. His mouth was dry, now, and he could hardly drink from the stream. Sadly he remounted and rode north.

Thrushes wrangled in the autumn sky.

At Linton he found life again. The town had burned down in the thirties, and was still not wholly rebuilt; but in amongst the weeded open plots there were many smart-looking new buildings, and the church, dedicated to the Virgin Mother of Christ, carried two broad glass windows in its front like great jewels. The people were suspicious of him, ambling in on his horse. Folk gave him a wide berth. A tavern had a bushel over its door, and Wycliff bought a tankard of weak beer: sour, despite the bushel's promise of a fresh batch. How old is your beer? Wycliff asked the tavern keeper, who scowled and said that his wife brewed the beer, not he, and she had been away two days visiting her sister in Trumpington who was sick. God send her health, said Wycliff, earnestly, and drank the vinegary brew. Did Christ on the cross not drink vinegar? Who was he to set himself over his lord, God himself? Later the tavern keeper, not coming too close, had asked him who he was, whither he was going. Fleeing the plague? Fleeing London? It will do ye no good, for the plague is faster than a palfrey. It is already in York, they say.

—It is God's judgement, said Wycliff.

—I wish he'd judge another way, said the taverner, and retreated to his back room. I wish, he called from the far side of his door, he'd rebuke us with words, and not with death.

On his way out of town Wycliff saw a cart laden with bodies trundling east, pulled by a bullock. In the sky overheard, leaf-shaped birds tumbled and circled. A great cloud hung over the north, shaped roughly like an escutcheon, parted per pale and per fig. The sun grew feverish as it approached the horizon.

South of Nottingham he passed through a village (he didn't know its name) where bodies littered the streets, some clothed and some naked. There were as many rats dead on the ground as people. It was good to put that place behind him, but images from what he had seen there loitered in his mind's eye.

He slept in the forest that night, and went on in the morning, but with a hot wrongness in his head, an ache, weepy eyes, a dry throat. He thought: it has come to me, then.

The day was cooler, as if autumn had suddenly taken hold of the country. The sky was all white. It pleased the ravens to todd about the sky like wind-blown leaves. White, and whites. Will the world end in white? Or perhaps we should say: winter construes the whiteness of the wind into something static. The birds are a mess against the whiteness. He found himself saying words aloud, not knowing why he spoke, or why he spoke those word *muster*, *mustard, book, fire, sparrow*. The copse of trees on yon hill: an acropolis. The west sucked the sun through its milk. His mind was blank. His skin was all soreness and weariness. His throat was horrid dry. Horrid dry.

He found a place, in amongst the trees, and let his horse go. This was as good a place as any. The horse would not leave him, but chewed such grass as it could find in the woodland. There was a stream and he drank, and then he wrapped himself in his blanket and tucked himself between two roots and readied himself to die. He would meet his maker humbly, and ready himself to be judged.

> *Lo, the book, exactly worded,*
> *Wherein all hath been recorded,*
> *Thence shall judgement be awarded.*
>
> *Liber scriptus proferetur,*
> *In quo totum continetur,*
> *Unde mundus judicetur.*

In the morning, he woke with a clear head. Not the plague, after all. He was thirsty, and a little shaky with hunger, but otherwise well. He saw this at once for what it was: a miracle. God had not abandoned him. He prayed and sang a hymn, croakily enough. It turned out his horse had not abandoned him either. Wycliff ate fruit and drank water and rode north. In three days he was home.

Newsreel (8)

CARTS FILLED WITH NEW CARGO
WEST COUNTRY DEPOPULATED

Flagellants are the new craze, and if you've a mind to join in, you'll need – 1 ironspiked knout or whip – 1 set of rags – 1 doleful face. The words that everyone is singing:

Dies iræ, dies illa
Solvet sæclum in favilla,
Teste David cum Sibylla

.

Commit *these* words to memory

Put not your trust in princes nor in the son of man in whom there is
no help. Psalm 146:3

+++JEWS BURNT+++
Likely cause of plague located and cauterised

FIRST THINGS AND LAST, THEIR HOLOCAUST: ALL MEN

in the Black Death which purveys aprioric roots for aposteriorious
tongues this is not language of any sins of the world

AQUINAS BEAUTY REGIMEN!
integrity, wholeness, symmetry and radiance

Around the house the flakes fly faster,
And all the berries now are gone
From holly and from cotoneaster
Around the house. The flakes fly – faster
 —faster

    —faster

        —faster

            —faster

The earlier that service is offered to the Lord, in the morning of the
day or the morning of a man's life, the more pleasing it is to him.
The lark, wakeful early in the morning, serves God with singing,
and so it will find food for that day though tempest lash down or the

sun's mirror blast drying heat. If the Lord of all things so generously rewards a bird for praising him in the morning, then how much more shall he reward one of us for serving him in the morning with appropriate vigils, prayers, attendance at mass and however else the holy spirit shall direct him?

BLACK PRINCE

The land was hot and dry. The land was the colour of sand, and there was also dust in one's throat, and grit in one's eye. The land was the colour of straw. The land was the colour of jaundice. The land was scorched white and taupe and yellow. You could not believe it could be hotter, and then it grew hotter. Knights rode through the tan landscape. One breeze primped the fanned-out spear tips of this dried palm, castanetrattly, like feathers from the tail of a brass bird showing off its rear plumage.

They passed through woodland, and the shade was some relief. There was a shrunken stream in the midst of the copse, and everyone drank, and the horses too. They rode on, and passed out the far side of the woodland.

A castle called (according to a peasant they grabbed) *Ornave* perched on a rock, with cypress trees around it like spears. Ornave closed its gate against the Black Prince. A dozen French nobles gathered on the battlements, and parleyed; Ned on his white charger, shuffling four feet backward, rearing, stepping forward, drifting a little to the side. The Prince as impatient as his mount. For half an hour it seemed that Ornave was going to resist. 'Monsieur,' the mayor called down. 'There are weaker castles to the east and the south. May we suggest you lodge there tonight?' 'Do you understand what it means to deny me?' Ned yelled back up. 'Do you comprehend what you are doing?' They shrugged and apologised and referred his anger to the new King, Jean, no giant of monarch as his father Philip, but a king still. 'Should we disobey our king, Monsieur?' 'Your king?' the Prince shouted back. '*Your* king is called Edward, and not Jean.' Then the main body of English men-at-arms came marching into sight, in none-too-impressive order, and the nobles of Ornave visibly quailed. Edward, angry now, formed his troops up before the gate and swore to the mayor that he would be welcomed into Ornave as a guest or he would hang the whole population with their left hands stuffed in their mouths, but that it must be one of the two. Still the castle held out, until the carts finally trundled up, and Edward ordered the carpenters to begin dismantling the empty houses of the village to build a siege engine. At this the Ornave nobles changed the tune they sang, opened the gates, threw together a hasty feast and welcomed the English. Edward told them that, since he had been made to wait outside for six hours, six nobles would be hanged, but he would give them the liberty of choosing which six. A little while later six trembling men in fine clothes and big felt hats were pushed into the centre of the main courtyard. Edward inspected them. Their fingertips were hard-skinned, their teeth white, their tongues fluttered and stuttered when they tried to speak. Their fine clothes hung about them, and they wore their hats like cowpats. Then Ned, going amongst the rest of the population, spied a humbly-dressed man, but a man whose teeth were brown from the sugar he ate, whose skin was white and soft – and in two minutes he had flung a noose about this one's neck and dangled him from a second-storey pulley spike. The whole castle stood and watched this fellow twitch and kick. His hands were not tied, but he pulled and gouged at the noose in vain. His right foot, flailing, caught against his left calf and pulled his hose half down, not only exposing his manhood but showing it sticking out stiff like a truncheon. The man's face was soon black as any moor's, and his tongue turned blue, twice the thickness of a normal tongue. Eventually he died. Edward let the faux-gentilhommes go, and went into the castle's chapel – a tall, echoey chamber. Here he prayed, alone.

Mercy touched his heart. He decided not to hang the other five gentilhommes.

At a village called Couffoulens they found only those the inhabitants had deemed too sick and too old to move. Warwick proved this incomplete evacuation merely a function of insufficient motivation by chasing them out of the place at swordpoint, and leaving them sitting under some arthritic old *oliviers* on the outskirts. Then the English took what food the departing citizens had left behind – not much – and set fire to the place. Then they rode on to a new town, with a central *château* of white stone, very pretty against the blue sky.

Sir John Henxteworth rode up and down, asking anybody who would listen *but what is the name of this town?* He was writing an account of the most noble and heroic *aventure* of the chivalric and notable Black Prince of England, and wanted to get all the details right. But nobody knew the name of the place; the locals had all either scarpered or else were holed up in the little castle in the middle. It hardly mattered. Edward quartered his troops in the place – his long and rather straggling line of foot soldiers – men were still marching in by noon the following day: something needed to be done about that. Discipline won battles, not numbers. Which was fortunate for him, since he didn't have numbers. There was a stylish stone fountain in the town, *la source* the French called it, olives studding in the trees round about, game in the forests, some early vegetables nestling unharvested in the bronze-yellow soil. The French inside the chateaux attempted no parley, and were clearly hoping that Edward would grow bored and march away. But he decided here to attempt some of the drill his father had perfected on his Scots campaigns. Early reveille, no breakfast, marching in step up and down a dry field on the outskirts, archery practice, plenty to keep the men busy.

After a week, Sir John relayed the news that a certain Guy de Pépin-le-Sarrand wished to parley with the Prince. Ned had his servants dress him, mounted his charger in full armour and colours, red and blue and gold glorious in the morning light, and rode to the gate. When the fellow – his face still chubby after only a week of siege, and with an insolent shape to his mouth – began to try and bargain over the top of his battlements, Ned cut across him. 'You have kept me here a week, and two of your people must pay with their lives for each day, one man and one woman.' 'My lord of England,' Guy returned. 'We sent our women and children away before your coming.' 'Two men then,' Edward snapped back, growing angry. 'You should have opened your gates to your lawful lord as soon as we arrived. Seven days tries the patience, and the patience of a prince is violent when trespassed upon.' 'My lord of England,' the Frenchman began again, but Ned had had enough. He turned his horse around and rode away. Three nights later, in the small hours of a moonless dark, his men carried a ladder to the side flank of the castle. The ladder only got them two thirds up the side of the wall, but there was enough to enable the first of them, a noted climber from the north of Wales, to slip over the battlements with a rope tied to his waist. The men were able to get up and onto the battlements, and so down again to open the main gate. Edward's force then surged inside, killing first in darkness and then, when the defenders' panic overcame them, by torchlight and with more leisure. Blood spread over the flagstones black as polished leather. There were many screams, and only one English casualty – a knight from Essex called Sir Edmund de somewhere-or-other who was chasing a knight. This panicky Frencher ran, foolish in his fear, face-first into a stone wall and fell to the ground stunned. Sir Edmund found this so richly comic that he had to stop where he was, and lean on his sword, incapacitated with laughter. And as he stood like that, some French laddie snuck up behind him and slipped a knife into his back up near his neck, and that's how they found him. By dawn they had survivors drag the corpses through the gates and pile them on open ground. Then they hanged the rest from gibbets on the outskirts, for the birds to devour. There were women, too: not noblewomen, but serving maids and the like, retained for the various comforts they could provide. Ned disposed of these amongst his officers. For himself, he abstained. Had one of the lasses looked anything like Joan it might have been a different matter; but they were all small and swarthy, and he resolved not to defile the purity of his memory of the woman he loved by indulging in any such baseness as to lie with one of them.

William de Montacute, Earl of Salisbury, was one of his knights on this *chevauchée*. Indeed, Ned had asked him personally to accompany them. For your renown in the fight and the good duty of your noble family name, he had said, but they both knew something else informed their chilly friendship. It was that William had been married – ought not to say married, now that the Pope had spoken, but how else to describe what had passed? – to Joan. That William had known her body, naked in bed, slim and white and shivering with pleasure as he moved his spur within her, as his broad, tawny-coloured shoulders clenched. There had been a child, rumour said, but it had been miscarried. Ned did not, of course, ask Sir William about this. He did not mention Joan at all. The Pope had taken his wife away, on some priestly pretext uncovered in Hainault, but actually because of the fox-like plotting of Tom Holland, that sly man. Brave, a very help in present trouble at Cressy – but sly, and sleekit, and far from the chivalric ideal. William had married again of course. Or not again, for that again would contradict the incontrovertible word of the Holy Father. Say, then: married. Elizabeth de Mohun, a noblewoman from the West Country someplace. Somerset, was it? The couple lived in Berkshire, and Ned had met her when she had been formally presented at court. Handsome enough, though black where Joan was fair, and buxom where she was slim. But she had already given him a son, and was now with child again.

As he always did when he took a castle, Edward went to pray alone in the building's chapel, on his knees in the echoey space. There was still blood on the wall, here, but he ignored it. He prayed to God the Father, whom he always pictured with the King his own father's beard; then he prayed to the son, who understood the hardship Ned suffered, living in the paternal shadow, the cup to be drunk of strenuous living and danger on the battlefield and self-denial, the cup that he must not ask to pass by him. Finally he prayed to the Holy Spirit, and at this something strange occurred; his heart quopped softly. He felt somebody else was in that holy space with him, but when he looked to the right and to the left he was alone. The dove of the Lord, invisible as his grace, and a great sense of presence. He rose, his armour clanking, and turned to face the great white block of light coming in through the high east window. Light, leading him on. He walked, as in a trance, out of the chapel, and down the steep little cobble road, and through the main gates. He could hear the white rush of the wind rummaging in the leaves of the fat-headed sycamores, making a noise exactly like a shower of rain. God was with him, the Holy Spirit closer to him than the arteries of his neck, more central than his own heart. He was, he realised, weeping. His cheeks were wet.

One of the knights of his household was at his side. 'Highness?' It was Sir John Henxteworth, that scribbler. Ned pushed the heel of his hand across the left cheek, across the right, and said: 'good Sir John: of this you must *not* write.'

'My lord.'

The next day Ned left a small troop to hold the castle and rode on with his army.

Newsreel (9)

TO THE KING – A SON. Thomas of Woodstock Prince of this Realm and 1st Duke of Gloucester, 1st Earl of Essex, fourteenth child of our Glorious Monarch King Edward III, born in good health at Woodstock Palace in Oxfordshire.

Riot on St Scholastica Day
PLAGUE-AFFLICTED CITY WRACKED WITH VIOLENCE
Disturbances begin in Swindlestock Tavern
2 DAYS OF RIOTOUS DISORDER

63 scholars and more than 30 citizens of Oxford are dead and many more injured after two days of ungodly, unscholarly and riotous behaviour in the city of Oxford in the shire of Oxfordshire.

Students Walter Spryngeheuse and Roger de Chesterfield assaulted taverner John Croidon by flinging beer in his face, calling it *pissy vinegar* and *not fit to wash silverware*, afterwards striking him and smiting him and knocking him oft about the chops. The mayor demanded the arrest and apprehension of the two students, and their punishment, but more than two hundred scholars rallied to their defence.

> *Havoc! Havoc! Smite fast, give good knocks!*
> *Havoc! Havoc! Smite fast, give good knocks!*
> *Havoc! Havoc! Smite fast, give good knocks!*

ALICE OF HENLEY

They brought her in for my lady of Salisbury, wife of the noble warrior William, Earl of Salisbury, who was away in France fighting alongside the Prince of Wales. They brought her in because she had a reputation as a wise woman, and a skilful hand in the pains of birth. This, she freely admitted to any who asked her, was a matter of her knowledge of herbs, only: a tea made of birch bark and leaf mixed with sweet marjoram took away much of the pain of cramps. And besides, the Lady Elizabeth liked her. They had met several times. Alice was a freewoman, and though now widowed seven years she felt no compulsion to wed again. From time to time she took a lover, and ensured that no children would follow with the use of an herbal pessary, but often she was content simply to live her life: attending church, tending her garden, looking after the younger children of villagers for a farthing a day, doing her best to cure the sick when called on for a halfpenny a time. The big house, where my lord of Salisbury stayed when he was in the country, rarely called upon her. But she had helped with the birth of the lord's son and heir, and now that my lady Elizabeth was experiencing stabbing pains in her round belly she was called in again. So she presented herself at the gate, and was taken inside: a young women dressed as an old one, in modest shawl and headscarf, carrying a basket.

They let her in. The young lord, not yet six years old, came running out to see who the visitor was, and was hotly pursued by his tutor. 'Oh,' said the boy knitting fingers into his blonde hair and tugging it out left and right, 'it is only that old witch woman from upriver.' 'You must return to your studies, my lord,' said the anxious-faced tutor. Alice curtsied at the lad, and kept a placid expression on her face. *Witch* was a dangerous word, though.

A waiting-lady led Alice up some wooden stairs to a chamber where the Lady Elizabeth sat upon her bed – a fine tester bed, feather-packed mattress and a dusty canopy hanging from the ceiling. Her hair had lost lustre and there were boils upon her neck, but the lady looked well enough otherwise. Alice slid the lady's nightgown up and placed a hand on her naked belly. She saw at once that the child was a daughter.

'A girl, my lady,' she said. 'And a healthy one.'

'You speak with assurance,' said Elizabeth, and waved her waiting-lady away. This latter, a pinch-faced matron in a green kirtle so faded it looked almost yellow, went out tutting. 'They say you are a witch.' A Somerset lass rather than a fine London lady, she spoke English better than French, and was easy with Alice. But again with that word, witch. Alice could do with that word being uttered less frequently.

'My lady,' said Alice, putting her basket on the bed near her patient's feet. 'I am fortunate that my own mother taught me about herbs, and that is as close to witchcraft as ever I have come.'

Elizabeth clenched, puffed unsweet breath between rounded lips, scrunched shut her eyes. Then, with ponderous, bear-like grace, she pushed forward and got on all fours. Her huge belly sagged in a perfect curve. Her face relaxed. 'There were never cramps like this,' she whispered, 'when I was large with young Will.'

'Do they come regular, my lady? Or some now, some whenever?'

'I am large,' Elizabeth said leaning forward, lowering her head like a cat stretching, and the great nippleless breast of her stomach touched the mattress. 'But not yet ready to birth him – her, you say?'

'A girl,' Alice said, unsure where her certainty came from. 'If you call back your maiden-in-waiting, we can heat up some water and make some of my tea, which will ease away your pain.'

'Wait a moment,' said Lady Salisbury. 'I would ask you – of your sight. Can you see my husband?'

'No, my lady,' said Alice, calmly.

'I mean: see if he is well, if he is alive? He is in France, and war is a dangerous matter.'

Elizabeth had not invited her to sit, so Alice remained standing. 'It is not, my lady, that I see as you see me standing here. It is more akin to memory than to sight. You, my lady, must remember things from your youth, from your childhood. So it is with me. You remember birthing your noble son? So of course you know that at that time you carried a boy in your belly, and no girl. And so it is that, when I touch your belly, I seem to remember, as from a great distance, that you have a fine healthy girl.'

'So,' pressed the lady, 'remember me your memories concerning my husband.'

'You are anxious about him, as is natural, my lady,' Alice said. 'And, being anxious, you make your pain greater than it need be.'

'Does he die in France?'

Alice smiled. She suddenly thought of William Montacute, Earl of Salisbury, riding to tourney in an English field, the sun polishing gleams off his armour. But the memory slipped, suddenly, and the thunderdrumming of horse hooves brought a lance square on the Earl's chest, folding the metal plate in like foil, snapping ribs and stopping his heart still, such that he was dead even as he fell from his horse. But: wait. This was not the present Earl. This was his son – the lad who had sneered at her in the courtyard below. A sigh slipped from Alice's mouth: dead, and childless too. This was some future year. The Montacute line broken off by a single lance.

'What?' Elizabeth demanded. 'What do you see? Why do you sigh?'

'I see your husband returning home safe from France,' Alice said, hurriedly, and then looked inward to see if it was to be so, and was relieved to discover that it was.

Elizabeth scrambled back and sat down with her legs before her, smoothing her nightdress over her modesty. She breathed a deep draught of air and blew it out. There was a fall of old soot inside the chimney, making a noise like pigeonwings. 'Does he come back with honour?' she asked, but before Alice could answer she said: 'of course he does. How could he not? And he is with the Black Prince, whose defeat of the French is as sure any the sunrise and the sunset.'

Alice was tactfully quiet at this point, but Elizabeth was canny enough to read the nature of her silence. 'Do not tell me,' she said, half in wonder, 'that the Prince fails in France?'

'My lady,' Alice said, as forcefully as she dared, 'it would be treason against the king's great name and the great name of his son, that noble warrior, to say anything of the sort.'

'Of course,' Lady Salisbury said, automatically. 'And I would not bait you, upon such ground.' She breathed in, and puffed out air. 'Still! If he dies he will never be king. He would always be known as the Black Prince, and never as the Black King.'

'Permit me to call back your lady-in-waiting, and to burn some wood and heat some water,' Alice said. 'My tea will ease your pains, I assure you.'

Elizabeth said nothing for a while. Then she said: 'when he won that mighty victory at Cressy.' Then she stopped. Then she said: 'he established the Order of the Garter. The Prince, you know. And he inducted my husband as one of the first knights of that most noble fraternity. They fight together as brothers, my husband and the Prince.'

This was such common knowledge, Alice reflected, it was hardly needful to speak it aloud. But she only said: 'Yes, my lady.'

'You know to whom the garter belonged?'

Alice bowed her head, and said nothing.

'No woman can be happy sharing her husband with another woman.' Her face was contorted again, and Alice thought: if this be another contraction, then the child is coming, will-her or nill-her. But the face cleared, and it was surely a vexing memory and nothing more. 'Still: she has to live with a knight so low-born he is virtually a commoner. And I am the Earl of Salisbury's wife.'

'You are, my lady.'

'They say *she* is a witch, too.'

That word again. 'In truth, my lady, I know nothing of witchcraft, nothing at all.'

But the lady's thoughts were not running on Alice. 'She certainly seems to have a way of bewitching men.'

Alice waited, but it seemed Elizabeth expected an answer to this. So she said: 'she is reputed beautiful, my lady.'

'Did you ever see her?'

'No, my lady.'

'Skinny and thin, like a mink, with an evil eye. White, yes, but white like leprosy. Her husband – do you see any misfortune for him?' Eagerly now. 'Does he die in France? Can you tell me that?'

'I never met the gentleman, my lady, and cannot speak to his fortunes.'

The Lady Salisbury grunted. 'My husband, though, prospers, you say? Comes home in one piece? Two days ago I received a case from him. From France, I mean. He had taken some fine cloth and three silver knives in horn handles from a French castle, and a painted icon of the Virgin Mary too, very delicate with lapis paint and gold paint. These he sent to me as gifts. The fellow who brought them told me all was well, but then he got drunk in the kitchen and he told the servants that the expedition is in a poor way. He said the land is all drought, and they have so little water they have to give the horses wine instead. Can you imagine it! He said that they would march to a river, hoping to water their horses and drink and wash, only to find the riverbed nothing but parched boulders and white dust. He said there was much disease in the troop, and that anyway it was a small army. He said that the French king Jean has an army seven times as big, and far better armed, and that the peasantry supply Jean and spurn the English. He said it was going to be a disaster – that King Jean of the French is chasing the Black Prince all over the countryside, trying to press him to a battle, and when that battle comes we will be defeated and the Prince of Wales captured and the ransom we must then pay to get him home again will cripple the whole country.'

After such a long speech, she paused and retrieved her breath. Alice stood patiently. Finally she said: 'my lady, the Prince of Wales won the battle of Cressy, and there he was outnumbered. Who is to say that he cannot do so again?'

'The French were not ready for us, at Cressy,' said Elizabeth.

'We surprised them. But we cannot surprise them a second time. Surprise does not work that way. They have had ten years to prepare. Everyone knows they have forged thicker armour, against our arrows. And they could not be so foolish as they were before. You see them victorious against us?'

'My lady,' said Alice. 'I do not see . . . that is not the way of my wisdom. God's grace, and the saints, gives me a sense of now as yesterday, or yesteryear. I cannot *see* . . .'

'Well,' she interrupted. 'It needs no witch sight to see it, nohow. The Prince of Wales cannot defeat them this time.'

'We must trust in God, my lady.'

'At least my husband lives. That is something. You tell me that the Prince fails,' said Elizabeth, her eyes flashing sudden force, it looked almost like joy. 'And yet you do not, for it would be treason. Yet *he* is another that loves her above all women.'

Alice did not need query the identity of *her*.

'And they say that she loved him, as I'm sure she must, dwelling with her commoner-knight in obscurity. It would hurt her heart were the Prince to die, or be captured, or lose honour. It would,' and she closed her eyes slowly, 'hurt her heart.'

Alice considered. The Prince, she thought, would never be king. He was always to be remembered as the Prince, and never Edward the Fourth. His name, she thought, would always be linked with the Battle of Cressy, and if that was his finest military achievement then perhaps it was true that he was doomed in France. And then she thought: if the Prince dies, the King has other sons. They say John of Gaunt is a fierce and clever man. They say that we have taken north-east France as our own, and treated with the Dukes of Normandy to make it a vassal state; and that the Prince now fighting in west and southern France has already added to the Empire of the English. If he falls at his next great battle, he has already done enough, surely, to guarantee the honour of the realm. And then she thought: what did all this have to do with *her*? She was more concerned to take out her spring onions and to find a wash what would stop the slugs devouring her cabbages in the ground. So she said: 'it is not treason to say that God's will be done, whether for victory over the French or defeat. And whatever happens to the Prince, I see your husband returning whole and strong to this, your fine home. So I beg of you, my lady, permit me to make you some of my special herbal tea.'

Elizabeth, her eyes closed, her hair stuck to her high brown forehead, seemed to have fallen asleep.

So Alice curtsied, and went off to find the lady-in-waiting.

THE BLACK PRINCE

He essayed a new strategy: sending out raiding parties of half a dozen knights, to move quickly north and south as he marched eastward. Attacking villages and farms before the inhabitants had time to evacuate. This proved effective. Many French were killed. Sometimes the looted supplies were too capacious for six men on horseback to carry home, and further parties had to be sent to retrieve the rest. It hardly mattered how much food and drink he seized; his army gobbled it up and seemed ever hungry for more. An army is like a baby, sleeping, waking, crying out in hunger.

One such party came upon a tall, narrow castle: white-walled and flying a flag upon which was a golden star, crowned with three smaller stars, against a blue ground more intense than the blue sky behind it. Edward himself, his coat of regal colours over his armour, rode to the gate, with his bannerman beside him and five other knights. It was hot, and he was sweating inside his steel; he had taken his helmet off and tied it to his saddle. The castle that stood before him, though too small to be strategically useful, was one of the finest and most pristine he had ever seen: white all the way up to tiered crenulations and orange-pottery tiles on two sloping roofs, like a painting from an illuminated manuscript. Around were bushes and trees of dark green, and fields with twisty *oliviers* whose teardrop leaves were the colour of copper that has been exposed to the open air for many years. Lavender grew in shaggy bushes, and its purple scent drifted sweetly across the whole. And when the bannerman called hello, and announced Edward's rank and name, it was no man but a woman who came to the battlements over the high gate.

'Good day to you, madame,' cried Edward, shielding his eyes as he looked up. 'Has your lord sent you to treat with us? Is he too cowardly to meet us himself?'

'My lord is in the grave six years, by grace of the plague,' the lady called down, 'and this castle is mine and mine alone. I am the lady who commands it.'

'God send you good fortune to match your beauty, madame; never before has castle been in the charge of a ruler so fair. What is your stronghold called?'

'The castle of Villenave-d'Ornon,' replied the lady. 'And I am Eleanor d'Ornon, its mistress, alone in my fastness.'

'Madame d'Ornon,' said Edward. 'I am come on the command of my father, the king, to regain this land, rightfully his, from the usurpations of King Jean.'

'You,' said the lady, 'are *le terrible prince noir* of which everybody hereabouts speaks, the author of countless murders and violations. Corpses line the route of your march, and wherever you go you turn fertile France into a desert. I defy you.'

'I commend your bravery, madame,' said Edward. 'And though war is terrible, as you say, yet all the sufferings of France would cease tomorrow if Jean relinquished his claim upon these lands. And to you I say: I am guided by the spirit of chivalry, and give you my word as prince and knight that no harm will befall you. I shall pass the command through all my army that the beautiful castle of Ornon, and its beautiful mistress, be left in peace, though the whole country around you burn. And I shall leave at your gate a barrel of wine, and a dozen cheeses, and one goat, and when we have ridden away I ask only that you pledge one cup to me, to help my soul to heaven should I die in these adventures.'

'Good give mercy into your heart, noble prince,' replied the lady. 'I thank you for your graciousness, and your gifts, and though I do not abate my loyalty to Jean le Bon, yet I shall send you down a favour to mark the honour of your chivalrous deeds today.' And she disappeared to reappear with a square of white gauze, air woven with cloth most marvellous, and so light it took a full minute to drift down to the ground beside the Prince.

They marched on, and through a forest so dry the leaves were parchment and the ground crackled beneath hoof and foot with a noise like a fire burning. Actual fire was a danger, too; smoke on the horizon where a forest blazed and no water to put it out. They came out of this covert and surprised a medium-sized town, whose inhabitants were in the process of putting up chains across their main street to impede horsemen. The town houses were already barricaded, and a lid was fastened over the town well. But they had not been warned of the English approach, and so were not yet ready. Edward cleaned the town out quickly enough. Warwick gathered together all the town's smiths, metalworkers and handymen and made them sharpen all the English swords, and then he cut their necks, one by one. 'The sharper you make my sword,' he told them; 'the quicker your death will be.'

Bodies littered the gutter.

Most of the townspeople had been thus disposed of when a rider came hurrying in, saying that the French king was only seven miles behind them, and with a much larger host than Edward had originally been told about – either the earlier estimations were wrong, or Jean had reinforced himself. It meant they had to be fast. Fourteen women and girls, many looking bruised and sorry for themselves, had had their hands tied behind them; one knight, Sir

Hugo of Ham, had his men tie one long rope in loops about all their necks in a chain, and fixed each end between two of the strongest horses he could find. A whip on the hind quarters of each and much yelling sent them away, pulling their chain of kicking figures behind them, and this gave the foot soldiers a laugh, which added spirit to their work. They grabbed what they could from the town and set the place on fire and they moved on briskly.

Trit-trot, trit-trot.

Though Edward prayed nightly and every morning too, he had not been visited again by the sense of grace he had known in the chapel of that taken castle. He tried not to think that God had withdrawn his grace.

A forced march – more orderly, now, than before – and they crossed a hill and made camp on an eminence with a good view of the land through which Jean must come if he were truly following them. All of the men and most of the knights slept under the stars, although tents were raised for the Prince and for Warwick, Suffolk and William Montacute of Salisbury. These three Earls gathered in the Prince's tent.

—We may be able to flee back to the coast. I would not recommend holing up in any of the castles we have taken upon our *chevauchée*.

—Assuming they are still deputised to us, agreed the Prince. No: we would fare badly if we were besieged. Jean has men enough to lock us in, and still march north and win great victories in battle. We must fight him, I suppose.

—Highness, said Montacute, stiffly, not meeting his prince's eye. We would lose such a fight.

—Come, cousin! Edward tried, in a cheering voice. Do not say so! Have we not come here to fight Frenchmen? And now Frenchmen press themselves upon us, keen to fight. We should thank them for the opportunity they present us!

—We are very largely outnumbered, noted Warwick.

—We were outnumbered at Cressy. We did well enough there.

Montacute blushed at this, could not control the colour rising to his face. It was a point of personal annoyance to him that he missed this battle, whilst the lowly fox Thomas Holland not only fought in it, but won honour and renown for doing so. And now Thomas had his Joan.

—Cressy was ten years ago, Warwick said, stretching his face into a grimace. He added, a moment too late: Highness.

—And so am I ten years older and more experienced.

Warwick looked at the Prince. It was true: the years had changed him from the youth he had once been. And it was true that he was now a better military leader, with other strategies at his disposal than merely *charge and swing your swords!* But, still: miracles happen in churches, at holy days, not on hot battlefields with an exhausted army, pursued by fresh troops better armed and disciplined than they.

—I hear, he essayed, that they have thickened their armour, and better protected their horses. There is no guarantee our archers will have the effect they had at Cressy.

—My lords, said Ned. I shall say to you: good night, and beg you return in the morning with more heartening counsel than this. Fight, we must; and if we are marked by fate to die, then let us commend our souls to God and pray tonight for the intercession of his saints.

And so the others went away, though none went happily.

In the morning they struck camp at dawn, and marched rapidly along a valley, over a hill and into the town of Descartes. Jean had been here, not long before, and this had given the inhabitants hope, so there were many still in that town to kill, and Ned's men went at it with a right good will. The younger women they locked in the chateau, and took them out in ones and twos for their pleasure. The men they hanged from the town walls, in a great necklace of corpses facing north-east to discomfort Jean when he came back this way in pursuit of them.

That night Edward had a dream of Joan, and for a while his heart lifted. But then she turned away from him and took Thomas Holland's arm, and walked away, over hills bright red and purple, beneath a yellow sky. He ran after her and pulled her from her husband, but she said: do you not know, Ned, how the son must die for the greater glory of the father? What else does the Passion teach us, but this? He became angry then: will Jean kill me? he asked. And if he does, will you care? She only laughed, and he woke in the morning angry.

That fury did not leave him, and as his men packed up ready to march on throughout the town, he had Lord le Desparre bring him a woman from the chateau, to his rooms: the fairest in colour, if there be any that are fair. And in half an hour a muddy blonde woman, trembling a little but not weeping, was brought in; and he used her after the manner that man uses woman. Then she was taken away and he felt a bitter disgust in his belly. He tried to pray, but his prayer seemed hypocrisy, and his words did not mount. It seemed to him that God had pulled back from him, and that he was destined to die in the coming battle. He wondered if his seed would quicken in the French girl's belly, and thought that it would be best to set all the women free. So he ordered it.

News came that Jean was closer now, and that his men were singing battle hymns loud enough to be heard from miles away. Camp sickness had taken hold amongst his men, and the lack of fresh water was making this worse. People died by the hour.

—A damned dry summer, said Lord James Audley to Lord Peter Audley (his brother). Both men were drinking wine. Descartes was already smoking; and soon they would be gone, assuming their horses, also fed wine, would walk straight enough to carry them.

—Not a drop of water to be had anywhere, agreed Lord Peter Audley. I need a wash.

—A man cannot wash in wine, agreed the Prince.

—We march today, I believe, said Lord Peter Audley. And there will be water at the end of it. That river: what's it called?

Nobody seemed to know the name. Edward called his nobles about him.

—What is the name of that river? he asked.

—The Vienne, Highness, said Denis de Morbecque, who was charged with knowing such things. But the bridges are broken down, and the river level is very low this year. As for the strength of the French army, it is, by a calculation I hope your Highness is minded to accept, eight or nine times your own.

The Prince whistled, vulgarly. A strong mistral of a whistle.

—This King Jean, he said, is a cleverer man than his father, he says. Cleverer and more persistent. *Dare* we fight, my lords?

The Earl of Warwick said: we must send to your father for more men. We cannot fight when the numbers are so steep against us. It would be suicide, and not chivalry at all. The King has poured men into Scotland, I know; and I know as well that the plague has rendered ordinary men to be rare and precious things, and costly. But still . . . money ought not to be an object when the honour and the safety of . . .

He ran out of steam. Everybody was hot and tired.

—Our horses dance, Ned pointed out. I wouldn't mind, but that they dance so badly.

The nobles said nothing. Water was also a rare and precious thing. But horses watered on wine became sluggish, or skittish, or trotted sideways, like a crab.

—The King of France's army outnumbers us eight or nine times, said Edward. And we have drunken horses, and camp fever killing our men, and those who do not die of it are much weakened.

Edward led his ailing army towards Châtellerault, and the river Vienne, which might or might not still be flowing. Stragglers among the men-at-arms at the rear were being picked-off by raiding parties from the French main force. He began to ponder a parley with Jean: on what terms might they be able to withdraw, and keep their lives?

Not advantageous ones, certainly. And it would be a fatal stab in the heart of the honour of English arms.

Men were muttering of thirst and inhospitable France and saying openly that they wished to return to England. Every morning, ensigns reported to their knights that more men had slipped away in the darkness.

At Châtellerault they found the river so low that it had shed its fish to turn to rotten leather on the dry pebbles. Yet a thin stream still ran, in the very centre of the stony riverbed, and the men drank and washed and the horses were refreshed. Edward's heart was not lightened by this small mercy. He prayed, and again his words refused to go upwards. It came to him in a flash that he had sinned, and gravely, by forcing himself on that woman in Descartes. It was partly the violation of the girl, but mostly it was the violation of his oath to forswear such camp antics. It had uncleaned him. He told Suffolk to find him a priest, and the holy man was brought in after an hour or so.

—Hear my confession, Father, he said.

The priest was old. One of his eyes was blank as a boiled egg. There were warts on his forehead like two trimmed-back horns, and he stank of sweat and vinegar. He could not disguise his surprise at this command: your confession, your Highness? Do you not have your own priests?

—They are warrior priests, and have killed men. So they may neither marry couples, nor hear confession.

—Very well, said the priest, sitting down on the stone windowsill beside the Englishman, and turning away. How long is it since your last confession?

—Three months. More. Nearly four. I have sinned, Father.

—Tell me.

—I do not account the men I have killed as sins upon my conscience, for just war is permitted under God's laws. But yesterday I lay with a woman, and it was not with her consent.

—You are married?

—No.

—Still, this is a grave sin. What else?

—I own pride. It is a grievous thing, I know. But, truly, Father, I seek forgiveness for the sin with this woman. I took an oath to abstain from such things, and the breaking of a vow is a grave matter.

—It is, my son, said the priest. And your penance must be grave too. You must quit this land, and not return within seven years. You must give up making war upon French people. That is your penance.

Edward stood up sharply. Are you truly a priest, you fox? he asked hotly. Or one of King Jean's men in disguise?

—I am a priest, your Highness, said the man, mildly, turning to face Edward as if waiting for a blow.

Edward left him and walked briskly from that room unshriven. He was angry, true; but with the dense, inner anger that is closer to despair than any other emotion. That evening he feasted on what could be scratched up from the scanty supplies of Châtellerault's larders, and drank too much wine. Then, though he should not have done it, he told Suffolk what the priest had said, and the Earl laughed. But in the morning news came to Edward that Suffolk, drunk, had got together with three other knights, and gone and killed the old priest for his presumption – pushed a sword down, in between his collar bone and his throat. Ned was angry at this, and Suffolk, his head hurting from too much wine, met his anger with anger. He was no true priest, said the Earl, but a very serviceable villain and a meddler. What right had he to speak to you of such a penance? He deserved to be punished and we punished him.

—It is bitter bad luck, Edward shouted, to murder a priest on the eve of a battle! This shut Suffolk up. He only clutched his head and moaned.

It could not be helped. The army, a good proportion of its men-at-arms limping and sickly, marched from the town and followed a tributary of the river, called the Gartemps, with the forest of Moulière to their right. Foray. Forêt. The big trees moved with an underwater slowness in the forceful summer wind. Word came that the French were making for Poitiers: emptied by the ferocious Earl of Derby years before, but repopulated at the king's command and newly fortified. Edward decided that a bold stroke might revivify his men. So he sent the baggage train trundling on down the old Roman road, and led his horses and men through the Moulière trees. Jean had brought his troops down the eastern flank of this, and if he reached Poitiers then he would reinforce his army with the garrison soldiers and become all the more unbeatable. But, Ned thought, if we burst from the southern border of the woods and fall on them as they march, we could devastate—

—devastate—

—devastate—

—devastate—

A rustle in the undergrowth, and much coughing and grumbling.

Emerging from the trees, it was clear that Jean had already passed by. From his saddle, Edward could see the citadel of Poitiers and could see moreover that the king's oriflamme battle standard was flying over it. Below them was only the tail of the great force. He yelled charge anyway, and the other knights repeated his cry, and the horsemen led two hundred Anglo-Gascons over the dry grass and stones to attack the rearguard. The attack was a surprise, at least; the Frenchmen were wearing felt caps garnished with ostrich feathers, and they scrabbled to put on their hard bascinets, and their swords, and were easily cut down. The men further along did not hesitate, but broke running for Poitiers' walls and safety. Edward, his arms strong with sudden fury (where had that come from?), rode amongst the enemy hacking and slashing. In half an hour it was all over. The rest of the English army emerged from the trees, and the computation of French knights and men-at-arms slain reached two hundred before breaking off – more lay on the dusty road. Suffolk had captured the Duc d'Auxerre, and was pleased with having done so.

Edward brought his men, tired now as the elation drained from them, a mile or so east along the road towards the town of Nouaillé; and as he did so he sent horsemen on to meet up with and double-speed the trundling of the baggage train. Of course the French would soon muster, and attack. The town was small, a square and a dozen brick houses, with more wooden domiciles on the outskirts, all abandoned. They had dropped a dead dog in the well.

With Nouaillé behind him, Edward drew up his exhausted troops into as much order as he could manage. To his right the land was forested. To the left it was open ground, descending at a shallow angle. At his back the wood of Nouaillé, a low thicket of hedge bushes and twisty thorn trees. It was all the cover his men could be given. From his horse the Black Prince looked about at the field on which he would presumably die – or, more shameful, be captured. There was no water in this place. His men, and his horses, would be thirsty in the morning, or drunk on wine (men and horses both) as the might of 35,000 French troops rode out to make war upon his exhausted five thousand.

—Highness, said Suffolk, riding up. We must hear their parley.

—William, said the Prince. I suppose we must.

Newsreel (10)

Gascons are loud-mouthed, talkative, given to mockery, libidinous, drunken, greedy eaters, clad in rags, poverty stricken; but they are skilful fighters. The Pilgrim passing through their lands must take all care.

For every man that lovés chivalry
And would he hope to have a lasting name
Has prayed that he might be of that game
And ride into the lists with company

MARINER IN NEWGATE

A mariner named Dennis, of which parish it is not known, has been committed to Newgate for being present when a Spanish ship, that was peaceably docked at Sandwich, was plundered and her crew slain, in violation of the law that any merchant ship, even such as belong to an enemy nation, be entered into any English, she is to have *frith*, that is peace and freedom from molestation, provided only it was not driven or chased into port, but even if chased into port, and it reached any frith burgh, and the crew escaped into the burgh, then the crew and whatever they brought with them were to have *frith*, that is peace.

surplices to be washed sixteen times a year against the great feasts, eighteen surplices for men and six for children, and seven albs to be washed sixteen times a year, and five altar-cloths for covering the altars to be washed sixteen times a year

Ora ora ora
Ora ora ora
Ora ora ora
Pro nobis ora

Camera Eye

and the walls too bloody to be cleaned without

leaving a brown stain, he orders them whitewashed again   and again, until the sullying is covered over. The servants, pressed from neighbourhood villages, are surly and unhappy: French peasants, hating the English.

He has been given too few men, really, to keep the peace. He must compensate for fewer numbers with greater cruelty. It is the only way, and it holds order, although it does not soften the scowls on people's faces.

Best get used to it, he thinks: this land is England now.

Dusty, though, with a white and throat-clogging dust, and too hot in the day. He rides out to hunt, and comes back caked like a mummer with a paste compounded of sweat and dust. The castle has its own well, thank the Lady herself, and he has a bath drawn and filled and placed waiting in his room.

He strips off, and looks at the greentinted water, and steps in: cold and startling and   ah, sweet in this oppressive *chalêur*   sits   washes the dust into a scum on the water's surface. Through the arrowslit a white finger of afternoon sunlight lengths on the opposite wall, and slides upwards.   A hound slinks in, sniffing for food   turns its whipcord haunches on him, and goes back down the stone steps   then, turns again, and comes in. He rubs the dog's head, narrow and hardboned under its suede pelt, like the pommel of a sword. Encouraged, the dog drinks from the dustfilmed water, and then pads out.

His man comes in: apologies, my lord. Apologies. Fuck the rood, what now? He rises, dresses in a loose shift, and goes barefoot up to the top of the tower, and looks out.

Mistral in the one big tree below blows like rushing water. Sunlight shares out sky and clouds: blue and white, superbly clean-looking.   The pennants of the French king Jean are winking and waving in the distance.   He feels a curious lightness in his head as he counts the host that follows the mounted foreguard. Thousands upon thousands – a number so much larger than the Prince of Wales' compact troop it is almost comical.

We must warn the Prince, he says. The Prince must be warned.

My lord, says his man, and he is crying, like a fucking little babe at the breast. There is a troop at the gate. There are rangers in the grove to the east. I have ordered the gates locked, but we surely cannot hold out for long?

He looks again, and knows the approaching crowd for what it is: his own death. He had thought death a lone knight, bonefaced and drywhite, black armour on his thin body, bringing a sword down sharp. But this is the truth of it: death is a swarm. Flies in the hot air. Inescapable. Arm, he tells the man. All of us. Dress the horses.   His own charger, exhausted after the hot ride through the late morning, needs resting. It hardly matters though. We will break out, he declares. But he knows: the only thing he will break out from is life itself. Fuck the rood, he yells at the man, who is still snurling and weeping like a child, bestir! Bestir!

Newsreel (11)

John le Whyte, an animal skinner having travelled down from Cambridge, did at night break into the mercer's shop of Geoffrey Punte, of good character, on the Lane of St Lawrence Jewry, nearby the London Guildhall. Whyte therefrom feloniously stole gold and silver rings, pearls, thread and bracelets to the value of 100 shillings. John le Whyte was afterwards hanged.

STATUTE OF LABOURERS
King sets maximum wage

That every person, able in body and under the age of sixty years, not having enough to live upon, being required, shall be bound to serve him that doth require him, or else be committed to gaol until he shall find surety to serve, and that the old wages shall be given and no more.

> *You shall have harp*
> *Sautry and song*
> *And all other mirths*
> *You among*
>   *You among*
>   *You among*

IN POITOU
Gathered at Poitiers: The Prince of Wales; Thomas de Beauchamp, 11th Earl of Warwick, William de Ufford, 2nd Earl of Suffolk;

William de Montacute, 2nd Earl of Salisbury; John de Vere, 7th Earl of Oxford; Reginald de Cobham, 1st Baron Cobham; Edward le Despencer, 1st Baron le Despencer; Lord James Audley; Lord Peter Audley (his brother); Lord Berkeley; Lord Basset; Lord Warin; Lord Delaware; Lord Manne; Lord Willoughby; Lord Bartholomew de Burghersh; Lord of Felton; Lord Richard of Pembroke; Lord Stephen of Cosington; Lord Bradetane; Lord of Pommiers from Gascon; Lord of Languiran; Lord John the 69th of Caumont; Lord de Lesparre; Lord of Rauzan; Lord of Condon; Lord of Montferrand; the Lord of Landiras; Lord Soudic of Latrau; Lord Eustace d'Aubrecicourt; Lord John of Ghistelles, and two other strangers; Lord Daniel Pasele and Lord Denis of Amposta, a fortress in Catalonia; Edward le Despencer, 1st Baron le Despencer and Sir Thomas Felton, a veteran of the great battle at Crécy and Poitiers.

> *And other mirths*
> *You among*
> *You among*
> *You among*

FRENCH ARMY VAST

The King himself in command, with twenty-six dukes and earls and more than 120 banners, and the four sons of the king, Duke Charles of Normandy, the Duke Louis, the Duke of Anjou, and John, Duke of Berry, and Lord Philip

> *Among*

BREAKING NEWS: SCOTS JOIN KING OF FRANCE

It has recently been announced that the French army now includes a sizeable contingent of Scots commanded by Sir William Douglas, who declares himself causeless to love the English or their king.

Robert Branunche, merchant of Lynn, trader in wool, has endowed in his will for two chauntry priests to say mass for his soul upon his death, the chauntry to be added to the great church at Lynn. Robert has also left an endowment to add windows to the Trinity Guildhall, and for light to be thereby admitted to the guild meetings within.

CARDINAL OF PERIGORD

Sunday. There could be no fighting on the Sabbath day, of course. Jean had declared himself pleased at this, for the English force – small and visibly weakened by their rampaging around the countryside – did not have access to fresh water. 'Let them sit in their thorny hedge and be scratched to pieces,' he announced, in good spirits. 'Let them grow thirstier and thirstier, and so weaker for when battle comes.' 'My King,' the Cardinal said, 'if there is blood that must be shed, let it be pagan blood, in the Holy Land, not here. I suggest that it is more seemly for two great Christian princes to confer and bring this warfare to an end. Then, together, you could ride under the gate of a restored Christian Jerusalem.' 'Ride out, Your Eminence,' said the King, in a careless tone. 'By all means.'

Hélie de Talleyrand-Périgord put on his cardinal's colours, and had his man help him into the saddle. No natural chevalier, he. Two riders accompanied him, one carrying the cardinal's colours: three lions on a red shield, one lion for each of the attributes of Holy God, a flattened cardinal's hat over the top of the assemblage and twin pyramids of tassels coming down on either side. RE QUE DIOU the banner declared. The other rider was his nephew Robert de Duras. He had fallen into a habit of coughing nervously when introducing the fellow as his nephew. Everybody knew what it meant. Still, the lad was a good knight, valiant and upright. They couldn't laugh at that.

And so the three of them rode out, trotting through the great mass of French troops, most of them seated in knots of three or four, lounging on the ground, husbanding their supplies, shielding their heads from the sun. There was a holiday mood among the men, spirits high, laughter and song everywhere.

The Cardinal clasped his skullcap against his pate and spurred his horse over the open ground between the two armies, one much bigger than the other. Soon enough he came to the English advance guard – Gascon soldiers, traitors you might call them, although then again there were plenty of Scots fighting with King Jean, and Scotland notionally belonged to King Edward now. So it was change and change about, really. The English forward guard sent back for an English noble, who came trotting through the hazy September sunshine. 'Good morning, sir.'

'It is proper,' the Cardinal replied, 'to address me as Your Eminence.'

'Your Eminence, it is,' said the Englishman. His French was strangely accented, and delivered with a kind of insolent slurring of the vowels. 'And what can I do you for?'

'Take me to your prince, that I might parley,' said the Cardinal, impatiently. 'I am here to prevent the spillage of Christian blood.'

'You stay here, emi-ponce,' said the English milord. 'You stay *right* here, me old beauty. I'll go fetch our Terrible Black Prince pronto-pronto.'

He rode off.

'Insolence,' muttered Robert, to his left. 'That will be punished on the battlefield.'

'We are here,' the Cardinal said, piously, 'to prevent precisely that, my boy.'

So the Cardinal and his attendants must needs wait, his arse growing stiff from sitting astride a horse – not born to it, the way these English were. It was a warm morning and he was soon thirsty. After a long wait – too long for dignity or chivalry, a deliberate insult on behalf of the English, those dogs – a party of a dozen men came trotting up. The Prince of Wales was easy to spot, dressed in a long red-and-blue lozenge surcoat over his black armour, and with a crushing-looking heavy helmet topped with a gold-coated metal figurine of a lion. The Cardinal cleared his throat, and readied to address the blank metal visage, but at the last minute the Englishman pulled his helmet free, and shook his long yellow hair. 'Stuffy,' he said. 'So. Your Eminence?'

'I am come to parley,' said the Cardinal. 'Highness, if there is blood that must be shed, let it be pagan blood, in the Holy Land. Reclaiming Jerusalem. Let us not let Christian blood stain the soil here, in a Christian kingdom. I suggest that it is more seemly for two great Christian princes to confer and bring this . . .'

'Yes, yes, very good. Terms?'

The Cardinal cleared his throat again, a resonant noise like something heavy being dragged over a floor. 'My son, quite apart from anything else, you must consider of the superior strength of France.'

'Eminence, it is only that superior strength,' said the Black Prince, smiling, 'that brings me to this conference.'

'Well. What, then, are your concessions?'

'The Prince of Wales,' said the Prince of Wales, 'on behalf of the king his father offers to . . .' Edward raised his right hand, turned it over, looked at it, turned it back, '. . . to restore all the places conquered during this expedition, to surrender all prisoners—' one of the English nobles growled at this '—and to, let's say, to swear not to bear arms against France for seven years. To give up,' he added, as if in afterthought, 'Calais, Guisnes and all the places we won in Gascony.'

The Cardinal nodded, and announced that he would take these terms to the King, and brought his horse about. He rode slowly over the land between the armies. To his right the Moulières forest clung to the horizon like a serpent of dark green. Thin white cloud had diffused itself across the sky, giving the brightness a weirdly generalised quality. It was still hot. A film of sweat made his red skullcap slide over his scalp as he trotted, and he had to take it off and hold it in one hand for fear of losing it. The French forward guard saluted him as he rode through.

The King in his tent was praying, but he broke off without an amen when the Cardinal entered. 'Well? Well?'

Skullcap in hand, he repeated the English prince's offer. But it only provoked fury in Jean. 'You rode all the way back with such a paltry offer? Wasting my time. Wasting everybody's time.'

'My King.'

'No, no, no.' He shook his regal head with surprising violence, and his red hair flew out, like a miniature oriflamme. 'This will never do. Go back: the Prince must surrender at discretion and yield his person up to me, along with, let's say, one hundred knights. I'll have him ransomed at two million crowns. Think what the money will do, to help restore the prosperity of my kingdom! And the hundred knights will bring in several hundred thousand more. No, he must surrender, or he must face the consequences.'

'Shall I return at once, my King?'

'At once.'

The Cardinal paused, however, to drink a beaker of wine, and then a second. Thirsty work, this parleying. Then he had his man lever him up into the saddle once more, and once more they trotted off: the Cardinal, his nephew and his standard-bearer. Through the French lines. Halfway across the field to the English, he regretted drinking so much. The pressure of the hard saddle hammering beneath his delicate buttocks, more used to a padded chair, filled him with the urge to pass water. He looked about him, but there was nowhere discreet, and he – a cardinal of Avignon – 30,000 French. His physical discomfort provoked spiritual sourness. This was all pointless. The English prince would surrender now, or he would put up a show of fighting and get captured anyway. Or perhaps die. Why could they not see the foolishness?

At the English front rank, he was forced to wait once again, his bladder cramping and pressing down like an overfilled wine sack. The English made him wait, because they had the devil's humour in them, or because they had no manners. He eyed the long thorn hedge, and saw faces in amongst the prickles, like field mice or nesting birds. *That* must be uncomfortable. And that thought, in turn, turned the Cardinal's mind to his own discomfort, and he shifted his weight in the saddle. 'Robert,' he hissed to his nephew. 'I need to relieve myself.'

'Your Eminence?' replied the fellow uncertainly.

'To piss. To piss.'

'Your Eminence, I . . . I don't know what to suggest.'

'Oh never mind.'

Finally the Prince emerged, trotting with leisurely motion. When he was close enough the Cardinal called: 'King Jean the Second of France says that you, my Prince, must surrender at his discretion and yield your person up to him, along with one hundred knights. It must be surrender, or you must face the consequences.'

'Very well, then,' said the Prince, cheerfully. 'The consequences!'

Impatient to be back where he could relieve himself, and angry at the vanity and pride of princes, the Cardinal turned his horse and rode quickly across the open ground, his two attendants spurring to catch up.

JOHN OF GHISTELLES

He wasn't scared of dying. That was, after all, always the prospect a soldier faced in battle and being scared of it would be as absurd as a woodworker being scared of wood. And (as he told himself before every combat) if he did die, it would be good to see his father again.

Catch up. This morning, though, he mounted his horse and looked across the parched French landscape at so enormous a French army and something quailed within him. Not cowardice, or fear, or even despair, but rather a swamping sense of the *pointlessness* of it all. He was thirsty, ill-rested, weary of yomping up and down France killing people and burning their towns, and now that matters had finally been brought to a *proper* battle it would, evidently, all be over very quickly. The French would hammer the English. Their numerousness would wash over like the Red Sea drowning the Egyptians, and that would be that. It was, he supposed, the sense of anticlimax that offended him. So much hardship and horror, and all to end like this.

Still: duty was duty. Honey twat. Key: manny prance, and so on. He urged his horse forward, and the wheezy creature staggered to the left, then plodded ahead. Poor old nag, he'd had a hard time of it in France. Not properly looked after, neither watered nor fed adequately, and now wheezy and broken.

Men were readying themselves. That damned thorny hedge was going to be a problem. Would hem them in. He saw men with cuts on their arms and faces from stumbling into it. And here was Old Sir Tom Felton, who had fought at Cressy, and who told everybody all about it every bloody day and twice on Sunday. His horse looked clapped out too. You can't properly water a horse on wine, after all. 'Good morning to you, Sir Thomas,' he called.

'I suppose we're just waiting on your Franky namesake now,' Old Tom growled back, and went into a spasm of coughing.

'It's in God's hands, Sir Tom.'

A third knight, young and perky, came trotting up: Sir James Audley. 'Isn't this sky wonderful? Now that the clouds have cleared away! Mostly. Look at that blue!' he said, and put his head back. 'Hello sky! I greet you, clouds! What a great day!'

'We're stuck between this thorn-bush on the left,' complained Sir Tom, interspersing his words with coughs, 'and that woodland over on the right. It will crush us as a vice does.'

'There are men *in* the bush you know,' said Audley, patting his horse's twitchy neck. The biting flies were buzzing already, though the morning air was cool. 'How they aren't scratched to pieces I don't know.'

John peered at the distant French host, counting banners. There was the oriflamme; there the banner of Duke Charles of Normandy. And there, God curse him, was the flag of that treacherous Scot Sir William Douglas, may haggis tear his heart out. Assuming haggis was an animal. Perhaps it was the name of a girl?

And – suddenly – *he is here, he is here,* said the bright Monday morning, and the very birds spiralled upwards in an ecstasy of liquid twittering song. The red-and-blue of his padded surcoat was bright in the early light, and the black armour beneath, and his fine, long, thick yellow hair. 'Good morning good knights,' he said in English, and laughed.

'Your Highness.'

'Highness.'

'Highness.'

The lords and nobles who followed behind him looked dour. They, clearly, felt some of that same weight of pointlessness that oppressed John's chest. 'Let's get it over with,' growled the Earl of Salisbury. 'No point in delaying the inevitable.'

'Patience is Victory's lady-in-waiting,' returned the Prince. He peered, from the little hilltop, at the sea of men facing them less than a mile away. 'Is that the Cardinal's banner?'

'I believe so, your Highness.'

'*That* is poor form. Only yesterday he was going between the two camps suing for peace. He should not be fighting. It's not proper.'

'And yet,' said Salisbury, 'there he is.'

'He is a man who likes to be on a winning side,' coughed Sir Tom. 'You don't get to wear the Cardinal's hat without having that instinct.'

'Brave Sir Thomas,' laughed the Black Prince. 'Come now. Were you this glum before Cressy?'

'I am glad to die, with honour, fighting beside you, Highness,' said the old knight, sitting up straighter in his saddle.

'Well now, let me see,' said the Prince, casting his eye over the French. 'At Cressy they charged, and we shot them to rags with arrows. They'll not make that mistake again, I think.'

'It seems they have thickened their armour, and added protection to their horses,' said Salisbury. 'Highness.'

'It's what I would do, if I were in Jean's gilded leather shoes. Well – Audley?'

'Sir?'

'You'll lead out a troop, go south and swing round. Get at them from the side. I'll send a larger force north. With God's help, we shall win this day. Do you know *why*, Sir Tom?'

'Why what, Highness?'

'Why we shall win?'

'Because our deaths will glorify the king your father's campaign,' returned the grizzled old knight, immediately, 'and so ensure that the rest of France be captured. In our defeat is our victory.'

At this Edward put his head back and laughed, loud, at the morning sky. 'God be praised that I have such warriors about me, this day,' he said. 'I'd better go and make a speech, I suppose. To the men-at-arms. But, Audley, you start your feint. Go south, and they'll think you're slinking away. And you, Beauchamp, ride to the baggage train. Tell them to cut across land towards the forest, only make sure the French see it. They'll think we're retreating in disarray. Sir Tom, bold Sir Tom, you agree with me that the French believe they will win?'

'Yes, your Highness.'

'And do you hesitate to tell me what all my highest noblemen are too scared to say – that my own men are certain we shall lose this day?'

Thomas looked startled at this question, unsure how to answer. 'Highness . . .' he grumbled, and then he stopped.

'Those men,' said Edward, peering into the distance, 'are already living in the morrow. They are already, in their minds, back in their chateaux and farmhouses, boasting to their wives and wenches how bravely they fought and how glorious their victory was. *They* are not in the here-and-now. Our men are looking only at death, where there is no forward point from which to *look* back. That means they are fully present, all in the moment and alive with a fierce life. A man will fight harder for his life than for a future twice-told tale. We have our backs against the thorn, and so we will press forward. The French will run at us, but their thoughts are all behind them.'

'Highness,' said John Ghistelles, addressing his prince for only the second time in his entire life, 'may I go with Lord James Audley?' He spoke French.

'Speak English, man, English,' Edward replied, grinning at him. 'This day of all days. But yes, brave sir, of course you may.'

And the next thing John knew he was trotting with Lord James Audley and two dozen fine knights, through bright sunshine and into proper battle. None of your piss-on-the-ground little sieges, or riding through towns chopping down olive-merchants. A full battle. His spirits began to lift. This was why he was here, after all.

They passed a great crowd of English men-at-arms, all clustering around the Prince on his horse, listening to his words. '. . . gallantry. You have heard we are fewer than they, and indeed you have eyes in your head, so you can see it. But battle,' his voice rising, 'is not decided by the numbers, but by the will of God.' A great cheer. 'If we die, then God be thanked that battle will have taken so few from the great army of the king my father – and we shall take many more of them with us! But if we live, and victory is ours, then how much greater the glory, divided between so few! And therefore, brothers and men, fight with me as . . .' The words became less clear as John rode off. He still strained to hear: *true* and *knight* shouted to the air, and a second great cheer, and then indistinct sound and then *Saint George* and another cheer. Then the sound of birdsong and the hushing of the breeze, and the hoofs of a dozen horse over dry ground.

They rode down the gentle slope, and the land became softer. No stream, though. The horses picked a way less surely. Here they came into the positions of four or five hundred archers, who had camped there overnight, holding the southern approach. Audley rallied them quickly enough: they were stiff and tired, having been on guard since Sunday morning without relief. At least a proper fight would be a change, bach, which is as good as a rest, see. With many complaints and bad words they stood and shook as much of the stiffness out of their legs and arms as they could. John looked back, and saw the English army forming up. He looked ahead, and saw individual French riders, small as toys, galloping up and down the fore of King Jean's French lines. They would be doing all that pre-battle flimflam: boasting of what they were about to accomplish, challenging the Black Prince to single combat, all that sort of stuff.

A fly bit John's horse on its underbelly, and the drunken beast reared on its hind legs, like a preacher, whinnying in outrage. John slid from the saddle and landed flat on his back on the ground. All the wind went out of him, and it took him long minutes to get back up. 'Alright there, bach,' said an archer. 'Never trust a *ffycin* horse, as my old gran used to say, and you've got a right horse, here. A horse in Llaregub bit her littlest finger clean off – *clean* off, look you, from her left hand. My nan, that is. Nine-fingered Lynne, they called her after that.' I'm alright, John wheezed. I'm. Alright. A second archer joined the first, and between them they got him upright again. It hurt to breathe. To breathe. Hurt to. Had he broken a rib? Damn and dammit, that was poor timing. Couldn't be helped. Maybe he was just bruised. He took a deep draught of air and it felt like a lance was piercing his side. 'Fuck,' he said. The Welsh liked this. 'It's not every *ffycin* English nob will speak like a true soldier, look you,' said the first archer, approvingly. 'Assist me back onto my horse,' John said, and they guided his iron foot in the stirrup and helped him haul his iron body onto the beast's spine again. He sat for a minute, his whole torso humming with pain. Shallow breaths, shallow breaths. But there wasn't any time: Audley was leading his small cavalry troop away at a brisk walk, the archers jogging alongside. John spurred his horse, and the motion sent horrible jags of agony up his chest and along his spine. When he had caught up he was able to slow to an amble, and that went a little easier on him. Still hurt though – Christ, how it hurt.

Shallow breaths. Shallow breaths.

The French were a blur of men on the horizon, far away, and still far, and then they had approached close enough for John to make out individual faces and drawn swords and the great flank of a massive army, turning its steeds to face this puny assault. 'We'll go in once,' Audley was yelling at the Welshmen, 'and come away again, and when they chase us I want you to knock them all over with your arrows. Alright?'

Then the charge was happening. John didn't even hear the word: they were just in motion, and the fiery glow of pain suddenly intensified in jolting barbs of agony in time to the motion of the horse beneath him. The thicket of French arms darkened and swelled. The pain in his ribs was so overwhelming it pushed the thought of drawing his sword quite out of his head, and then next thing he knew he had ridden hard against a French rider. There was the sudden apparition of a howling helmeted head close to him, and a great jolt as his horse shouldered into the armoured flank of the other beast, and then the other rider disappeared. John's horse staggered like the drunkard it was, stepped sideways, and started trotting back. John held on, just about, but by the time he realised what was happening he was already on his way back to the archers. Audley and the other horsemen overtook him on this retreat and then the air was full of the serpentine hissing of arrows. He saw these as fuzzed lines, or saw them not at all but only heard them, and then he followed Audley in wheeling his horse about. A thousand mounted French knights came pummelling the turf towards them, and arrows drew lines through the sky and John, gasping, saw them clattering off the armour like peas from a peashooter. Saw them slide and bounce, shafts wobbling, harmless.

'Christ and his fucking virgin *mother*', shouted Audley, lifting his sword to lead a second charge. John couldn't breathe. He gulped at air like a carp in a greenscum pond. Couldn't. Couldn't catch his breath. Finally got his sword out. Dug his heels in, and his horse danced forward three steps, stopped sharply, throwing him painfully against the beast's neck, then jumped forward casting him off for a second time.

This time he rolled, and though the collision with the earth hurt desperately he didn't break anything else. Didn't think he had, anyway. Once again foot soldiers reached him, and helped him up. John had no idea if these were the same archers as before. 'Problem is the *ffycin* glue, bach', one told him. 'Been so dry, see? It's parched the glue holding the arrowhead to the shaft, is the *ffycin* issue, and so the pointy bit is liable to come away, see.'

'Help me up', rasped John. 'Help me.' The French had turned and were assembling for another charge. The action of clambering up on his horse again was twice as painful as the last time, but John got back in the saddle, and paused to try and scrape together some breath. The French were coming. He could feel the vibrations through the ground, hear the low thunderous rumble, see the swarm of armed men pouring forward. He lifted his sword, although raising his arm hurt his chest sorely. Away to his right, in the middle distance, he could see a huge body of French foot soldiers advancing upon the main English position.

'Saint George', he gasped and then felt a surge of shame at the feebleness of the noise he was making, shame that felt, oddly, like exhilaration. For *fuck's* sake, come on. He tried again: 'Saint George', he screamed, and the action of his lungs was burning fire inside his torso, and the pain was so intense a strange narrowing and paleness descended upon his field of vision, but he ignored this and leant forward and spurred his horse. He was riding. 'Saint George,' he cried, a third time. The French were almost upon them. He saw two things, one following quickly upon the other. The first was an arrow, fired from somewhere over to his left, sinking flight-deep into the rear of a French horse, and that horse shrieking and falling, dragging its rider down with it. The second thing he saw was a burly rider heading straight for him, mace held at the end of an outstretched metal arm, looming up at him. John lifted his sword, but the collision of mace and the front of his helmet broke the bones of his face into a cloud of hard particles, and these passed swiftly back through the matter of his brain as a whisk passes through cream to froth it up. He was off his horse. He was horizontal, on his back in plain air. He was upside-down and vertical, heels-over-head, in plain air. When his body landed, front-first on the dirt, John was no longer a part of it.

Camera Eye

He feels a strange elation, and this is a feeling for which he cannot account, since things are not since things are not going

      not going well.

From the little hill he took in as much as he could: Audley's attack dissipating itself without effect upon the south French flank.   The larger attack to the north was beyond his view.   Directly before him came the main body of Jean's force: the marshals' battalions, pennants brave in the clear air, red and gold and red and blue and red   pinkred and spottedred   bloodred.

He hears them: *saint denis*, they cry.

and the cry is taken up

sundeny sundeny sundeny

and they were coming in their thousands to break him suddenly, as a hammer descends upon the smith's anvil. And now the hedgerow was to their right, and the scrubland and bush-primped space to their left   and to *his* left Edward saw men squirreling out of their places in the hedge and running away like cowards, and saw other men, small as birds in the distance, sneaking off into the woods, and he saw the whole in a sudden vision: not one thing, a single army, but a mass of differentiable individuals, flies in a swarm, all pulling in different directions. And God the Father sends down orders, but men are legion like the devils that Christ faced, and some obey and some do not, and that fractures the whole, and the son must stand in full view of everyone and die to so redeem their scrabbling, petty-minded selfishnesses

sundeny sundeny sundeny
sundeny sundeny sundeny
sundeny sundeny sundeny

—Saint George, says the Prince, as loud as he may. And he lifts his sword into the bright air.

and with a suddenness akin to grace, the whole scene changes in his eye. The men are not abandoning the hedge, but moving to better positions within it. Audley's charge, following up another volley of arrows, and another volley, is routing the French left flank. The marshals' battalions are almost upon them   and he understands that there is a third thing, beyond the unyielding authority of the Father that says die if you must, and beyond the pity of the son who says let me die so you may live. It is a mysterious third quality, imperceptible to sight or taste or feeling, yet somehow palpable as well. And it works through the whole body of the English army. It turns the myriad clustering mass of *I* into a *We*. It says: only in *We* do we live forever. Edward's excitement is so intense now it almost closes his throat and prevents him breathing.

The whole force works as one

Archers

Archers loose from the hedgerow, from the bushes. Arrows snap instantly into the unarmoured rear flanks and back legs of horses. Horsemen tumble and fall, and are ridden over by those behind them. In minutes the space between the two bodies of bowmen is dammed up with fallen men; but the force behind is too large, its momentum too great, to be able to stop. Men and horses keep piling in. Arrows sting and whisper in the morning air.

This time, louder: Saint George, cries the Prince, and the men behind him echo and

KING JEAN THE GOOD

It is no crime, nor sin, to read books. It is no sin to be able to play an instrument, he thought. None dare say it to his face, but they thought him a pale and feeble son compared to his father. Yet Philip had lost Cressy and so France, and bankrupted the nation; and he, Jean, had spent ten years drawing that nation back together again. He had deferred the royal debts not once but twice, and that took more courage than riding pell mell into battle – a different kind of courage, for sure, but a courage nonetheless. These old nobles with their heads full of chivalric romance and fables of knights fighting blatantbeasts did not seem to realise that nations ran on money, on money, only on money, and money was hard to come by. The plague had attenuated the peasantry worse than it had the nobility, and the fields grew half what they used to. Everything cost more, and armies cost most of all, and he read books to learn how to win wars, not how to lose in a glory of pointless chivalric bravery, like the old King of Bohemia after whom he had been named. Riding blind into battle to die, very noble but very, very foolish too – they were all riding blind into battle all the time, and that was why they were always losing, and that was why France was in so terrible a state.

Not this time. No, no, no. He read about Alexander the Large, and Pompey the Big and Caesar the one and only, the unique and the marvellous, whose horse had toes instead of hooves and who lay with boys and men like a Biblical sodomite, yet who won battles, by God, won battles whenever they presented themselves. You did not win a battle by riding in blind and trusting to your own boldness. You planned it. You made sure you assembled a larger force – much larger, if you could muster it. You ensured your men were well-fed and well-watered, with the best armour that borrowed money could buy. You had the knights tell the ensigns to drill the bastards, marching there, marching here, until a thousand boots struck the ground with a single thump. You scouted the land. You learned from your previous errors.

The English were mere bandits. The English were robbers and rapists and thieves, the sort of men that any good lord hanged from a gibbet on a Saturday as a warning to the others to obey the law. They hurt his country, and pilfered from the peasantry, and burned a few towns. But now Jean had them. They were stuck, like a pig trying to squeeze under a fence and trapped by its own fat belly. Jean himself had ridden to the front of his formation to see: a thorny hedge would stop them being able to retreat, and to the right the land was debatable, pocked with raspy bushes before giving way to the woods. No army could pass that way in good order, and if they tried to run then his knights would have it easy, riding them down, bashing their brains out. English Prince Edward was all reputation and no reality. He had picked a terrible position for his small army, and now Jean's much larger army would crush him.

He slept poorly, and was pacing up and down his tent before dawn. No matter: he would sleep well once victory was claimed, picked up from the ground like a discarded trifle. He stood outside and watched daylight enlarge out of ruddy quiet. It was beautiful, an augur. Sweet dimness broadening into the red of his own oriflamme, and then a glorious rosé yellow blue, growing over the head of the doomed English. Soon enough it was hazy light, and he was hectoring his people. To arms! To arms!

Wideawake.

Up on his horse, he gave out orders once more, but he was only repeating what he had told his marshals a dozen times before. It had the beautiful precision of inevitability.

—Saint Denis!

—*Saint Denis!* roared the army.

The whole enormous organism pulsed into life. He had borrowed a fortune, and it had not been easy to get the money. He had gathered the money and then he had spent the money. Some had gone to merchants and traders and smiths and all the petty people who supply an army. A great trunk of coin went to Douglas, the Scot: not buying his service, of course, merely thanking him as one prince to another for the part he would play in defeating their common enemy. A great pile of wealth had gone into the purses of German mercenaries. It would all come right. Jean understood, as his father never did, that money works by a different logic to everything else. The money he spends today will return to him, like birds flocking north in the springtime, when he has the Prince of Wales in custody, and a herald has sailed to the English with a demand for two, or two and a half, or – why not – three million crowns in ransom. Money will flood back to France. The fields will become fruitful again, and industry will revive, and order and honour return to the state.

The monster he had created shuddered into life.

—Great King, Geoffroi de Charny called, riding towards him. He had been given the honour of carrying the oriflamme on this day. The English are attacking to the south.

—So attack them back, said Jean, his voice high and querulous. Onward! Onward!

Somebody else rode in: the Count of Eu. My lord, my king, the English are retreating.

—That was easier than even I thought, Jean declared. He thought of the cheering there would be in Paris, when he paraded his booty through the streets.

—They are pulling their baggage train back, and their main force is in disarray.

—Strike now! Strike! Now, I want to join the battle, I want to be in at the kill.

So he rode forward through cheering troops and a swell of pride in France, God's land and his, and the restoration of his and his people's honour. It took a while to pick through the mass with his troop. Then he came further forward and saw a mass of dead. These must be the English dead. Beside them were many banners, trampled and toppled, and all of them were French. How could his people abandon their colours in so dishonourable a manner! Were they so eager to crush the English, that . . .

Wait a moment.

—My king! My king!

Who was this? Yelling. There was a long, drawn-out, sucking sound, as if the very sky were drawing in breath, and then the collective breath was expelled in a great hiss. The serpent in the garden. Bowmen filling the sky with their seed. Arrows clattered and hailed down all around. One struck the king's own shield, and skeetered away. Another lodged in his charger's plate armour, but thankfully did not penetrate. Around him men were squealing and writhing, and horses were tumbling.

No.

—My king! My king! We must go back. You are in danger.

The hissing again. Panic swelled behind Jean's ribs, and he rode his horse back in amongst his men. What is happening? he cried. What is going on? There was a lot of shouting and yelling and screaming, from, it seemed, every side.

—Great king, gasped the Duke of Normandy, his own brother, but with blood all over his face and a left arm that dangled limply at his side. There has never been a battle like it, in the history of war!

—What are you *talking* about, brother?

A wave of horsemen pulsed across the battlefield, and Jean was separated from his brother. His personal guard were drawn away, and struggled to re-form around him. It was not possible for Jean to see exactly what was happening. Whole vision was denied him. All around were men, surging, and jostling, and up ahead the sky was stitched with arrows. A crush of foot soldiers pressed behind him, and his horse, spooked and whinnying, stepped forward through the mass of men behind him. Everybody was being drawn forward as if by some riptide of humanity. His horse did not like treading on the bodies of the dead, but there was no help for that.

Frustration burst his heart. Yelling, incoherent, he began hacking at the men around him with his sword, even though they were his own men. He had to break out from this crowd of fools and knaves and – *my king my king* somebody was shouting.

A corridor opened amongst the seething humanity, and he rode his horse along it. He came out amongst a flat space cobbled with corpses. His charger did not wish to tread upon these prone human bodies, but he spurred the beast on. French bodies. German bodies. Where were the dead English?

—My king!

Who was this? One more panic-faced noble.

—Slain. The Marshal of France, Highness, he is slain.

—Jean de Clermont? the King replied, as if there could be another marshal of France.

—My king!

—This is proving an unlucky battlefield for those called Jean.

—The Count of Eu is sore wounded, sire, and captured by the English. Geoffroi de Charnay is killed, my king, and the oriflamme he carried taken by the English. Your brother, Prince Philip, has been captured.

—We shall free these noblemen, all, Jean yelled, when we defeat the English. Advance and take them back! But he thought to himself: not the dead. We shall never take the dead back.

A knot of English foot soldiers was running at them, leaping over the dead bodies, axes and swords. Drawn by the prospect of capturing the King of France himself. Six men of his guard drew and charged them, and Jean, startled, galloped with them, and hacked about with his own sword. Four, five Englishmen fell to the ground, howling, or silent, and blood splashed the royal leg.

—We have lost thousands, sire!

—And so? We have tens of thousands more – why are they not grinding the English under their heels? Where are the Germans?

The sky hissed, and hissed, and the mounted knights shrank into their saddles. The tuneless choir of many men screaming, weeping, gasping.

—My king, said somebody leaning in close. Who was this? It was the Duke of Orléans. It was the Duke, and he was saying something. Jean concentrated, and the words swam into comprehension. The Germans are broken, the Duke was saying. They tried to move against the English archers, but those bowmen drew so fast and fired so fast they could not approach. The Count of Nassau, the Count of Salzburg, the Count of Neyde, all dead.

—I gave Nassau eleven thousand gold crowns, with my own hands, cried Jean. He was weeping now, tears were running on his face. I might as well have tumbled the coins into the Seine. Duke, ride back and bring the rearguard into the fray. Take the Dauphin with you, my lord; we cannot allow him to be captured by the English too. Take him back to the camp, and return with all the men in the rearguard, every one. Bring them quickly. A gold louis for each English head, tell them!

The Duke needed no second order. He rallied his men and rode off, west, away from the fighting. He continued riding west. The rearguard saw him pass through, and many knights rode with him, and they rode wild for the far horizon, and so they did not die that day.

—The Duke of Athens, the Constable of France, is killed by arrows, my lord!

—It is impossible, Jean said, to his right-hand horseman. It cannot be. I am mired in a bad dream and cannot wake. The English could not win, and cannot win, and will not win.

—This is not a safe place, my king.

They rode, and soon came upon the Scotsman, his dark blue banner sluggish in the low breeze and a thousand men-at-arms around him. Douglas had taken a small hillock, and surrounded it with spearmen, and was watching the fight from his horse. The Scots parted to permit King Jean and his guard through.

—We must attack, always attack, my lord of Douglas.

—I have attacked all morning, sir, replied Douglas, in his accented French. The battle has been turned against us.

—Such a thing is not a possible thing, Jean cried, and then pointed and yelled: there! The Black Prince, that's his helmet! Following the outstretched arm with their gaze the soldiers saw the great lion-helmet bobbing through a combat affray, and a black sword flipping up and cutting down in a mist of blood.

—Charge him! Kill the Prince and the day is ours!

Nobody was listening.

—Did you hear what the Black Prince did, King Jean? Douglas asked. He found the Cardinal's nephew, Lord Robert of Duras – dead, or nearly dead and finished him off, I don't know which. Anyway he found the Old Cardinal's sin, lying there, spreadeagled. Now, the Prince was angry at the Cardinal de Périgord for fighting today, fighting for you, my lord. Yesterday he was pretending to be an emissary for peace, and today he was fighting for you. So he put the body of the Cardinal's bastard son on a horse with a parchment stuffed in its visor and sent it back to the French camp, so that the Cardinal should know his displeasure, that men of God and emissaries for peace should not fight.

Tears of pure frustration and vexation were making Jean's vision wobbly.

—Charge, my lord! he shouted. Cut straight through to . . . but as he said it he looked again, and saw how many English stood between this place and the Prince's troop.

—Not I, King of France, drawled Douglas. There's a path free south, and I shall take my men that way. I'll circle round and come eventually to the coast, and so back to Scotland.

—Then you'll return my crowns to me, sir, before you depart!

—The crowns are lost, Douglas grimaced. A crown will soon be.

He rode off, and did not look behind him as the King swore and cursed him. His men filed after him, and rode briskly away, as on a parade or in tourney. Jean no longer had the oriflamme, and so rode back to the west to retrieve an alternative, to bring the banner of his house out to the battlefield.

At the camp everything was in confusion. The impossible sentences kept tumbling from people's mouths. The Count of Tancarville, captured. The Count of Marche and Ponthieu, captured. The Count of Joinville, captured. Guillaume de Melun, Archbishop of Sens, captured. The Duke of Athens, Constable of all France, killed.

—This is old news, Jean snarled. Bring me some new.

—You must retreat, great king. You must ride west.

—This battle has just begun, Jean cried, and his bannerman raised, since the oriflamme had been mislaid, the blue-and-gold chequered blazon of the House of Valois. Defeat was a simple impossibility. It was as if a wolf should take a lamb by the throat, and the lamb knock the wolf's brains in with its hooves. Or, he thought, as he rode east again, or as if a wolf should begin to swallow the lamb, and choke to death on it.

He found a large force of French soldiers, true Frenchmen, no mercenaries, and their knights had kept them in good order. Jean's heart lifted: it was not over. Then he heard, or rather felt, a rumbling that made the grass shake, and that transmitted itself through the general clamour and howls of the wounded and the dying. A charge. Jean looked up: two great flanks of English were coming down the slope, from behind the main French army. How had they gotten behind? The rows of men-at-arms at the rear were crumpling, men scattering north and south or falling dead before the assault.

—Majesty, said Jean's bannerman, and then he added some ghastly guttural tangle of syllables, as if he were mocking his role, or speaking Dutch or Scotch or something. Jean swore at him for his insolence, and then saw that an arrow had struck him from the side, and bisected the profile of his Adam's apple. Jean saw the flesh puckered in and pushed out, and then watched blood ooze from the wound, and slosh down. The gentleman slid from his horse, and the royal blue banner fell with him.

Panic was now general. Jean could almost smell it. Pick up the banner, he shouted. Somebody pick up the banner. Groans and screams and yells all around. Hundreds were scuttling along the road to Poitiers, hoping to get inside the city and save themselves.

Pick up the banner, he called.

Then, instead of the banner raising, he himself was lowered. His horse was going down, but slowly, as in a dream. It went onto its front knees, and then onto its rear knees, and then slowly slumped to the left. Jean scrambled his leg free, and stood on the ground. There were three arrows in the steed's neck, bunched close together, the flights like a parody fleur-de-lys.

His personal guard were all dismounting around him, to defend him, swords out. The Count of Dammartin stood closest. Orléans will bring reinforcements, Jean shouted. Horses were approaching. The battle is not over. It is still early in the morning.

—Majesty, said Dammartin, it is late afternoon. We have fought all day.

The time had warped and shrunken around Jean. He could not believe it.

Horses were approaching. In amongst the confusion of voices, words yelled in French and in alien tongues, incoherencies from the dying, came the cry of: surrender, your Majesty. Surrender, Majesty. And here were the horsemen, almost upon them.

—Surrender, Majesty, or you will die.

—Who are you, sir? Jean realised that he was very tired, tired to the very bone. But he held up his sword.

—Majesty, I am Denis of Morbèque, a knight. I was banished from France as a youth for causing the death of a man in an affray in Saint-Omer, and so I have fought with the English for five years, and I have guided them around this land.

—Talkative, aren't you. Jean lowered his sword. The fight was going out of him.

—You must surrender, Majesty.

—To whom? Not to you, evidently, little Sir Denis.

The knight was a large and burly-built man, and looked confused.

—Where is my cousin, the Prince of Wales? Jean demanded. I would speak with him.

—Majesty, if you surrender to me, and give me your right glove, I will take you to him. I serve the King of England and therefore I serve his son, the Prince.

Jean pulled off his glove, noticing for the first time that there was a good quantity of dried blood upon it. Where had that come from? Here you go, knight of France who serves the English. I surrender to you. He handed him the gauntlet.

Men crowded around him, and voices shouted confusedly, I have him, I have taken him, he is mine. But Sir Denis was big and powerfully-built and pushed his way through. It was a slow walk, for Jean kept tripping over dead bodies and people kept crowding in around him as though he were a holy relic to be caressed for good luck. But soon enough they came to the Black Prince, no taller than Jean, and certainly not as clever or as well read. He took off his helmet, and his yellow hair was dark and wet with sweat, and as they saw whom Sir Denis was bringing the king's bannermen shouted out *give way give way there on pain of death* and the crush relented a little.

Silence fell, broken only by the continuing variegated moans and curses of the fallen, and the shriek of the many birds that had now gathered in the sky. Jean, walking towards the Black Prince, became aware that his left leg was sore. He tried not to limp, but each step was painful and he could hardly help himself. How had he not noticed the pain earlier? The Prince of Wales stood there smiling. As he approached the English lords and knights dismounted, one by one, and bowed.

—Cousin, said Edward. You have come to surrender?

—Cousin, said Jean, grimacing with the pain in his leg. I have.

They led him away, and he limped through the ruin and the dead bodies, and eventually to a tent. He was given wine, and food, and this he devoured with a ferocious appetite, for he was parched and starved. Then he was helped from his armour and bathed, and amazed to find a deep gash in his left leg, running along his thigh to the side of his knee. He had no memory where this had come from.

—You evidently to fight bravely very good bravely, said the fellow who washed him, in bad French.

Dressed again, they brought his son Philip to him, who embraced his father, and Jean wept over the lad, for he had hoped he was escaped into the west. With Philip came a half dozen French noblemen, likewise prisoners. A bad scene at Poitiers, said Dammartin. A thousand of our men ran to the gates and begged to be let in; but the citizens did not open the gates, for fear I supposed that the English would flood through, and so those thousand were cut down by the Englishmen who pursued them.

—Terrible, said Jean. He tried to focus his mind, but he felt immensely sleepy. Terrible. Then, no longer caring for his dignity, he lay on the ground and slept.

When he awoke he experienced a heart-breaking moment when he thought the day yet to begin, battle all before him and victory to be claimed. Then he sat up and saw his son, bruised and despondent; saw his nobles lying and sitting, and reality of defeat crushed down upon him.

It was still light outside the tent; the evening of the same day. It had all happened, and in so short a space.

Then the sun finally set, and a decent darkness shrouded the fields of dead bodies. People came and went. Word was that three thousand of Jean's men had surrendered. It would be a costly complex of ransoms to return them all home. Costly to France.

—Majesty, said an Englishman, in accented French. The Prince of Wales begs you do him the honour of dining with him.

Wearily Jean went with the fellow, and half a dozen like him, through the camp. The smell of congealing blood was in the night air. Corpses killed in the morning had had long enough in the sun to begin to ripen with decay. The Prince's tent was shining from within with shimmering torchlight, and Jean stepped through.

—Cousin! said the terrible Black Prince, now in the clothes of peacetime, his yellow hair washed and tied behind.

Jean sat at the table, and Edward waited upon him as a servant, as befitted their respective ranks. Ever a stickler for the chivalric law, this Prince. The Englishman brought the Frenchman fruit upon a golden dish, and when Jean had taken some, and drunk from his goblet of wine, Edward sat down.

—Well, we are done here, at this battle, he said.

—*Consummatum est*, said Jean. Edward looked up sharply at this, as if at a blasphemy, but then smiled again.

—We take no pleasure in the slaughter of men, said the Englishman, but we rejoice in God's bounty and look forward to a just and lasting peace.

—My land is poor in money, said Jean, and will now be poorer. You have taken much of God's bounty already.

With a boy's ingenuousness, though he was now a full-grown man, Edward said: trunks and trunks of the stuff! Clothing, horses, armour. I took a jewelled belt and a scarlet robe from the Mile de Noyers, must be worth two hundred livres. From your own pavilion, cousin, we took one of your crowns, the jewelled insignia of the Order of the Star – which is your imitation of my Order of the Garter, I think? And also we found this absolutely *amazing* silver ship, gorgeously worked and huge, just huge, *really* heavy.

—The centrepiece of my table, said Jean.

—Of my table now. And I took a splendid illustrated Bible, which the Earl of Salisbury has promised to buy from me for a hundred marks.

—And, in addition to all that, said Jean, holding one grape before his left eye, you have me.

Edward looked serious. Jean ate the grape and picked up another.

—Cousin, the Englishman said, shortly, if you'd taken me, as I – by the grace of God – have taken you, what would you have done with me?

Jean did not answer.

—You would, I think, have had me humiliated and ransomed at so high a price as to break the land of England. My spies tell me you talked much to your troops of giving no quarter. That we were bandits and thieves, not warriors. No?

—I am not yet out of your hands, Jean said. My future is, shall I say, uncertain.

—It is *most* certain. You will ride on a fine white charger through the streets of London, followed by your son Philip and a guard of French horsemen. I shall ride by your side on the smallest black palfrey I can find. You will reside at the Savoy Palace, or at Windsor Castle if the building of it is yet completed. You will not know yourself to be a prisoner at all. And then it will be but a matter of paying a small ransom before you are restored to your own fair kingdom.

All the bitterness of the day returned to Jean in a single reflux, a palpable burning sensation in his chest. That, he said, this is all your chivalry means, then. Loot, ransom, decking the bodies of your women with French silks, swilling French wine by the hogshead. It is a strange way of life. The smallest peasant farmer at least grows his own wheat and bakes his own bread. The banners wave and the cannon roar, and you talk of glory and honour—

—You too, Edward put in. Were in the same trade.

—Trade! Jean is actually outraged. He stops, and rethinks. Though the revulsion he feels at the description is automatic, he cannot deny its accuracy. They are both kinds of tradesmen, and that's the truth. It's a poor sort of trade, cousin. Better to sweat honestly, feed grossly, snore beside the wife of one's bosom. We miss a lot in our . . . trade, as you call it.

—Well, said Edward, and now his mood had again shifted about, like the youngster he was, and he was wistful. You're probably right. He munched his fruit, and then got up to serve Jean the next course, again on a golden platter. Tomorrow we shall decamp and move some miles south of Poitiers. We cannot stay here amongst so many rotting bodies!

—French bodies, said Jean, gloomily.

—And German ones. And Scots. And even some English. I'll leave a force to pen in Poitiers, of course; but over the next week or so we shall withdraw to Bordeaux. I've sent people ahead to prepare for a triumph. He grinned at Jean, and it almost seemed as though he couldn't quite believe the Frenchman would not share his puppydog happiness.

—Bordeaux, said Jean. It is a fine town.

Newsreel (12)

GREAT ENGLISH VICTORY. GOD IS PRAISED

Letter from the Prince of Wales arrives in London

was agreed that we should take our way, flanking them, in such a manner that if they wished for battle or to draw towards us, in a place not very much to our disadvantage, we should be the first; the enemy was discomfited, and the king was taken, and his son; and a great number of other great people were both taken and slain

CROWD ATTACK FRENCH KNIGHT AND HIS SQUIRE
ON THE ROAD IN NORMANDY

'There go the traitors who fled from the battle'

Peacock costumery rebuked: pride goeth etc etc
Bombans et vaine gloire, vesture disoneste
Les ceintures dorées, la plume sure la teste

From this time all has gone wrong with the Kingdom of France and the state is undone. With the King taken a captive to England, thieves and robbers have risen up everywhere in the land. The nobles despise and hate all others and take no thought for the mutual usefulness and profit of lord and men. They subject and despoil the peasants and the men of the villages. In no wise do they defend their country from enemies. Rather they trample it underfoot, robbing and pillaging the peasants' goods.

PART 5. ARMOUR

Newsreel (13)

Shall we define chivalry, in a single matter? To love a lady truly and honourably is the right position to be in for those who desire to achieve honour. What delight it must bring to a knight's beloved when she sees him enter the hall where all at the table honour, salute and celebrate him. Such will make the noble lady rejoice greatly within herself at the fact that she has set her mind and heart on loving and helping to make such a good knight.

IT'S WIN-WIN AT GOLDEN WINDSOR

King gives go-ahead for building two new towers and one magnificent hall
Greatest peacetime single expenditure of money

William, son of John de Brich, died of starvation in prison, having been attached for burglary of Geoffrey le Rook of Litelburstede.

John Harper, slain by John of Hanchet by force, using a staff, a bidowe, a buckler, a gambison and a palet.

Maud, daughter of Richard of Dunchurch, died by accidentally falling into a ditch.

John Heir, killed when struck by John Skinner with a pole hatchet after 'abusive words' were exchanged.

A man, villein, by falling from a haystack. Price of the stack, 11s.

We forbid to all servants of God hunting and expeditions through the woods with hounds; and we also forbid them to keep hawks or falcons. *Corpus Juris Canonici* (C. ii, X, De cleric. venat.)

ESTATES GENERAL IN TURMOIL AT PARIS

Camera Eye

Cold and up at dawn to pray with the other monks ora ora ora in growly unison   then: chores whilst this stomach growled an after tune of the prayers, and so to the scriptorium.

first pangs of actual joy here HERE here   A poor man's son, then a poor monk living on alms, and sometimes getting them but as often being called a beggar's brat and mocked for his ambition to be a bishop ho-ho, then one of three chantry priests bestowed by Sir Walter Murray in his will. Now another young priest visited the corner of the church and stepped behind the screen to pray for Sir Walter's soul, and he is here, in the monastery mixing the black ink in a metal pot, and uncapping little horn containers of coloured powders.

wainscot cells led off the cloister   birds in twos twining their flights around one another sang, and it is possible to look through at a geometrically separate shape of blue sky. The summer warmth. He pares his nails with his knife, so they do not scratch the parchment. Today he is to work on an illustration for the *speculum humanae salvationis*   King David's victory in battle and the wickedness of heathen kings. He draws Evilmerodach dismembering the exhumed corpse of his father, Nebuchadnezzar the Great with an axe   he knows only one fashion of axe, and so curves the lines to a pole of a woodsman's axe   and feeding

the body parts to the birds, in ungodly heathen manner.
A shocking mode of burial   as Evilmerodach is king,
howsoever evil, he draws the crown and head together,
and gives his face the severe dignity of royalty tucks

the figure's left thumb over the handle and draws in
the four other fingers coming round from the other
side to meet it. The right hand is just fingers. The
dismembered body looks, when he has finished, like
a discarded piece of clothing, the cuts on its flesh a
pattern in the weave.   No matter. Each bird is alike,
as birds are; though facing in different directions   all
in flight   in each beak a different bodypart: foot,
knee, hand. In one beak he draws a circle, with a smaller

circle inside and a dot at its heart: the wicked king's eye   finally he draws the rest of the corpse's head. As this man was also a king, though wicked, he adds a crown.   He peers again: the head looks too heavy for one bird to carry, especially crowned in gold. He draws in two birds supporting the severed neck.   The scratching of the quill on the parchment as he draws each line. Some of the brothers draw with an uninked pen to make a web of indentations to be inked later. He does not.

Evilmerodach had ruled the kingdom when his father Nebuchadnezzar had been mad, and driven into the wilderness. A king roaming the wilds like a beast, chewing grass, naked   desperate and unkingly. And then Nebuchadnezzar had regained his wits, by grace of God, and cast his own son into prison   heathen   and in prison Evilmerodach had languished, with a noble Jew called Joachin, and the two had become friends. Then the old king had died and been buried and Evilmerodach had been released into his inheritance. But then: when he began to reign, he raised up Joachin, whom he had a companion in prison, and fearing that his father would resurrect, who had returned from being a beast into being a man, took Joachin into counsel; at whose counsel, he exhumed the corpse of his father, divided it into 300 parts, and gave the 300 parts to 300 vultures. And Joachin said to him, *Your father will not resurrect until these vultures return together.*

He stretched and stared through the entrance of his wainscot cell at the patch of blue he could see outside   the day before he had gone into town to buy necessaries for the monastery; and Hugh the Colour had measured out powdered lapis in his narrow shop, and had said   there is money to be earned, brother monk, by your talent   and he had laughed, but Hugh the Colour had gone on: I have friends in London who make and sell books – books – books – how hard to find good men to illuminate their product? You could earn enough to buy fine clothes, and a house. You could earn enough to be a wealthy man, in London. The plague has thinned the population so, that folk with skills such as yours—   I am sworn, I say, to the church, I say, to the monastery, to Christ

        I say

        I say

yes yes, but did you not tell me yourself you were once a chantry priest? And now a monk. The past, says Hugh, grasping his arm, is not a prison. We may make ourselves.   If God will it, he says, and breaks away   he thinks of the past: towering, dominant, by turns insane and, when restored to its mind, vindictive. The past dead. His own father a villein. The rumours were he had killed his mother, but he had never faced justice for that, if it had happened. He grew up in the cot with him and his stepmother and his three sisters, and watched his father beat his stepmother with a switch

yes yes yes yes yes

taking care to strike a different part of her writhing body with each blow as she wailed and begged mercy mercy   face legs hands   and after she would lie whimpering in the corner like a hound. He had never loved his stepmother. If anything he had despised the woman, her weakness. Christ teaches us to love all, and perhaps he was a bad priest, and perhaps he loved drawing better then praying or helping the poor. He made his way back to the monastery with supplies in his satchel and pondered Hugh's words. The past was dead, and only one part of it – named Christ – had overcome that fact to be alive in the present. Perhaps the past should be lawfully interred, and remembered by a lone monk in a chancel   or chopped into pieces and fed to three hundred

birds   birds   birds
birds   birds   birds
birds   birds   birds

It began to rain, a drizzle soft as chenille sifting out of a silver-grey sky and   he clutched his satchel to his chest and picked up his pace

THE BLACK PRINCE

Aquitaine being so hot in the day, the best time for a hunt was dawn. Ned rode out with five companions, and stopped at the head of the shallow valley to look down: stubby trees and many bushes all wrapped about with a groundmist, and half a dozen Englishmen on horseback. Six spears straight up like poplars. As they descended, goats scattered into the brush. Towards the bottom, where the stream clanged over its stones, the trees grew bigger. By the time they had ridden into position the sun was properly up, and the mist all sucked away into a sky metallic with blueness. The six waited in the spotty shade, and soon enough a mother boar came to the stream to drink, and three barrel-sized youngsters, and without giving any command Edward spurred on and ran at the creature. It bolted, looked almost to have got away, but then swung about and charged straight at the party. Its three young went bowling off in three different directions. Ned got one of the piglets stabstraight through its bristly back with a single downstroke of his spear and the creature writhed and shrieked like a seagull. Sir Hugh blooded a second boar cub on its hind leg, but it wriggled past and vanished into the bushes. Back at the stream two horses danced aside as the mother boar galloped through, turning its monster head left and right to brandish its tusks. Long as swords, and curved like pain, yellowwhite, diabolic. Sir Ian of Honnockbrae got his spear into the boar's rear, but the monster called in a voice that sounded almost human *ho ho* and *oh oh*, low and guttural, and shanked left, dragging Sir Ian half from his saddle. If he had not let go of his spear he would have been pulled to the ground, but he let the weapon fall and gripped the mane of his horse. His struggling back upright incommoded his mount, which whinnied and trotted briskly away. Ned extricated *his* spear and charged the boar, but the old monster was canny and darted left to miss the strike, and it made a run for freedom, dragging Sir Ian's spear behind like an oversized clatterly tail. But then Sir Hugh caught it on the belly from the side, and soon enough all the knights but the spearless Sir Ian converged on the carcass and stabbed it. That was that. They tied one leg to Sir Hugh's saddle and the other to the Prince's and dragged the heavy mass of meat up the stone path out of the valley and back towards the castle.

It was mid-morning now and the sun and its brute châleur had transformed the land. It was a forbidding place, really: brassy and dusty, the rocks like curls of old leather, the greenery a less lush, more pinched dark-verdance than was found in England, intermittent amongst the white and yellow dirt. Cicadas sawed the air raspingly in every direction.

They passed down the main street of the little village, dragging the corpse behind. No longer black, now a freakish white spectre. The dead boar looked as though it had been dusted with chalk. Several villagers stared sourly at the Englishmen, but Ned's gaze was up, at the battlements, and his colours flying. Mind you, though he was looking upward, he did not miss the oldest of the villagers spitting into the road behind his horse. Ned stopped, stood up in his stirrups and turned, but the men were already scampering away with the graceless lope of the old in a hurry. The one who had spat, he saw, was a lean old fellow with a bald red head. He vanished round the corner. If he hadn't had the boar tied to his saddle, Ned might have pursued – finish the hunt, he thought, with a flush of excitement, with a real quarry this time. But if he stopped to untie the dead weight, and then remount, he would never catch the man. He would, he thought, recognise the rooster-hue of his bald head, though he'd only seen it from behind, when he met with it again.

A lizard pulsed across the bright face of a nearby wall: fluid bursts of speed intermitted with cautious pauses.

Gone, into a crack.

—Highness? Sir Hugh asked.

—In, Edward nodded up the path to the castle gate. And so they dragged their prize in, and servants ran over with buckets in which they washed their heads of the dust, and the castle butchers, sour-faced Frenchmen, dragged the carcass to the kitchens, and Ned drank a draught of water to take the dust from his gullet, and then a goblet of wine. This latter was brought to him by Denis de Morbecque, his chamberlain in this small citadel.

—What more do the dogs want? he wanted to know, handing the empty cup and striding away. Little ghosts of white dust struggled from his footsteps. Denis followed.

—Highness?

—They are unburdened by excessive taxes. Our courts of law deal justly with them. One master surely is as good as another—

Up the stone stairs, three at a time. Into his chamber, pulling off the dusty clothes. Denis stood, his head deferentially angled. Edward was pulling on clean, or at least undusty, clothes.

Newsreel (14)

on on on account on on account on account of the lack of productive land around the city, it being mostly marsh. Yet yet yet the king holds that Calais remains a cannon aimed at the heart of France and must be maintained, such that ships travel from the coastlines of Kent and Sussex and over to Calais bringing all the necessaries: 350 ships crewed by nearly 12,000 men. The cost the cost the cost of this constant traffic is in excess of £14,000 per annum, and almost all must be met from the English exchequer. More than eight of every ten Calaismen belong to the garrison and they must be fed.

> Mid the war's great coise
> Stands the great red croise
> That shows England's the boise

fed

Citadels of Villepreux and Trappes occupied by English
Nuns of Poissy, Longchamp and Melun abandon their buildings

fed

between 40,000 and 50,000 moutons had been disbursed on the
Dauphin's personal instructions

Camera Eye

He is hound. His master is the Lord, Auberie of
Montdidier, though he does not know him by this
name   scent of leader and feeds him lifemorsels from
his own hand   he follows his master on the hunt,
sniffing in at the slots the deer's sharp hoofs have left as
traces in the ground; and growling at the fumes of the
excremental pellets, and running, and shouting loud
with dogshout and loud again   and waiting, where his
master is, the Lord, Auberie of Montdidier lays a hand
against the smooth pelt of his neck.

The Lord is on the back of a greathound, bigger
than true hounds and much dumber, but not prey and
therefore hounds. He is with another lord, also on a
greathound's back   the two human men together, and
they growl and whimper at one another after their fashion.

They are friends, from the same pack. He is hound, and can smell the deer reeking off all the trees   brushed again. He runs ahead shouting. He runs ahead, and hears his name called back.

He doubles back

His master is the Lord, Auberie of Montdidier, but the other human is behind him, and bites him with his bitingsword, from behind bites at his neck. The other human, who smells of oldsweat and the decay of his stool, still inside him, makes the little mouth at his belt swallow the whole sword and gets off the greathound.

He is stripping the pelt off   His master is the Lord, Auberie of Montdidier, and

in fury at his master being killed, and he runs at the other human shouting, shouting, shouting, and the human stands, unafraid   which is a fearful thing to see   and draws a stick and beats hound with it. The pain bites in at his back and bites all about and he whimpers and puts his tail down and shrinks away. When the other man has finished his master is naked, and the other man has taken his pelt and stuffed in one of the mouths at his saddle, and lifted himself high off the ground on the spine of the greathound. He calls to the other hounds, and they cluster around him, and do what he does, of course, and the pain of his beating still bites him, so he slinks after the one human and back to the big house.

Here he skulks. He is kicked out of the foodcave, though there is plenty of food. He sleeps outside where it is cold. Many humans come and go. New humans. He snatches a scrap and when the female human shouts at him he runs off. He dreams of his master the Lord, Auberie of Montdidier, and the dream saddens him.

One day he is called out and must trot alongside the greathound of a new human, all along a long road. He trots up the road, with his tongue hanging out. This new human acts like the Big Dog, and the hound follows him as such, although he knows the Big Dog is still his master the Lord, Auberie of Montdidier. They sleep when the sky sleeps, and run along the road together, these three, when the sky wakes. They come to Paris, although the hound does not know this is its name   the biggest house he has ever seen, with the most rooms, and many many humans   houndsmell and rich odours and intricate patterns of fantastical scent.

here the human who pretended to be Big Dog gives him over to another, who spends a long time patting him and pulling wide his jaws to look at him. The men whimper and growl at one another, and then the first man goes away and the new man takes him.   He is led into a vast room, clogged with grey and blue clothhangings and many men standing in their bluegrey greyblue clothes, but complexly woven of a hundred scents, including some scents the hound knows   knows   in the centre the Man Big Dog of Men sits in his hard chair, with his grey crown and bluegrey clothing, and hound knows him, and

Kneeling before is the other human, who used his hard sword to bite at his master the Lord, Auberie of Montdidier. Hound knows him. Hound runs, and leaps, and bites the other human, who rolls over yelping and shows himself to be no Big Dog at all by rolling and whimpering. Men are barking and shouting all around, and the Man Big Dog of Men is standing and pointing, and some have seized the other human, who used his hard sword to bite at his master the Lord, Auberie of Montdidier, and have pulled him away.

the Man Big Dog of Men slaps and strokes and tickles hound. He is good hound. He is good hound. Later they feed him fresh meat, and he drinks much water from the trough.

BLACK GEORGE

So it was peace, and Black George rode the unsteady sea back to England, and you'll let me off at fucking Dover captain my captain I'll *walk* to London if I have to, I thank you, no need to sail me all round the Kent coast and in at the Estuary in this shipwreck waiting to happen thank you *very* much. Glad to have feet on ground again, and a mule loaded with French wealth. Treaty of Brétigny signed and sealed and King Edward and French John brothers again, and the Frenchers have already paid hundreds of thousands of golden pounds of ransom, and now the news is they've fallen *behind* paying the new instalment of hundreds of thousands, the *bâtards*. And King Edward has thrown the whole mass of coins at these gigantic building projects. A new Castle at Windsor. A Fortress in the Thames Estuary. A Silver Ladder to the Moon for all Black

George knew. He cared not at all. He had his haul, and some of it he deposited with a man called Gareth, notionally a trader in fine cloth but actually a kind of unofficial banker for the more ordinary sort of man. Some of it George kept to himself, to have ready, and he spent a chunk of that buying a house near Cripplegate, and putting a wife inside it – his actual wife, his own actual wife, of good family and good looks – and making sure she had the finest dresses plundered French money could buy. Six happy months. Well, two happy months, then four unhappy ones when he became certain his wife was cheating on him with a lithe young apprentice boy who would walk past their house every day on his way to the glovers' shop and leer in at their windows. She denied it of course, and the one time George discovered the lad inside the house she swore she was only giving him a drink of water on a hot day. But it chewed his guts, it really did. He knew he wasn't the handsomest dog in the kennel: old, his skin scraggy, scarred from years in the wars, his manners rough. But he was paying for everything, wasn't he? His wife, Kate, lived in a fine house and her two older sisters lived with her for company, both widows from the plague, both too old for childbearing and neither wealthy – but happy to live on his charity whilst criticising him for pissing in the corner, or spitting on the table. His money. They all spent it like it was nothing. Like it was nothing.

Anyway it was all one, in the end. The plague was back in town in full force, and Kate fell sick one morning, and by the evening was clearly set to die. In the end she lasted a full week, and he nursed her, and tears fell down his scarred old face, for he loved her after all. Her two sisters – both almost two decades older than she, and in truth only half-sisters, stayed away. He didn't have to ask why they did so. He'd seen the plague up close the first time it had been doing the rounds, when he'd been in France-land, and so he had a superstitious terror of proximity to the victims. But he couldn't leave her. He loved her, and prayed loudly, and embraced her, and would have fucked her, tenderly – as tenderly as he was capable – if she hadn't pushed him back with trembling arms. She didn't want him to get the death, too, she whispered. He loved her, she was beautiful, or she had been beautiful and was no longer, but he still loved her. Towards the end it got bad: her fingers got black and her neck swelled so she could hardly swallow, and then something inside her was overwhelmed by the sickness and she vomited painfully and bloody, and shat herself, and wept and moaned with the pain. He tried her on water, and tried her on expensive wine, but she could barely swallow either. During the last day and night she begged him to make it stop, and he wept to think that he knew two dozen ways to kill a person but all of them would leave evidence of the act behind and that would surely hang him. He wept that he could not abate her suffering. He thought, finally, of a pillow, recalling that one of the Roman Emperors had been slain by one. But George and his wife slept with bolsters of wool and he thought these not soft enough to go in her mouth and stop her breathing. Then she vomited more blood, and then she cried aloud very pitiably for a full hour in terrible pain, whilst George chewed his own knuckles and wept, and then she stopped breathing.

He expected to develop the plague himself, but he did not. A boy wanted two full shillings – twenty-four whole pennies! – for cleaning and washing the house, and his neighbours agreed it was a scandal, people would take tuppence for such a job not five years before and be glad to have it, but nobody offered to do the work for any less, and so George paid. He paid to have her wrapped in a brand new sheet and buried in the Cripplegate Church and he paid for all the necessary rituals. His sisters-in-law came back then, and wept, and begged him to allow them to carry on living in the house, but he told them both he was selling the house and they would have to shift for themselves, and they wept louder.

He went to confession, and told the priest he had thought of murdering his own wife, in that last day, had even started to plan how he might do it. The priest told him this was a grave sin, and laid a heavy penance upon him, but also said that God knew the love he had in his heart for his wife, and God judged on the strength of that. So when he came out of church, George felt a little better about things.

One of the clerics at the Cripplegate church was prepared to act as mediator for the house sale – he often performed the act, he said, for people who did not know the town well enough to deal direct with purchasers. A lean, tall junior priest with a scar down his cheek like he had once cried a single tear of molten lead. The man's fee was small. George bought him a drink in a tavern, and asked after the scar on his face. Before coming here, the cleric said, he had been on the staff of a Great Company in the Limousin, in France. The administration and much of the organisation of these Companies was done by clerics, he said, and sometimes such men got mixed up in the fighting. George didn't press him on this latter detail. The captains-general, and constables, and marshals, and sub-marshals and corporals were all brave men, but the specifics of money accounts, supplies, ransoms, selling on prisoners and so on was not their strong point. George asked: whose Company? and the cleric said John Hawkwood. I know him, said George. I fought with him at Calais. A good man. A good fighting man, the cleric agreed, or perhaps, corrected.

How might a man such as I, decades in France, experienced in war, fought at Cressy and Calais and a hundred other battles – how might such a man take service in Hawkwood's company?

The cleric sucked his lips against his gums. The scar writhed on his cheek. You served with the King? With the Prince of Wales? Understand, these new Companies are not encompassed by the King. They are, rather—

I know all about the Companies, said George sharply. But how may I join?

What is your battle expertise?

I organised sieges, the smaller towns and citadels. I'm good at that. But I'll fight any old how. I can fire a bow. I'm happier with a sword in my hand than I am with . . . but here, at a loss for a comparator, he stopped.

And it is that you speak French?

I do.

Italian?

Why would I need Italian in France?

Yes or no, the cleric pressed, impatiently.

It's like unto Spanish I think, and that I can speak a little.

I will write a letter, said the cleric, for three pounds, and you will take it to a man in Southampton. You'll buy your own kit and weaponry of course. You'll organise your own travel and feed yourself until you join the Company, of course.

Good, said George. Good.

The following day he approached his sisters-in-law in more emollient mood, and promised them thirty pounds between them, half the sum he expected from the sale of the house. They thanked him, but soon began weeping again. Why must he sell the house? Why couldn't he stay, and they keep house for him. He rebuked them, told them to be grateful for the large sum he had promised them – a fortune, really – but then he caught the image of his wife's face in one of the sister's imploring eyes, and couldn't be angry any more.

I'm going to fight in France, he told them.

There is no more war in France, one of the sisters – Anna – said. In his last sermon Father Balliol said the war is over and we must give thanks to the King and to God that the scourge of war has been lifted from our fellow Christians.

War is never over, said Black George.

You will not be the man to call our priest a liar, said Anna, her temper rising. Joan, the other sister, tried to hush her, for she could see her fifteen pounds evaporating like a puddle in the sun of George's anger. But Anna wouldn't be shushed. Father Balliol said it in church. There is no more war.

There's no war in England, George said, and you two crones should be grateful of that fact, for you would last no time in France, no time at all. But there is still war in France, and there a great company of soldiers is fighting under Sir John Hawkwood, and I am a soldier and will go.

Stay in England where it is peaceful, urged Joan. Why risk your life?

Stay and do what? I am a soldier. When Anna rolled her eyes at this, he roared at them both: what would you have me do? God made me a soldier! I must go where there is work for soldiers!

God made you a man, was Anna's retort. The devil made you a soldier.

At this George walked away, for he could feel a killing rage come up at her words, and he didn't want his wife's sisters' blood on his conscience. Instead he spent the day in a tavern and drank down a vast sum.

In the event he did not sell the house, for the cleric fellow came back with an offer from a silversmith of only forty-four pounds, forty in coin and the rest in comestibles, plus two chairs for which George had no use. Forty-pound, he complained? I bought it not one year ago for sixty!

Back then London was full of soldiers newly returned from France, and every one had a sack of booty, said the cleric. Naturally prices went up. But now, with the plague back, and people leaving the city, few are looking to buy a house, and prices have come down. You should be happy to get so generous an offer. Happy to get any kind of offer at all.

Prices went *up*? George repeated in incredulity. Prices came *down*? What are you talking about? Prices are prices. Things are things. Has half my house fallen down that I should get less money for it?

This, said the cleric, with a curious and sly expression on his face, is not how the world is.

He can take his forty pounds and four pounds of comestibles and most especially his two fucking chairs and stow them snugly up his arsehole, George said. Still, he paid the cleric the three pounds of gold and took the fellow's letter down to Southampton. He even bade farewell to his wife's sour old sisters before he left, telling them to keep the house clean for now, and he would sell it when he came back. They wept and Joan embraced him, but it was Anna's grateful look that brought the twist of grief into his gut, for he thought again of his beautiful wife, his beautiful dead wife, who had died in such pain in his own arms, and he had to hurry away so that they did not see him weep.

From Southampton it was back on the shitting sea, shitting him up and down and sideways and back again until he grasped the side like a church gargoyle and vomited the shit of his queasy stomach into the water. Normandy was an unconscionable distance, and for the middle bit the ship was out of sight of both England and France, and George decided he was doomed, certain to drown there, and tried to mumble prayers with his mouth full of the sour residue of vomit. It was Noah's flood come again, and no Noah this time to save them. It went round his head *ah no noah no noah ah*. Then he fell into a kind of swoon, not exactly a sleep, and the thought got into his head that the whole world was covered now in water, and that he would never again see land.

But they got to Barfleur alive, and after that down the coast to Isigny. The whole of western France was Edward's now, more or less, and passage should have been easy. But actually there were dozens of small groups of bandits, and broad reaches of untamed land. Most of the smaller villages and towns were charred ruins and perfectly empty. Weeds outgrew crops in the fields, and harvests sprouted ungarnered in the fields. Towns rarely opened their gates. George travelled at first with a band of palmers, and kept his face hooded. Then his mule got sick and died, and he had to walk on foot for a while, his kit on his back. Then he bought a new mule, and continued, keeping company in a loose way with six Frenchmen who boasted about how they were going to make their fortune in Navarre. In Anjou a sheep murrain had killed all the sheep, and carcasses lay in heaps in the fields, untouched even by wolves so vile was the sickness in their flesh, and many were skeletons in woolly jackets. The six went towards Spain and George rode solus along the north bank of the Loire for many days, and was once attacked by four men on horseback – but he fought them away, old though he was, and mounted only on a mule though he was, and armed with a sword to their spears as he was. It was terrifying in the moment, and then exhilarating, and afterwards he looked back on it with equanimity. The men had looked lean, undernourished and weary. The fact that he had fought back at all had been enough to dissuade them from pressing their numerical advantage.

He often dreamt of his late departed wife, and some days, when the sun shone, and he found fruit to eat unpicked on the trees, or was able to snare a rabbit, or pluck a fish from the river, he had the sense that she was there with him, watching over him. Other times she came as the Night Witch on her black night mare, and terrified him by opening her cloak to reveal that it was lined with the dead bodies of everybody he had ever killed in his whole life, and that was a fearsome number indeed. Then he would wake up, gagging, or sometimes – shamefully enough – weeping and sniffling like a baby, and he didn't enjoy that at all.

The big mountains swelled on the horizon as he approached, like gavocciolos upon the body of France itself. He'd been this way before, and knew more or less where to cross east, into the rising sun, until he met the Rhone, and so to pass south. There was more life here, less disease, villages where he could spend gold pennies on food and supplies, and hear news of the terrible doings of the grand White Company of Monsieur Jean Haccoude.

He caught up with the Company itself in the Ardèche, and it was a ticklish business not getting an arrow through his throat introducing himself. But he showed his letter of merit, and a couple of the guys recognised him from Calais, and one old boy even remembered him at Cressy, so he was brought to meet the great Hawkwood, who grasped him on both shoulders and looked long in his eye, and then told him that he was alright, and he was in.

Word got about that he was a dab hand with a siege, so he went straight into the war councils of the principal captains. The news was that Languedoc, a huge rich country, had finally brought together a great treasure in coin, as their contribution to the ransom still owed England for the release of King John of France. This fortune was coming up the Rhone by boat, in its journey to the top of France and so on to England, and the plan was to fish it out of the stream as it passed. There was this little town, decent walls, good wooden gates recently repaired, that stood on the river: Pont Saint Espirit, and pont was bridge, like in Welsh, and espirit was soul, and if this place had the soul of a saint rather than a warrior it should be easy to take.

So George rode with them and gave the town a good eye-over. The walls were too fat at the base, and the stone too rugged, he told Sir John Hawkwood, to do their job properly. He, George, didn't know the men he commanded, but any decent youngster could shin up and over such walls. So when they saw the boats come up the river and dock there it was time. That very night, a thin moon like a curl of silver wire, and clouds blocking out the stars, they did just that: they were over the walls before the sentries saw them and got the gates open. After that the place was theirs in short order. The Seneschal of Beaucaire himself happened to be in the town, and offered to surrender himself for a healthy ransom, but Sir John threw him off the walls to his death, declaring that with so much coin as their prize they need wait upon no ransomed Frenchmen.

That was a pity, because it turned out that the consignment of coin had not come up after all. In fact it had been delayed in Avignon, in order for a portion of it to be counted out and so pay off another Great Company to stop them wasting the coastlands. Still the town was theirs, and the land around was pretty rich, so they contented themselves with raiding. Best of all, the town had a chain across the river, so Sir John was able to charge a fat toll for any merchantman wanting to go up or downstream, and to confiscate the cargoes of those who didn't pay.

News of this success passed all over France, and smaller companies of old soldiers flocked to the town. Soon enough Sir John and his captains commanded an army as big as the one that Prince Edward of Wales himself had led to victory at Poitiers, concerning which the people who had been there would never stop fucking going *on* about, Jesus Mary and *Jo*seph, and when George said he'd been at Cressy nobody but a few of the oldest boys cared in the least.

So the Pope excommunicated the whole Company, naming Sir John in person, and all his followers in general; and a marshal set up camp at a place called Bagnols to draw a huge army in holy crusade against them. But the Pope hoped to pay not with money but with indulgences so the army never materialised. It took nine months, but eventually the Pope saw sense: revoked their excommunication, agreed indemnities, and paid the Company a huge sum to go fight in Italy instead. Sir John almost didn't take this money, since holding Pont Saint Espirit was so lucrative, but they were soldiers after all, not tollbridge keepers, so they went off.

George had never been to Italy before. He didn't enjoy going over the Alps, when the wind was a relentless freezing gale and where he lost sensation in his feet. He never slept a complete night through during the entirety of that crossing; shivering himself awake over and over. Then they came down from the higher heights, and it was warmer, and sensation returned to his extremities, which was worse at the beginning, like his feet were being stabbed by a hundred knives. But he got over that, and soon enough was back to his old self. On the far side of those too-tall mountains he found a country pretty much like southern France, except that the villages were as yet unburnt, and the people unraped and unkilled.

The Avignon Pope had sent the Great Company to serve his Vicar in Italy Gil Albornoz, but when they got there the pickings were too rich to ignore. Through late summer the Italians sent armies against them, and some of these fought bravely; but they were consistently outwitted by the Company's habits of marching through the night, and of waiting until *after* victory to pass out food and drink. A sober and hungry army always fights better than a bunch of well-fed winebellies. Come the winter the Italian armies packed up, because it was not their custom to fight out of season, but the English soldiers cared nothing for custom and carried right on. By the following year pretty much the whole of Piedmont and Lombardy was theirs.

George enjoyed it too, at first. There were several fat towns to besiege, and inexperienced Italian burghers unused to being invaded made for sweet solutions to breaking gates, climbing walls and the like. He earned good money – twice what he had carried home from Edward's French wars, and he'd only been fighting a year and a bit. He hired a cart to carry it, and two Lombard servants to attend to him and to lead his mule about, and he himself bought fine new armour and rode a horse worth fifty pounds if it was worth a farthing. Sir John himself liked and trusted him.

But as the campaign went on he began to lose his savour for it. For one thing, the other old soldiers talked constantly about chivalry, and boasted how they had once fought right alongside the Prince of Wales – the finest soldier Christendom had ever seen – when most of the time George knew they were flat lying. It was the hypocrisy. It made his guts rumble unpleasantly. The hypocrisy. They were no army led by princes and nobles. They were people like George himself: nobodies, commoners, men with a talent for killing, nothing else. Chivalry was not for the likes of them, and the word issued from their mouths with a foul odour. Even Sir John their leader was a knight only by his own self-acclamation, and the rumour was his father had been a tailor, and he himself apprenticed to that trade before he ran away to France. Nor did this Company treat their captives with chivalrous courtesy. Those that looked like they were worth something were asked to name their ransom, and then tortured to encourage them to up it – flaming torches in the crotch, noses removed, fingers chopped off. One old boy from Shoreditch who called himself Sir Ajax (a tanner, before the war) had a special way of leaning an axe blade slowly on a person's knuckles to cut through with exquisite slowness. People screaming in Italian sounded very like people screaming in French. Italian women weeping and begging for mercy and knitting their fingers together imploringly were indistinguishable from French women performing those actions, and anyway George had lost the stomach for rape. Rape was a young man's game. He was rich enough to pay for the nicer-looking whores, so he spent some of his money that way. So much better to lie with a woman who wasn't scrabbling to get away from you, or weeping, or inert like a corpse. Who could at least pretend to be enjoying herself. It took him longer to grow tired of the killing, because where that was concerned . . . well, it was more of a specific challenge and problem, like planning a quick siege – how to kill quickly, where to stick the sword to produce the minimum blood for the maximum harm. But eventually he grew tired of that too.

He approached Sir John and requested a release from service. The old soldier praised his honesty in not merely slipping away, though they both knew the difficulty of getting a mule laden with gold out of a large military camp unnoticed, even at night. In the end they drank together, and George paid the old rogue a hundred gold florins, and went on his way. In his head he was thinking: I'll keep the Cripplegate house, and buy another – a manor, in the countryside somewhere in Berkshire. I'll be a country gentleman.

He got to Genoa without much difficulty, and there spent a month converting his two hefty boxes of treasure into more portable form. It was a great city for bankers, was Genoa, and traders of all kinds, and soon enough he had two thousand florins' worth of coin inscribed on legal letters and binding documentations. A remarkable metamorphosis this, worthy of Ovid: heavy gold into light paper. The men he dealt with had counterparts in London, for whom these fine-scribbled and wax-sealed documentations were as binding as a prince's word of honour, or as gold itself, or so he was told. He believed it too. Or at least he talked himself into believing it. Then again, he kept a couple of hundred gold coins in specie as well, and carried them with him. He was old-fashioned that way.

Then, because he couldn't face going over the mountains again – and certainly not because he had learned to love the sea – he made a deal with a Genoese sea-captain to take him to Marseilles. And you know what? It wasn't half so bad. This Middle Sea was bluer and sunnier than the northern channels over which George had previously travelled, and the voyage was almost pleasant. Until, that is, a red-sailed keel, leaner and faster than the Genoese merchanter, swept down on them like a hawk and pirates boarded and the captain begged for his life and lay face down on the deck, and two of the crew jumped overboard to swim for the nearby coast, the cowards. George sat belowdecks clutching his small box to his lap, and the two pirates who came down must have thought him a wrinkled old merchant, and nothing to fear. They told him to surrender the box, and when he didn't reply, one came over to snatch it. George pulled his sword out from beneath where he had been sitting and jammed it quick and hard in at the man's armpit. The trick with these things is to strike full, and not hesitate. The pirate bellowed like a heifer, and a lot of blood came out. Ill luck meant that the tip of George's sword got stuck, somewhere in amongst the workings of the man's shoulder joint, and he couldn't pull it out; but the fellow slumped to his knees and

George saw his corsair blade in its scabbard and was able to get that out and jab it at the other's face as he came for him.

The two men were on the wooden belowdecks floor bleeding and howling, so George cut the cords at the back of their two necks, which silenced them. Then he extracted his own sword with a foot against the first fellow's shoulder. Better his own sword than a stranger's uncertain blade. A third pirate put his head in at the hatch to see what the noise was, and George put his sword up hard, into the man's open mouth and through the back, and down the fellow tumbled. Then George roared, with all his voice, that he was coming *out*, by Saint George, by the Terrible Black Knight himself, and would have *blood*. His voice was larger than he was, and when he scrambled up top the remaining pirates were already backing away. He ran at them, and one tripped and fell backwards into the sea, and the other tried to fight but was no match, and looked horrible surprised when George's sword bit into his groin and hauled up through his belly, dragging a creased wake of red in its path.

Afterwards George couldn't stop shaking. That was not usual for him after a fight. Usually he had more stiffness to his spine. But he couldn't stop trembling. Shiver, shiver, shiver. He cleaned his sword, and hauled up a bucket of seawater to get rid of as much of the blood from his clothes as possible, but his hands were shaking like a shitting dog. The captain blessed him, and kissed his knees, and brought him out some wine; and then they continued their voyage, with a second boat in tow. At Marseilles the captain tried to claim this keel was his, but George wasn't having that. He told the Italian that a half-a-half was generous split, too generous really, the cowardly cunt had pressed his nose to his own deck at the first sight of the pirates, but the truth was that George hardly wanted to be saddled with a boat, so took a letter notarised by a French cleric for half the value of the craft in ecus.

The shaking left him eventually, and after it George felt a surge of new life and paid for a fancily-dressed whore in a private apartment, with sweetmeats and wine and all the trimmings. After the act he dozed, and dreamed again of his late wife; and once again she rode the night mare and opened her cloak, only this time she was naked and beautiful beneath, and in each wing of the cloak was one of her sisters – the two of them, miraculously, young and beautiful too – and they sang together in descant that he was to come home, he was to come home, he was to come home.

The plague was bad in Marseilles at that time, and a couple of days after coupling with this whore George started to feel feverish and ill. He had rented two rooms near the harbour, one with a window, and lay on the bed staring at the blue sky and feeling sorry for himself. When the buboes appeared in his groin he knew it was over. By that point he was almost ready to welcome death, or if not welcome exactly, at least admire the symmetry of such a demise, as bringing him closer to his late wife, his poor saint, and he thought of her, and wept at how he had once suspected her of fucking that scrawny apprentice boy, and how he had shouted at her and beaten her. He vowed that when he met her in the afterlife, he would beg her pardon most earnestly for this. He saw then the meaning of his dream. Home was not England, where his wife was not; but heaven, where his wife was.

Nobody came to nurse him. He didn't care. When the other people in the building realised what had happened they left him alone. He had a large skin of wine to drink, and no water; and there was nothing to eat. Very soon he grew ill with a kind of parched, trembling fever, and his armpits and his groin burned with continuous pain, and it seemed to be bright day through his window and then he would blink and it would be night.

But he did not die. He woke one morning, his mouth cracked with dryness like a parched leather boot, and his head clearer. His buboes had burst. He lay for a long time, then slept again, and when he woke he was strong enough to move about. There was a deal of mess, but he didn't care about that. His wineskin was empty, but he couldn't face the thought of drinking wine anyway. He dragged himself out of his rooms and down the stairs and out the back, to where the well was. He drank until his stomach creaked. Then he discovered he was very hungry, and gave a serving maid a gold coin to bring him food.

Within two days he was hale enough to pack up his box in a knapsack and go down to the docks. Riding a horse or even a mule was more than his weakened body could manage, and the illness had taken too much strength from his legs to contemplate a long hike, so he bought passage on a craft that was travelling up the Rhone. He thought vaguely of seeing Germany, and then taking one of the German rivers to the Northern sea and so home. That, he decided, was what his dream had portended. His real home, his English home, and a respectable manor house in the countryside outside London. Maybe marry again, and have kids, and tell them all about his adventures in the wars.

Passage on a riverboat was much less fraught than sea-passage. Since he was still exhausted from his illness he slept most of the time, usually abovedecks. When he wasn't asleep he sat watching the lands slide by, the mountainous horizon, clouds overhead in the shapes of shields and horses and engines of siege.

His luck ran out at Pont Saint Espirit. A customs officer recognised him as a member of Haccoude's notorious Company, seeing past his scrag-bearded, post-plague leanness, and George was arrested. His box was taken, and all his wealth. The constable of the town wanted to execute him straight away, but there was a delay: for a legal question remained over the proper deposition of George's box. Was all this wealth to go to the town, as the constable thought it should, or ought it be delivered to the Pope in Avignon? Lawyers argued the case for weeks, and during that time George languished in an unlit cell. An enterprising local advocate came to visit him, and George – with nothing to lose, and no other options – agreed an enormous fee for him to argue his case in the court: that the box belonged to neither party but was his alone, and that he would part with it as ransom for his life. This lawyer returned twice, to inform George of how proceedings had gone in court. George told him to stress that the Pope himself had hired his Company, which surely meant he, as a member of that Company, can have done nothing wrong. But it seemed that the Pope had since repudiated Sir John for his doings in Italy, and all his people were proscribed. So then George tried to say that he had resigned the Company, but that did him no good. 'Tell them,' George growled finally, 'that I'll gladly swear the Pope's allegiance and fight in his army. Tell him I'm a great captain who fought with the Black Prince.' 'I'll tell them so, seigneur,' the lawyer assured George, and departed. But he never saw him again. The first George knew of the eventual judicial decision was when he was brought out of his cell blinking in the light one morning, and his hands tied behind him, and shuffled up half a dozen wooden stairs, a heavy necklace of rope arranged about his neck. When his eyes adjusted to the light he saw that a disappointingly small crowd had gathered. There were two other men with him on the platform. George didn't recognise either of them. The priest reading the rites was very young, barely more than a child, and even George could tell that his Latin was execrable, poorly pronounced and mumbled. The lad got to the end of his speech in a tie of tongue, and hurried away. A bird flew down and perched on a branch, a couple of yards to his right, and sang a gloriously fluid song, apparently just for George's benefit. He had lived a long life and yet never before seen a quality of blue so pure as the blue of this sky, or heard a music so wonderful as the bird's trilling. A pot-bellied man in a black tunic laboured up the three steps onto the platform, and at the top leaned his elbows on his knees to regain his breath. He sounded like a sawyer at work. Then, without further ceremony, he shoved the man to George's left forward off the platform. George heard the fellow's neck go like a branch snapping, a loud retort as the rope tautened, and it gave him a sudden, weirdly precise memory of Old King Edward's cannons being discharged at the walls of Calais. Then he felt the shove in the small of his own back and staggered forward, and fell, and unluckily rolled with the noose so his neck was wrenched without breaking. A giant's hand clasped his throat. His sight shrank in, and it felt as if his whole head were expanding, swelling painfully. The pressure forced his tongue out. His cock hardened. He kicked his legs, frantic, struggling to drag down enough to break the neck – to pull the whole fucking head off if he could – anything to stop this hideous sensation of suffocating slowexploding pressure in his face and ears and lips and tongue and blood flowing gushing from his nose, and his lungs burning with the absence of air, and his sight swallowed into a tunnel of red-black and he kicked and he kicked and kicked and kicked

Camera Eye

Wheat flows under the caressing hands of the southern wind

     wheatfields in a landscape wheat coloured, and poppies throughout like sprinkled blood   cypresses sway like greenblack candleflames   twelve peasants,

     men and women, in a line, and the sickles hissing like the iron snaketongues they are, and so the field is consumed, bite and bite and   half a dozen binders tie the sheaves behind   the sun bakes the sky hard and a blue so dark it is closer to purple

     Jean had a toothache yesterday, and it was worse

today, his whole brown face bulging like a stuffed pocket, and sore, merde, sore, merde, sore. There was no helping it, for the harvest must come in, or the clouds over the mountains, black as shagpelt bears, would roll down and soak everything the night and the wheat would start to rot.   Rot.   Rot like his bemerded mouth.

A lord and a lady are riding, with a large gaily-dressed entourage, passing along the rough road at the side of the field.

The peasants gawp for a bit, and wipe their brows. Maybe it's a good time to stop for a rest   the coolblue shade of the trees   drink watered wine, and everyone except Jean chews bread, but Jean can barely open his mouth and whines *merde merde merde* over and over,   until Gaston and Pierre and hefty Marie have had enough, and grab him and Philippe pushes the top of his sickle into the grumbler's mouth.   A whole lot of *oh oh* and *ah ah* and some writhing, but they hold tight   Philippe fumbles a bit, and sticks a thumb in, but then he hooks the end of the sickle and yanks real hard   real hard

and

a thumbknuckle-sized clot comes free   hard stone of blood   and in   amongst it a three-horned nubbin, holed and black.   Jean spits blood and spits blood   drinks wine, and spits blood and spitpatters blood   and when he can talk he mumbles *you cut you cut my gum you merdeeater*   but it is time to go back to the harvest, so they all go.

      Jean presses soil into the wound inside his mouth, but it doesn't really stop the bleeding   works more slowly, and is doubled over, and keeps spitting blood, and stumbling back to the tree to drink more wine, and pack in more soil, so it would almost have been better if he'd just gone home. But they cut and stack the grain and as the sun sinks like a giant clot of blood he took one last sip of wine and fell over.

      Philippe and Pierre drag him, one foot to each man, back to his cabin where his old mother   —toothless now so no worry about mouthache for her—   is tending his two year old. His wife had died giving birth to a dead daughter so it was just those three.   He woke up and complained of the pain, and drank a deal of water, and fell asleep again.

      Come the morning Jean's face is swollen more, and all blueblack on one side, and the smell is bad.   He is better the next day, and the day after better still. On the third day he gets up, sans one tooth, and goes back to work.

JOAN

—Oh, says Joan, in startlement, or pain.

   —What is it, my love?

   The vision has already receded. She didn't so much feel as *intuit* the wrench, the slashed mouth, the blood. Gone now. She smiles at her lover, her lord, and they ride on through the bright sunshine until the harvest field is behind them and they are trotting between silvergrey olive trees, ranked like shaghaired soldiers, and up towards the castle.

And then she tucks her veil, gauze from Gaza, cloth woven marvellously with air, about her face; for the sun is hot and yellow-gold and huge in the sky. Her camera eye drifts, goes somewhere. She is somewhere else for a while.

It takes her a moment to orient herself. Where is she? Indoors, now. She is sitting at a table, with her lover, her lord, the Prince of Wales and of Aquitaine, beside her. They are in one of their castles. She was not paying attention. And now the sun has been replaced by a large golden disc, solid or bristling with precious stones. This is in the hand of a man, a white hand, soft-skinned, beringed, and so a nobleman's hand. She moves her gaze up and sees the face of John of Chandos.

—In imitation of the Round Table, he is saying. In the hope that it will remind you of the place you may yet fill in history – along with heroes like Oliver, Roland, Launcelot, Tristram . . .

Joan pats her belly, round and solid as a cannonball. She herself a cannon pointed at the heart of . . . of – suddenly she knows what this jewel is, and what it signifies.

Ned's eyes, she can see, are gleaming. Oliver. Roland. Launcelot, Tristram. Edward. A pentad of parfit and gentil knights. She knows she has to speak, although her mouth is dry.

Everyone in the room looks at her. She sees now that the room has many nobles within, although only she and Ned are seated. So she says:

—A belle gift, she adds. Though it may cost us more than money.

—Oh, my wife and love, Ned laughs, like all women, you are a witch when it comes to prophesy! Forebodings and forebodings. I may yet reject it, if you wish me to reject it. But Prince Arthur was never yet dissuaded from his duty by the words of a woman.

At this, the child inside her kicks, and she connects the inner impact and rolls it through her mind as a spurt of uncharacteristic anger.

—Duty? If you mean war say war, and if you mean pleasure in killing say pleasure, and if you mean glory say glory. These are better words than duty.

—*Cœur de mon âme*, he says, to her, though his eyes are still on the jewel, it is a duty to sustain the divine right of kings to rule as kings. If a brother prince has been unseated through wickedness and scheming and treachery, it is duty, and that is the plain word, to restore him.

John of Chandos speaks: the world knows your brother prince for a devil. A man does not pick up the name Pedro the Cruel by chance.

—What does his cruelty have to do with it? What does his character have to *do* with it? Ned says, firmly. His rights are from God, not from his dancing master. Don Pedro may be a very Belial for wickedness, but he is the ruler God chose for Castile. Yon Henry de Trastemere may wear a halo at the back of his hairy head, it doesn't stop him being illegitimate. Bastard is bastard. And so God disposes for Castile.

—The people seem to like him, drawls Chandos.

—The people? returns Ned with enormous scorn.

Joan thinks now this was why her camera eye showed her the image of the peasant's mouth being split with iron, the blood and blackness flowing out.

Now, though, her camera eye is showing her nothing. Sometimes she sees nothing but what her own actual eyes are gazing at. It can be that for weeks, or even months. She asks: why, my lord, do they call him Pedro the Cruel?

DENIS, PRIEST

He often thought of what the Abbot told him: to serve God alone, be a monk; but to be a priest means to serve God in the world, and the devil walks up and down the world with a long stride. The danger is not death, although there are brigands and desperate men and captainless soldiers who would think nothing of killing a priest as he travels about. But a swift death would be a martyrdom and access to the highest heaven. No: the danger is temptation. The danger is always to the soul, and not the body.

Denis was the youngest son of a Marseilles merchant, and the grandson of a ropemaker, but he studied hard and long and mastered five languages, and soon came to the attention of William de Grimoard, Abbot of Marseilles, and one of the most learned and pious men in all of Christendom. He accompanied the Abbot on his tours to Avignon, to Rome, as far north as Paris, where William lectured on canon law to large audiences. When the Pope himself selected William as papal emissary to Rome, Denis went with him. And when, to everybody's surprise – Abbot William not least – William was elected Pope, Denis returned with him to Avignon. Pope! He wasn't even a cardinal (although the conclave retrospectively corrected that); and he was a Provençal when all the Italian cardinals were clamouring for an Italian Pope, after near a century of Frenchmen. But he was certainly a very holy man, and Denis was blessed to be amongst his inner circle. It was God's work. No other explanation made sense.

Of course, the reason why the new Pope retained Denis amongst his closest men is that he understood how little ambition he possessed, at least in the conventional, secular sense. Like the new Pope – Urban, was the name William took – Denis was a Benedictine, and wore the habit as his master continued to do. It was for that reason that the new Pope so often trusted Brother Denis on diplomatic missions, sometimes accompanied by another

Provençal Benedictine, Brother Foulques de Bagnols. The English king was a scourge upon France, although he had mostly left Provence alone. But he was a Christian, and the king of France was a Christian, and who was better placed to promote peace between two Christian princes and brothers than the Pope?

Then Edward of Wales, the Black Prince of such renown, wrote the new Pope a letter. He had, he said, thought much and prayed much, recently, about the nature of the Holy Spirit, and begged the Holy Father for guidance in this matter. For had not the holy maiden Hildegard of Bingen declared the holy spirit a *viriditas*, or greening of the world, flowing like the growth of plants and the pouring of sweet water in a desert? And does not the love of God fall upon the parched faces of believers like rain upon a drought? Yet, if so, how can the Holy Spirit, whose denial is the one unforgivable sin, be a person, as God the Father and God the Son surely are? To this letter Pope Urban replied (Denis took the dictation, and marvelled that this violent English youth should be blessed with such treasure, words from the most learned Christian in Christendom): that these three persons are in the unity of inseparable substance, but They are not indistinct amongst themselves. How so? He who begets is the father; He who is born is the Son; and He who in eager freshness proceeds from the Father and the Son and sanctifies the waters by moving over their face in the likeness of an innocent bird and who streamed with ardent heat over the apostles is the Holy Spirit.

—Holy Father, Denis said, when His Eminence read the letter back, you know what this prince truly thinks.

—Nor I nor you know his heart, the Pope replied, open as it is only to God.

—Yet the whole world knows this prince's vanity, Holy Father. He thinks God the Father his own father, the English king. And he thinks himself the Son. And he thinks the Holy Spirit that flows from both is the falcon of victory that flies over his army as it marches through France, and the ardent heat of the castles and towns he burns. Such blasphemy should be rebuked, and not encouraged, Eminence.

—His letter to me contained no such heresy, Urban replied, mildly. And though God caused him to be born into the margins and wastelands of the world, far from France and further from Jerusalem, yet his is a Christian soul. And we cannot pretend he has not enjoyed success in this world, nor deny his chivalry, nor the need to accommodate him in the larger pattern of secular Christendom if we are to reunite the church and lead a great crusade into the Holy Land.

The following week Denis had a flux in his gut and was ill. But by God's great mercy he returned swiftly to health.

The bird flying over the wasteland of floodwater was not the dove. It was a hawk, a kestrel, a cruel raptor. The arm it settled on was not Noah's. Or if Noah, then a cruel antitype of Noah. A Noah who relished the flood, who gloried in the death of Christians, who pranced and preened over corpses.

But nonetheless he and Foulques rode along the coast, west, and then up to Bordeaux, and delivered the Pope's letter in person to the Prince. Edward kept a court of vainglorious magnificence: hundreds of knights and officials, hundreds more of courtiers, musicians, cooks, jugglers and bards; banners of gorgeous weave on every wall, feasts every day. Pedro of Navarre was there, big and pale and hard-eyed, the Prince's personal guest. Pedro the Cruel, they called him, always too close to the English, and now fawning upon Edward because he had been ousted from his throne south of the Pyrenees by his older brother, the bastard Henry of Trastamere.

After a week resisting the temptations of this place, Foulques and he returned east to Avignon with the Prince's reply. They rode all day, starting early and seeking lodgings only at dusk, and so they covered the ground quickly: in under a week they were back at the Papal Palace.

—I suspect this prince, Denis said, as they rode, has become so puffed up with sacrilege and pride that he considers himself a secular Christ, born of a secular God, whose secular Holy Spirit is chivalric war.

—God will punish him, if he thinks so, Foulques replied, in an indifferent tone. Abstracts and hypotheticals did not interest him. To him, God's revelation in Christ was a practical, worldly, tangible revelation. They were riding their rocking mules down into the valley of the Lot, and the sun was drawing the shadows of the cypresses long, as a wire-maker draws metal.

—I think God *will* punish him. In which case, Denis said, perhaps the Christian Kingdom of France is to be God's instrument.

—If what you say is true, then he will die before his Father. He will be secularly crucified, and never be a king himself, which is a sorrowful thought. For him I mean. For myself, I am more concerned with Pedro the Cruel.

—Pedro the Cruel, Denis agreed. A bigamist and savage man. He shot his first wife dead with a crossbow, they say.

—They say.

Only a month in Avignon, and the two of them were sent back to Bordeaux. Pedro was close to agreeing a treaty with the English to recover his throne, and His Holiness had his reasons not to prefer such an eventuality. Still, there was little they could do. Foulques thought that perhaps the discreet sowing of dissension might be achieved by spreading stories of Pedro's cruelty; but when they attended yet another of Edward's feasts they found the man himself openly boasting of his crimes.

—Intrigue, he laughed, chopping into a steak with his knife and gouging off chewable portions. Conspiracy. It has been a hard struggle, brother prince. You know what it's like.

Edward, seated regally with his beautiful Queen, Joan, at his side, inclined his head. The gesture said he might, or might not, have known what it was like.

—Bitches and wives, French bitches and French wives, whores of the Pope, of the whore of Babylon, Pedro boomed. Hateful French bitch my wife, a hateful Bourbon, she was plotting against my very life. It was my mistress, Maria de Padilla, who unveiled her plotting. And so, for her . . .

He illustrated his account with vicious knifestabs in his chunk of bleeding beef.

—If Henry had died in battle, Pedro went on. Henrico Trastámara – or if I'd crushed his neck with my boot when I'd had the chance, and I did have the chance, believe me – bastard-born of my father's despicable lust. A devil, dared to call himself my brother – if I'd snapped his neck he'd not have stolen my throne. I should have done it. I regret not doing it. At least I was luckier with his bitch mother, hateful Leonora of the hateful Gusman's.

Denis and Foulques were at the same table, close enough to hear all this blustery and unrepentant impiety. After dinner the two of them spent half an hour in prayer, in a small and ugly side chapel. There was a better chapel nearby, but their way to it was barred. The Prince was praying there, they were told.

After that they met with local priests, who reported on the latest news. Or gossip, but that was the same thing. What everybody knew, but nobody dared say, was that Pablo had sealed a pact with the Mohammedan King of Granada. He had kissed the heathen's hands, it seemed, and promised to pour Christian wealth into the coffers of Islam.

Denis spoke in a low voice.

—He speaks slightingly of the Pope, said Denis, and has executed honest Christian priests. And he was witnessed kissing the Jews.

—A bougre, said Foulques sadly, and a bad man.

But then, with a flush of insight, Denis embraced his companion, two Christians together, and said: Michael's lance is raised in heaven against Antichrist, my dear friend. English Edward and Pedro the Cruel are well matched. God is not mocked, my dear.

Newsreel (15)

PEACE DIVIDEND
PEACE DIVIDEND
PEACE DIVIDEND

Plague worst in South West. Families reporting loved ones dead of 'other diseases' so as not to compromise their chance of burial on holy ground.

Dispatches from the Holy Land

'Behold,' writes a Crusader poet, 'without renouncing our rich garments, our station in life, all that pleases and charms, we can obtain honour down here and joy in Paradise.'

SALE. Offered for sale at thirty florins, all the goods belonging to Belier le Gustet of Villaines, whom the English and other enemies of the Great Company took with them when they left Villaines at Christmas 1360. He has not since returned and no one knows what has become of him. The common rumour runs at Villaines that he has died in the service of said Company.

BATTLE OF GATASKOGEN

Swede battles Swede over which Swede is to sit on the Swedish throne. Albert III, the Sweet Swede of Sweden, sweeps swiftly the battleground.

MARIA, EMPRESS OF CONSTANTINOPLE,
DIES IN CHILDBIRTH.

Camera Eye

baby sleeps, mostly; or feeds; but sometimes he stares about him with poorly-focused and mute astonishment, an expression that borders on a kind of comical outrage   sometimes bleats like a little goat, and sometimes makes a series of rapid running-on e-e-e noises, for all the world like a dolphin. Occasionally he cries, which though never loud, for his lungs are still tiny, is nevertheless one of the most penetrating noises she ever heard. Unignorable. Then again, when he sleeps he looks more peaceful than any human she has seen; and sometimes his open eyes seem to articulate a kind of rolling bliss, an uncontending contentness, happy simply to look.   Sin, the priest says, soaked into his very bones, but she won't believe it. This flesh does not smell of sin; these eyes do not flash sin; even this soiled cloth, unwound from his little flabby bottom and washed in the stream, doesn't smell of sin.   He smells of newness come into the world, and dawn, and the renewed conquest of Death.

Another day, and then another day. The sky pours love

  hushing the earth
 mother and baby.

Cords of water, dark as any grey was ever dark. The earth is heavier after the rainstorm than it was before, but when a mother gives birth everything weighs exactly the same afterwards.

THE BLACK PRINCE

It is no mere figure of speech to say the winds howled. Painfully slow work getting the carts up through these mountain passes, but the men could travel no faster than the carts, because they needed the tents the carts carry. To sleep outside in this weather would be death. This tent was pegged into the ground, and this other tent was pegged nearby, and that tent was pegged too, but this tent had become a sail without a ship, a huge vulture of cloth flapping through the sky as men ran after it shouting.

The royal tent was of a larger and more substantial build, but its walls bulged and sucked in the wind, and the lords and princes inside must raise their voices to be heard over the waterfall roar of the gale outside, and the cannonshot retorts of the tent-walls banging out, and slapping back.

We shall pass, Ned told his nobles. We shall overpass and we shall overcome.

The snow, when it came, attempted to change his mind. White tumult out of the grey sky. Great burly wind-heaved walls of snow blown aslant across the line of men, of horses, and of carts, creaking their way. Horses began to die, and men at the rear of the advance to slip away and stumble back down the mountains into France and warmth. Beards and moustaches were frozen stiff, like tomb-effigy beards and moustaches. It relented for a day. Then it really started to come down: thick as curdled cream, cold as hell itself, filling the mountain passes hip-deep. They found a place to pitch camp, a little wider than the paths, though crowded and impossible to defend (let us hope, Ned said, that nobody is crazy enough to attack, up here). They tied the horses as close into the cliff face as they could, and dressed the beasts in blankets. Then they cleared the ground and did their best to drive tent pegs into the iron-hard soil. The Prince's tent was the first to go up, of course.

A messenger arrived as the royal servants were sweeping out the snow and lighting a small fire. Edward and his brother John huddled round a brazier. Smoke blurred the canvas ceiling. They each read the letter, and then Ned read it again. The world is full of traitors, though. Full of traitors.

It set him in a bad humour, and he quarrelled with his brother John. *His* son Richard, John's son, was the royal heir! The heir to the throne of France and England! John brooded on injustice. It was foolish – they might both die, here, where the cold bit deeper than a sword edge. They might both die in the battles to come. Abandoned by the French, this was a strong chance. A strong chance.

After a while, he stepped outside. He had men to look to. The snow had stopped falling, and the clouds were breaking up like suds in an obsidian basin and rolling way. The stars looked down approvingly on a world as cold and white and forbidding as their own. Moonlight crept spectrally off the whiteness like a guilty thing. Ned's breath came from his mouth in an impressively large feathery plume: one breath, two, three. He checked the horses; talked to the men. Some of them had managed to light fires. He plocked his way through the freezing softness to where the sentries were posted. Then he returned to his tent. John was not there. He had evidently found some other bed for the night.

In the morning the army struck camp quickly, and marched on. It did not snow again. By afternoon they were down below the white and into a warmer climate. An aide-de-camp rode alongside the Prince and reported the night's losses: so many horses dead; so many men who did not wake up; so many more deserted.

Things could, Ned pondered, have been worse.

Once in northern Spain, the campaign began to feel more like regular war. They crossed rivers, raided farms, vineyards and orchards to supply the men. They captured the small town of Navarette easily, and killed everybody inside. Reports began to reach Ned of his enemy's army – a hundred thousand men, it was said – three hundred thousand – a million men! He sent experienced scouts forward, and they came back with the estimate of sixty thousand, which Ned could believe. He had his troops counted as they rested in Navarette: of the thirty thousand who had left Aquitaine, some twenty-four thousand remained. Archers from Wales and Cheshire. Gascon and Mallorcan men-at-arms. His own weasel brother. On the other side, Henry the Second of Castile – as he now, blasphemously, styled himself – and his main general, Bertrand du Guesclin. The Black Dog of Brittany. The Eagle of Broceliande. He who had killed Sir William Bamborough in single combat at the siege of Rennes. Famous for avoiding pitched battles and instead wearing down the enemy with raids and withdrawals. He would be advising Henry not to confront the English in open fight. If his advice prevailed, then Ned's prospects looked very poor indeed. He could not long subsist in this place if his army were weathered away with attrition and sneak-raids.

Twenty-six thousand men. Three days later, Ned had 23,000 men. The shortfall was not due to desertion. The wells of Navarette, some said, had been poisoned; or else camp fever had come to them, that inevitable accompaniment of the marching army. Men were puking and shitting in every street-corner. The sounds of groans at sunrise drowned out the birds' dawn chorus. It was time to move.

Ned prayed: God, father, son and Holy Ghost, please let Henry meet me in open battle. On their own ground and with the whole summer to play with, it would be only too easy for du Guesclin to reduce Edward's force to a mere stub without ever properly fighting it.

He prayed.
He prayed.
He prayed.

The whole army marched in relatively good order from Navarette, leaving only a few hundred to hold the fort as a safe point in their rear. They forded a river, wide and shallow, green against the yellow-orange of the landscape, and Edward decided the further bank would make a good battlefield. Perhaps the Holy Spirit informed him. He made his men form into battle order; the archers on the flanks, the main body of men in the middle. They stood there, all day. The morning was cloudy, and not too hot, although very often men would groan at the pangs in their bellies, and some would crouch and shit where they were. Some fell over, and were beaten by their corporals, or else dragged away. Come nightfall it was apparent Henry's army was not coming.

—*Ego non comprehendere*, said brother John, for the two brothers had patched up their quarrel and were once again sharing the princely tent. We sent horse over the forward ways, and those scouts told us nothing?

—A vision, Ned said. I was spirited a vision, the Holy Spirit. There were twisting, stabbing pains in his intestines, and he scowled in his discomfort.

—What was it the Holy Spirit sang in your ear, brother? Henry comes to fight, stand ye here? Since the Holy Spirit cannot lie it must have been an alternate *spirit* that gave you such a mission.

—I drink no more than you, said Ned, primly. He called for his servant to bring him a shitting bowl. His guts were cramping.

—You drink twice what I do! John scoffed. Anyway, it hardly matters. The men wasted a day, exhausting themselves by standing in the sun all the hours.

—It was good discipline for them, Ned said. Discipline is never wasted. It is what wins battles. He went to the corner of the tent and squatted over the bowl. A stinking snake uncoiled fluidly from his rear end, and John groaned at the smell, and left the tent.

That night Edward slept badly, but in the morning he felt a little better. He drank his breakfast posset, and stood to be dressed and strapped into his black armour. Then he led his men out, and they marched all day, and the whole of the day after that, and on the third day the town of Nájera appeared on the horizon. Even from here the banners of Henry's army could be seen, thick as a forest. Scouts rode forward, and returned with confirmation: *at least* 60,000 men were assembled. At least that number, and probably more. Ned had barely twenty, and they were exhausted from their forced march, and many were ill.

Ned was ill himself. His head felt hot, his body trembled with incipient fever. His eyeballs boiled in their sockets. The time elapsing between the clenching in his guts and the inevitably foul, squirting hot release from his fundament was growing smaller, making it harder for him to withdraw from counsel or conversation and retire to some place where he might void himself discreetly. He was thirsty the whole time, and no matter how much wine or ale he drunk the thirst did not seem to abate.

Still: it was time. God determined the time. Fate did.

They all mounted, and rode out.

—*This* is the place, he told John, mounted beside him. This is where the Holy Spirit showed me.

—Highness? It was not John, it was Sir Robert Cheney, a good knight, a good man. Ned blinked, and blinked, and wiped the sweat from his brow. His surroundings seemed to be simultaneously retreating from him and rushing towards him. He dizzied, swayed in the saddle. Where was John? He'd been here a moment before. Get a grip.

Grip.

Grip.

—Highness?

—We shall do battle here, Sir Robert, Ned announced. In this shallow valley. Against the army hated of God. We shall be victorious.

His head cleared enough for him to sense Sir Robert's unease;

but then he went woozy again. Permit me to summon your princely brother and also the noble John of Chandos, Highness, said the knight, and rode away. Feeling lightheaded, almost ready to laugh, Ned ordered camp be set, right here, and then he dismounted, lay on the ground and fell asleep.

In Spain, in pain in Spain. Ill in Castile. Weary, weary.

He was asleep for no time at all; barely minutes. Or so it seemed. Yet when he returned to consciousness it was dusk, and the two Johns, of Gaunt and of Chandos, were speaking in low tones. *Terrible position for a defence,* the latter was saying. *If Henry claims the hills on either side of us, which with his superior numbers surely he will, they will be able to crush us as between two blades of scissors.* Then the former: *you don't know what it's like, Sir John. He won't listen to me.*

Wearier in Iberia.

He had to *grip.*

Edward jumped to his feet to surprise them although he underestimated the strength of his legs and fell back down. His brother helped him up. Come! he declared. Let us dine and discuss tactics. Then the griping took his guts again, and he had to scurry off to some bushes nearby.

A glum feast, in the princes' tent, and then a sour council of war. Let us fall back, John of Chandos said, for here we will be between the hammer and the anvil.

—Brother, urged John of Gaunt. This is no defensible position.

—Then no defence shall be tried. We shall attack.

—Attack, Highness? John of Chandos repeated, as if he could not believe the words.

—Attack, said Ned, and belched foully, and struggled not to be sick. The air swirled visibly around him. The ground shifted left, then right, then left again.

—The enemy are well presented, your Highness, Chandos said, in a tentative voice. They are well situated at Nájera, and outnumber us three to one. We would waste our strength on their very substantial defensive positions, and when we drew back, they would charge and crush us. This is not a well-situated battleground.

—The Holy Spirit! Ned cried, standing up. He was, he realised, quite drunk now. It was hard for him to stand upright. Then his guts grinched, and he had to dash from the tent.

He slept poorly. Feverish dreams of carnal love upset him, his member a sword, his conquest a plump lady, and he stabbed her belly and front but she bled diarrhoea when cut open, and oh! the stink. He woke in the small hours, and went to sit outside his tent. The moon was a fat sickle that appeared, when you looked at it, to be harvesting the pale clouds scudding just beneath its blade, but those it passed through them they swept along the sky, still whole. How was it he could cut down his enemies and cut down his enemies and still there were always enemies?

His servants brought him water, and he drank and drank and was still thirsty. Then he stared at the night sky, the landscape, the distant warm pricks of light that marked the campfires of Henry's army. The sky to the east was beginning to pale, revealing a snowlike bank of white fog filling the valley between the two armies. Haste. Haste was the key.

He ordered the two Johns roused, and sent the order about the camp to wake the men. By the time his servants had strapped him into his armour the whole camp was alive.

—Sir John, he told Chandos, swaying a little where he tried to stand. The world possessed a fondant strangeness, it would surely deform if he touched it. The stars were much closer than was usual. The whole of the east was on fire, just beyond the horizon. Oh, his aching guts! Flatus passed messily from his fundament.

—Highness.

—You shall take the whole body of horsemen, into the mist of the valley. Go right, ride rightward, up the slope, and when the dawn has burned away the mist you will have a clear charge upon the left flank of Henry's army. They will be unready, and you shall smash them.

—It bids fair for a cool day, John said, uncertain. April has bare begun. The mist might stay until noon. It might stay all day. Highness. It would be madness to charge through fog.

—The morning sun will shoo it away, said Edward, in a voice louder, and more like singing, than he intended. His head turned all the way around, or else the whole world turned all the way around his head, or else nothing happened and his senses played him tricks. Hornets were buzzing inside the insides of his ears. He felt like doing a little dance. Brother, he said, panting, brother, brother—

—My prince?

—When Henry's force tries to turn to face the attack, you must lead the remaining horsemen down, go down, down into the middle to strike there. When you have both done as much damage as you can, and pull back, come fast, to give our archers clear shots.

The two Johns looked at one another. Brother, said John of Gaunt. This is not how . . . not how war is made, you know.

—War, said Edward, gripping his serving man to stop himself falling, is made of the commander, who is God, and the soldier, who is the son, and by a third thing that is the same as the other two and yet distinct from them, which is victory.

Within half an hour, John of Chandos had led his trotting force away, to be swallowed by the mist. Ned felt a pang of clarity in his feverish head: it was this thought – that he would never see them again. Perhaps they were lambs into the jaw of the tiger. He thought: how huge would the ransom be for him, the Black Prince, if he were captured? It would bankrupt England. But then the fever swirled into his head again, and he called for more wine. Nothing was real. Or it was real, but not really real. Not really really real. Jug jug. Glug glug. Spiders crawled over the sky. Grass grew upside-down underneath the earth. Under the oceans were other oceans. His vision pranced, and pranced, and every time he blinked it made the people around him seem to dance and prance. The land was all flood.

The sky was bright now, and the mist, though not entirely banished, had been reduced to a few cloudy patches in hollows. John of Gaunt was forming up his cavalry. Trumpets sounded to bring the men together. The foot soldiers were grumbling, as they tried to scrabble up breakfast. Ned, his head lighter than breath itself, was helped up into his saddle, and the fever gave him preternatural hearing. He heard one Welshman saying to another, *bloody Castile bach* and the second replying *that black boyo can stick that bloody trumpet right up his arse*. Joy flooded Ned's heart. That was funny! That was very funny!

Lights swirled and scooted. Rainbows edged his vision.

And then he decided it was time to address the men. He rode over to where the horses stood, snorting and shuffling and twitching their flanks. All the way along, at the far end of the valley, very faint, tinkle-tankle, the tiny yells of men, the fingerdrumming on a table top of far distant horsehooves, all the sounds of battle were just about audible. John of Gaunt had done as his prince had commanded. Charged the enemy's flank, coming from a position unsuspected. No: it was Chandos who had done that. Why, look! *Here* was John of Gaunt, beside him!

Right. A bit of show. He had never felt so drunk. A cannonclap fart bounced him from his saddle. He unsheathed his sword. Resheathed it. Unsheathed it.

—Gentlemen! he bellowed. Everyone was silent. Of course they were: they needed to be quiet to hear him. Or they were respectful, as in church. Though their faces (the lucid portion of Ned's mind insisted) looked sombre, scared, uninspired. Nonsense! Ignore that!

His armour chafed him, in at the groin, and around the waist. He would have to have that looked at.

—Gentlemen, he shouted again, and waved his sword. *There* are your enemies. They are in possession of the utmost plenty, while we have nothing. Be valiant, be loyal. I trust in God and in you and in the Holy Spirit that this day shall be yours.

There was murmuring amongst the men. Ned flourished his sword at the clear sky above him.

—O God of battle, he yelled, grant that victory be ours. We fight a usurper. We seek to restore to his lawful rights your own anointed.

He could not hold the flatulence. Perhaps they didn't notice. A foot soldier somewhere away to the right said, distinctly: *load of bloody balls*. Ignore him, Ned thought. Ignore. Ignore.

—Forward, he cried. Forward, banner, in the name of God and Saint George. And on went the helmet.

And they were off. Edward trotting in the van, the motion repeatedly lifting him an inch from the saddle and each lift releasing a prrblllrrrr little noisy pbpbpbpb parcel of flatus. Couldn't be helped. He felt his guts close in on themselves like a fist, and grimaced, but the pain passed. He almost swooned, but managed to hold on to the reins, to grip the flanks of his horse with legs. Wouldn't do to fall off his horse. Oh but he was tired, and his head felt like cheese cooked before an open fire, and he might even have slept as he rode, for he couldn't remember how he had covered so much ground. But here they were, and battle was all around him, and he saw the polished armour and blazon of John of Chandos, so not devoured by the tiger after all, except he had lost his horse. But the knight dealt great blows, on foot, with his battleaxe. Ned cheered, and the sound resonated inside his helmet. But then a Catalonian – Ned knew him, by repute, from his blazon, it was Martin Fernandez – burlied into Chandos and knocked him over, and toppled on top of him. The two metal men grappled on the ground. When Fernandez rolled away and John of Chandos struggled back up, he was holding a bloodied knife. Then there was a roar to the left of him, or it was to the right of him, Ned wasn't sure, and he spurred his horse and swung his sword to and fro, and the blade met no resistance. And here was Don Pedro, also on foot, helmetless. Don Pedro! Ned cried. Don Pedro, we fight together for the divine right to rule! Didn't hear him. Couldn't hear him. Pedro struck a man down, and stabbed him between the legs, looked around with a wide grin. Everywhere men were fighting. The English had more desperation in them, for they were fighting for life, and for the food with which they knew Henry's army was supplied. Suddenly, without knowing how he got there, Edward saw that he was at the river, and so at the town itself. Spaniards by the hundreds were tumbling over the banks and into the water, fleeing the English pursuit. But Englishmen are not thuswise to be fled from. Men went over the banks and into the river too, as happy to kill their prey in water as on land. The river ran red. Something struck Ned's helmet, and it rang like a gong. His whole head seared with pain. By the time he had gathered himself, his personal guard had killed the assailant, but the highpitched flute sound would not leave his ears. He rode back, waving his sword, but the next thing he knew it was late afternoon, and the whole of Nájera was on fire.

Was that true fire? Or was the sunset rubying the walls and roofs?

Or fire? True fire.

So hard to tell.

A man on foot led Edward's horse back to the English camp. He had so much disgraced himself as to shit in his armour, but his people washed him and took the armour away, and dressed him in clean clothes and his red-and-blue heraldic surcoat, and the next clear moment in his mind he was at supper with his nobles.

He drank some wine. It cleared his thoughts. For a while he observed the others, and thought to himself: we won.

None of it felt in the remotest part real.

Don Pedro's greasy fingers were tearing up a chicken. One of ex-King Henry's chickens, presumably.

—Now I shall have at them, he was growling. Exterminate all the brutes. Gomez Carillo de Quintana, leader, kill him first and make his death the worst.

Edward looked down at his own meal, as yet untouched. Another cup of wine, and his rational mind was further restored to him.

—First and last, the Prince told Pedro. His own voice sounded inside his great empty skull like a roaring of wind, a mocking echo, a boom, and booming boom. He heard the sound of surf. He heard the cooing of doves. None of the sounds were in the world. All of them were inside.

—You say? Pedro leered.

—Study the arts of being liked, Ned told him. Pedro's two eyes appeared to multiply on his face, until his face was nothing but eyes, like boils all over a plague-victim, and Ned stared with a kind of horrified fascination. The man who usurped your throne was liked. You must needs be liked more. Or you won't keep your throne.

Everybody stared at Ned. But then Pedro grinned. But, he said, a bastard, and a usurper and if he were in my grasping fists I'd . . . I'd . . .

He dinged one of those grasping fists into a dish of thick gravy, and its russet lumps bespattered his own front. And the griping in Ned's guts took him once more, and he excused himself and scurried away.

Camera Eye

passing the landscape as a hawk does.

Eyes of amber, not the colour but the hardness, and the sense   of something gnarly, tangled, insect inembedded, inward lurking looking at eyes of sapphire, not the hardness so much as the colour, and the knowledge this is beauty long gestated and pressure-crushed and cataclysmic.

dreaming of his wife

THE BLACK PRINCE

For a week, the Prince was desperately ill. Since there was no immediate need to prosecute the war he gave himself into the care of his physicians, who reduced his consumption of wine, and made him drink foul stoops of tea made from strange herbs. He spent three days and two nights in a babbling excess of half-mindlessness, in which weird phantoms bobbed up at him and dreams and reality intermingled, as fingers lock together in prayer. Then he slowly began to improve. At the end of the week he could feel his strength start to return.

He was in Burgos. Pedro was back on the throne and he was in Pedro's palace.

Over a second week, he ate little, drank more of the foul tea, and took stock of his victory. Letters arrived from Aquitaine. It took him a long time to read these, and even when his servants read them aloud to him he found it hard to concentrate on the words. Still: he had reason to be pleased. It was true that the Usurper had escaped; but they had captured Bertrand du Guesclin, and would ransom him for a hundred thousand crowns at least. The victory had cost very few English lives, though the kingdoms of France and Castile had lost many thousands of men. Ned's main worry was the flittery tremble he couldn't seem to banish from his left and right hands. Still: now he was the Count of Biscay. And he could return in triumph to Aquitaine and see his wife and new son.

At the end of the third week he was too impatient to wait longer. Though he still felt weak and trembly, he announced he would lead his army home. The Bishop of Burgos visited him, and sat on a chair at the end of his bed.

—I administered last rites, my son, the Bishop told him, in heavily-accented bad French. When you were at your worst with the sickness. Thank God you have recovered.

—Pray God I will, said Ned.

And here was Pedro himself, looking as shifty and bestial as ever, coming in to make sure his ally and his Bishop weren't plotting. With him were certain of his grandees, like hyenas in fine cloaks and fur caps. Edward's adjutant brought up their letter of accompt. Pedro had reaffirmed, by this document dated – dated – (he had to check) – the 2nd and the 6th of May in the year of our Lord 1367, that your obligations amount to one million gold pieces.

—My obligations are more, dear prince, Pedro replied, with a wolf's grin, much more. There is a gratitude that can hardly be computed in trashy gold and silver. He was shifting his weight from foot to foot.

Exhausted though he was, Edward felt anger stir in him.

—Give that gratitude to God who granted us the victory. I will be satisfied with the trashy stuff. And at once, if it is no trouble. I have an army to pay.

Damnable trembling in his hands. He pressed the both to his sides.

But at this Pedro positively writhed, like a dancer, or an eel, and began a long complaint about his grandees, and how they were withholding their lawful taxes and right tribute, and that without it he could not pay. But he had friends who would advance him the money, if Edward had no qualms about taking Mohammedan gold, and as Edward coughed, Pedro launched into a lengthy speech, like a lawyer, about whether the status of Edward was a friend and ally, or else whether he was an invader in Castile, as his (Pedro's) grandees said, and as the Mohammedan heathens to the south feared, and that to resolve all these issues in one, and to settle all lawful accounts with Edward, he would pay him the gold he owed only when his army left Spanish soil.

Edward's stomach groaned, outwith his conscious control. It may have sounded as though he was sighing.

—Oh, my friend, my friend, you have my word, on God's holy bones, that the money will be waiting for you in Bordeaux.

—Another waits in that kingdom.

—*Your* kingdom! urged Pedro, wringing his hands. And then: another? What?

—The usurper Henry.

—He?

—My princess writes to me, Ned drawled, and her words are that Henry de Trastamere is looting and burning villages in Aquitaine.

Pedro started forward eagerly. You see? he said. Is there a greater devil at large in the world? First he robs me of my kingdom . . . now, praise God and your Highness, restored to me . . . and then he tries to rob you of yours!

Ned is too tired to get into all this here. He fixes Pedro with his eye, and says: the money.

—As I am a Christian king I swear by Christ's sacred body that it will be yours, once you are off Spanish soil. And now, if your Highness will forgive me—

He swept from the room, and his chattering courtiers followed him. A solid sense of dread and unhappiness had distilled in Edward's stomach. The Bishop was still there.

—The devil dragged me into this, he said.

—And now, my son, the Bishop replied, you must pray to be dragged out of it.

Still, there was no help. He had to take the army home, and the sea voyage across the Bay of Biscay, though quick, would not carry the many thousands of men he had to take with him. It would be unchivalrous to abandon his men. So he rode out of Burgos and he was still managing to stay in the saddle, just about, as they passed the charred ruins of Nájera. It was a miserable ride, and his whole body shuddered and complained, and he clung on as long as he could. But at some point he had to concede he no longer had the strength in his shivering limbs to stay on a horse.

It was humiliating, no question, but it could not be helped. At least his head was clear. But his body felt as shaky and weak as a baby's. He lay on a litter and was carried by his men over the summer scorchness of northern Spain. His brother, and John of Chandos both kept him company for much of the time, but they too looked exhausted and ill. And here was Denis. The men were dying. His men were dying. How many?

How many? Christ and his saints!

Very many.

The sun was a nail of heat and light in the centre of his own forehead. He took another drink.

—It cannot be much less, my lord, said Denis.

—A fifth? Reduce *by* a fifth?

Murmuring.

—Mother of God. Reduce *to* a fifth? That is, what, twenty-odd thousand men . . .

—And most of them, John of Chandos intoned, without proper Christian burial.

Dust under their feet, the sky furnacebright, there was no shade anywhere. The smaller rivers were all drunk entirely away by the sun, rolled up into white boulders and a million dead white pebbles. The land, having been picked clean by Edward's army on the way in to Spain, was still clean on the way out. John of Gaunt's horse plodded wearily alongside Ned's litter, and John of Gaunt himself slouched in the saddle.

—I suppose, brother, Ned addressed him, the time has come again to talk of the succession. Of whether the next king after me shall be Richard II or Henry IV.

—Such talk, groaned John, may well be purely academic.

Denis, on the far side of the litter, was audibly shocked. A sudden dry-wind sucking in of breath. Such talk was treasonous, of course, for divine law dictated the succession of kings. But treason meant something different to princes.

—My lords, Denis rasped. This is hardly in the best of taste.

—Nothing so far has been in the best of taste, John of Gaunt returned. An expedition damned from the outset. A starving army. Twenty-odd thousand men dead. His Highness may as well drink the whole cup. If Henry of Trastamere is in Aquitaine, he will strike as high as he can.

—No, no, no, groaned Edward.

No, no, no.

No, no, no.

No, no, no.

Newsreel (16)

URBAN V QUITS AVIGNON FOR ROME

April: Cruel news. King Peter of Cyprus: Murdered. Chivalry in Cyprus Discredited.

O O O O that shake

Omne Bonum: copious encyclopedia of all medical knowledge, gathered together in one place. 1100 folia, more than 600 illustrations, bound in finest calf leather. One previous owner – Jacob the Palmer of London, a clerk of the King's Exchequer. Regretful sale, but circumstances dictate etc etc. All reasonable offers considered.

Le Prince d'Aquitaine à la tour abolie

fragments

—have you insured against your ruin? Competitive new rates for **all** your fragment insurance needs. Mad again? No need to worry. Contact directly, or send your servant to HEIRONIMOES.

Honi shantih mal y pense

Honi shantih mal y pense

Honi shantih mal y pense

JOAN

The baby appeared to Joan's camera eye as a perfectly blank thing, all exterior and sounds, gurgling, or screaming, occasionally, if rarely, silent. It wasn't a bad baby, as babies went, but there was a distracting *nothingness* there. With her earlier children Joan had had glimpses of lives nested inside them, ready to unwrap themselves over the decades to come like ferns. With tiny Richard: nothing. For a while she wondered if this meant he was doomed to die young; but as the months passed it seemed not. He was a lusty little thing, and his two wetnurses giggled and cooed over him. Joan didn't feel any animosity to him, but at the same time the thought that he might die left her feeling unmoved, and the realisation that he was going to live left her feeling unmoved.

She pondered this. It wasn't good, surely. She had loved each and every one of her previous children from the first time she had held them.

Still: it was what it was.

The Bordeaux spring turned into summer, and it became too hot to do anything very much in the day. Administration of the principality was mostly handled by the Bishop of Bath, her husband's chancellor, a tubby man who sweated a great deal and always smelt slightly of vinegar. He made a show of consulting her, titular princess of this land as she was, with respect to the larger issues. Mostly the peasants got on with growing crops and the lords got on with governing the peasants and the priests got on with praying. The ones who fought were away over the southern mountains, and her eye gave her no glimpses of that either, so she schooled herself to pray and hope for the best. The Bishop worried mostly about money. There was never enough money, it seemed. But then, at some point soon, the Prince would come riding back with carts full of booty and every debt would be paid, and the splendour restored. Joan never worried about money. It was demeaning to worry about money. A merchant offered her a fine kirtle, cotton woven with silk, and bejewelled buttons, and she took it. Later that day the Bishop came in person to rebuke her, or to try and persuade her to return the garment. It cost all the year's tax yield from all the provinces of Lot and Garonne! My lady, Highness, I beg of you! She did nothing but gaze at him with her eyes, and this was enough to shut him up.

'My husband will like me in it,' she said, 'when he returns. It will please him. If money does not please, then what use is it?'

She had been in the habit of going to the Bishop for her confession, not because she liked him, or because he was liable to go easy on her – rather the reverse – but simply because he was the senior cleric in the principality and her own status required nothing less. But for the following few sessions, after his little show of temper, she approached a lowlier priest. The Bishop understood this for the snub it was, and made efforts afterwards to appease her.

Oh, but it was hot, and slow, and dull! The shadows lengthened and dawdled and then finally they shortened. The sky whitened and heat fell down with palpable pressure, and grew dark, and the stars chilled the skin. In the middle of the day the crickets were louder than human ears could endure.

Afternoon. Costance, her lady, read aloud to her from a romance. The story was this: beautiful Florence was daughter of King Otes of Rome, and must marry Garcy, the King of Athens, but she cannot love him because he is old and ugly. So Garcy brings his whole Athenian army to Rome and attacks the city, and Mylys and Emere, sons of the King of Hungary, come to the city's aid. It is Emere with whom Florence falls in love and the two become betrothed, but . . . during Mylys's absence Emere, no, wait, during Emere's absence his brother Mylys is overcome . . . overcome with the beauty of Florence, declares an impious passion for her and . . . and . . .

And?

'Costance? Costance!'

But Costance had fallen asleep in the heat, her chin on her collar bone, the book open in her lap.

A snagged fly snored in a spider's web.

Joan called for water in a bowl and washed her face. She went through to another room in the castle, with two other ladies-in-waiting padding behind her, and found baby Richard asleep in his cot. He looked peaceful. A handsome child, really.

Nothing. Again, nothing.

The Bishop of Bath dined with the noble lady, queen of beauty in all womankind, Princess of Wales and Aquitaine, and kept patting at his brow and chin with a cloth, and simpering at her. They ate *à deux*, fowl dressed in a rich sauce, tasting of olives, and they drank a warm white wine. The bread was coarse. She mentioned this.

'Poor bread, yes I agree. Rough bread. But I have some smooth news!'

She settled her calm eyes on him, and said nothing. He patted at his face with his cloth.

'Henry de Trastamere,' he said, 'your Highness – well, we are sure he is out of Aquitaine. And if he has quitted Aquitaine it can only be for one reason.'

'You mean,' Joan replied, her heart hurrying a little in her slim chest, 'that Edward is safe? That Edward is coming home?'

'Henry de Trastamere will not wish to meet his Highness. It would be his final meeting, his – shall we say – ultimate meeting with anyone. But there is other news. And that is that Henry de Trastamere is back in Castile. That he had not merely deposed Don Pedro for a second time. That he has ensured that there will never be another occasion for such a deposition!' The priest chuckled. Unseemly, really.

'You mean he has killed Don Pedro?' This was terrible news. 'You mean that the whole expedition has been wasted?'

'Well,' burbled the Bishop, cutting a piece from the fowl and spearing it on his knife, 'nothing is ever really wasted. Not in God's eyes anyway.'

From the adjoining chamber, baby Richard began to cry weeeeh weeeeh, and Joan could hear the wetnurse attempting to soothe him.

'But I fear,' said the Bishop, after he had swallowed this morsel, 'that his Royal Highness is going to be sadly short of money.'

The wetnurse's efforts were in vain. Tiny Richard cried more lustily still.

Three days later the message reached her that the Prince was in Pessac. From the castle balcony she was able to watch the first few hundred members of his troop enter the city and march through the streets. The population lined the way, but none cheered. And Joan, scanning the riders for her husband's helmet – no, none of them were helmeted: so she scanned the riders for her husband's blond hair. She could not see it. It was not until the party was almost underneath her, at the main castle gate, that she saw he was being carried on a litter. He was ill. She hurried through and swept up their child, Richard, and in moments was down to greet him. And when she saw how thin he had grown, how old and ill he looked, how lank his hair, so dull his eyes, she burst into tears herself.

ROBERT HAWLEY

Money moves slow. That's my main conclusion from the whole business.

We took Alfonso Count of Denia at the great Battle of Nájera, where we fought under the command of the mightiest warrior Christendom has ever known, the Black Prince Edward. Few can make such a boast but we can. The Black Prince! Anyway: the Spaniard had been bloodied a little in the fight, and then had vomited up his breakfast as I and another squire, Richard Chamberlain by name, had approached him, swords out. After that he at least surrendered with some dignity, for all that there was sick in his beard and that his eyes didn't seem to focus very well. He handed us his gauntlet, and Robert took him back, out of the battle. That was near the end, when the mass of the Spanish army had broken and run for the town of Nájera itself – five thousand valueless foot soldiers killed in that last hour, or winkled out of hiding places in the town that evening and the following morning, and throatslit or bludgeoned or hanged. Bodies everywhere. One arch of the town bridge became clogged with corpses. The next afternoon the stench was already rising under the stark Navarre sunshine. Richard C. had grabbed two other minor nobles, but the Duke of Alfonso was our major prize – £20,000 in ransom, I thought, and Richard reckoned it would be even more. For the moment, though, he had to be fed, and the two other men we took were only squires, without much access to ready cash. Still half of twenty thousand is ten thousand. And ten thousand pound is ten thousand pound. And when the army picked up its feet and marched west towards Burgos, I was still daydreaming how I would dispose of the money. A nice manor in England. A proper escutcheon. A good name to pass on to my children. It was hard, though, hauling all these prisoners. Richard lost his temper with one minor Castilian nobleman, £40 worth of ransom if that, and struck the fellow in the face. He complained to an English knight that he had surrendered and given his word, and ought not to be treated so, and there was a *contretemps*. Richard Chamberlain let the man go on his parole that he would send the full sum of ransom directly to England within the year, to which the man agreed – he walked off, and Chamberlain never saw the money. Instead he received a letter, three years later, when we were back in England, asserting that the fair damages for the assault he had suffered exactly matched the ransom he had promised to pay, and that therefore the matter was settled. Chamberlain was ill by this stage, but he paid a lawyer to write a letter in return denying the honour of such a claim, unilaterally declared and not negotiated, and further denying that the fellow had ever been assaulted. Forty pounds for a quick slap on the chops? Bollocks to that.

In Spain, Dickie and I were buoyed to discover that our main prisoner, the Count of Denia, was cousin to King Peter IV of Aragon, no less. So we asked him to set the value of his own ransom: too low a price and he would bring discredit on his name, too high he might bankrupt his house. He named 150,000 *doblas* – something like (we reckoned it there and then) £28,000 in good English money. Oh, this was marvellous. I begged leave to approach the Prince, who, it was known, was buying up the more valuable prisoners; and he not only granted me an audience he readily agreed to take the Count of Denia off our hands for twenty-five, promised to us as compensation. We were only too happy to agree, of course: since that was real money, even split two ways. So then we went on with the campaign – we were soldiers, after all. It was damn hard, that year. Damn hard.

The other of our prisoners got camp fever and died, which was a shame. As for our big prize, well he was released by the Prince, on his word, and after delivering his two sons as hostages, and a guarantee from the Count of Foix.

Coming home was a long hard slog. We got back to England, though not soon enough, and it was a long time waiting around for our money. The pickings we'd acquired were soon spent, and then my friend Dickie Chamberlain grew sick and died and the money he was owed passed to his heirs. Jesus, it's hard: a gentleman can't be badgering the Prince of Wales for a debt, when the Prince himself is waiting for *his* money from a dilatory Spaniard. We would get paid when the Prince got paid – we understood that. Anyway, the Prince gave over one of the Count's sons to Foix, who I heard locked him in a dungeon and piled him with heavy chains, though he kept the other lad in England and treated him well. But after a few years, the ransom proving hard to extract and he having better things to do, the Prince sold the debt on to his father, King Edward himself.

Edward was always picking up cut-price ransoms like this, and he knew what he was doing. A shrewd man where a debt of honour was concerned, no question, our big king. Edward the Great. But even *he* couldn't extract the fucking money, and having sat on it for years more, he sold it back to us – at a discount, of course. Richard's heirs and I didn't have the money to buy this debt outright, of course; but the King was persuaded that his son had promised us compensation, and such compensation had not been forthcoming. So the ransom debt was to quit his house of any obligation to us, and we were fucking happy to take it. We'd not seen a penny of the ransom, at any point.

It was no easy matter, though. We had new letters drafted and sealed and sent by ship to Denia, demanding our money. We reminded him that his debt to us had precedence over subsequent debts he had picked up getting captured and ransoming himself on his word at later battles. It was eight months before a reply, and that was full of pettifogging bollocks about the return of his son from the Count of Foix. I didn't care about any of that. I wanted my money. I was no longer a young man. So, borrowing what I could, I put together a small party and we sailed to Navarre – weeks at sea, all of us at the side of the boat spewing green into the green water – and what a fucking waste of time and money that whole expedition was. I'd carried the Prince of Wales's colours, because I figured his involvement in the ransom gave me the right. But diplomats at Bayonne were very angry at this, and insisted I hadn't the right, so letters had to be sent back to England, and that was months more, whilst my people ate and drank and whored away the money I had brought with me. Then there was a small riot, where my people beat up a group of people who declared themselves for Denia, and one of the Spaniards died, and four of my people were arrested, and one of this four, a good lad from Hertfordshire called John, lost an eye and most of his teeth – if Denia had just given me my fucking money all of this would have been avoided. But eventually the letter came back granting us the right to carry the Prince of Wales's colours in the Prince of Wales's lands, which certainly meant Aquitaine and Gascony, and I figured meant Navarre as well. So we presented at the courts in Denia, and the right of the ransom, and the value, were affirmed. But then we learned that Edward, the Black Prince, Prince of Wales, the fucking Flower of English Chivalry and one of the greatest warriors ever to have lived, was dead. Got sick, got worse, passed over to his eternal reward. Desperate, desperate news.

It didn't affect the debt, of course; but we sailed home with a heavy heart. There were more letters. The brawl, where the Spaniard lost his life, became caught up with the matter, legally speaking. The Count of Foix – the Cunt of Foix, I called him, though never to his face, oh but the trouble he'd given us – finally surrendered up his captive. Some money was paid out of Denia, but none of it to myself, or to Richard's heirs. Bitter business.

Do you know when it was settled? How long we had to wait? 1391. Twenty-three years after the battle, near enough a *quarter century* after the pot-bellied Count of Denia had surrendered to Richard and to me with sick in his beard, and afterwards given his word – as a nobleman and gentleman – to pay us one hundred and fifty thousand doblas in return for sparing his life. It rode my life like a night-mare, that fucking debt. Still, we got the money in the end: not the £28,000 we had been promised, but a fair sum. Eight thousand came to me, and that's a pretty tidy sum.

FEAST

The charges of the feast were twofold: that for liveries and that for entertainment. Liveries were of coloured cloth, or else of another variegated patterned mode that is called *stragulatus*. There were two qualities, the *secta generosorum* and *valettorum*, the material for the suit of gentlefolk and servants. The garments of the highest born were trimmed with fur. Some of the cloth was trimmed with swansdown.

The banquet lasted two days. The quantity of beef and mutton consumed was not large; but pork, lamb, and veal were abundantly supplied.

Swans and geese, fattened in coops on oats and peas, were consumed.

Forty rabbits were eaten.

The poultry consumed in the feast was the largest item. Fowls and capons, partridges, teal, wild ducks, *gastrimargii*, snipes, plovers, owsels, thrushes, and fieldfares. The centrepiece of the second day was four roasted hoopoes, arranged with their feathers on a central plate. Gascon wine and Gascon beer were in great supply.

The cooks were well-paid. The walls were new painted with delightful scenery of England and of Aquitaine for the occasion. Musicians and dancing. Through the afternoons a scop told tales of heroic chivalry, some of which concerned the daring of the Black Prince himself.

Chess was played.

Edward returned from siesta. He was, Joan could not help thinking, looking bloated and flushed. Too much wine. And as his man helped him into his chair at the highest table, and as people – as word passed about that the Prince was present again – came hurrying back into the main hall, Joan had a little vision. Not a full-fledged camera eye, nothing so immersive, but a flicker of something. It was: pearls. Or, bubbles – except hard-edged bubbles rolled about with light, or ivory, or ice. It was difficult to say. These little spheres were filled with fluid (was it?) and they were located inside her husband, in the lining of his stomach, and inside his liver, and kidneys, and in his brain. For a swift disappearing moment she had an overall sense of the constellation of all these dots, or bubbles, or seeds, or whatever they were. And then it was gone.

PART 6. LIMOGES

Newsreel (17)

Cockadoodledoo! A rooster, raucous in the rain. The symbol of France, here it craws and crows and makes its tiny thunder in the dampness of this barn. Pokes its pathétique head through the circle of this hole in this barn door.

WAR OF THE CENTURY RESUMED!

Vitalis of Assisi Dead. The noted hermit and holy man passed away without fuss in Santa Maria di Viole, as he had lived, in utter poverty. His one possession was an old container from which he used to drink water from a nearby spring. His reputation for holiness has already spread across Italy, and his intercession was often sought against sicknesses and in particular against diseases affecting the bladder and genitals.

PRINCE ON THE MARCH!

On manoeuvres: an Anglo-Gascon force of some 3,000 men, led by three sons of Edward III, including that flower of chivalry Edward, Prince of Wales, and accompanied by John of Gaunt the Duke of Lancaster, and Edmund of Langley the Earl of Cambridge, also accompanied by the Earl of Warwick and the renowned Sir John of Chandos, as well as such experienced soldiers as John Hastings, Earl of Pembroke, Sir Walter Hewitt, Guichard d'Angle and the Captal de Buch.

CORRECTION: In our previous bulletin, we announced that Edward the Black Prince, that flower of chivalry, Prince of Wales and Aquitaine, Count of Biscay, was 'on the march' in France with an army of 3,000 men. We have been asked to point out that the Prince, owing to some slight and temporary infirmity, is not marching, but is rather being carried in a litter.

CORRECTION: In our previous bulletin, we announced that Edward the Black Prince, advancing through central France, was accompanied by 'the Earl of Warwick' and 'John of Chandos, Earl of Hereford'. It has been brought to our attention that both these noblemen are recently dead, and as such are not presently in company with the Prince.

> *Saw an eyeball peepin' through a counterpane that hid*
> *the gree-een knight*
> *Don't know what they're doin' but they laugh a lot, Gawain*
> *and gree-een knight*
> *Wish they'd let me in so I could find out what's there behind*
> *the gree-een knight*

The procession marches, though the rain makes the banners dark and heavy to carry, and several of the bannermen drop their poles and bemerde their colours. The otherwise bright colours of Du Guesclin, the Duke of Bournon, the Duke of Anjou, the Duke of Berri . . .

The rain eases, and then comes down harder at dusk. This man is trying to cut edible meat from a mostly rotten pig carcass.

The procession continues: Jean de Kerlouet, Louis de St Julien, Guichard d'Angle, Louis de Harcourt, Thomas de Percy, Robert of Sancerre, John de Vienne.

THE BLACK PRINCE

He had good days and bad days, physically. Oh, but his *will* was iron-hard. Ah, but his *will*. He would march. Or his men would march, and he would be carried. Denis, always at his side, brought good news. The Duke of Anjou has chickened out of confronting you, Highness. Learned somehow of your preparations at Cognac. Too scared now to march on Bordeaux. He has dispersed his garrison.

The first goblet of wine did little for him, but the second dissolved and unknotted some of the pains in his torso and legs, and by the third he was able to feel a little more himself. He said:

—Fame. The hart we hunt. Our notoriety aids us.

—Highness, Denis agreed.

—Notoriety. It aids. But thank God the Father we have more than notoriety now.

He is God the Father, and his obedient army, ready to die for him, is his Son, and his great reputation is the Holy Spirit, that flies about the countryside like a dove, or burns through the late summer fields as fire. He checks himself: it is too close to blasphemy to compare himself to God the Father. Another beaker. Warm red and a little sour in the mouth, and afterwards he began to feel nauseous.

He asked after the levies. Specifics, to take his wandering mind off such thoughts.

Denis brought out a list and started to read: many of the levies are in, Highness. Poitou, Saintonge, La Rochelle, Quercy.

—Limoges?

—That city, my lord, Denis replies, uneasily.

—Limoges, Denis? What is it?

—That city has made declaration for the King of France.

As with any blow, first you feel nothing but a kind of disinterested registering of the impact, of the fact that you have been struck. Then, you pause, and note again, and only then does the pain and violation occur to you. Edward coughs, and rubs his face, and scowls, and says:

—Well, they are all traitors. We must deal justice to traitors.

He stops. Denis is looking at him.

So the force must alter its direction, and swing down towards the town of Limoges, with its high walls, and wide river. At least there will be no trouble keeping the horses watered. But the town is ready for them, and its walls are too tall and straight to permit climbing, or ladders. No hope of entering it, says the Earl of Pembroke, no hope at all. Look at those battlements!

—If not over the top then underneath, and we must give employment to our engineers, says the Prince. My lord of Cambridge, is there no chance we might make a swift breach in at the north wall?

—North or south or any, grumbled Cambridge, it will be like piercing an iron mountain. It would take at least a week.

He means a month, but courtesy does not permit unpalatable truths to be directly spoken. The Prince understands, though. Today is one of his better days, comprehension-wise.

—So so so, says Edward, struggling to contain a sudden wild tremor in his legs and feet, and holding back what would, he knows, be a noisome and possibly fluid breaking of wind. Set up camp here, my lords. And send the captain of sappers to me. His temper tips, and he barks at his litter-carriers to bear him somewhere discreet where he can void, and be quick. As he goes he calls:

—They call me black, and they mean my heart. They shall soon discover, lords mine, what colour my heart truly is.

It takes two days to set the camp up, and another day to clear some ground to the south where the horses can be exercised and knights can practise their battle riding. Edward feels a little better on day three, and then much worse on day four. The arbitrariness of this makes him furious. Days pass. The weather is mild and sunny; the nights display an improbable treasure of stars to the world, and Edward despises the way his mind cannot *free* itself from its own resentment. He seethes. He grinds his teeth at night. He is in pain all the time, except when he is so drunk he can no longer speak, and even then the pain does not entirely leave him, but lurks, wolf that it is, at the margins of his being.

The Earl of Pembroke attempts to beguile his time with a game of chess, but the Prince cannot concentrate on the board. Chess is the game of warriors. He must try. He sees an opening in the Earl's defences, and pushes a knight through.

—Check.

The wind flaps the tent-wall like a sail at sea. There is a pleasant odour blowing in through the open door: citrus, herbal, dry. Pembroke grimaces.

—I regret this, your Highness, he says, countermoving. Sincerely. A queen captures the knight and checks Edward's king. He moves the king, changes his mind, and moves it in a different direction. But it makes no difference. Pembroke moves a bishop up and the game is over.

The Black Prince stares at the horncarved pieces and wonders how much muscular strength it would take to grind each and every one to dust. More than he possesses, certainly. He tries to swing his legs over the side of his couch, and his man, seeing the action, rushes to help him up.

—How long, he asks, struggling across the tent to his shitting bowl.

—It will have to be soon, Highness, says Pembroke, averting his eyes. The garrison of Limoges is countermining. They will blow our sappers to the moon unless . . .

—Please, gasps the Prince, do not let me detain you, my lord. Pembroke hurries out. After he has voided, and drunk a posset, and slept for a short time, Edward feels a little better.

He calls his secretary, and dictates a letter to his wife.

—My dear and beloved wife, he says. And at the words he pictures her, her unreadable eyes, her whiteness. The parfait balance of her visage.

The secretary has written, and is waiting.

—I have had news of the death of my mother. Scribble scribble went the secretarial pen. She was a good woman and I regret. He waits for the scratching to cease, the secretary to catch up with him. And I regret I knew her so little. You once said to me that my father the king converted her into a kind of machine for. Stop. Wait for the writer to catch up. A machine for for machine for the birthing of of of princes. Scribble scribble. But she played an heroic role, once, that the world is not likely. Wait. Likely to forget. The town of Calais has good reason to remember her kindly. As for the town of Limoges . . .

The secretary holds up his left hand, and Edward stops. The town of Limoges is there, outside his tent, in all its massy intractability. The town of Limoges is also down there, on the parchment, in still gleaming ink rebuses. So much more manageable. The scribe's hand goes down.

—What were my last words? the Prince asks.

—'As for the town of Limoges . . .'

— . . . there will be, if things go as I plan, nobody left there to remember anything. For a man must pursue his own destiny, bowing down before his own evil. It was granted only to a woman to be born with no trace of original sin.

The scribe is not writing, but waiting, uncertain, to see if the Prince really wants such words to be written down. Edward looks past him, through the open mouth of the tent.

Camera Eye

at the head of the valley in the dark of the hills on the strawspread floor of a lurchedover cabin a man halfsits halflies propped by an old woman two wrinkled girls that might be young   chunks of charcoal still gleam on the fire, and the straw around the blaze are scorched and singed   the flicker rubs red and yellow from his doughsaggy face the taut throat the belly swelled enormous

the barefoot girl brings him a claycupful of water wipes sweat from his streaming face with her own hair   the firelight flares in his eyes and in the blanched faces of the women.   He will die, they think, and then the women will lay him out, because that is women's work, and they will pay a neighbour some sous to dig a hole to bury him, for digging is man's work.

foreigners   what can we say to the sick? foreigners what can we say to the dead?   He came nearly two decades before, with the swarm of English and Gascon who fought over this territory, and the olives were plucked unripe from the trees or the trees burned in a great bush of fire five times the size of the tree   farmhouses smashed down, animals killed and eaten or simply killed   and the people hurrying away with as much as they could carry belted round their waists or packed on their backs. He had peeled off from the mess of soldiery and hidden in the woods for a week on sourberries and rabbits, and then when the plague had passed over had come out and slowly made friends.   He was skilled at bricks and stones, and helped rebuild, and learned the tongue, and made a handfast marriage with a local girl, and when she had given birth to her rapebaby he drowned it and told her it was stillborn, and then had given her two girls of her own. And from time to time the English and the Gascons

would come back round and he would take the three of
them up into the hills to the abandoned ancient caves,
where people lived before Noah's flood, they say, and
moved as the waters rose, though God's wrath caught up
with them at the end

vistas over the lowlands with smoke rising in seven
smudging pillars

until the morning came when there was no smoke
and they went home

and   foreigners   what   can   we   say   to   the
sick?   foreigners what can we say to the dead?   the
women have told him that he has camp fever, picked
up from a trip down the valley to talk with some of the
soldiers in the hope of picking up some extra food. But he
does not have camp fever. He has the death, the plague,
the blackness in his blood   buboes big as ripe apples

seven towers of Jerusalem

news of the black devilprince's return and the town
locked itself away and the peasantry fled and he stayed,
too sick to move.   Once she asked him: why did you
not stay with the army? and he said: killing makes for a
dysentery of the soul, and I had had enough of it.

we have only words against
breathe
breathe

seven views of Jerusalem

CASWORON

His Da said: they used to call this Cornwall *the Silver Lands*, and not on account of the rain. The wealth of the world is hidden, and our job is to unhide it. His father dug tin out of the ground at Bere Ferrers, and then came to Somerset for the silver mining, on account of it being more lucrative, and Cas came with him, of course. But the most of the silver was all dug out long before he came along, and there was precious little to scrape from the belly of the earth. Then one day he was digging a long tunnel under the brow of rock and it chunked down upon him, all in one shuddering reposition of ground, like the hill shrugging. That was the end of him. The priest said, saves us the bother of burying him, and said a quick mass over the land, but still charged Cas the full fee. Bohemia's your land for tin now, they told him, and with his Da dead and no other skill, he gave some thought to going over the sea and finding this place wherever it was, and digging at rich bright-coloured seams. He thought: to hand over most of his ore to his masters, but to keep enough for two coins in his cheeks, each day, and so get rich. But then his pal Bryn said: the army needs miners. Digging for tin, is it, for their tinpot helmets, is it? *Ddim o gwbl* you foolish Cornishman, said Bryn, it's for digging under the walls of French cities and making them to tumble down, and from far below in the Somerset ground he heard his father rumbling or grumbling or bidding him swear to serve the king. *Swear!* So he and Bryn presented themselves in the city of Bristol (*swear!*) and were soon marched with three dozen other miners down to Portland and so over the seas to Normandy, and then across land to another port, and on the boat again for days. A big place next, *pur dha* city, called Bordeaux. This was the seat of the Black Prince himself but they were told they had just missed him, he was off on his wars again, and Cas didn't even spend a night in the place before they were all marched along beside the river and inland. A week of sleeping under hedges, and once in an old barn with huge holes in its walls, and then they caught up with the carts, slowrolling their way along dust roads, cannon strapped underneath them and supplies piled high. The horses looked thin and uneager to Cas, but that wasn't his concern.

Thunder grumbling over the horizon.

Swear!

Still, they were part of the army now, and not just any army but the army of the Terrible Black Prince himself, and when he got back to Cornwall, whenever that happened, he Cas would be able to say *Ev yw ow howeth*. Better than that, it was threepence a day, it was, which was a penny more than the soldiers got, and for a while Cas was happy enough. They marched for many days, and the food wasn't good. Bryn approached a knight and explained how they needed to keep their strength up for the sort of work they were to do, and received for his pains a smite upon the head with a sword flat that made blood go in his eyes. Bryn was always a bit funny after that blow, prone to fall asleep at a moment's notice. Had a lump the size of a goose egg on his scalp for some days, until it went down.

They stopped finally at another fine city, not so big as Bordeaux, but highwalled and called Limoges, with the *shh* sound lovely and soft at the end of the word. Here there was a big siege, and the Prince gave orders the place was to be taken, so a knight and two sergeants came to talk to all the miners. They had selected the best place, they said, to dig under the walls and pack in gunpowder, but it was exposed to the defenders above, so we will need to build a protective roof to carry with us (they said) called a sow, you see. So, they scrounged some wood and pegs and tools from the carpenters and said, the Prince's command was such and such, and could we have some nails, please, and they said: fuck off, you Cornishmen, fuck off back underground with the gnomes, which was hardly pleasant. So they had to build the sow with wooden dowels instead of nails. They built a sow on legs, and the knight strode by and said, pull it apart and make it bigger, and so they did that and strapped leather to the top and got up early one day with their kit and carried the whole lot to the wall. The ground was soft enough, and the defenders threw down some big stones but the sow held. But at the end of the day it was clear enough to Cas that they were digging in the wrong place to bring the wall down. Not that he had a lot of experience of this sort of thing, but it was common sense, really, to any miner. They needed to be taking the ground away from the wall near the tower – not digging through the solid rock on which it was erected, which would take months. They needed to be excavating next to the underground rockcrop and chipping away where the tower was slightly unbalanced on its foundations. Bryn agreed with him. Cas discussed the matter with the other miners but they took exception and there was a fight, and he got a punched head and swollen nose and spent a day lying under the trees feeling sorry for himself and fuck his threepence a day he was going home. That was the day the Limoges folk poured burning oil on the little structure of the sow and set it alight, and two men burned to death, and another one was shot in the shoulderblade by a crossbow bolt as they all ran for home, so it was a disaster, except for Cas, who missed all that. The man who was shot was called Aneiran, and when they pulled the bolt out it broke the shoulderblade clean across and he howled and rolled on the floor. The knight, a bastard from Surrey called Sir Wifwaf or Gifgaf or something, was all choler at this, and raged at them. He seemed to regard Cas as in charge now, and nothing the Cornishman said would dissuade him. Fetch some more diggers, you bastard, and build a new sow and get back at it.

So they built a new and bigger sow, on wheels this time, and Cas foraged some shields for them all to wear on their backs, and since he was in charge now, he took the team in closer to the tower. It was harder packed ground, and they needed to chip away some of the rock too, and things went more slowly. Exhausting work. They needed more muscle, so he asked Sir Wifwaf or whatever he was called, said 'can we have more bodies, your honour?' and was given four surly-looking youngsters from Wiltshire. The hardest part was the first week, when two of these boys got shot in the legs from not tucking in tight enough under the canopy, and a proper Cornish miner called Pen got his back broken by a throwndown rock and took three days to die. But once they cut through under an overhang, things got easier. Comfortable, back inside the womb of earth, his proper place. But it was slow work, and every time they got back to camp a succession of fucking knights and nobles came to badger them, why is it taking so long? Can you please hurry it up, sixpence a day my good fellows, a shilling a day. Cas had no objection to the extra money, but you can't cut rock like it's sand at the beach, your honour, my lord. There were bad words spoken, and Cas had to tighten his fists at his side, for striking a nobleman would be death. Then, sensing matters were growing dangerous, the town of *Limogessss* seemed to wake up, and started really counterattacking: scalding oil, rocks, bolts. Once a troop of a dozen men came out of a postern gate and came at them with swords. The first Cas knew – he was at the rock face, fully underground – was shouting and screaming behind him. Some canny Cheshire archers saw the attack and fired a bunch of arrows, and the Limogeans lost two men before they ran back, and by the time Cas got his head out of the hole the attack had been and gone, as had the English counterattack and the English being beaten back by crossbowmen on the battlements. Three of his miners were dead, including Bryn, his old friend. He waited until darkness, and then made a run back to the English camp.

Ceasing the mine was not an option. He recruited more men and went on with the digging. Then they heard a countermine tic-tic-ticking away in the earth, not far, and had to come out. This was not news the knights and lords wanted to hear: but there was no help for it, except to start a new excavation. So they moved right round to a new tower, and this was perhaps an even better site, should have chosen it from the get-go. But the delay meant that the nagging from the knights and lords grew more insistent. An old sick man was brought through on a litter, carried by four soldiers, to look across the ground to the wall. After he had been carried away somebody told Cas that he was the Black Prince himself. Cas couldn't believe it. More skeleton than warrior. Weakness in human form. There was something wrong about the whole show, Cas thought. Some malign spirit was joking with him. The Prince, as everyone knew, had conquered half of France more or less single-handed. This one was some sickly lordling, not the true Prince. Even if he *were* Edward, Prince of Wales and Aquitaine, he was in some truer sense not the real Black Prince. Reality, Cas knew, lies at a lower level than mere surface appearance, and can only be liberated with much backbreaking and dangerous work.

They needed to move quickly before the city got another countermine going, so Cas asked for and was given some more boys to help with the digging, and went back at it. The Limogeans threw down an absolutely massive piece of masonry, taken, Cas guessed, from the cathedral, or some building of similar bulk. It hit home. The sow was shattered to splinters when he wriggled up from his hole and one of his boys had a broken thigh. Getting back to the camp was a tricky matter that day, dragging the lad with him, and Cas was almost back when a crossbow bolt thwacked into his head and he fell straight down on the dry soil.

The bolt had struck the back of his head, just under the lip of his metal helmet, and gone in. He lay for a long while, on his side. There wasn't any pain. The afternoon wore on. Somebody noticed that he was still breathing and dragged him into the camp, where a surgeon pulled the bolt from his skull – that hurt, a little – and packed the hole with strawy mud. 'You're lucky,' he was told. 'It didn't go in very far.'

'Didn't go in very far,' said Cas. 'I'm lucky.' Miners in Cornwall shouting *chons da!* to one another before going underground.

He stood up, a little wobbly but able to walk, and he made his meandering way down to the river, where he was in the habit of washing himself after a day's digging. He stripped naked, got in up to his neck, and scrubbed his skin with some river weed, the slime of which was good at removing dirt. Then he splashed himself with clean water.

He felt like a door had been opened in his head, his very head itself. He felt that glory was pouring into his soul.

Back on the bank he sat watching the sunset and it was the first sunset he had ever seen. There was such a treasurehouse of colour and light heaped up on the horizon that he was amazed. He was astonished. He was astonished by the colour, and astonished that he'd never noticed it before. He peered at his own skin, dotted and tattooed with dirt that would never wash off. And around him the world had gone dark. The moon was a silver coin at arm's length and he could reach out and pluck it and put it in his pocket. There were more stars in the sky than he had ever realised. But then, he thought to himself, there were so many stars because there was so much sky to fill.

He was cold now, so he dressed and went back to the main camp and found a fire and warmed himself up. The flames were an intricate dance of fluid snakes, white-yellow and red, and this is where the stars were being born, in their great profusion, a constant upstream of bright sparks floating up to take their place in the firmament. He'd seen fire a thousand times, yet evidently had never really seen it before this night. The fire fizzed as a new branch was put on it. The sound was like the sea in the cove at Trethgowan.

In the morning he helped build a new sow, and the following day he was back underground as if nothing had happened. His head throbbed a bit when he exerted himself, and once his plug of mud popped clean out. But he simply fitted it back in and went back to work. The subterranean space in which he worked was transformed:

the soil a wadding of fine fabric, the stone solid gold. And his Dad was down there with him, digging away.

'Dad,' he said, when he took a break for some water, 'I'm glad to have you with me.'

'I was never properly buried, son,' his father replied, speaking Cornish. 'I've been an unsettled spirit since that day. But if you can dig this grave, the grave of a whole city – if *you* can dig it – and leave me here, under the weight of this tall tower, then I'll be at peace.'

'*Gonvedhav*,' he replied. I understand.

'Oh, you understand, my lad,' said his Da. 'You've always had your quickness for understanding. But for how long do you intend to remain content?'

Cas had no answer to that. That evening he ate his ration beside a campfire, and talked to nobody. Then he wandered off.

Afterwards he looked again at the moon. Not living, like the sun, but not dead and gone either. A bright ghost, in the sky. The flames in the fire were spectres, too: ghost snakes still writhingly in motion. The whole world was a kind of shimmering, beautiful haunting. He was weeping. Tears were cutting through the grime on his face. He wasn't sure why. It wasn't on account of his father. It had something to do with the brimming excess of beauty that there was in the world, and the weak foundations on which that beauty had been erected.

Newsreel (18)

He came as still
To his mother's bower
As dew in April
That falls on the flower.

POPE URBAN V DIES IN AVIGNON

Most learned man of his generation?

Let his epitaph be: he tried to move the papacy back to Rome, failed, and returned once again to Avignon, the fool the fool the fool the fool the fool.

The Fate of Aimeric. In late 1349 Geoffroi hatched a plan to retake Calais from the English by stealth. The scheme involved bribing one Aimeric de Pavia, who was commander of one of the city gate towers, to open a side-gate to the city so that Geoffroi and his accomplices might come inside at night. Aimeric was happy to take Geoffroi's money, but happy also to take Edward III's, and so betrayed Geoffroi to the English. They ambushed Geoffroi as he came through; his men were killed and Geoffroi himself badly wounded and taken prisoner. He languished in England for several years until a substantial ransom for his release was finally paid in July 1351. It so happened that Aimeric fell into Geoffroi's hands some years later. Geoffroi had not forgotten. He had Aimeric taken to St Omer, where, in front of a large and enthusiastic crowd, he had him tortured with red-hot irons and dismembered, limb by limb, with an axe.

Solitary I am, and solitary I wish to be,
Solitude is all my sweet love left to me.
Alone without a friend without a mate
And all appalled and mournful and irate.

LIMOGES FALLS

Town's futile resistance to the glorious Black Prince overcome

Walls tumble to the sound of Edward's mighty trumpets

TOWN AFIRE

for an old man he is old
for an old man he is grey
but a young man's heart is full of love
get away old man get away

underlying such year by year fluctuations it is easy to detect the swell of a secular tide the latter rose slowly and gently but with sufficient consistency to bring the prices of what on the eve of the black death of 1348 to a height nearly twice as great at the point at which we find them in the first two decades of the century whereas in the twenty years from 1210 to 1230 the price of wheat fluctuated around 3/– it climbed eventually to a bidecennial average of 6/– in that period of the second half of the fourteenth century the prices rose to a new

RENEWED CONCERNS FOR THE HEALTH OF
THE BLACK PRINCE

but a young man's heart is full of love

BULGARIA WEAKENED

Rival half-brothers Ivan Sratsimir and Ivan Shishman become co-Emperors of Bulgaria after the death of their father, King Ivan Alexander. Bulgaria is weakened by the split, according to reports from the capital city

LATIN PATRIACH OF CONSTANTINOPLE DIES following long illness all Constantinople instructed to mourn

but a young man's heart is full of love

SIR GUICHARD D'ANGLE

The order was no quarter, so no quarter was given. D'Angle had been a personal friend of the Black Prince for a decade now, and knew the man well enough to know he meant what he said. The wall came down with a strangely muted thunder, like a storm on the other side of a hill, and threw up a new wall twice as high, but this battlement was composed only of dust and soon this curtain fell away too. D'Angle was in with the first men at the breach, choking and coughing, swords out. No quarter meant none for ransom, but then again there would be plunder enough inside. Prince Edward was making an example of Limoges for disloyalty, and it would be a poor idea to disobey his commands. The city had it coming, anyway. They shouldn't have made the Prince wait for so long. A month!

Then again, a month is not so long in terms of a siege, so Limoges was still well supplied. The people he met on the other side of the breach were generally plump and well fed, and that disconcerted him. He was used to breaking down cities, sure, but by the time you get inside the folk are usually scarecrows and skeletons in old rags, covered in sores, eyes bulging and shining with suffering, and you're doing them a favour by cutting them down. But these people were like . . . well, they looked like *people*.

Ah well.

The first people they encountered were soldiers, but they were easily killed. Hundreds of English and Gascons were running through the gap, as the dust sifted down and cleared, and hundreds more lining up behind them, axes and swords ready. The men were bored, and now they had something to do, and the something was no quarter. So d'Angle cut down two Limoges soldiers, and by the time he was ready for the third the defenders were already throwing down their weapons and kneeling and begging for mercy. No mercy, though. A kneeling man's neck is at exactly the right height for a hearty swordswing. He cut a third of the way into one neck, hauled the sword out, and chipped away a glancing blow at another – it wasn't a good blow, but it nonetheless drew a bright red springspout of blood – and by then the others had grasped the fact that kneeling and surrendering would do them no good, so they were scrambling to their feet and trying to run off, only to get an axe in the back, or a sword, or get bashed over with a shield and stabbed on the ground.

They had the nearby gate open now. Archers were coming in behind him, and taking positions. The Limogean crossbowmen were giving up their weapons and attempting to surrender. Not that it did them any good. The sight of these men – paid by the city to defend it, throwing aside their heavy crossbows, the cowards, and screeching for their lives – made d'Angle furious. Cowards! He ran at the nearest and swept his sword right-left with full strength. The blade cut through the man's left leg entire, and chopped through to the bone of the left, and the coward went down in a pissgush of bright red. Screamed like a hog in the shambles. D'Angle swept his sword back left-right, pulling it up and the top scored across a second soldier's face in a rattle of flying teeth and blood: cleaving his upper lip, his nose and eye and sending his metal helmet popping high up in the air. D'Angle roared, and turned, but the remaining half dozen men were already running, so he leapt forward and cut at a retreating back, straight through the padded cloth, but the blade bounced off the shoulderblade and although the man stumbled he did not fall.

D'Angle stopped to regain his breath. The fury was draining out of him now. The street was full of English and Gascon raiders, hurrying forward, eager to kill and even more eager for plunder. D'Angle ran down a side street, stopping at the houses and shops on the way. Some had locked doors, some of the doors had no locks, and some had no door at all. He entered where his fancy took him to discover cowering and shrieking women, children, men in their dotage with liverspots on their bald heads like splash patterns of blood. They were mostly down on the ground, huddling against the wall, and that meant a series of sharp downward chopping motions, which was a problem because the blood tended to splash forward and wet his legs. But downstrokes were at least quick, since of course none of these people were wearing helmets, heads could be eggcracked easy enough; and the blows put an end to their skreeks of *ayez pitié! ayez pitié!* His hose was sodden by the time he emerged. He made his way towards the cathedral tower, and the streets were full of people killing other people.

He left bloody footprints as he stalked.

D'Angle was starting to get tired. Killing people with a sword is like chopping wood: the muscles of the arms soon enough begin to ache. Still: best press on. Best get it out of the way. The sooner we crack on, the sooner we finish. A mob of twenty or so people were running towards him, mouths wide, eyes terrified, some already bleeding, chased along by some leisurely-jogging Gascon axemen. D'Angle took his stance; and as the crowd came on he cut right-left, left-right, right-left. They were a mixed bunch: various old men, half a dozen men in uniform, a nobleman holding an expensive looking hat in his hands to stop his head-wound getting blood all over it, some women, some children. As a nobleman himself, d'Angle was of course taller than the commoners, so his chest-level sweeps tended to cut into their faces. He managed a particularly good strike at the Limogean noble's neck that severed everything except the skin at the back so that the fellow's head flopped over against his spine in a spurt of red. Of the twenty, only four got past him, and one of those slipped in the spilled blood and lay on the ground sobbing. D'Angle stamped his leather boot – absolutely dripping with blood, it was, surely stained forever and the pair had cost him fifty shillings in Southampton – on this one's head, but that proved an error. The sobbing stopped, yes, but the thrust unbalanced d'Angle and he almost fell, as if tripping over a boulder. He had to dance along on his other foot to regain his balance. He could hear the Gascons laughing at his impromptu ballet. This fired up his anger again, and he ran at the civilians who had run past him and cut them all down with sharp strikes to the back and neck.

He stopped at the corpse of the near-decapitated noble, just to see if he had been carrying a purse or anything of the sort, but there was nothing except a ring on one finger. D'Angle took this. With all the blood it slipped off easily enough. Then he was off again, jogging in the direction of the cathedral. Some Welshmen were joking and laughing, bows slung over their backs, daggers out, stabbing at figures kneeling, or writhing on the ground, or pressed up against a wall. The plaster behind them had a vineleaf pattern, complete with grapes, all of it overpainted with fresh blood. And here was another coward-soldier, hurrying round the corner. d'Angle took pleasure in hacking into his flank with his sword. The man went down on all fours, like a dog, and d'Angle swiped down and took his head off, and then regretted having given him so honourable a death. Two of his comrades, cowards both, were limping after him, trailing blood over the pavingstones, and d'Angle cut at their faces, and when they turned away screaming, cupping their shredded visages in their hands, he cut at their legs and buttocks, taking chunks of flesh out like a butcher.

Round the corner were some priests, tubby-bellied and weeping, trying to run but getting tangled up in their own robes. No armour here, so d'Angle impaled the first on his sword, forcing the tip in just under the ribcage. The others were begging, *ne occide me! ne occide me!* as if Latin would save them. d'Angle took an ear off with a swift upcut, and then brought the blade down again and cut the same man's arm clean off at the shoulder. Hoicking the sword up again opened a new mouth in the fellow's fat belly.

Limogeans were rushing up the steps to the main door of the cathedral, as if that would save them. Nothing would save them. The *terrible prince noir* had ordered their deaths, and so death was inevitable. It annoyed d'Angle that they couldn't simply accept it. He waded into the mass of people, hacking and chopping. A head bounced free like a dropped cabbage. People tumbled left and right. He splashed through puddles of gloop. A bloodsoaked cloak got itself tangled around his sword and he had to stop a moment to pull this free. With one stroke he took a woman's jaw off, and it fell away, tongue and all.

Some of the English foot soldiers were going into the cathedral after the civilians, but d'Angle stopped for a while, leaning on his sword. The steps were carpeted in dead bodies – or most of the bodies were dead, and some were dying. A noblewoman came hurrying towards him, arms out, shrieking *ayez pitié bon monsieur ayez pitié douce monsieur ayez pitié*. A good-looking woman. Very expensively dressed. He swung his sword and it stuck in her chest, in amongst her ribs, and when she dropped down clucking and gasping and spitting blood the motion of her falling body yanked the sword from his hand. He retrieved his weapon and examined it: getting blunt: a great many little indentations and pits in its two cutting edges.

He sheathed his sword and took out his dagger. Then, walking unhurriedly back towards the gate, he took stock. Here were three citizens banging at a housedoor begging to be let inside, but the folk inside were not loosing the lock: d'Angle stabbed one in the side, grabbed the hair of another and slit his throat, and watched the third – a woman – dash off in so blind a terror that she ran straight into a wall and fell down. He went over to her and *coupez*'d her *gorge*. He walked on. Here were half a dozen children, all gripping one another in a shuddering mass cuddle, eyes wide, and he cut all their throats. Here was an ancient old man, maybe a hundred years old, and he had a fancy engraved buckler in his left hand and an antique sword in his right, and he staggered towards d'Angle, offering combat. D'Angle sidestepped him and knifed him in the flank. The oldster dropped to both knees, weeping, letting the sword go, and d'Angle stabbed him again in the other flank, and left him. Here were more of those civilians pestering *ayez pitié ayez pitié* and he swept his knife very rapidly in a series of Z patterns and they went down clutching their faces, or else ran off. As if running would save them. There was nowhere to run.

D'Angle left the city through the breach in the wall, and washed himself quickly in the river. Then back to his tent, where he told his boy to sharpen his sword, and be quick. Then he presented himself at the Prince's tent and was received. 'How is the passage of arms, my friend?' Edward asked him, in English. He was increasingly prone to speak English these days, which forced d'Angle to reply in his awkward, accented version of that barbarian tongue. 'It will be quick, Highness,' he said. 'The Limogean soldiers have all thrown down their weapons, the cowards, and the civilians are sheep, bleating and flocking together, as they always are in this situation. You have men beside all gates? They will try to open them and flee to the countryside.'

'Oh,' said the Black Prince, his face set with determination. 'We have men at *all* the gates.'

D'Angle gratefully accepted a flagon of wine, which he drank in one draught. His hammering heart relented a little. He closed his fingers into two fists, and then opened his fists, like a flower greeting the sunlight, and felt calmness trickling back into him. Some knights brought in the Bishop of Limoges, his hands bound, his face bruised, into the Prince's presence. *'Ayez pitié de moi, grand prince,'* this cleric begged. But Edward was in no pitying mood. He lectured the Bishop about his disloyalty in closing the gates of the city against him. The Bishop tried to protest, swearing on the Holy Cross that he had personally counselled against such treachery, that he had begged the lords and constables of the place to uphold their oaths to the English crown, but that he had been ignored and overruled. The Prince was having none of this. 'Take him outside and cut his head off, right away,' he ordered. And so the prelate was dragged outside.

Now the Prince declared he wanted to see the city, so his people took up his litter and carried him towards the gate. D'Angle begged the honour of accompanying him, and ran back to his own tent to retrieve his sword. His boy had done an indifferent job sharpening this, but it was better than it had been, so he changed out of his bloodsoaked hose and strapped on his now-clean breastplate and ran back to the Prince's litter.

Back inside the city, every street was strewn with dead bodies. The Prince's men had some difficulty stepping over the corpses to keep their charge on a level, unjolting path. Some Limogeans, seeing the Prince's blazon on his litter, ran forward to beg mercy. D'Angle, and some others, made short work of these: a downstroke opened a V in the skull of one, and sliced across to open the belly of another and so permitted the guts to come roping out and down. A third tried to run, and d'Angle sprinted after her, and speared her with swordpoint through the small of her back. This cut made her legs stiffen abruptly, such that she leapt into the air like a hare and fell with a thump to the ground, which was comical to watch. Other citizens, poorly dressed and whimpering, were crawling on all fours along the gutter beneath a high wall, and d'Angle strolled along, holding his sword with two hands, point down, and jabbing at them, one after the other.

Two English foot soldiers, armed with axes, were chopping at a locked door, and from the other side the shrieks and wails of a large group could be heard. The wood was soon shards and the men went inside, and d'Angle and four others went in too. A merchant's house: several items of furniture, and hangings on the wall, and a dozen Limogeans cowering against the wall. One held his hands out at d'Angle, palms front, and a sweep of the sword took the fingers off. But d'Angle's muscles were starting to ache with all this heavy swinging and swinging, so he sheathed his sword and took out his dagger. The English axemen had gone through to the back of the house, from where the sound of axeblows and screaming could be heard. D'Angle worked his way methodically along the line of people with his knife *ayez pitié grand chevalier ayez pitié ayez pitié* and found the easiest thing was to grasp a hank of hair with his left hand and push the knifeblade down behind the collar bone with his right. The blade was long enough to kill quickly, and there was less blood that way. On his way out he spotted a golden candlestick, and tucked it into his belt. It was, he reflected, surprising that there was only one. He could imagine somebody had already pilfered the other, but if they had taken one why not take both?

Outside d'Angle set off to rejoin the Prince's litter. Round a corner he came upon a little scene: some Welshmen had dragged a priest out of his church, stripped him naked, and castrated him. They were holding the severed testicles in the direction of his church and genuflecting, drinking wine from the rich-looking communion goblet they had presumably taken from that very building. The priest writhed on the floor. On the far side of the road, behind a little heap of corpses, two more Welshmen were ripping the habit from an elderly nun. D'Angle hurried past, over a carpet of civilian corpses.

He chanced upon some youngsters, apprentices perhaps, judging by their clothes, wringing their hands and hooting like little birds with *ayez pitié milord ayez pitié*. He beat one of these on his head with his metalled fist until the skull caved, stabbed another, and tripped a third who tried to run, and then put his knife in at the back of the lad's neck. Four got away, but ran straight into some Welshmen, who struck them down with maces and left them motionless on the ground. Here were three nuns, and d'Angle was made inexplicably furious by the sight of them – strange, really, for his own sister was mother superior of a convent – and he battered them with his fists and cut them with his knife and left them dead and their flesh all ripped and tattered.

By the time he caught up with the Prince's litter again, the Earl of Cambridge, blood smoking on his armour, was trying to persuade Edward to permit the taking of prisoners. 'It would be a mistake to lose so many rich ransoms, sire, surely,' he said. 'No quarter, I said, the Prince croaked, not looking at the noble lord. 'No quarter, I meant. Kill them all, my lord.'

Cambridge loped off, looking piqued. D'Angle understood his anger of course; but then again – this was to be a long campaign, all the way across country to Paris, and there would be plenty of chances for rich ransom and plunder before the end of it. For now the best bet was to finish this town quickly. No point in drawing everything out. Half a dozen young women, maidens of good family according to their own cries for pity, tried to approach the Prince's litter and beg mercy, or ransom, but Edward turned his face away from them, and soldiers made quick work of them. D'Angle stabbed a plump youngster in the breast, and cut the throat of a skinnier girl, perhaps her younger sister. He noticed that the first was on the floor but still alive, and decided he hadn't cut her deep enough; so he crouched down and drew the knife along her throat to her wet-sounding gasps.

Some soldiers had set fire to a small church, and the people inside – scores and scores of them, hoping perhaps for sanctuary – were tumbling through the door coughing and vomiting and barely able to voice their *ayez pitié pitié pitié*. Most ended up in a writhing heap, and d'Angle joined in the killing: stabbing down with his dagger right-handed, left-handed, into backs and fronts, faces and arses, cutting and slicing. He stood back when he thought he had finished, but one of the soldiers – a Spaniard, by his face – said he knew how these heaps of civilians went, people lay quiet but alive under the press of corpses and hoped thereby to survive the assault. So the men-at-arms pulled dead bodies from the top, and soon enough they uncovered a layer of the still-living, who tried to wriggle away, or who begged for mercy, or thrashed in panic. All these must be cut to pieces. One wormed its way along the ground towards d'Angle, and as the other men-at-arms stabbed and hacked he put his foot on the small of this thing's back and slid the knife into its fundament, slicing up and away to release a quantity of blood from the lower end and a quantity of screaming from the other. Smoke was spewing blackly from the door of the church now, and rolling into the sky. The Prince had not specifically given the order to fire the town yet, so this was premature and possibly dangerous, but surely such an order would come. There were yelps and shrieks from inside, but they were soon silenced.

Two musicians ran at him, holding their musical instruments in front of them, perhaps believing they could buy their lives with a song. A lute. A horn. D'Angle cut one in the throat just under the Adam's apple, and chopping the other across the face so deep that his brains were put on show, and that was the end of them.

A large group of Limogeans had been herded into a street impasse, or else had run down there in panic. Some Englishmen with axes and cudgels were working away this group but the clogging of the narrow way was making progress hard. D'Angle joined in. Never let it be said he shirked his duty, no matter how laborious. He cut left and right with his sword, and outheld hands were lopped clean off, elbows smashed, as the citizens tried to protect themselves. He pushed out with three swift backhand strikes, flexing at his elbow, and cut deep gashes into the fronts of two wailing women. Back again and he heard the collar bone of one haggard-looking man snap like a stepped-on twig. He was an elderly fellow in a stained linen shirt, but his moustache and beard were well-trimmed and his skin was pale, so perhaps he was a nobleman hoping to disguise himself as a poor man and so escape justice. Justice was not to be avoided, though. A couple of the Englishmen recognised d'Angle, and cried joyfully 'Sir Guichard! Sir Guichard, you French bastard! Welcome to the coal face, Sir Guichard!' and he grinned at them and went at it again. A woman was trying to protect her baby by huddling round it: d'Angle cut several times into her back and then she slumped to the side, spilling the wailing infant onto the floor. This latter d'Angle speared with the tip of his sword, like a piece of meat on a plate; but that only made it scream louder. Its little face was as red as the setting sun. D'Angle stabbed it again and again, but the tough little creature refused to die. Annoyed, he set his foot on it and cut away at its little neck until the wailing stopped.

He pulled back from the impasse, and looked at his blade. It was getting blunt again, but it would be bothersome to go beyond the walls, sharpen it and return. If he did that he'd miss all the rest of the killing. So he went on and set to with his sword, using it now as a club. It worked pretty well at fracturing bones, breaking open skulls and so on, although this resulted in rather more bloodspatter than was ideal in terms of his own cleanliness. Couldn't be helped. Eventually all the civilians in that blocked-off street were dead.

D'Angle wandered back out to the square. There were civilians on the roofs, and several fell off, or perhaps jumped. There were children running naked through the streets covered in blood, their own or others'. One young girl grasped d'Angle's knees. He hadn't seen her coming, and was startled by the pressure on his legs. But it was not enough to topple him, and he cut the back of the kid's neck with his dagger, but though this killed her she didn't release her grip and he had to prise her off. A very old woman stood in one small square, apparently unnoticed, back straight, singing *en contemplant la croix benie* in a clear, thin voice. It was a hymn he remembered from his childhood. There was something rather fine about this, so d'Angle put his knife away, and caved-in her head with a single heavy blow of his sword. Her head lolled at a crazy angle, but she dropped to her knees as cleanly as if she were at prayer.

The Prince's litter had been set down, so that Edward could watch the combat of three French knights: Sir John de Villemur, Hugh de la Roche, and Roger de Beaufort, this last gentleman son to the Count of Beaufort – governors of the city, and leading figures. Panting a little, splashed all over with blood, d'Angle came to stand beside his leader, and watched. The three knights were fighting well, holding off three English lords with a series of fluent moves.

The Duke of Lancaster was engaged with Sir John de Villemur, who was a hardy knight, strong and well made. The Earl of Cambridge had singled out Sir Hugh de la Roche, and the Earl of Pembroke was fighting Roger de Beaufort.

D'Angle might have been watching a practice bout at tourney, or on a training day. It was clear that these three knights had resolved to sell their lives dearly, and for the first time since the wall had tumbled d'Angle felt a twinge of pity that such chivalrous gentlemen must die. But must is must. He was about to say something to that effect to Edward, when, astonishingly, he saw tears rolling down the Prince's lean face. 'Oh,' he croaked, slipping into French for the first time that day, 'oh, give them quarter, such chivalrous brave knights, they must have quarter.' Several other nobles shouted the words through to the English lords, who drew back and rested on their swords. The Frenchmen grasped what had happened. 'My lords, we are yours,' shouted one, in a clear voice. 'You have vanquished us. Therefore by God we beg you, act according to the law of arms.' 'By God,' replied the Duke of Lancaster, 'Sir John, we do not intend otherwise, and we accept you for our prisoners.' As these three knights were taken, English and Welsh cheers echoed around the little square.

Still, some three thousand Limogeans had been killed to these three prisoners spared. Prince Edward ordered the sappers to stay back. There was no need to dig a pit, he said, for they would not occupy the city, which would instead burn, and so provide a decent pyre for the fallen. D'Angle supposed the sappers were happy at this news since it saved them an afternoon's labour; though it also meant that some plunder would inevitably be lost. He strode back out of the city, stripped, washed in the river for a second time that day, and regained his tent in that pleasant state of physical weariness one experiences after prolonged physical labour. He ate a little food, and drank some wine, and then he lay on his couch and slept for an hour. When he woke it was still afternoon, and he dressed and returned. A great deal of booty had been removed from Limoges, and more was coming out. The fires were not supposed to be set until the following morning. But then somebody or other got too eager, and a line of houses was aflame by dusk and the flames spread quickly. By nightfall the Black Prince's camp was pitched alongside the world's biggest bonfire. There was grumbling at this, at the loss of treasures yet to be winkled out of Limoges. The shrieks from inside the flames suggested that people had hidden in upper-rooms and cache-holes, hoping to escape their fate, and were now being burned alive – and if people were hidden, then surely treasure was too. But when d'Angle joined Edward in his tent for a select victory feast the Prince was blithe about the loss of money. 'There are a hundred towns between here and Paris,' he told the half dozen lords assembled around the table. 'After today it will be a brave town who shuts its gates against us. We shall have rich pickings through the heart of France.'

They all toasted the Prince's victory.

D'Angle complimented the Prince on the wine he was serving.

'Where is this from?' Edward asked his secretary.

'From the Bishop's own palace, your Highness.'

'A very treasonable bishop,' Edward grumbled. The memory of the treachery lit his eyes with a hectic flame. He really, d'Angle thought, did not look very well. 'At any rate,' the Prince said. 'I suppose he will bring a handsome ransom.'

There was some discussion amongst the noble lords as to whether the Bishop had indeed been beheaded as the Prince had ordered, or whether he had been pardoned at the last and so could be ransomed. Edward was in no mental condition to confirm or deny. He was barely awake. His hands were shaking so hard he could only drink when an attendant held the cup to his mouth. He made a series of odd wheezing, whistling, keening noises. He kept drifting off into a stuporous doze.

'A fine word, *chivalry*,' announced the Earl of Cambridge, to the company as a whole. 'It means what is appropriate to a chevalier.

And what is a chevalier? A man on a horse.' He laughed at this, as if he had said something very witty.

'Treasonable bishop,' murmured Edward. 'Bishopable treason.' His attendant once more angled the goblet of wine at his mouth, but the red juice fell from his lips and dribbled down his neck. He closed his eyes. When his attendant attempted to mop this spillage up Edward made a series of indignant baby noises. His arms flapped vaguely at his side.

The Earl of Cambridge drained his drink, and stood up. 'And a man on a horse,' he announced to the company, 'is little different to a man on foot, or on a litter. Man is man, man is damned. Man is God's one mistake.'

There was total silence in the tent, until the Prince farted, giggled at his own emission and then slid down his couch. The Earl of Cambridge unbuckled the garter he was wearing, and threw it to the ground. 'So much,' he announced, 'for chivalry.' And with that, he left the tent.

BLACK GEORGE

He was in some place he did not recognise. It was hard to make out the sort of place it was, France or England, summer or winter. There was light, but of a strange quality, like the light of twilight or early dawn except that it filled the whole sky. George looked up and saw, isolated against the brightness, spots of intenser brightness like great sprawling constellations of stars. Beneath his feet a table-flat green field stretched before and behind, left and right.

George's hand went to his neck. It felt rough, but then it always felt rough. It didn't feel – what? Stretched? Raw? He wasn't sure, now he came to think of it, that it felt at all. Then he noticed his arm was clad in a sleeve of feathers: a sleeve of blue feathers, green feathers, black feathers, each plume streaked with lime or purple or maroon. Both his arms were so sleeved, as was his torso. He brushed at the feathers covering his left arm, and puffs of golden dust came off.

He had noticed his approach, but the cleric was standing beside him – the same cleric he had paid three pounds, back in London, for the letter to introduce him to the White Company. Was it the same cleric? He appeared, now, to be wearing a bishop's garb, although one with strange colouration. Or was that the odd light? But he recognised the man's face. Did he?

'What are you doing here?' he growled at the cleric, fondling his own throat again.

The fellow was reading something from a small green-bound book, occasionally marking something in the margins with a feather-pen. He looked up at George, and his eyes were owlbig and gleaming.

'I am not here,' he said. 'Only you are here.'

'Where?' George demanded. 'Is this still Provence? I was in Provence until a moment ago. Unless I was in France. Not London though, I think. Or I don't think.'

'Where,' agreed the cleric. 'When.'

'This?' George growled, looking around. 'This is what being dead is like?'

'Being dead,' said the cleric, a little primly, 'is like being alive. Only – less so.' He showed George the open two pages of his book, but the writing was in a strange squaresquiggly alphabet George couldn't read. To be fair, he could barely read English. This, though, was well beyond him.

'So is this Purgatory? Am I to be purged?'

'You were dead already,' the cleric said. 'You were always already dead. All in Adam are dead. Only in Christ are you made alive.'

'Christ is indeed my saviour,' George said, feeling oddly inhibited from saying so. Why the reluctance? These were the proper things to say. 'Christ,' he growled, pushing the words out, 'is truly my salvation.'

'There is the question,' said the cleric, 'of sins.'

George didn't reply. Of course there were many sins. That surely goes without saying. He was born into sin, and people don't rise above the station into which they are born. Society requires order and harmony, heavenly society just as much as earthly society, and any too-rapid zigzag changes in one's circumstances would destabilise that. It would have done a violence to the structure God ordained to have shucked off his original sin, and therefore this was not a thing even to be attempted.

He waited.

'Paperwork too,' said the cleric. 'That's more pressing. We have to determine that before we can go any further. There is, for instance, an earthly documentation from the Pope at Avignon excommunicating you.'

'Ah, no,' George was eager to explain. 'He *did* excommunicate us, yes, on account of the captain I was fighting under. But he undid that.'

'And later redid it.'

'I wasn't told about that.'

'Whether you were told or not,' said the cleric, mildly, 'is hardly relevant.'

'Surely,' said George, 'that won't stand in my way? Of getting into heaven?'

The cleric looked hard at George. There was something odd about his eyes – beyond, that is, their bizarre size and luminosity. 'Let's run through the order of judgements. Were you always obedient?'

'I served in the army of Edward the King and Edward his son, the Prince of Wales,' George said, standing up straighter. 'I followed orders.'

'That's not a very full answer, now, is it? You see, obedience is the prime thing, and from what I've got written down here, you've never been awfully good at it. Remember: Adam and Eve's first sin was disobedience, and the divine judgement for that was death, and the infirmities and miseries of mortal life. Then there are the sins of violating love, insulting the Holy Ghost and so on. Shall I tell you what is highlighted in my book, here, under your name?'

'Tell me.'

'You shall not kill.'

'I have a clean conscience, on that front,' said George, firmly. 'It doesn't mean *all* killing, that commandment. It means unlawful killing. Well. I was a soldier, and I killed a lot of people. But that's what soldiers do.' Something came back to him and he spoke it: 'God made me a soldier.'

'God made you a man,' replied the cleric. 'You made yourself a soldier.' George got a sudden flush of realisation as to whom it is the cleric recalls to his mind. Not his wife, who was love and beauty and gentleness in a single human form. But his wife's sister, who was sharp and insightful and full of judgement.

'I am damned, then?' he demanded, trying at least for the rude dignity of the dying soldier. Jesus may promise life, but soldiers know that there is a deeper truth, one that was true before Christ came into the world, and which remains true even after his mission. That everybody dies. That death cannot be defeated, or shirked, or avoided. That the only thing that matters is how you encounter death. Very well, he thought: I'll not snivel.

'This heaven will pass away, and the one above it will pass away,' said the cleric. 'The dead are not alive, and the living will not die.'

'You'll have to run that past me again,' said George, narrowing his eyes.

The cleric, looking increasingly ambiguous between masculine and feminine, smacked shut the book in his, or her, hands. 'Well, let me explain what happens now. There are, I'm sure you'll remember from your Sunday School, two judgements. One when you die, individually; and another when the whole world dies – the last judgement, when Christ himself comes to separate the, well, you know.'

'So,' said George. 'And what follows?'

'Now,' said the cleric, 'I will take the amount of pain you have caused other people and the amount of pleasure you have caused other people. I will subtract the smaller amount from the larger, and you will experience – you yourself, all at once – the remainder. The remainder of pleasure, perhaps. Or of pain. Depending on how you have lived your life. It might be a blast of pure bliss that will carry you, wonderfully, through to the end of time. Or it might be . . . otherwise.'

'That's not fair,' George complained. 'Nobody told me that my business in the world was to bring *pleasure* to other people.'

'I think, if you look back,' the cleric said, 'you'll find that everybody was telling you that, all the time.'

A flicker of hope. 'Well, this depends, I think, how we are to define the two terms. If the French army had invaded England,' he insisted, warming to his theme, 'there would have been a great deal of pain to a great many people. I fought in the army, and prevented that. Surely that counts for something?'

The cleric said nothing to this, although his, or her, expression was eloquent enough.

'Do I have a choice about this?' George asked, quietly.

'Life is when a person has choices,' the cleric said, briskly. 'Choices stop when you're dead. That's very nearly the definition of death, you know. Shall we?'

'Let's get it over with,' George grumbled.

The whole green world tilted, swayed, rolled back. The rocking was centred on his body. His body was swaying. What is happening? he asked. But the cleric was no longer a cleric, and was now unmistakeably a vision of his sister-in-law, clothed in light, a bird, a beautiful bird, holding in her winged arms a book made of light. They're loosening the rope, she sang. Untying it. In a moment you'll drop to the ground. Untying the rope, he said. Dropping the body, she said. You'll feel the release, and then the plunge will register in your stomach and the sensation of falling in your inner ear. But, for you, it will be a very long time, a very long time, a very very long time, before you feel the thump of striking the dusty ground. He reached out to her then, for he could sense gravity shifting the terms of its grip upon him. He was about to say something else when the whole world dropped, and him with it.

PART 7. ENGLAND

Newsreel (19)

PREORDER *THE BRUS* TODAY. John Barbour's epic poem of Knights Errant and Chivalrous, a vivid recreation in verse of the celebrated Battle of Bannockburn: available from all good escritories and parchment titivators today.

'Al fredome is a noble thing'

ANGLO-PORTUGUESE ALLIANCE SIGNED

PHILIP II OF TARANTO HANDS OVER RULE OF GREEK ACHAEA TO HIS COUSIN, JOANNA I OF NAPLES

DANCING MANIA IN AIX-LA-CHAPELLE

Prince returns to England. Edward, Prince of Wales and Aquitaine, Count of Biscay, heir to the throne of England and France, experienced a worsening of his medical condition in the town of Cognac, and has returned to England to seek the expert medical care only English doctors can provide.

The following statement from his office has been released: 'the noble prince's health has taken a temporary downturn, but with proper medical care we fully anticipate that he will be able to resume his military duties before the end of the year.'

FOR SALE. Treatises

A Treatise, entitled, The Enchantment of the Lullillus, and a Tract against such as Pray to Dæmons;
A Treatise against those that oppose the Pre-eminence of Jesus Christ and the Virgin;
A Tract against the Oath taken by the Pope and Cardinals after the

Death of Urban V. and against the Letter of the University of Paris, proving beyond all doubt that Eymericus was not dead in 1370 as some have assured us;
A Treatise against the Chymists;
The Correctory of the Reprimand: A Treatise against those, who will define the Time of the End of the World;
A Treatise against Astrologers, Necromancers, and other Diviners;
A Treadle against those, who had broached this Heresy, That St. John the Evangelist was the Natural Son of the Virgin Mary;
A New Treatise of the Admirable Sanctity of the Mother of God-Man

---

THE BLACK PRINCE

He lay in his chamber at Westminster Palace, and listened to the sucking and cooing of the great river as it flowed. Sweet Thames. There was a wisdom hidden in those endless vowels, as in the hushing of the breeze, some hidden message the world was trying to convey to him. He had better nights and worse nights, but never, it seemed, good nights. His doctors said the wine was unbalancing his humours, but he was not beholden to doctors, and he drank a good deal of wine. One morning he woke to the cry of gulls and the splashing of the river as the tide fought the flow, and he felt he was on the very cusp of understanding what the waters were saying. But comprehension slid past him, and he let it go.

His whole body was covered in sweat, and his legs were shaking. A servant came to help him up, pointedly not mentioning the stink of piss – came to remove the sheets and wipe him all over with a square of damp linen, and feed him some gruel, like a baby. He preferred a posset of milk and wine to start the day, but the physicians had forbidden this. No wine at all until lunchtime, they said. He was a prince and they were mere commoners. How dare they command him? How could they? Yet he didn't fight them. The fight was all gone out of him now.

He had them set a chair by his casement, so that he could look out. Down at the shores of Thorny Island, across at the far side of the river where buildings snaggletoothed the bank. A boat passed slowly upstream on four oars, in a pulsing forward-two-yards back-one-yard motion: forward two and back one, forward two and back one. There was something profound in that pulse – wasn't there? He pondered it idly and didn't plumb its mystery. Thorny Island was where King Canute had bid the waves retreat, and been made wet for his pains. And now there was a palace built here. One day the palace would be nothing but the outline of rooms, mud banks and river-grass, not one brick standing upon another. A seagull coasted the air like a skater, turned its head and shrieked at him: *qui-ose? qui-ose? qui-ose?*

—Begone, he yelled back, and shook a wobbly arm. But even so feeble an action wore him out. Once on a time city walls had tumbled, and a thousand fine French knights had died, from one gesture of this right arm. Now it ached and shivered even in the warmth of day. Allez! *Allez!* he croaked.

The bird took him at his word.

He thought of asking for Joan, but then remembered she was not in London. His son was in the palace though, so he struck the bell and summoned his servant to get him dressed. That took them both a long time. He had heard Wycliff preach, and would hear him preach again, he decided. But not today.

He was carried out onto the small well-kept lawn of one of the palace's inner courts, and settled in a chair. The sun was warm on his face. Two thrushes bickered in the branches. A bird-husband and bird-wife? A maid-of-honour cleared her throat.

And here was Richard: sweet-faced but sombre, dressed exquisitely in a miniature surcoat with the three lean lions and clusters of trifoil feathers. He greeted his father with his piping boy's voice. Like a woman's voice.

—The feathers, said Ned, in a creaky voice. Did I tell you where they come from?

—Yes, Father.

Ned didn't hear his son's reply, or didn't understand it, and so explained yet again how he had fought at Cressy in France when he was not much older than the boy was now (the boy was not yet nine, so this was not quite the truth). How he had discovered the corpse of the good old King of Bohemia, dead honourably in battle, blind but brave, fallen on the ground.

—Yes, Father, said Richard, obediently. His two nurses hovered in the background.

—So that's where it comes from, said Ned, truncating the story, his tiredness suddenly swimming up and taking him. The three feathers and the motto as well. The King of Bohemia had a son who was fighting for the French. Blind and old he was, the father I mean, and he asked to be led into the fighting. He was killed – not by me, thank God – and I took over his emblem and his motto. I was only a boy, not much older than you are now. Sixteen I was.

—Yes, Father.

—Blind, but brave. His son was fighting for the French. I suppose he knew he would die in that battle, but he rode into the fight anyway. That's where I got it from.

Something in his son's expression stung him. He realised he was rambling. He tried to gather his strength, inwardly, and sat up a little straighter.

—*I serve*, he said. I didn't realise what a responsibility it was.

—I serve, repeated Richard. And then, in his clear, flute-like voice: I serve what?

—Oh, something very vague – honour, chivalry. God. What it ought to mean (he thought, for some reason, of the endless song of the river) what it ought to mean is doing something for the people.

When you become Prince of Wales – if you become Prince of Wales – try and do something for the people.

—You said *if*, Richard said, quickly. Sharp little eyes.

—In the first place that depends on your grandfather. But in the last place it depends on Parliament.

—The little men?

—Not so little, said Edward, feeling a huge weariness pushing up inside him, like a tide. Not so little.

Not so little. He was exhausted and trembling, and the nurses led the boy away. His people took him to the main hall, and he ate some fowl and creamed turnip, and drank two goblets of wine, and almost immediately threw the whole lot straight up into a bowl they had ready. He was sweating. His whole body was trembling, his arms like pennants in strong wind, and he was sweating so hard it dribbled into his eyes. He was carried, as a wounded knight is borne from the battlefield, by two strong men and taken to his chamber. A physician bled him with sharp little knives, and in his increasing delirium he thought he was being attacked by Frenchmen with crossbow bolts, or that he was Christ on the cross and the Romans – Italians, Genoese, mercenaries – were stabbing him in the arm with their spears, aiming for his flank but striking only his side. He wept, and railed, and struggled, and his man had to hold him against his bed whilst the physicians took more blood. Eventually the letting calmed him, and he breathed shallowly, and felt very thirsty. When he tried to say *j'ai soif* the words stuck in his throat and would not come out, but when he said I am thirsty the words came babbling out.

His people brought him something to drink. He dozed, and woke with a gasp. A dove was perched on his windowsill, but it was much too big to be a regular dove, and there were many brilliant hues somehow tangled in with its white feathers, and its beak was red like a ruby, and its eyes were blue like a sapphire, and the whiteness of its feathers was of a clearness like snow or milk or the desert sky at noon or bleached bones that have lain in the sun for decades or the central whiteness of a star that has looked, coldly, down upon humanity for unimaginable eons and will continue to look down for eons more, equally indifferent to caring or uncaring.

—Sir? Sir?

His man is touching him on the shoulder. Ned comes fully awake.

—What? he croaks. What?

—You were shouting, sir. A tree, a sword, a great crowd of leaves.

Ned looked about.

—Bring me something to drink, Ned croaked. Then fetch my priest.

The priest came, clutching one of Ned's fine illustrated Gospel Books. He heard the Prince's confession, and absolved him, and set him the kind of penance a very sick man might be capable of, and afterwards Ned told the holy man his dream. He had planted his sword in a wide, flat, green plain, and the ground had bled like it was flesh, but afterwards his blade had turned into a tree and branches had creaked out, and many leaves – a great mass of leaves – an uncountable number of leaves. And each leaf bore a human face. Pray to Christ, was the priest's advice, and to his holy mother, and to God himself. Pray for peace and recovery. Pray for understanding, too, of your dream and of anything. For understanding only comes from God.

Ned tried eating once more, but once more vomited up his meal. An hour later, as the light over the Thames dimmed and sweetened, and a golden hue lay upon his windowsill, he drank a little milk, which he was able to keep down. He was too weak to stand. Each breath was a little hill he had to, as it were, march up and over. Each exhalation was a struggle and a small victory.

The vision of the dove had been the Holy Spirit. Or he had feverdreamed something along those lines. Idly he thought to himself: why three? Why not seven? Or many millions? Would not that speak more magnificently to the splendour of God? But then he knew from experience that though a larger army might overawe the eyes, it was in reality a tiresome entity: more mouths to feed, more people to discipline. The smaller army beats the larger, as at Cressy and Poitiers, provided only it is tighter and more disciplined. And so, with the divine. What God prized was not hugeness, but purity. So the real question was not *why not three million?*, but rather, as the Mohammedan might ask, *why so many as three? Why not one?* It must, Ned thought, drowsily, speak to something fundamental about the cosmos. Above, and here, and below. Father, son and what? What? Spirit, spirit, spirit. As opposed to: body. To body. To body. He looked at his own wasted and uglified corpus and told himself: you have been too concerned with the things of the body, the pleasures of the body, and the discipline of the body. Bodies fighting other bodies on the battlefield. Bodies arrayed in glory. Bodies tangling with one another in the bedroom. He had neglected the spirit. And that was what the Holy Spirit meant: that there was spirit, and that it was holy. It was so obvious it almost shocked him. He began to sweat, as if with fear, or exertion. God was – God, Himself, neither body nor spirit but rather the ground of everything, the page upon which the manuscript of the universe was illuminated. Christ was the body, who must have experienced the blisses of the body when he was on Earth, and who certainly experienced the pains of the body when he was crucified. If it were merely God and Christ, then religion would be saying: the cosmos is God, and inside it God has created these puppets of flesh. But of course that would not be enough. That was the impious parody of God he had made himself, as a general – seeing not eternal souls, parading in rainbow beauty past him, but only manikins of flesh to do his bidding, to go when he said go and come when he said come. To encounter others of their kind and chop them to pieces. The Holy Spirit was also God, because God was spirit as well as Everything.

And the Holy Spirit was Christ, because Christ was a man and so more than just a body, was a spirit himself. And the Holy Spirit was itself because the whole universe was suffused with spirit, and was the Father and the Son because they were both spirits too. And Edward thought to himself: I have neglected spirit, and abused spirit, and repudiated spirit. I was too focused on God the father, on my father, on the Son, on myself, and though the spirit was some emanation of me, or my military victories, or or or. Peace is harmony and wholeness and tranquillity and balance and war is the undoing of that. The Holy Spirit is both a dove, which is of peace, and a flame, which is destruction. The screeches of people trapped inside their houses as Limoges burned. The birdsong outside his window, right now, right here. A green force that erupted after fire had made hospitable ashes of the old order, and fresh rain had fallen from God's sky. A viriditas. The Earl of Derby had smashed Poitiers to pieces, and yet only a few years later it was restored, its walls built back up, its people working and growing and making and paying taxes. The same was probably true of Limoges, by now. And the Prince thought: I break them down, they build them up again.

Grass and trees and wheat are powered by this greenness, but in them it is a hectic and a wilderness force. Only in men and women is it something more harmonious, something more controlled, the rule of order in place of chaos, the force as a calm, inner stability: whole, complete, orderly, stable, and poised for blessing. And with a pinprick sense of total realisation, enough to bring tears to his weary eyes, the Prince understands, at last, for the first time, where the Holy Spirit dwells.

In the morning he would go and hear Wycliff preach.

After that, he slept.

WYCLIFF

The holy gospel tells by a parable how by right judgement of God men should be merciful. The kingdom of Heaven, says Christ, is like to an earthly king that would reckon with his servants. And when he had begun to reckon, one was offered unto him that owed him ten thousand crowns, and when he had not to pay of, the lord bade he should be sold, his wife and his children and all that he had, and that that he ought the lord should be always paid. This servant fell down and prayed the lord and said, Have patience in me, and I shall quit this whole debt. The lord had mercy on him, and forgave him all his debt. This servant went out and found one of his debtors, that owed him an hundred pence; and took him and strangled him, and bade him pay his debt. And his servant fell down and prayed him to be patient, and he should by time yield him all that he owed him. But this wicked first man would not, and went out and put him in prison, until he had paid the debt that he owed him. And other servants of this man, when they saw this deed, mourned with grievous hearts, and told all this to the lord. And the lord said unto his man, wicked servant, all thy debt I forgave you, for you begged me to do it. Behoved it not thee to have mercy on thy servant, as I had mercy on thee? And the lord was angry, and the anger of lords is a terrible thing, and he gave him up to prison and to tormentors, until he had paid all the debt that he owed him. On this manner, said Christ, shall My Father of heaven do to you, but if you forgive, each one to his brother, of your free heart, the trespass that he hath done him.

The kingdom of heaven is holy Church of men that now labour and struggle in this belowplace; and this Church by his head is like to a human king, for Christ, head of this Church, is both God and man. This king would reckon with his servants, for Christ has will without end to reckon with men thrice, thrice, thrice. First, Christ reckons with men when He teaches them by reason how much they have had of Him, and how much they owe Him; the second time Christ reckons with men, when in the hour of man's death He tells them at what point these men shall ever justly stand; the third reckoning is general, that shall be at the day of doom, when this judgement generally shall be openly done in deed. As concerning the first reckoning, Christ reckons with rich men of this world, and shows them clearly how much they owe Him, and shows by righteousness of His law how they and theirs should be sold, and so make amends by pain of things that they performed not in deed. But many such men for a time have compunction in heart, and pray God of His grace to have patience in them, and they shall in this life serve to Christ truly. And so Christ forgives them upon this condition. But they go out into the world, and sue not Christ their Lord in mercy, but oppress their servants that owe them but a little debt, and put them in prison, and think not on God's mercy; and other servants of God both in this life and in the other tell to God this fellness, and pray Him to serve their vengeance. No doubt, no doubt, God is filled with wrath at this, and at two reckonings with man He reasons this cruel man, and judges him justly to pain.

And therefore, Christ bids, by Luke, all men to be merciful, for their Father of Heaven that shall judge them is merciful.

Newsreel (20)

+TREATY OF BRUGES SIGNED+

Conference called at the instigation of Pope Gregory XI leads to treaty. France represented in the negotiations by Philip II, Duke of Burgundy; England by John of Gaunt, 1st Duke of Lancaster. A truce has been agreed was initially for one year, and the territory lately reconquered by the French king recognised as his.

The gift of wisdom corresponds to the virtue of charity.

The gifts of understanding and knowledge correspond to the virtue of faith.

The gift of right judgement corresponds to the virtue of prudence.

The gift of fortitude corresponds to the virtue of courage.

The gift of fear of the Lord corresponds to the virtue of hope.

The gift of Reverence corresponds to the virtue of justice.

COLUCCIO SALUTATI APPOINTED
CHANCELLOR OF FLORENCE

'Florence will flourish' he tells shocked assembly. 'I will prove salutary to this city.'

The gift of fear of the Lord corresponds to the virtue of hope.

WALDEMAR IV, KING OF DENMARK, DIES IN HIS 55TH YEAR. The ruler they declared 'a New Dawn' has seen his sun set.

The gift of Reverence corresponds to the virtue of justice.

Plague Returns. New cases reported in Wales, Bristol, Southampton and Bordeaux. Simon Sudbury, Archbishop of Canterbury, advises earnest prayer to God, Christ and the Holy Spirit from all quarters.

The gift of wisdom corresponds to the virtue of charity.

IOWERTH

Three times, as a baby, he had fallen into sicknesses they were sure would kill him: once with a speckled pox, once a fever that turned him redder than robin's breast all over his body, and once he slept for seven days and nights and grew cold and clammy as a fish. Yet he survived all three, and by the time he was seven years of age Iowerth was as strong as any lad of his parish. He lived on a farm in Brecknockshire, and his father was a freeman, and travelled widely – often as far as Hereford and Bristol, and once even to London by boat. Iowerth kept his mother and sisters company on the farm at Llanfaes when his father was away, and he rode a pony, and sometimes dreamed he was a chivalric knight on adventures, and he helped with services at the church.

It was a fine church, dedicated to Saint David, and had a slate roof, something not even true of the big church at Cardiff in those days, where the roof was only wooden. Inside there were half a dozen pews, and benches for the rest, and the tiles on the floor alternated blue and white, the colours of the blessed virgin herself.

Pigeons had nested on the roof. He could hear them, when he was inside the church sweeping the floor alone, hear them overhead murmuring to one another in their bird-voices like running water.

There were stories about the Church. One was that the foundation stone had been laid by Joseph of Arimathea soon after arriving by boat from the Holy Land, and that therefore it was the oldest church in the land. There was a story that a local nobleman had spent the night in the church with his hounds, ready to go hunting at first light; but when the dawn came he found his dogs had all been driven mad, and he himself was blinded, presumably for the blasphemy of using a church as a hunting lodge. This story bothered Iowerth: for what had the dogs done to deserve such divine punishment? And when Dafydd told the story the nobleman was Sir Richard of Hay, and when Owain told it the nobleman was William of Braose. It would hardly be both.

Still, Iowerth always felt the shiver go through him when the priest said mass, and once a bishop came through asking for volunteers to take the cross and fight to regain Jerusalem, and

Iowerth almost stepped from the crowd and presented himself, child though he was. He didn't, of course. But he daydreamed often of riding a great warhorse across the pristine yellow plain of the deserts of Judea, armed with a sword and wearing the red cross on white over his breast, and doing great deeds.

One week it rained every day from Sunday to Sunday, and the house flooded, and there were great shallow pools of water standing about. Another time there was no rain for a month, and the leaves on the trees grew dry and brittle as fine crusts, and rattled together with a noise like tin.

Iowerth listened to the smug cooing of the pigeons on the church roof.

One day Iowerth thought he would take the pigeon-eggs, and present them to his mother. Then he thought: he could take the pigeons too, and snap their necks, and his mother would be happy with the free meal. So he climbed up the wall of the church, putting his bare feet on the outcropping flints, and hooked his elbow about the top, where the roof slanted away. He could see the nest, and the brooding bird sitting on its eggs, and it looked at him with one inkdrop eye. Iowerth reached out with his free hand, and, almost losing balance, slapped it onto the stone just in front of the nest. He kept his balance. But when he came to withdraw his hand, he found it would not come free. He tried to pull it, to lift it straight up – a simple matter. But it would not come free. It would not release itself from the stone.

At first Iowerth was more puzzled than afraid. But after a while it became clear that the hand was not going to come loose, and he grew very afraid. The wind got up and rummaged through his hair, and dried the tears on his cheeks. His left armpit, where he was supporting himself, grew painful with the unrelieved pressure, and then grew numb. Iowerth tried sliding the hand along the stone, but it would not move. He tried a sudden tug, and tried pulling with all his might. He called out with the frustration and the pain.

Soon enough somebody heard him, or saw him from below, and came and stood at the base of the wall and shouted up at him. He tried to answer, but he was crying so much his words were smothered. The fellow went away, and came back with several others.

They put a ladder up, so Iowerth could rest his feet, which took some of the pain out of his armpit. But then they tried hauling him down by main force, and that hurt his arm more. It felt like they would yank his arm clean off, and that surely would kill him, so he begged them to stop and the copiousness of his tears persuaded them. His mother came – his father being away – and climbed the ladder, something she would not normally have attempted, to hug him and weep and ask what was going on. She helped him up, so that his knees were just about resting on the narrow stone ledge, but it was a precarious position. Why could he not release his hand?

Was there some strange substance or glue upon the roof of the church? Then the sun set and everybody went home except his mother and one of his sisters, who lit a candle and prayed and sang hymns; but when the candle went out and it grew cold they threw a blanket over Iowerth and went to their home.

Iowerth slept barely at all. From time to time exhaustion propelled him into a stupor, but then the pain in his arm, or the numbness in his hand, or his shivering from the cold, despite the blanket, woke him up again. Twice he slipped from the ledge, and yanked his pinned arm painfully, and had to scramble and struggle back up onto the narrow rim.

He tried praying to God, and then tried bargaining with God, and then in the darkest hour of the night, as a wolf snuffled menacingly around below him somewhere, and owls blew a cold wind through their beaks with hooo and woe, he cursed God, and railed that he had only wanted an egg, one solitary egg, to feed his hungry mother, and how was it fair that he be punished so? When dawn came he wept again, this time with relief. He soon became warm, and when people returned they brought him food and some milk to drink. But he could not unfix his hand. Trying to pull it, he fell from the roof again and dangled.

By noon his whole arm had lost sensation. The skin looked greyblue, something like an unusually uniform bruise, spread over the whole area. People had come from neighbouring parishes to see the strange event, and many of them were sceptical. They said Iowerth was shamming, only pretending to hold his hand there, that he ought to be ashamed, that it was blasphemy. So up the ladder came two men from a strange village, to heave and haul at the boy. His arm was so numb that it hardly hurt, though it hurt a little, and he moaned. They gave up after a while. People came and went, and a bonfire was built in the churchyard, although the priest complained it was disrespectful. People sang, people played dice, people came and went. The second night was a little easier than the first: for though he was still horribly uncomfortable it may be that he was growing accustomed to his strange posture. Or perhaps he was simply worn out. At any rate he slept for hours and woke before dawn with a new clarity in his head. People were snoring on the ground below him. The bonfire had burned low, and glowed ruby under a web of black ash. He prayed to the mother of God, Mary in her mercy and beauty, to intercede for him; and then he prayed fervently to Saint David, in heaven, for forgiveness for what he had done. As he prayed he began to feel the stone under his hand soften. Though his hand was numb as with great cold, and he could feel almost nothing, he was able to flex the fingers, just a little. It felt, very distantly, as if he were gouging into dough. Then, as the sunlight broke over the horizon, his hand came free, and he almost fell down the ladder, but was able to clutch at the stones with his tingling left hand. He clung there for a while, and eventually he came tremblingly down the ladder, half stepping, half falling. He woke his mother who wept and embraced him, and soon everybody was awake, and people were coming from all around to clasp him and look at his hand – slowly regaining its colour, painfully stabbing as sensation returned – and to praise God, and thank the virgin Mary, and the saints, and redouble the sanctity of the human heart, which is, after all, the only kind of sanctity that exists in the world.

Acknowledgements

Many thanks, of course, to Andrew Biswell and the Burgess Foundation; this novel could not have happened without them. Thanks also to Simon Spanton and the team at Unbound, to Jim Clarke, Rachel Roberts, Alan Jacobs and Francis Spufford. I am especially grateful to Dr Catherine Nall, of whose knowledge in medieval narratives of battle, and the medieval period in general, I am in awe, and who very generously lent her time and expertise. I have corrected all the errors they helped me spot, both historical and aesthetic, derived from my own carelessness and stupidity, although of course there still remain traces of these not totally liquidable human qualities in the work.

Unbound is the world's first crowdfunding publisher, established in 2011.

We believe that wonderful things can happen when you clear a path for people who share a passion. That's why we've built a platform that brings together readers and authors to crowdfund books they believe in – and give fresh ideas that don't fit the traditional mould the chance they deserve.

This book is in your hands because readers made it possible. Everyone who pledged their support is listed below. Join them by visiting unbound.com and supporting a book today.

Rose Biggin

Andrew Bishop

Doug Bissell

Andrew Blain

Cecilia Blanche

Whit Blauvelt

Steve Blundell

Sarah Bogle

James Boocock

Robert Borski

Mark Bould

Lucas Boulding

Julie Bozza

James Bradley

Simon Bradley

Glenn Branch

Jessica Branch

Matt Breckons

Catherine Breslin

Nathan Bridgman

William Bridgman

Al Brooke

Steve Bryant

Gareth Buchaillard-Davies

Jim Buck

Jonathan Buckmaster

Yves Buelens

Miriam Burstein

Michael N. Butera

William Butler

Brendan Byrne

Michael Caines

Max Cairnduff

Tom Callaghan

Elspeth Cannell

Sarah Carrick

Andrew Carter

Stuart Carter

Adèle Casey

Lindsay Catt

Ash Charlton

Anne Charnock

Ilona Chavasse

Joshua Christensen

Alisha Chromey

Jim Clarke

Jane Clements

Julian Clyne

Gabi Coatsworth

Jeffrey Cohen

Catherine Coker

Jim Compston

Dom Conlon

David Connolly

Robbie Constable

Mark Cooper

Brian Copestick

Erik Corry

Neil Coupland

Douglas Cowie

Robert Cox

Mitchell Cram

Colin Crewdson

Katherine Crispin

Alison Croggon

James Crossley

Tony Cullen

Andrew Cupples

Kim Curran Goodson

Patricia Daloni

Owen Dando

Elizabeth Darracott

Nick Davey

Máire Davies

Sue Davies

Geoff Davis

Marsha Davis

Henry de Vroome

Catherine del Campo

Paul Dembina

Roman Demidov

Steve Dempsey

Jane Dickson

F.M.A. Dixon

Andrew Donaldson

Bryce Doty

Stephen Dougherty

Connor Doyle

Richard Drew

Catherine Duerden

Suzanne Dwight

Gwilym Eades

Robert Eaglestone

E. Edwards

Phil Edwards

James Elder

Rod Ellis

Iain Emsley

James Ervin

Jonathan Everett

Alison Fairchild

Dylan Falconer

Gareth Farmer

Melanie Farrow

Peter Faulkner

Stuart Faulkner

Heather Fenoughty

Peter Fermoy

John Mark Findlater

James Firkins

Susan Fisher

Sam Fitzpatrick

Tony Flavell

Stuart Flynn

Paul Foth

Susan Foushee

Matthew Fox

Adam Fransella

Jamie Fraser

Robert Friel

Rx Frost

William Gaffey

Mark Gamble

Jane Gardiner

Annabel Gaskell

Amro Gebreel

Mark Gerrits

Tyler Giles

Marcus Gipps

Attilio Giue

Andrew Godden

Sophie Goldsworthy

Alice Gorman

Paul Gorman

Daniel Grader

David Graham

Susan Gray

Brian Green

Julie Green

Kim Griffiths

Vincent Guiry

Jukka Halme

Stephen Hampshire

Robert Hampson

Robert Harden

Andrea Harman

David Harris

Niall Harrison

A.F. Harrold

Dan Hartland

Judith Hawley

David Hebblethwaite

Alex Hewins

Philip Hewitt

G K Hiebert

Duncan Hill

Gail Hitchens

Timothy Hodler

Christopher E Holden

Walter Holland

Bryan Hollier

Ryan Holt

Antonia Honeywell

Stephen Hoppe

Paul Howard

Conrad Hughes

Peter Hughes

Michael Humphries

Tom Hunter

Dave Hutchinson

Thomas Hutchinson

Hermione Ireland

Deborah Irwin

Paul Jabore

Alan Jacobs

Maxim Jakubowski

Aleksi Jalavala

John Jarrold

Harley Jebens

Paul Jenkins

Ric Jerrom

Michael Johnson

Simon Johnson

Antony Jones

Julie Iler Jones

Miriam Jones

Abraham Kawa

Joanne Kaye

Matthew Keeley

David Kennedy

Ruth Kennedy

Ida Keogh

Toby Keymer

Sohail Khan

Katrina Kidder

Dan Kieran

Robert Killheffer

Paul Kincaid

Marc Kingston

Chris Knight

Pirkko Koppinen

Rebecca Krahenbuhl

Richard Kunzmann

Aleksi Kuutio

Ray Lakeman

Jessica Langer

Suzanne LaPrade

Duncan Lawie

Sing Yun Lee

Dainis Leinerts

Roger Levy

Tracey Lindsay

Ruth Livesey

David Llewellyn

Camille Lofters

Jack Lord

Nick Lowe

Tim Lucas

Roger Luckhurst

Brian Lunn

Brian Lycett

Conor Mackey

Mog MacLaughlin

Ross Macpherson

Yvonne Maddox

Patrick Mahon

Rohan Maitzen

Andrew Mamo

Philippa Manasseh

Alan Mann

Paul March-Russell

Andrew Marsden

Anthony Martin

Robert Maskell

Olwen Mayes

Jonathan McCalmont

Seth McDevitt

Martine McDonagh

Anna McFarlane

Anthony McGowan

Martin McGrath

Andrew McKie

Stuart McMillan

Patrick McMurray

Bairbre Meade

Megan Medina

Glen Mehn

Farah Mendlesohn

Diana Metcalfe

Sean Miller

John Mitchinson

Ian Mond

Will Montgomery

Tom Moody-Stuart

David Moore

Glyn Morgan

Richard Morgan

Steve Mosby

Geoffrey Moses

Charlotte Mounter

Duncan Muggleton

Arthur Murphy

James Murphy

Christopher Myers

Carlo Navato

Chris Newman

Conor Newman

Abigail Nussbaum

Tyler Nute

Ben O'Connell

Rodney O'Connor

Jenny O'Gorman

Cian O'Halloran

Hugh O'Neill

William O'Rourke

David Odell

Victor Okpe

Richard Owens

Alison Page

Richard Palmer

Neale Paterson

Mike Pennell

Peronel

Sarah Perry

Diana Peschier

Philip Phil

Mark Phillips

Nicholas Pierpan

Zakris Pierson

Edo Plowman

Philip Podmore

Justin Pollard

Tom Pollock

Stephen Potts

Larry Prater

Rich Puchalsky

Deana Rankin

Dan Rebellato

Gillian Redfearn

Helen Reid

Wil Reidie

Michael Reilly

Jon Rennie

Mike Reynolds

Rachel Richmond

Ian Roberts

Martin Roberts

Shauna Roberts

Anthea Robertson

Ian Robinson

Justina Robson

Robert A. Roehm

Adam Rosser

Paul Rydeen

Ian Sales

Gregory Sanders

David Santiuste

Andy Savidge

E. Saxey

Katharine Scarfe Beckett

Gabriel Schenk

Arthur Schiller

Andrew Seal

Lynsey Searle

Carol Seger

Dan Sellars

Tim Sheehy

T Gautham Shenoy

Clare Shepherd

Jim Shine

Jared Shurin

Donald Warren Sickels, Sr.

Neil Simmons

David Slater

Graham Sleight

Michael Marshall Smith

MTA Smith

Nigel Smith

Paul Smith

James Smythe

K Sommerville

James South

Rob Spence

Kari Sperring

Ted Spilsbury

Francis Spufford

Jim Steel

Karl Steel

Gabriela Steinke

David Stevens

Christopher Stuart

Christopher Sugden

Jennifer Sugden

Dom Surlis

Jonah Sutton-Morse

Emma Swift

Audrey Taylor

Tot Taylor

Christopher Taylor-Davies

Douglas Texter

Stephen Theaker

Matthew Thomas

Orin Thomas

Tony Thomas

Al Topping

Norman Towler

Robin Triggs

Kevin Trott

David G Tubby

Russell Turburville

Christopher Upham

William Vaughn

Paul Vincent

Sherryl Vint

Nigel Walker

Andrew Wallace

Steve Walsh

Jo Walton

Gareth Watkins

Ian Watson

Mark Watson

Stephen Watt

Andy Way

Ian Whates

John White

Lawrence White

Stephen White

Traci Whitehead

Lindsay Whitehurst

Aliya Whiteley

Nils Wieland

Will Wiles

Daniel Wilksch

Arnold Williams

Catherine Williams

Eley Williams

John Williams
Liz Williams
Caleb Wilson
Derek Wilson
John Wilson
Mark Wilson
Pete Windle
Stephen Witkowski
Gretchen Woelfle
Philip Womack
Rachael Wong
David Murakami Wood
Nick Wood
Wendalynn Wordsmith
Alex Wright
John Wyke